Sign up for our newsletter to hear
about new and upcoming releases.

www.ylva-publishing.com

OTHER BOOKS FROM
FLETCHER DELANCEY

Chronicles of Alsea:

The Caphenon

Without a Front: The Producer's Challenge

Without a Front: The Warrior's Challenge

Catalyst

Vellmar the Blade

Other Books:

Mac vs. PC

CHRONICLES OF ALSEA

CATALYST

Fletcher DeLancey

For anyone who has ever taken a leap of faith.

TABLE OF CONTENTS

CHAPTER 1: *Bonding break* 5
CHAPTER 2: *Well met* 11
CHAPTER 3: *Confession* 17
CHAPTER 4: *Mahaite Island* 28
CHAPTER 5: *Stories* 37
CHAPTER 6: *Reassignment* 43
CHAPTER 7: *Memories* 53
CHAPTER 8: *Sholokhov* 56
CHAPTER 9: *Revelations* 64
CHAPTER 10: *Absolution* 76
CHAPTER 11: *Watching* 78
CHAPTER 12: *Simplicity* 82
CHAPTER 13: *Data jack* 91
CHAPTER 14: *Covert agents* 98
CHAPTER 15: *The gift* 107
CHAPTER 16: *Taking it for a twirl* 119
CHAPTER 17: *Unexpected guest* 138
CHAPTER 18: *Different worlds* 141
CHAPTER 19: *Brainstorm* 149
CHAPTER 20: *Family circle* 159
CHAPTER 21: *New orders* 163
CHAPTER 22: *Briefing* 168
CHAPTER 23: *Transition in* 176
CHAPTER 24: *Symptoms* 182
CHAPTER 25: *Dr. Wells* 187
CHAPTER 26: *Transition out* 196
CHAPTER 27: *Language chip* 201
CHAPTER 28: *Lexihari* 204
CHAPTER 29: *Unexpected ties* 214
CHAPTER 30: *Evacuation* 227
CHAPTER 31: *Iceflame* 241
CHAPTER 32: *Decryption* 252

CHAPTER 33: *Meetings and greetings* ... 256
CHAPTER 34: *The right thing* ... 261
CHAPTER 35: *Grace* ... 267
CHAPTER 36: *Question and answer* ... 273
CHAPTER 37: *Mistake* ... 280
CHAPTER 38: *First lesson* ... 281
CHAPTER 39: *Second lesson* ... 284
CHAPTER 40: *Missing* ... 292
CHAPTER 41: *Obedience* ... 298
CHAPTER 42: *Third lesson* ... 301
CHAPTER 43: *Cowardice* ... 306
CHAPTER 44: *Hope* ... 309
CHAPTER 45: *Plan of action* ... 313
CHAPTER 46: *Through the door* ... 319
CHAPTER 47: *Teamwork* ... 321
CHAPTER 48: *Control* ... 336
CHAPTER 49: *Breathing* ... 343
CHAPTER 50: *Gift-wrapped* ... 349
CHAPTER 51: *Home* ... 355
CHAPTER 52: *Secrets* ... 363

GLOSSARY ... 375

About Fletcher DeLancey ... 381
Other Books from Ylva Publishing ... 383

ACKNOWLEDGMENTS

Writers often vanish into their own little worlds (or in my case, an invented universe) for hours and days and weeks at a time. If they're lucky, someone is waiting for them when they emerge for a cup of tea and a reminder that another world exists.

I'm lucky. So my first thanks always go to the woman who waits for me and who understands why I vanish: my own tyree, Maria João Valente. I also have to thank her for spending a romantic vacation brainstorming over a plot point that had stopped me cold. We managed to be romantic *and* solve the problem, which is kind of like winning the lottery.

Because I was out of my depth in several areas with this book, I am grateful to four experts in their fields who fact-checked my ideas and gave me different ones if mine didn't quite pass muster. They are Dr. Ana Mozo, who made sure that the many medical references, devices, and procedures made sense; retired Deputy Sheriff Ally House, whose tactical background helped me through an armed incursion; Saskia Goedhart, whose expertise in hand-to-hand combat was a gift I poured into Ekatya; and Maj. Chris Butler, USAF, Retired, who helped make my flight scene comply with physics and reality. (He also taught me what flight helmets are really for, so I could come up with alternatives.) Any factual errors remaining in this manuscript are in spite of their efforts.

Rebecca Cheek and Rick Taylor were indispensable for their willingness to spend hours upon hours reading my work, finding the weak spots, and helping me hone my craft. My writing has grown and changed in part because of their input.

Sandra Gerth is the best editor I could ask for at Ylva Publishing and has finally, by dint of many discussions in the margins, altered my comma habits with compound predicates. Cheri Fuller is our copy editor extraordinaire; Sandra and I consider it our goal to leave nothing for her to find. (She still tries hard.)

I had some help thinking up alien names for this book, so credit goes to Alison White, Shay, Kelly Parker, Cheryl Hanson, and Lisa Lub, all of whom lent me their creative brains. I modified a few of their suggestions, but it sure was nice to have so much to work with.

And finally, many thanks go to Karyn Aho, my Prime Beta. I have had so many discussions with her about plot arcs, character motivations, psychological underpinnings, and other details of storytelling—many of which took place at ridiculous hours of her night, thanks to our eight-hour time difference—that I honestly can't imagine writing these books without her.

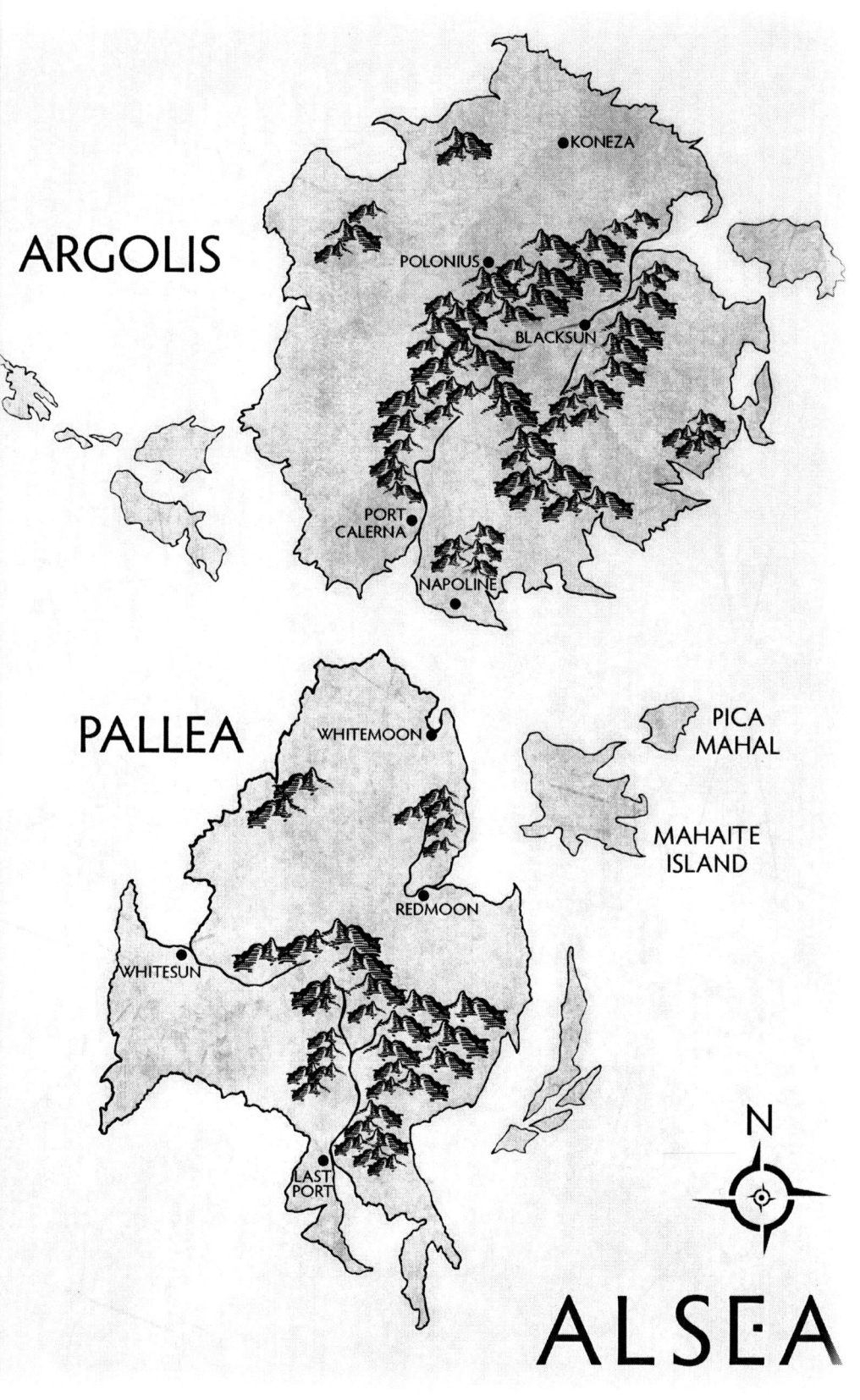

CHAPTER 1
Bonding break

Ekatya Serrado stood at the floor-to-ceiling window of their suite, looking north over the domed roofs of Whitemoon to the sparkling bay beyond. The luxurious inn commanded a spectacular view from its hilltop perch, second only to the view from Whitemoon Temple.

At the bottom of the hill lay a large park, its central open space a colorful contrast of grassy meadows and immaculately landscaped gardens. A narrow but dense belt of tropical forest surrounded the park on three sides, separating it from the city. The fourth side backed up to the hill, where a stone path meandered up to the front arch of the inn.

Though normally full of Whitemoon residents, for the past three days the park had been closed to the public due to its current occupant. Crouched in the largest meadow, looking wildly out of place, was Lancer Tal's state transport. Ekatya and Lhyn would be boarding soon, and even now she could see the tiny figures of Guards and guests milling around.

She glanced to the left, where the temple shone on its hill in the morning light. It looked so different now, an imposing edifice of black stone that absorbed the sun. Last night that same stonework had glowed, giving back the day's light and reflecting the moons as all Alsean temples did. Impressive though that light had been, it still came in a distant second to the brilliance of a tree catching fire from the mere touch of two women's hands.

That little display was still making her head hurt. She had questions, Lhyn had questions, the Protectorate government would have questions…and she suspected that they would all be unsatisfied. The Alseans simply accepted it as a sign from Fahla. Even Andira, with all her pragmatism, showed no desire to look beyond the surface. "Fahla has legitimized our bond and Salomen's position in a way I could not have done with a hundred speeches," she had said. "And you think I should ask why she chose to bless us?"

Sometimes she envied Andira her beliefs.

She turned away from the view and crossed the tiled floor to the bed, which sat beneath a skylight and could have slept four. Currently, it held two travel bags and several piles of clothing, most of which were hers. Lhyn had nearly finished packing her bag while Ekatya lingered at the window with her morning shannel. Shippers, but she had missed that brew.

"It still feels odd," she said as she rolled up a shirt at the foot of the bed.

"What, taking a real vacation for the first time in over two years? You're right, it does." Lhyn held up a scrap of fabric, wrinkled her nose, and squished it into a corner of her bag. "I don't think I'll need this. Andira said most Alseans don't wear swimsuits in the ocean."

"She also said it was optional."

"Sure, if we want to look like Protectorate prudes. I'd rather blend in."

As if that were possible. "The less clothing you wear, the less likely you are to blend in. You're missing a few ridges on that lovely body of yours."

Lhyn smiled from where she was bent over her bag. "What makes you think anyone will be looking at my body?"

"Because they have eyes, tyrina."

"Yes, and those eyes will all be directed at the Lancer and Bondlancer on their bonding break. As long as those two are around, nobody will be looking at us."

"I think you're underestimating the amount of attention a Fleet captain and the famous Doctor Lhyn Rivers will attract." Ekatya added another rolled-up shirt to her bag. "That's what feels odd. I can't get used to the idea of us going along on someone else's honeymoon. They're supposed to be off by themselves, having sex twenty hanticks a day. Not entertaining us."

"Oh, I think they'll manage plenty of time for joining and Sharing." Lhyn sat on the side of the bed next to her bag. "And you have it backward. They're not entertaining us; it's our job to entertain them when they want it. Weren't you listening when Lanaril explained?"

"Ah…not really. I was talking to Salomen." Ekatya folded a pair of pants and avoided eye contact. She was not comfortable around Blacksun's Lead Templar, a woman who lived and breathed religion. But Lhyn adored her, so at some point she would have to work past this.

"An Alsean bonding break isn't about the couple being alone," Lhyn said, and Ekatya could hear *that* tone of voice. A mini-lecture on Alsean culture was about to begin.

"I mean, yes, it's partly about that, but it's also about the two families getting to know each other. Family is such a foundational part of their culture." Lhyn's eyes were wide with interest as she added, "It permeates the rituals of bonding. The words of an Alsean bond proposal are really a request to be taken into the family, and the bonding break is the time when that request is put into action. Everyone tells stories, so the new members can learn family history and the families can learn more about their new members. We're going to learn so much on this trip!"

"It's not a field study, Lhyn."

"I know, but don't you realize what it means that Andira invited us? She's made us her family. She wants the Opahs to get to know us. She invited Lanaril for the same reason. Lanaril can hardly keep her head on her shoulders, she's so honored."

"I do know what it means. And I'm just as honored." But she wasn't at ease. Her friendship with Andira Tal, hard-earned in the middle of a global crisis, was an anomaly in her life. She didn't make friends easily or quickly, and she certainly didn't make friends whose absence never stopped aching. She had known Andira for all of two months before leaving Alsea, yet she had spent nearly two years since then being constantly aware of their separation. Hugging her the day before yesterday had felt like coming home.

But now she was expected to fit into a family dynamic, with Shippers only knew what kind of ramifications involved. She would rather have negotiated a treaty with the Voloth. At least then she would know how to act and what to say.

"Lanaril said that Andira and Salomen will spend a lot of time alone with each other," Lhyn said, blissfully unaffected by such concerns. "But part of our responsibility is to be there whenever they want us. Essentially, we're on call. Oh, and we're supposed to make sure they eat properly. I guess newly bonded couples don't always plan ahead for meals."

Ekatya had to laugh at that. "I should hope not. If those two are meal-planning, then I might have to take Andira aside and give her a few pointers."

"I see you missed that part of the conversation, too." Lhyn shot her a smirk.

"What? What part? Andira did not talk about—" Too late, Ekatya saw the look in her eyes. "You little spark. You had me going."

"And it was like netting trayfish in spawning season. No challenge at all."

Ekatya strode around the corner of the bed and shoved her onto her back. "I'll show you a challenge," she growled, her fingers finding the sensitive places along Lhyn's ribs.

Lhyn gasped and squirmed, laughing as she tried to catch Ekatya's hands. Then her laughter stopped and she went much too still. "No," she said in a panicked voice. "Get off. Get off me."

As her heart dropped into her stomach, Ekatya took two hurried steps back and turned slightly to the side, making herself as nonthreatening as possible. "I'm sorry."

Lhyn sat up and wrapped her arms around her torso. "It's all right. I'm all right. It's not you." Her breathing was fast and shallow, and Ekatya stood helpless as she watched her fight a battle all alone. If she saw a panic attack coming, she could often help to head it off, but sometimes Lhyn simply fell in the hole before either of them knew it was there.

At last Lhyn looked up, her face appearing ten years older. "Come here?"

Moving slowly, giving her every chance to say no, Ekatya stepped into the space between Lhyn's legs, slid her arms around her upper back, and dropped a kiss on the top of her head.

With a sigh, Lhyn rested her cheek against Ekatya's chest. "Much better. I can breathe."

"Sometimes I wish I'd taken that third strike," Ekatya said darkly. "He would never have breathed again."

"But then Sholokhov would have owned you. It was too high a price to pay."

"Sholokhov can never own me. Remember…"

"It's not about owning. It's about who you give yourself to."

"And I've only ever given myself to one person." Ekatya kissed the top of her head again.

"Ask me," Lhyn whispered.

It was their ritual, and Ekatya did not hesitate. "What is the first rule of capture?"

"Survive. Do what I have to, but survive."

"What is the second rule?"

"Delay. Say anything, do anything to delay any act that might debilitate me or make me unable to assist my own rescue."

"What is the third rule?"

Lhyn looked up. "Find the piece of you inside me."

"It's always there." Ekatya held her gaze. "Always."

"And thank Fahla for that." Lhyn tucked her head against Ekatya's chest again, a position she had never cared for before but found great comfort in now.

It was an odd physical reversal, given the height difference between them. Ekatya always looked up to her taller partner, but in these moments she looked down, providing shelter, and she would do it until her legs fell asleep beneath her.

After several silent minutes, Lhyn gave her a final squeeze and pulled back to rest her hands behind her on the bed. "You know that I'm never leaving Alsea again."

"I know."

She inhaled deeply, a smile returning to her face. "I can breathe here. It's so safe."

"It is. And we could hardly be safer than where we're going. Between Andira's and Salomen's units, we'll have forty Guards patrolling the place."

"Not to mention Andira. She would have made short work of him, just like you did. I still wish I could have seen it."

Ekatya ran gentle fingers through Lhyn's long hair, the silver strands shining against the mass of dark brown. "Are you going to tell them?"

"I already promised Lanaril that I would. That's what a bonding break is about, telling stories and getting to know the family. I want this family, Ekatya. This is my home now. They have to know." Lhyn's eyes closed, as they always did when Ekatya touched her this way. "Will you tell them your story?"

"Yes. Though I might have to hide the shuttle, or Andira will want to jump in and fly back to the Protectorate to teach a few lessons. She's not going to be happy."

Lhyn's chuckle was music to her ears. "Wouldn't you love to see her in Sholokhov's office?"

"Are you kidding? It's one of my daytime fantasies."

Now Lhyn laughed outright. "And here I thought those revolved around me."

"No, those are my nighttime fantasies." Ekatya hid her relief at seeing Lhyn return to normal. These moments happened less and less often, but it still tore a hole in her heart every time.

To this day, she had no idea how she had held herself in check. It would have been so easy to kill him.

CHAPTER 2
Well met

"Well met, Lead Templar Satran." The little boy held up both hands solemnly.

"Well met, Jaros." Lanaril touched his palms and smiled at the unguarded innocence of his emotions. Jaros Opah was thrilled to be here and quite proud of his maturity in introducing himself.

"I've heard so much about you from your sister and bondsister," she said. "It's a pleasure to see you outside of the ceremony. But you mustn't concern yourself with titles now; we're all family here. Call me Lanaril."

He shook his head, his freshly cut brown hair showing red highlights in the sun. "I like titles. They mean something."

Andira stepped up next to him and rested a hand on his thin shoulder. "I still can't get him to call me by my first name."

"I think I understand," Lanaril said. "I'm not certain I can call Colonel Micah by his first name, either. He doesn't look like a Corozen, does he?"

"Oh, no. He's the *colonel*." Jaros turned toward the enormous state transport, which took up most of the park's central meadow. In the crowd of Guards gathered near the ramp, Colonel Micah stood out for his lack of uniform and the fact that he was the only Guard with a full head of silver hair. He kept it in a short, bristly cut, a style common for younger warriors but not often seen on warriors his age.

"Do you know the other Guards, Lead Templar?" Jaros asked. When Lanaril said she did not—which was mostly true; she knew only a few of them by sight—he proceeded to point to each and give their rank, name, and a short description of their accomplishments.

After spouting more names than Lanaril would ever remember, Jaros indicated one of the few Guards taller than Colonel Micah. "That's Head Guardian Gehrain. Lancer Tal promoted him two moons ago, right after her challenge moon on our holding. And the warrior next to him is Lead Guard

Vellmar, but I don't know her very well. She took Gehrain's place as Lancer Tal's Lead Guard."

"You might get to know her this moon," Andira said. "She's been working very hard since taking over my unit, so I've promised her some leave time. That's why she's not in uniform today." She leaned closer, her bright blonde hair looking even lighter next to his dark head, and spoke more quietly. "She's better than me with a sword."

"Really? Speedy! Will you spar with her?"

"Oh, most definitely. If Salomen leaves me with any energy."

His brow furrowed, bunching the skin along his forehead ridges in an endearing manner. "I thought this was a bonding break."

"It is."

"Then why is Salomen making you work?"

Lanaril pressed her lips together as tightly as she could.

"Because your sister cannot bear seeing me idle," Andira said, smiling at someone coming down the stone path behind Lanaril.

"Don't believe her, Jaros. I wish she would be idle more often." Salomen joined them with her father and older brother in tow. "I thought you two were out for a stroll around the inn property?"

"We were, but Jaros saw the Guards here and was afraid the transport might leave without us." Andira ruffled his hair as he rolled his eyes.

"I was not. I just wanted to see it."

"And he has already introduced himself to Lanaril."

"Very nicely, I should add. I'm most impressed with Jaros's manners." Lanaril watched the boy light up and thought she could happily spend a day absorbing such uncomplicated emotions.

"That's my influence," Salomen said, nudging her brother. "Now that Nikin is taking over some of the daily upbringing, I expect a steep decline."

"You mean a decline in temperamental outbursts? Yes, I expect the same." Nikin's white teeth flashed against his tanned face as he grinned.

The family resemblance between all three of the siblings was quite pronounced, with their dark brown hair and eyes, strong chins, and transformative smiles. Salomen and Nikin were both taller than their father, Shikal, and judging by the length of his legs, Jaros was well on his way to matching them. His facial ridges were still small on his forehead and nonexistent on his cheekbones, but the thick, masculine ridges on both Shikal and Nikin were an indication of what he would grow into.

Salomen's ridges were attractively narrow, the fan-shaped trio on her forehead curving gracefully from the bridge of her nose to either temple and straight up to her hairline, while her cheekbone ridges cast faint shadows as she leaned over to tug Jaros's collar straight. He bore the attention stoically, lifting his head to make room for her hands. The action made his chin dimple more obvious, a twin to Salomen's own, and not for the first time Lanaril thought they could easily be mistaken for mother and child.

Shikal looked over Andira's casual clothing, his eyes crinkling in amusement. "You seem more approachable today. I could hardly believe that shining warrior in the full cape and breastplate last night was the same person who spent a moon working in our fields."

"What about that shining producer in the full cape and breastplate? I thought she looked like Fahla walking among us." Though Andira's front was perfect as always, the smile she directed at Salomen would have advertised her thoughts to a sonsales. Salomen's answering smile was just as easily read.

"Our Lancer seems to have been mentally compromised, don't you think, Father? It must have been all the spirits she drank. Oof!" Nikin huffed when Salomen elbowed him in the ribs.

Shikal shook his head. "You deserved that. And I believe our Lancer sees very clearly." He stepped forward and slid a finger beneath the fabric at Andira's throat, flipping out the upright collar that had been rolled under on one side. "But not when she dressed this morning. You must have been distracted, eh?"

Lanaril had never seen Andira blush before, nor stand so obviously speechless. She wondered how long it had been since anyone but a lover or Colonel Micah had touched her in such a casual, familial manner.

Shikal turned to his daughter. "I thought your mother taught you better than that. It's your job to make certain your bondmate is fit to be seen in public. Fahla knows Nashta was always stopping me before I walked out the door."

"And how many times did you stop her?" Salomen had not taken her eyes off Andira, who still looked as if she had been hit over the head with something large. "Father, Andira might need a little more time to adapt to her new family before you start trying to parent her."

"As if I could," Shikal said. "I would never presume to usurp Corozen's role."

Jaros frowned. "Colonel Micah is Lancer Tal's father?"

At last Andira found her voice. "Not biologically. But in every other way that matters, yes, he is. Just as you're not biologically part of my family, yet here you are."

The frown had not left his face. "We won't stop being friends just because we're family, will we?"

"No, of course not. Why would you think so?"

He stepped closer and spoke in a low voice that everyone else could still hear. "Herot is my family. But we're not friends."

A pained expression crossed Andira's face before she crouched down with her hands on his shoulders. "I believe your brother is thinking very hard right now about his family and his choices in friends. You may find that when he comes back home, things will be better between you. But you're right, family is no guarantee of friendship. I forgot that because I've spent so many cycles without either one, but you know what?"

"What?"

"I get to choose both now. I'm choosing friends to be my family. And I choose…you." She tapped a finger to the tip of his nose.

He launched himself into her arms, and she held him tightly, resting their heads together. Then she opened her eyes, looked up the pathway, and smiled. "Here come two more people I've chosen. Didn't you tell me you missed meeting Captain Serrado last night?"

"She's here?" He pulled away and looked around before spotting the two Gaians walking toward them, bags over their shoulders. "Oh…"

To Lanaril's surprise, the previously confident boy took a half-step behind Andira. "What do I say to her?" he asked.

"You say well met," Salomen answered. "They may be Gaian, but they know our ways."

He nodded silently, radiating both awe and trepidation as he watched the women approach.

They made a striking pair. Lhyn was tall and slender to the point of seeming fragile, and her startling green eyes were almost too large for her face. After all this time and many quantum com calls, Lanaril was used to the lack of cheekbone and forehead ridges. She had certainly seen the same alien smoothness on the faces of the Voloth colonists, who were physically indistinguishable from the Gaians. But seeing it so closely was…different.

Lhyn wore her long brown hair in a complicated braid that brought out its silver streaks, giving her a look of dignity that was usually dispelled the moment she opened her mouth. She was one of the most open and enthusiastic people Lanaril had ever met, and her words rarely strayed from the truth of her emotions.

Ekatya Serrado was much shorter, with shoulder-length hair as solidly black as Lanaril's own and dark blue eyes that sparked with intelligence. Though her height and slim build made her look small, she had the confident stride and aura of restrained power that inspired others to get out of her way. Lanaril could easily imagine her commanding more than a thousand people on her ship.

But where Lhyn was open and true to her emotions, Ekatya was closed and cautious. She maintained an outwardly friendly facade, behaving with impeccable politeness, but she held people at her fingertips. Especially Lanaril, it seemed. She hoped this bonding break would provide the opportunity for both of them to move past that, for Lhyn's sake if not her own.

"Good morning, everyone." Lhyn dropped her bag on the grass and shaded her eyes with one hand as she looked toward the transport. "This is a crowd. Are we late? Blame Ekatya; she had to have a third cup of shannel."

"Making up for lost time, Captain?" Andira asked in a teasing tone.

"Absolutely and without shame. I hope you've packed at least a case of it somewhere on that transport." Ekatya smiled at the group, and when her gaze reached Jaros, he slid a bit farther into Andira's shadow. "I don't believe we've met. You must be Jaros."

"Ah…" He looked at his sister for help, but Salomen tilted her head toward Ekatya. Reluctantly, he moved away from his protector and held up a hand. "Yes, I am."

Ekatya met his palm touch. "Well met, Jaros Opah. I'm Ekatya Serrado."

Lanaril was fascinated by the way she could physically project so much assurance when her emotions told a different story. Like all Gaians, Ekatya and Lhyn were sonsales, unable to sense emotions and equally unable to front their own. Everything they felt was free for the sensing—all the unguarded emotional power of children, but with the complexity and contradictions of adults. And this battle-hardened, accomplished warrior was nervous about meeting a small boy.

"Two hands, Jaros," Salomen said. "Andira has invited Ekatya and Lhyn because she has chosen them for her family. Which means they are your family as well."

Jaros obediently lifted his other hand. "Well met, Captain Serrado."

"There's no need to call me Captain. I'm not on duty right now, and I'm not your captain. Call me Ekatya."

"But you're the Savior of Blacksun," Jaros said in an awed voice. He let go and shoved his hands in his pockets. "I read a book about you. We learned about your ship and battle tactics in my history class this cycle."

Lhyn laughed. "Look at that, you're already history. I guess you can retire now."

"Which battle?" Ekatya asked.

"The Battle of Alsea," Jaros said as if that were blindingly obvious. "There was only one battle. Not counting the first ground pounder, I mean."

"After the *Caphenon* crashed, yes. But what about the battle we fought before we crashed? When we destroyed the first Voloth invasion group?"

His mouth formed an O. "We didn't learn about that! Not any details. Just that you blew up three ships before crashing."

"You didn't learn about a battle that took place right over your heads? It seems we need to update the Alsean records." Ekatya drummed her fingers on her thigh as she raised her eyebrows. "Should I start with you?"

"Yes! How did you know they were here? Is it true you fought them all alone? What was it like? Were their ships even bigger than the *Caphenon*?"

Jaros had forgotten the meaning of the word shy, and Ekatya had forgotten her nervousness at the same time. She smiled at Andira, who gave her a quick wink.

Lanaril watched, her curiosity rising. There was an oddly intimate nuance to Ekatya's emotions, a private thread between her and Andira. An intimacy like that would make sense had they been lovers, but…

She glanced at Salomen, wondering if she had felt the same thing, and found her staring at Andira with a speculative expression.

Well. This trip might be more exciting than she had imagined.

CHAPTER 3
Confession

Tal had arranged for several platters of refreshments to be brought to the conference table in her private cabin, intending to use it as a place where both guests and Guards could stretch their legs and enjoy a nibble. But the transport had barely lifted off when Salomen grabbed her by the wrist and dragged her out of the main cabin. Quiet laughter followed them down the short corridor, the others assuming that they couldn't even wait to land before joining again.

Unfortunately, joining was the last thing on Salomen's mind. As soon as the door shut behind them, she dropped Tal's hand and said, "I think you have something to tell me."

"Shek." Tal ran her hands through her hair. "Please don't be angry with me."

"Oh, how I love conversations that begin with those words. Tell me, on a scale of being half a hantick late for our third date, to letting me find out in front of three hundred people that you might die in ritual combat, how angry am I likely to be?"

"Being half a hantick late for our third date is the *bottom* of your scale?"

Her attempt at stalling failed. When Salomen silently crossed her arms over her chest and assumed a waiting stance, Tal sighed.

"Remember when you told your family about your empathic gift?" she asked. "And you said that the longer a secret is kept, the more entrenched it grows?"

"Vividly. And now you're worrying me. What is going on between you and Ekatya?"

"More than I realized," Tal muttered, half hoping she wouldn't be heard.

Salomen took her wrist again, led her to the four large, comfortable seats by the windows, and pushed her down. Taking the opposite seat, she said, "You told me the two of you never joined."

"We didn't. But…we Shared."

Salomen sat up straight, reeling from the impact of that news, and Tal scrambled to mitigate the damage.

"I wanted to tell you earlier, but there was never a good time. I'd hoped to bring it up after my challenge moon, but then there was the whole disaster with Herot and Parser and Shantu, and after that we were cleaning up the mess, and then it was all the politics of electing two new Primes and getting ready for the matter printers and the bonding ceremony…" She dropped her head into her hands. "I know I should have said something. I just didn't know how to start the conversation. And the longer I left it, the harder it became."

"You *Shared* with her? A woman you loved? And not only that, but a sonsales alien who was probably overwhelmed by it? No wonder she's connected to you!"

"I didn't know she was!" Tal lifted her head and faced Salomen's ire. "Not until the same time you did. I thought it was just me."

Salomen's eyes narrowed. "How could I not know you still felt that way?"

"Because I don't! Or I didn't. Agh!" Tal threw up her hands. "I felt that way before, yes. And you know all about that, but that's not what's happening now. This is something different, something I'm…" She rubbed her forehead ridges. "Rather nervous about."

"No, I don't know all about that, because you somehow left the Sharing bit out of your explanation. You said she never knew how you felt until the very end. How is that possible when you gave her everything you are? I would have preferred it had you joined with her." Salomen slumped back into her seat. "And I cannot believe I just said that."

"It wasn't that kind of Sharing."

Salomen gave her a sideways glance that dripped with skepticism.

Stung, Tal said, "And you wonder why I didn't want to start this conversation."

"Don't even *think* of shoveling this back on me. I am not the one bringing my past love and your greatest competition on our bonding break!"

Tal snapped her mouth shut and stared out the window, where the coastline of Pallea was passing beneath them as they flew southeast. It was difficult to think clearly with the weight of Salomen's emotions rolling through her, a tangled ball of jealousy, anger, and fear. But underneath the knots, pulsing steadily, was the power and solidity of their tyree bond.

A memory rose to the front of her mind, something Salomen had said on her first day in their State House quarters.

"Nothing has changed." She met Salomen's eyes, willing her to believe. "She still has her tyree, and I still have mine. Ekatya did not light up a molwyn tree with me."

Salomen blinked, inhaled deeply—and relaxed. The sudden shift as the knots slithered apart left Tal light-headed.

"You're right," Salomen said. "Whatever is between you, it's not what we have. Maybe I overreacted, but I'm just not used to…" She made a helpless motion with her hands.

"Sharing your toys?" Tal asked with a small smile. "Your father did mention that about you."

"It's much too soon for jokes. You know she's the only person I would ever worry about."

She sobered. "I do know, but there's no need."

"And I understand that, mostly, but she's not a ghost any longer." Salomen pointed at the bulkhead behind her. "She's right there, and she has a deep connection with you. Which is a little unsettling to discover the day after our bonding ceremony."

"I'm sorry, but I really had no idea. I didn't feel it until now." Tal hesitated. "There was…something, when she gave me that warmron the night they arrived. But I hadn't touched her in seventeen moons. We were both so happy to see each other—I thought it was just her unfronted strength."

"I did, too," Salomen admitted. "Their emotional nakedness does take some getting used to."

"It does. Ambassador Solvassen has learned to keep his emotions a little more ordered, and Chief Kameha has always been more muted. His mind tends to be focused on engineering details and projects. I've grown accustomed to working with them, but I forgot what it was like to be with Ekatya and Lhyn."

Salomen nodded, her posture slightly more open though she was still guarded. "Perhaps you could just tell me the whole story this time."

Tal winced at the reminder. "There isn't that much to tell. It started with the honor challenge Ekatya told you about. That was when I Shared with her the first time."

"The first ti— Oh, for the love of Fahla." Salomen rested her head against the seat back. "How many times?" she asked the transparent ceiling.

"Only once with Ekatya alone."

That brought her head back up. "You Shared with *both* of them?"

"I didn't plan it. I didn't even know what I was doing. And it really wasn't safe, which became abundantly clear when they left and I…well. Let's just say it wasn't a good time in my life." Tal pushed down the unpleasant memory. "I didn't Share myself with Ekatya that first time. I used the Sharing to push my memories of Lhyn's emotions to her. They were tyrees and didn't know it, and Ekatya refused to believe me when I told her. She didn't think it was possible. So I showed her."

Salomen stared at her in silence until a tiny smile lifted one side of her mouth. "You Shared with her to prove she was tyree."

"I told you it wasn't what you were thinking."

"I know." The smile spread. "Trust you to have protective instincts even toward an alien. One you had just beaten after she insulted your honor."

"Well, there was some guilt involved. I owed her. And it seemed like a crime against Fahla that there could be such a thing as sonsales tyrees. They couldn't feel the gift they held."

"I can understand that." Salomen drummed her fingers on the armrest. "What about the other times?"

As often as Tal had imagined this conversation, she had yet to come up with the right way to explain.

"This is where it gets complicated," she said slowly. "I've never told you exactly what I did to make sure that Ekatya stayed with us to help in that battle, and I promise you that I will, but not right now. Suffice to say that because of my strategy, their bond was strained. Deeply strained. I kept waiting for them to resolve it, but…" She shrugged. "They're sonsales. Neither of them knew how the other felt, and they weren't talking about it. At least not with each other. It was driving me insane. I dreamed my whole life of having what they had, and they were letting it slip like water through their fingers because they were too afraid to trust each other."

"And we wouldn't know a thing about that." Salomen was softening, her hand reaching out for Tal's as if she wasn't aware of it.

Tal gladly laced their fingers together. "But we had our bond driving us. We couldn't turn it off even when we wanted to. They couldn't turn it on."

"I think I see where this is leading."

"I connected them, yes. But I didn't know what I was subjecting myself to. They had so much power and no control; it was like completing an electrical circuit. I became part of their bond without realizing it. And we did that for fourteen days in a row. Only on the last day did I drop my own blocks and make it a true triad Sharing."

"Fourteen days." Salomen gazed out at the towering columns of clouds they were now flying through. "With both of them. That is…not what I expected."

Tal could almost hear her thoughts as she followed the shifting emotions. She braced herself when Salomen met her eyes.

"I'm not your first tyree."

"No. But you are the tyree I was meant to have. What I did with Ekatya and Lhyn…it wasn't my bond to join, but they had no barriers and I had no idea what I was doing. And none of us wanted to stop."

"But then they went home, and you were left behind with a broken tyree bond. Goddess above, now it makes sense—the way you were still so affected a full cycle later."

"It wasn't a full bond," Tal said. "But yes, it was enough to be debilitating. I didn't even realize it until I had already made a mess of my life." She smiled, tightening her grip on Salomen's hand. "Then I met an obstinate, disrespectful producer who pushed me past every border of propriety, and despite my acting like a dokker's backside to her, she gave me a shining gift. She understood how I felt, even without knowing the whole story, and she told me that Ekatya was the dream I could only touch."

Without releasing their grip, she shifted into the seat beside Salomen and slid her free hand around the curve of her jaw. It was an intimate gesture, half of the hand positioning for a Sharing, and it said more than her words could.

"But you are the dream I can hold," she said softly. "And the one who holds me."

With an inarticulate sound, Salomen wrapped a hand around the back of her neck and pulled her in for a kiss that left no doubt as to which dream was real. Drawing back, she said, "Now I really wish you had told me earlier. Perhaps then I wouldn't have made a fool of myself jumping to conclusions."

The sun pouring in through the ceiling lit up her eyes and brought out their many different shades, darker at the edges and lighter toward the center. The golden ring encircling each pupil was the sort of intimate detail that Tal delighted in, knowing that very few people were privileged to see it.

"You were never the fool," she said. "I should have told you."

"Yes, you should have. But I know now, and I'm sorry you had to go through that."

"I'm not, if it's what led me to you."

That was exactly the right thing to say. As Salomen leaned in, Tal tilted her head back, offering her throat in full trust. The sudden suction made her breath hitch.

Salomen let go and blew across the now-warm skin. "I wish I had known you then."

"I wish you had, too. Imagine if I had met you instead of Darzen, back when I was first starting to heal."

"Well, for one thing, I wouldn't have stopped you from ordering horten soup."

Tal's laughter was cut short by a gentle bite, followed immediately by the suction that sent her skyward. While she was losing herself in the sensations, the back of her seat began to recline.

"You do have a golden tongue." Salomen left the seats in a half-reclined position and straddled Tal's lap. "You can talk yourself out of any situation, even when I'm angry with you."

"Does this mean I've talked you out of your clothes?" Tal asked hopefully. "You know that's what they all think we're doing in here."

"No, but you may have talked yourself out of *your* clothes." Salomen's hands were busy at the buttons on the side of Tal's wrap shirt, and in another piptick she pulled the top layer away, exposing one breast. "You looked ravishing last night in that bonding suit and breastplate, but I have to say, I prefer this for easier access." She bent down and took the nipple into her mouth.

"Oh, Fahla." Tal's head slammed against the seat. "And to think I put off this conversation." Her fingers wound into Salomen's hair, holding her in place.

Salomen smiled against her breast, then pulled Tal's hands away and sat upright. "Let this be a lesson to you, then. Had you told me earlier, we could have done this much sooner."

"I'm a grainbird," Tal said, trying to get her hands loose. She needed them on Salomen's body.

"Yes, you are. Which is why you're not touching me now." Salomen pushed her hands back. "Hold on to the back of your seat, tyrina."

"What?" Her resistance was purely instinctive, a warrior's reluctance to be at any physical disadvantage. But Salomen's grip was very strong, and she was using her body weight.

"I'm not about to reward you for keeping the truth from me." Salomen's efforts won out as she pressed Tal's wrists against the top of the seat. "Hold on to this if you want me to go any further."

"You're joking."

"I'm not, and you know it." She leaned in for a deep, possessive kiss, then slowly pulled away. "It's your choice. Either you let me take control, or I fasten your shirt again and we bring everyone in here to attack those platters." Releasing Tal's wrists, she sat back and waited.

Tal was caught in an agony of indecision. She loved it when Salomen was assertive, but this was a step beyond. She had never completely given up control before, and it was not an easy role to accept.

But that was the point, she realized. Salomen had something to prove. If it were easy, it would have little value.

Silently, she turned her wrists and rested her fingers on the top of the seat.

Salomen's smile was somehow predatory and loving at the same time. "Good choice, my Lancer."

She unfastened Tal's trousers, then slid to the floor and began pulling off her boots. It was an act of humility that Tal had hated for most of her life, having been forced in her early training to remove the boots of any older trainee who demanded it. Salomen had memorably redefined its significance the night of their first joining, when she made it an act between equals.

Now she was redefining it again. Tal discovered that having her boots pulled off while she was in this position, with her hands above her shoulders and her body presented as a gift to be opened, put all of the humility squarely back on her. The feeling intensified when Salomen told her in a no-nonsense tone to lift her hips, and her trousers and underwear joined the boots and socks on the floor.

"Open your legs," Salomen said. It was all the warning she gave before she gracefully dropped to her knees and leaned forward.

"Oh," Tal whispered, jolted by the touch of her tongue. "I thought you would—"

A bite just this side of painful interrupted her, and when she felt long fingers slide inside, she forgot most of her vocabulary.

Keeping her hands still was far more difficult than she expected. But the enforced passivity enhanced her other perceptions, adding a layer that felt raw and dangerous—and all the more pleasurable because of it.

Salomen's presence in their link took on a fierce edge. Despite being fully dressed and untouched, her arousal was not far behind Tal's as she took her to the brink and then withdrew, not allowing her to finish. With sure hands and a devastating touch, she eased Tal back into a rhythm, pushed her to the edge again…and again withdrew.

The third time Tal was denied, she thought her fingers might punch through the seat fabric. She bit her lip rather than ask.

"I know this is killing you, but you are so competitive," Salomen murmured as she rose from the floor. "And so damned beautiful looking like this."

She straddled Tal, who by now had been driven high enough that the mere brush of Salomen's trousers against her molwine made her gasp and arch her back. Then she gasped again at the bite on her throat ridge.

"I've been neglecting these terribly," Salomen said into her ear. "And you refuse to ask me to finish you, so we'll do this the hard way." She began a slow rocking with her hips, applying delicious pressure while simultaneously working her way along the length of first one throat ridge and then the other.

Gradually she ramped up the intensity of her bites, but kept the same damnably slow pace with her hips until Tal was trembling beneath her, desperate for her release and silently praying that Salomen would not stop a fourth time.

"Ask," Salomen said, and bit down so hard that Tal nearly lost her grip on the seat.

"Ask," she said again, and began to suck where she had just bitten.

"Goddess," Tal choked out.

"No. Ask me." She bit down once more and this time did not let go.

"Salomen—" Tal strained her hips upward, trying to increase the pressure. Her fingers were going numb.

Salomen surged against her without relenting from the power of her bite. It was almost more than Tal could bear…and then it abruptly became too much.

"Please!"

The sudden absence of pressure on her throat ridge nearly pushed her over the brink. A shudder ran through her body.

"Let go," Salomen said. "Hold on to me."

With a groan of utter gratitude, she wrapped her arms around Salomen and held her close. "Fahla, I need you."

"I know. Hold on." Salomen slid her hands beneath Tal's shoulders and shifted into a higher gear, her hips moving twice as fast as before. She lowered her head and returned to the throat ridges, this time sucking just firmly enough to keep the sensitivity high without distracting from the deeper pleasure of her thrusts.

Tal could not keep her hands still, her previous inability to touch making her starved for it now. She pressed and rubbed and squeezed, worshipping the curves and planes that made up this precious body. When the release finally roared through her, she pushed Salomen's head up and kissed her, crying out into her mouth. Shaken by the aftershocks, she buried her face in the warm fragrance of Salomen's throat and thought she might never leave this place.

Salomen remained still, stroking her hair and the back of her neck and murmuring words that Tal could not process. Gradually, sense returned, and she heard "my beautiful tyree" and "even more stubborn than me, but I love you anyway."

The last made her laugh. "I am not more stubborn than you."

Salomen kissed the top of her head. "You put yourself through torment just to avoid asking me to finish you."

"But it was a very pleasant sort of torment."

"I know. I felt it." Salomen's amusement shook her body. "And Great Goddess, but you were glorious like that."

Tal finally pulled back enough to look in her eyes, which were full of love and an only partially slaked lust. "You didn't have anything to prove to me."

A knowing smile brought out the lines at the sides of Salomen's mouth. "Perhaps I had something to prove to myself."

"Did you succeed?"

"Oh, yes. Fabulously."

"Good." Tal snuggled in again. "You're overdressed."

"I'm fine. We do eventually have to let our guests in, you know. I didn't plan to spend half the flight joining with you."

"Let's shove the platters out into the corridor and lock the door."

"Yes, because that would be the height of courtesy, and who would explain it to Jaros?"

"Oh, Fahla." Tal suddenly remembered who was on the other side of the bulkhead behind her. "I've never been so glad that this cabin is soundproofed."

Salomen laughed, kissed her one more time, and pushed herself onto her feet. "Much as I love making you sound like that, I'm very happy not to have to answer any questions. That job I'm leaving to Nikin when the time comes." She leaned down and refastened the top layer of Tal's shirt. "I feel as if I should apologize to your other breast. Poor thing never even got free."

Tal rubbed the side of her throat, where the hot skin was evidence of numerous marks. "I think you made up for it with my throat ridges."

Salomen scooped up the underwear and held it out. "I'd apologize for that, but I'm not one bit sorry."

"No, you're proud as a moonbird in full feather." Tal rose and began dressing. "I'll be going out there covered in bite marks while your throat is pristine."

Salomen offered the trousers with an unrepentant smile. "It's a bonding break, Andira. They expect it."

"I'm going to get teased," Tal grumbled as she settled the trousers in place. "Micah will be positively gleeful." She pressed the control to bring the seats back into their normal position, then sat down to pull on her socks and boots. "And if you wanted to avoid Jaros asking any questions, you made a tactical error."

The realization washed over Salomen's face, and now it was Tal's turn to laugh. "Didn't think about that, did you?"

"Shek," Salomen muttered. Then she brightened. "No matter. It's Nikin's job anyway. He'll just have to do it a little sooner than he might have planned."

Now fully dressed, Tal stood and drew Salomen into a warmron. "Thank you, tyrina," she said quietly. "Both for that lovely joining and for understanding."

"You're welcome. Thank you for giving me what I asked for. I know it wasn't easy for you—either part of it."

Tal nodded, suddenly serious. It had to be said. "It's still there. That piece of a tyree bond between Ekatya and me."

"I know."

"I swear I had no idea—"

"I know that, too. It's all right."

"It doesn't change anything."

"Yes, it does." Salomen ran soothing fingers through Tal's hair as she spoke. "I don't know how, and don't worry, I'm not afraid of it. It's only a piece, and what you and I have is beautiful and whole. But the truth is that you and Ekatya are not just friends, and if this little piece of a bond has survived seventeen moons of separation, then you will never be just friends. You created something permanent."

"I know," Tal said. "I just don't know what to do about it."

"And this is where you keep making the same mistake. It's not for you to do anything, not by yourself. This isn't about you. It's not even about you and Ekatya. It involves all four of us, and we will all decide if anything needs to be done."

Tal stared at her, and Salomen shook her head with a smile.

"Come, my Lancer. Time to stop being rude and give our guests a chance to enjoy that food." She laced their fingers together and tugged her toward the door.

"Wait!" Tal let go and diverted to the cabinets to the left of the door, where she pressed a hidden control.

"What is that?"

"Air circulation. No need for Nikin to answer any more questions than necessary."

This time, Salomen actually blushed.

CHAPTER 4
Mahaite Island

Lanaril watched the island flashing beneath them, fascinated by the rise and fall of the landscape and its varying textures after a hantick spent flying over the ocean. It was hard to believe how many cycles had passed since she last visited Mahaite Island, on a celebratory trip after completing her novice studies. She had been twenty then, an official adult at last, with a certificate of academic honor in one hand and an admissions letter to the Whitesun Academy of Templars in the other. She and four friends had come here to swim, hike, drink, and join before burying themselves in another five cycles of study.

"It's lovely," Lhyn said, leaning halfway over Lanaril's lap to stare out the window. "When I first saw Mahaite Island from orbit, I thought it looked like an upside-down hand with six fingers, and three of those fingers are trying to grab Pica Mahal."

Lanaril smiled. "There's a legend that the volcano on Pica Mahal is the beating heart of Mahaite. But Mahaite fell in love with a different island, one that sank beneath the waves, and when he lost his love, he tore out his heart and threw it away. It hurt too much to keep it. Since then, he has regretted his impulsive act and always reaches out to pull his heart back. But he threw it too far, and it has remained forever out of his reach."

"Probably a good thing for Mahaite, given how many times his heart has erupted. Have you ever been there?"

"Shortly after my Rite of Ascension, yes. My friends and I thought we could climb to the top of the volcano in one day. We took a ferry from the eastern tip of Dahal Ridge—that's the northernmost finger on the east side of Mahaite. It's only a hantick by ferry from there to Pica Mahal, and the trail up the volcano starts right out of the ferry terminal."

"Did you make it to the top?"

"Yes, after our guide laughed at our intentions and booked us into a shelter just below the summit. We were young and stupid, and forgot that after climbing to the top of a mountain, we would eventually have to come down."

They were in one of the rows that had facing seats, and Ekatya sat next to the window in the seat opposite Lanaril. "What time did you reach the summit?" she asked.

"Shortly before sunset."

As Ekatya chuckled, Lhyn said, "Young and stupid is right. Good thing you hired a guide."

"I think the island authorities are accustomed to dealing with stupid mainlanders. It's impossible to get a permit to climb Pica Mahal without reserving a guide. We thought it was a scam to bring money into the island treasury, but after barely making our shelter before nightfall, we were ready to rain the blessings of Fahla upon our guide."

"Are you planning a repeat visit while we're here?" Ekatya asked.

Lanaril shook her head. "When I was twenty, I could climb a mountain on a whim. These days it would take a little more preparation time. Besides, we won't be near Dahal Ridge."

"Right," Lhyn said. "We're going to the crooked finger."

"Lina Stille." Ekatya held up her pad, where a map of the two islands glowed in full color. "Some of us did our homework."

"Some of us didn't need to."

"Of course. Which is why you called it the crooked finger."

"Sometimes descriptive terms are more fun."

"Because fun is always more important than accuracy. Are you sure you're a scientist?"

"The best in my field." Lhyn was suddenly drained of all happiness. "Or so I've been told."

Ekatya gave no outward sign of her own shift in emotion, but grief and regret snuffed out the sparkling light Lanaril had been enjoying. "By numerous people," she said. "Including everyone at your institute, and their opinions should count for something."

"They do." Lhyn could not hold Ekatya's gaze.

Lanaril looked back and forth between them and debated for a moment. "Does this conversation have anything to do with the story you didn't tell me last night?"

She listened to Lhyn's indecision and Ekatya's self-control, as the captain held back her own answer and waited.

"Yes," Lhyn said at last. "I'm sorry, Lanaril. I thought I could tell you a short version last night, just so you'd know, but that ceremony was so beautiful…and the eclipse, and the music, and everything else…" Her smile held too much knowledge. "I couldn't do it. And I realized this morning that I can't do it more than once. So I need to wait for a time when we're all together. Probably when I've poured half a bottle of grain spirits down my throat."

Lanaril shifted to face her. "Will you be all right while you wait?"

With a choked laugh, Lhyn said, "And this is why I love Alseans. Yes, I'm all right. I became much more all right the moment we arrived in orbit. Thank you for asking."

Lanaril held out a hand and smiled when Lhyn took it without hesitation. "I am very sorry for whatever happened to you," she said, projecting her affection and sympathy. "Know that if you need to talk, or even just to be emotionally heard, I am here. And I seem to have very little on my schedule for the next two ninedays."

Lhyn blinked back tears. "Sometimes I really hate your cultural restriction on warmrons."

Lanaril offered her other hand. "Since we are family now," she said quietly.

Lhyn interlaced their fingers and held tight, and for the second time in three days, Lanaril wished she could flout a lifetime of training the way Andira did.

The transport dropped altitude as it neared Lina Stille—or as Lanaril would always think of it now, the crooked finger of Mahaite. Wrinkles and shadows in the landscape became ridges and valleys, and then she could make out individual trees in the unending carpet of green. Here in the tropics, where the growing season lasted nearly the full cycle, some of the trees reached enormous proportions. She remembered climbing one on her last visit to the island—an endeavor made considerably easier by the ladder fastened permanently to its trunk—and thinking, as she looked down on the tops of the smaller surrounding trees, that it was like being on a ship sailing a verdant ocean.

Their destination was the very tip of the finger. Soon the last trees flashed beneath them, revealing a grass landing pad which ended at the water. Though marked off for multiple transports, it was vacant now. The entire resort had been reserved for their group.

A pedestrian bridge led from the landing pad to a small island in the protected bay, perhaps half a length offshore, where the resort was hidden in the trees. Lanaril had read up on it the moment her invitation was delivered, and approvingly noted that no transport traffic was allowed at the resort itself. In fact, the airspace over the bay was closed to all traffic except emergency transports, so their pilot had taken an indirect route along the water's edge, turning north shortly before landing.

In the bustle of both guests and Guards exiting the transport and collecting luggage, Lanaril moved off to one side and closed her eyes, simply breathing the air. Whitemoon had felt so different from Blacksun, with its warm, scented breezes at a time when Blacksun Basin was experiencing the crisp coolness of autumn. But Whitemoon was also a busy port, full of the noise and odors that came with its traffic. Here the air felt heavy with the fragrance of flowers and the decay of leaf litter in the forest behind her, and beneath it all ran the clean scent of seawater untouched by industry. The only sounds of civilization were those of her fellow passengers, as Guards called orders, luggage was shifted, and low voices commented on the beauty of the area. Beyond that she heard the slap of water against bridge pilings, the lower swoosh of wavelets upon the shore, the rustling of leaves and branches, and the cries of birds that never flew over Blacksun Basin.

She opened her eyes and began making her way toward the bridge. Guests had the option of crossing on foot or taking the cable car, which was slung beneath the bridge deck. According to the resort's information, the car had a transparent bottom and afforded perfect views of the local waterfowl, as well as an occasional glimpse of the giant wingfish that lived in the quiet bays around Mahaite. Lanaril thought she would try that later, but for her first approach, she wanted to walk over and enjoy the views of both their resort island and Pica Mahal.

The other guests had the same idea, leaving a group of Guards free to load up the cable car with luggage and take it across ahead of them. Some of the remaining Guards made a second pile of luggage for the next trip, while the others stood in a ready posture, scanning the area for danger. It was difficult to imagine any threat in this paradise, but even with her unprecedented approval ratings, Andira still had enemies. And now, by virtue of their bonding, so did Salomen.

Sensing Lhyn's need to be alone with Ekatya, Lanaril angled her steps to intersect with those of Andira, who was walking onto the bridge next to Colonel Micah. Salomen was with her family on the landing pad, where a last-tick discussion of housing appeared to be taking place.

"I'm still a little concerned about the attack you suffered on the transport," Colonel Micah was saying. "Are you certain you don't wish to file a report? Assaulting the Lancer is a serious offense."

"I'm not listening, Micah."

"On the other hand," he said with vast enjoyment, "perhaps your reluctance to name the attacker indicates something else. Perhaps it was not an Alsean at all, but a treecat. One could have gotten aboard while the transport was parked in Whitemoon. I've heard they sometimes get confused and climb people just like trees, which could also explain the marks on your neck."

Lanaril covered her mouth to hide her laugh.

Andira shot a glare at her Chief Guardian. "You never did learn to swim very well, did you? Something about being too dense to float. I wonder how deep the water is here."

"Happily, I'm also too dense for you to throw me over the rail."

"I could ask Gehrain to do it."

"Gehrain just zipped under our feet, along with half the luggage."

"Senshalon, then."

"He's with Gehrain."

"How convenient that you sent my strongest Guards on luggage duty before harassing me."

"I'm wounded. I show concern for your well-being, and you call it harassment."

Lanaril increased her speed, closing the gap between them. "I wonder, Colonel, why you seem so unconcerned about our Bondlancer? She may have escaped injury this time, but there's no guarantee that the attacker won't return."

Andira twisted around and frowned at her. "You're supposed to defend me against him, not join ranks with him."

"I must admit some admiration for our mysterious assailant," Lanaril continued without remorse. "Who appears to have easily overwhelmed the leader of the warrior caste."

"Not so easily," Andira muttered. "She did have to work for it."

Lanaril and Micah burst into laughter, and Andira let go of the grin she had been holding back.

"Truly, I'm happy for you," Lanaril said. "Salomen is your equal in so many things, including passion. Fahla could not have sent you a better bondmate."

Andira looked back to where Salomen was now stepping onto the bridge, with Jaros at her side. "No, she could not."

The three of them chatted easily as they crossed the long span, occasionally stopping when local wildlife made itself known. A flock of pure white sailtails passed overhead, softly calling to each other, and a great school of fish appeared on the landward side of the bridge, their dorsal fins breaking the water's surface in such numbers that it sounded like a rushing stream. Lanaril saw more waterfowl than she could identify, and at one point thought she glimpsed the shadow of a wingfish. Across the water, Pica Mahal watched over them, its top hidden in clouds.

They had dawdled enough that when they reached the end of the bridge, Salomen and the Opahs had caught up. Ekatya and Lhyn were still out on the span, along with quite a few Guards.

Somewhere on this island, Lanaril knew, there was a black sand beach perfect for relaxing and swimming, but on this side the land came to a sudden edge before dropping off into the water. A trail followed the rocky edge, encircling the entire island. Andira had already declared her intent to run it first thing tomorrow.

A second trail led straight from the foot of the bridge into the giant trees, where it quickly vanished behind thick trunks. Brilliant flowers outlined it in the shaded dimness, too evenly spaced to be anything but carefully cultivated.

They followed the trail into the forest, through two sharp curves and over a slight rise of ground before arriving in a clearing where a ring of nine cabins stood on stilts, each with two sides open to the warm breeze. In their center was a much larger cabin, built on the same design but with four solid walls and a broad wooden deck surrounding it on all sides. A wood-chip path encircled it and sent spokes out to each of the smaller cabins.

Though Lanaril did not have a practiced eye, she noted several Guards already watching from various points around the clearing. They must have been in the forest as well, though she had neither seen nor sensed them.

Two men were walking toward their group, the taller of whom wore his gray hair in a braid and moved with the upright posture of a retired warrior. He confirmed Lanaril's guess when he stopped and thumped both fists to his chest in the warrior salute to a Lancer.

"Lancer Tal, Bondlancer Opah, well met. You do us great honor with your visit."

The shorter man, whose thick torso and bulging arms bore testament to a lifetime of manual labor, held up his hand for a palm touch. "Well met indeed! This is my bondmate, Galon, and I'm Jarnell. We're delighted to welcome you and your family to Stilletree Resort."

"Well met, Jarnell, Galon." Andira touched their palms in turn, then smiled at Jarnell while Salomen greeted them. "Builder caste, yes? Is this your handiwork?" She gestured at the ring of cabins.

He drew himself up proudly. "Designed and built. I may not have driven every nail, but they're mine. I'm particularly proud of the Bondmate Bower." He pointed across the clearing.

Lanaril did not know how she hadn't noticed it before. On the other side of the clearing stood an enormous delwyn tree, its massive trunk at least three body lengths in diameter. High off the ground, above the tops of the surrounding trees, the trunk divided itself into three lead branches, which grew horizontally before curving straight up again.

Nestled into the space created by the three branches was an octagonal cabin with walls made mostly of glass. A cantilevered deck lined with colorful planters jutted out from the branches, seeming to hover in the air while providing space for a table and four chairs. Wooden stairs wound their way around the tree trunk, descending from the deck to the ground.

"Holy Shippers," Lhyn said. "That looks like something out of a storybook."

"It's lovely." Salomen smiled at their hosts. "I cannot wait to see it, and the views it must command."

Andira took her hand, silently adding her agreement, and Jarnell beamed. "The view is magnificent in every direction, and the glass is of course privacy screened. One of your Guards already took up your luggage, and we left you a welcoming tray of food and drink. Now then!" He took a reader card out of the pouch on his belt and unrolled it. "We assigned cabins to five of you and had the luggage delivered, but I understand there was some question about where Raiz Jaros would sleep."

"I get my own cabin," Jaros said. "Father and Salomen agreed."

"Fortunate you are! In that case, your cabin is that one right there. You'll be between your father and your brother. We put your bag into your father's cabin for now, but it will be a matter of pipticks to move it."

Barely pausing for breath, he pointed out the cabins reserved for Shikal, Nikin, Ekatya and Lhyn, Lanaril, and Colonel Micah. Three cabins remained unoccupied.

"But where are the Lead Guards sleeping?" Jaros asked. "Shouldn't they be here?"

Galon spoke for the first time since the initial greeting. "The Lead Guards and the Head Guardian are each in their own bondmate bowers, watching over their units. We have three other cabin rings in our resort." He gave Andira a respectful nod and added, "It is truly a pleasure to have so many warriors staying with us, and of such a high caliber. If it's not too much of an imposition, I wonder if I might be allowed to watch some of their training?"

"I'm certain they'll enjoy an audience," Andira said. "You have the bearing of one with considerable training yourself. Alsean Defense Force?"

"Mariner."

"Which is why he cannot bear to be out of sight of the water." Jarnell nudged his bondmate. "And so I find myself retiring here and working harder than I did before I retired."

"Warriors never retire; did you not know that?" Andira put a hand on Colonel Micah's shoulder. "Sometimes they make the attempt, but they never get very far."

"So I've noticed," Jarnell said with a wink as he rolled up his reader card. "You must be anxious to settle in, so we'll leave you to it and go take care of the rest of your Guards."

They took their leave and joined the crowd of Guards waiting at the edge of the clearing. With a quick exchange of words, the entire parade moved down the path and soon vanished into the forest, leaving their small group alone.

Jaros tugged at Colonel Micah's sleeve. "Why do Gehrain, Ronlin, and Vellmar get bondmate bowers while you only get a cabin?"

"Because I'm part of Lancer Tal's family," he said. "Which means she treats me worse than her Guards."

Lancer Tal laughed. "Pay him no attention, Jaros. He just needs to go for a swim."

CHAPTER 5
Stories

"Stars and Shippers, I didn't expect this," Ekatya said as she stood in the center of the room.

"Neither did I. They look so plain from the outside, but…wow." Lhyn stood next to her, gazing around their cabin.

The worn wooden steps leading to the front porch had given Ekatya the impression of old, simple construction. Stepping across the threshold ended that supposition in a hurry.

Their cabin was floored with hand-painted tiles polished to a shine, and the ceiling was made up of colored wood slats carefully arranged into geometric patterns. It took a moment for Ekatya to realize that the painted tiles represented a forest floor, and the ceiling represented the branches and leaves of trees. Each corner of the room was anchored by an unpeeled log—the trunks of the trees. Sconces on the two solid walls were housed in hand-blown glass shades of a rich rose-gold and would no doubt continue the theme with the soft glow of sunrise or sunset when they were lit.

One of the solid walls held detailed wooden cabinetry for their clothes, decorated with the same patterns as the ceiling, and the all-important shannel dispenser. Based on the sheer quality of the rest of the cabin, Ekatya expected that shannel to be top-notch.

Against the other solid wall was an enormous bed covered by a quilt in undulating shades of blue and silver. It had no headboard, but the wall itself was carved in ripples that were inlaid with matching colors of blue and silver, going all the way to the ceiling. Ekatya stared at it in puzzlement until Lhyn said, "Oh! It's a waterfall. And the bed is the pool at the base of it."

"You're quick. I wasn't seeing that at all." Ekatya trailed her fingers along the smooth quilt. "Sleeping in a pool; that will be a new one."

She walked through the door to the left of the bed and discovered a bathroom, which, while narrow from front to back, made up for it by utilizing the width of the cabin. Here the forest theme shifted to one of rocks and pools: the surface areas around the sink were made of flat stones, as was the flooring, and the shower at one end was elevated on what appeared to be a pile of darker stones with steps cut into them. Standing on the first step, Ekatya could see that the shower's base had been laid with hundreds of tiny tiles in varying shades of blue and green. Windows at each end of the bathroom were opaque and faintly tinted in green, making the bright daylight appear as if it were being filtered through thick trees surrounding a hidden pool.

"Did he say he was a builder?" Lhyn poked her head into the bathroom. "He's not a builder. He's a crafter. This is art."

"Why shouldn't a builder make art with his hands?" Ekatya asked. "There must be overlap in the castes. I saw some of those Guards carrying what looked like musical instrument cases. They can't be wholly defined by one aspect of their lives."

Lhyn ran a hand over the stonework surrounding the sink. "No, it's never that simple. And the castes encompass a lot. When I first figured them out, I thought, only six? How would I choose?" She scooted past Ekatya and walked up the shower steps. "But then I thought about it. Even when I was a teenager, I would have known that the warrior caste was out of the question. And the producer caste, and crafter…"

Ekatya watched her examining the shower tiles and shook her head with a smile. "You couldn't have been anything but a scholar. Though I think you have some warrior tendencies, too."

"I think you had too many drinks last night. But speaking of warriors… did you notice that Andira and Salomen already turned on their privacy screen?"

"What? They could hardly have gotten up the stairs yet." Ekatya went back into the main room far enough to see the Bonding Bower. Sure enough, the formerly clear glass walls had taken on an opaque sheen.

Lhyn's arms slid around her waist from behind. "They could be having sex up against the glass right now," she said in an amused tone. "With one Hades of a view. I'm envious."

"What do *we* do if we get in the bonding break mood?" Ekatya gestured at the open sides of their cabin. "I feel a bit on display."

"We close the walls. Didn't you read your brochure?" Lhyn released her and walked to a switch on one side of the bed. With a faint hum, a thick cloth slid out from one of the unpeeled logs that braced that corner, stretched itself across the entire length of the cabin, and snicked into place in a slot Ekatya hadn't noticed in the opposite log.

"Hm." Ekatya crossed to the other side of the bed, found the matching switch, and tested it. Soon their cabin was fully enclosed with two cloth walls, their off-white color letting in plenty of light while offering a large canvas for the hand-painted murals that covered them. Flowers of varying heights, trees, birds swooping through the air, animals she didn't recognize perched in the trees and rustling through the underbrush, fish leaping out of water—Ekatya had a feeling she could examine these walls for hours and not find everything.

Lhyn already was. "This is incredible!" she exclaimed, her finger brushing over a tiny rodent in the shadow of a tear-shaped leaf. "Like tapestries on spools. There must be spring tension inside the log, to keep the cloth tight when the walls aren't fully open." She went back to her switch, retracted the wall halfway, then stepped over and rapped her fingers against the cloth. It remained solid, with no ripple showing the impact of her knuckles. Next she moved to the far edge of the cloth and held her hand on the outside of it. Nearly touching her lips to the inside, she blew hard for a moment and straightened. "Thought so. Windproof."

"I'm guessing waterproof as well," Ekatya said. "Ingenious. And so much easier than building a wooden wall. Probably cheaper as well."

"Sure, if you use plain cloth. These murals must have taken weeks to paint. Two cloth walls times nine cabins times four cabin rings… Jarnell kept some crafters very busy."

They fiddled with their walls a bit more, finding the perfect compromise between privacy and maximum breeze, then unpacked their bags into the beautiful cabinetry. Ekatya couldn't leave without trying the shannel dispenser, so they sat at the tiny table for two—they were clearly not being encouraged to eat here—and shared a cup.

"It tastes great to me, but I'm not as picky as you are." Lhyn handed over the cup. "What's your verdict?"

"Divine," Ekatya moaned after one sip.

Lhyn watched her with a smile. "You do realize that's your fourth cup and it's not even midmeal. Shouldn't you be starting a bit lower than full addict level?"

"I *am* a full addict; what's the use in pretending? Besides, it's only three and a half cups."

When Ekatya finished her shannel—which made her total closer to three and three-quarters cups—it was nearly midmeal, so they walked across the circle of grass to the main cabin. Shikal and Colonel Micah were already there and enjoying a pink drink, which they explained was Jarnell's specialty fruit blend. Greetings were shared, new glasses were poured, and before they had taken a sip, Nikin came in with Jaros. Lanaril was only a few minutes behind, and the group settled around the spacious dining table, making conversation as they waited for the new bondmates to arrive. As Shikal explained to a fascinated Lhyn, on this first day the bondmates would be expected to keep regular mealtimes, but after that all bets were off—unless they forgot to eat altogether, in which case the family would perform their duty and drag them out of the Bonding Bower.

"Oh, I hope they forget," Colonel Micah said.

Shikal laughed and tapped their glasses together. "I'll help you drag them down."

Ekatya was content to sip her spirits, listen to the others, and watch Lhyn in her element. She had not seen such a relaxed, happy expression on Lhyn's face in too long. Then she noticed Lanaril watching her from across the table and knew she had been caught staring…or worse, caught feeling.

Embarrassed, she took in the sights of the room, which was decorated with the same themes as their own cabin. Comfortable chairs and couches were sprinkled about in such a way that two or three people could converse quietly, or the entire family could gather in a large group. One wall was taken up by a food prep area, which Ekatya learned was stocked with pre-made meals for their first day and would continue to be stocked daily thereafter, depending on choices they all made from the electronic menu attached to the wall by the cooling unit. Guests would rotate through cleanup duties, though the bondmates were exempt.

A roar of greetings brought her out of her thoughts, and she looked up to see Andira and Salomen entering hand in hand. They were not in the same clothing as when they had arrived, and Salomen's throat was now as thoroughly marked as Andira's.

Ekatya grinned at them and raised her glass, but they were spared the worst of the teasing thanks to the presence of Jaros. Though Ekatya wasn't certain when Alseans began their sex education, apparently it was sometime after the age of ten.

After a delicious meal of a tender white fish, the name of which Ekatya did not catch, Shikal and Colonel Micah volunteered for dish duty while Lanaril cleared the table. The others wandered over to the sitting area, where Andira and Salomen took over a wide chair that forced them to sit close together, which did not seem to be an issue. Lhyn pulled Ekatya down on a couch opposite them, while Nikin and Jaros chose smaller chairs. Jaros, who had been somewhat quiet during the meal, took this opportunity to grill Ekatya about her ship and share his own impressions of the *Caphenon*. Andira had taken the Opahs on a tour not too long ago, and Jaros was particularly fascinated with the bridge.

"How often do you use the full display?" he asked.

"Quite a lot, because I appreciate knowing where I am visually. Without it, all we have are our control boards, and most of the information on those takes the form of numerical data and graphs. There's nothing quite like being able to look around and *see*. But not every captain feels the same way. I know one who only uses the top hemisphere, because he says his crew gets queasy when all they have under their feet is space." She leaned forward and added in a conspiratorial tone, "I think his crew is fine. He's the one who gets queasy."

Jaros grinned. "But he can't admit it."

"Oh no. Captains do not admit queasiness."

"What happens if he has to fight a battle and needs the whole display?"

"Then he probably forgets all about feeling queasy until the battle is over, after which he turns the bridge over to his second-in-command, retreats to his private washroom, and...does something very uncaptain-like."

"You mean vomit?"

"What charming conversation we're having over here," Shikal said. The cleanup crew had arrived.

"Captain Serrado says not all captains can use the full bridge display," Jaros explained. "They get sick."

"Seems as if Fleet would screen for that sort of thing." Colonel Micah settled into a chair next to Shikal.

"They screen for everything you can think of and a few hundred more, but the captain I'm referring to flies a support ship. If he ever ends up in a battle, then something went very wrong." Ekatya noticed that Lanaril moved across the room before sitting, choosing a seat that closed their circle. Did the woman do anything spontaneously, or was she always playing her role?

"But you've fought so many. It must have been speedy, going home a hero," Jaros said dramatically. "How many awards did you get?"

Ekatya couldn't stop the derisive snort. "I didn't go home a hero."

It was as if a bolt of electricity had gone through the room. Andira in particular had straightened and was watching her with a keen stare.

"I didn't tell you everything," Ekatya said. "There wasn't anything you could do, and I didn't want you to worry."

"What happened?" Andira demanded.

Ekatya looked around the room, debating how much she could say given her current audience. Lhyn rested a hand on her thigh, offering silent support, and she relaxed. Other than Andira, no one here was involved in Protectorate politics. She would tell what she could and reserve the rest for later, when Jaros was not around.

"It took us half a moon to get home," she began. "By home, I don't mean my own planet. I mean Tashar, where both Fleet and the Protectorate government are headquartered. Then it took another half moon to get through all of the debriefings. Then I was finally called in to Admiral Tsao's office to get my next assignment."

CHAPTER 6
Reassignment

Tashar, 22 stellar months (16 Alsean moons) earlier

EKATYA STOOD STILL AS THE retinal scanner dropped in front of her face, lit up her eye, and returned to its position above her head.

"Captain Ekatya Serrado. Pass," said the computer.

The thick door in front of her slid open, and she stepped onto the platform where the train was already waiting. Uniformed people streamed through its doors and jostled for seats, but the officers' car was nearly empty. She chose a seat on the left side, knowing from long experience that it would have the best views as they traveled from the city of Galiomet to Command Dome.

While waiting for the train to finish loading, she adjusted the cuffs of her newly altered uniform shirt and smoothed out her jacket. She had only brought two of her tailored uniforms out of the *Caphenon*, and in the past two weeks of her involuntary sequestering at Protectorate Fleet Central Command, her access to laundering facilities had been limited. Apparently, her superiors did not care how well her uniform fit. She had been forced to wear standard-sized uniforms to the unending debriefings, and when the days grew too long and the questions too repetitive, she found the chafing and ill fit to be a form of torture. On her bad days, she wondered if that had been intentional.

When she was finally through and released from her "guest lodgings," which were nothing more than nicely appointed prison accommodations no matter how Admiral Tsao tried to spin it, she had wasted no time getting out of Command Dome and into the blessed anonymity of Galiomet. The first thing she had done was get her tailored uniforms laundered; the second was to visit a well-regarded tailor and drop off six new generics for alteration. The tailor expressed surprise at being asked to alter Fleet uniforms when there were so many specialist shops inside Command Dome, but Ekatya had no intention of entering that dome again until she had to.

Now she had to. After a mere two-day leave, most of which she spent in Lhyn's arms wondering why they had ever left Alsea, she was headed back in.

The train began to move, smoothly at first and acquiring a slight vibration as it picked up speed. It climbed onto the elevated track that allowed rapid passage across the city outskirts, then entered the agricultural fields and dropped to a lower track. Vehicle traffic could still pass beneath, but anything larger went to special crossings.

Soon the city had been left far behind and the train began a gradual ascent, leaving the valley floor and moving into the higher elevations. It wound around a hill, passed through a tunnel, and emerged on the side of another hill looking down into a new valley.

Command Dome took up all of it. At its center, the tall spires sparkled in the sunlight, their beauty belying the politics and short-sighted power mongering that took place inside. Surrounding them were vast warehouses, training facilities, housing, classrooms, laboratories, three hospitals with different specialties, restaurants featuring foods from all over the Protectorate, shops of every description, and countless offices. But the true power resided in those spires, and every Fleeter with an eye toward advancement dreamed of eventually having an office inside. Ekatya had once imagined it herself, and as a young ensign and then lieutenant, she had believed a captaincy would be her stepping stone into those buildings. Getting her own command taught her two things: she liked running her own show, and she hated politics. It had been some time since she wanted an office anywhere but onboard her own ship.

Though her dreams of working here had changed long ago, she still loved her occasional trips back. This first view of the dome, after emerging from the tunnel, had been one of her favorites.

But that was before she arrived from Alsea and was ordered to remain in her rooms on the fifty-eighth floor of Spire Three "for security purposes" until her debriefings were concluded. Being held a virtual prisoner did wonders for dulling her appreciation. She had not been allowed contact with her officers, which she expected, but being denied contact with her grandparents or Lhyn was shocking. Even if she had been taken into custody prior to a court-martial, she would have had the right to communication.

Coming back here now felt like walking into a trap.

She gazed out the window and tried to loosen the knot of anger in her stomach. For most of her adult life, this view had symbolized the best ideals of both Fleet and the Protectorate. The good people working and training here strove to protect the weak from those who would use or abuse them, to keep their part of the galaxy free from despots and their transport routes free from pirates, and to maintain a peace in which many planets with different cultures and political systems could coexist without prejudice.

Those ideals had failed spectacularly when the Protectorate tried to sell Alsea to the Voloth. While it was true that most of the Fleet brass had not known the real facts of the deal, it was also true that even when they did know, they had punished her for doing something about it. She might have escaped court-martial, and she still had the promise of a Pulsar-class ship somewhere down the line, but two weeks of being imprisoned and subjected to the questioning of her loyalties had proven to her that not everyone in those spires believed in Fleet ideals. Worse, many of those who did not believe held very powerful positions—and she had angered them.

The train twisted around a switchback, giving her a more relaxing view of the grassy hillside and the swathes of orange malkin flowers covering its flanks. She deliberately did not look across the car, did not look at the more open view, until the train rounded another switchback and Command Dome was once again looming outside her window.

Arching over the entire gigantic complex was a dome-shaped shield, more easily visible now that she was closer. The central location of the spires was no accident—they were outfitted with shield emitters that linked to those on the perimeter, providing a seamless and redundant system of protection. In the early days the shield had been transparent, since that was easier to construct, but there had been issues with wildlife. Birds flew straight into it, died, and slid down to pile up all around the edges; other wildlife either ran into it at ground level or got too close while scavenging on the carcasses. The city inhabitants had campaigned for change, but Ekatya wasn't certain that anything would have been done about the issue if not for one prosaic fact: the piles of carcasses rotted and stank. The shield stopped weaponry; it did not stop airflow.

Nowadays the shield was tweaked with a system that gave it visible form. While the buildings beneath were still in view, they seemed to be under a hazy dome with swirls of colors constantly moving over its surface. That was how Protectorate Fleet Central Command acquired its nickname of Command Dome. On the other side of the continent, the Protectorate government buildings were sheltered beneath a similar shield. No one called it anything but Gov Dome.

The train rounded one more switchback, found its way to level ground, and then dove into an underground access, one of five around the dome's perimeter. They were the only ways in or out. Ekatya sat quietly, watching the lights of the tunnel flash by, until the circular walls vanished and the train rose into the daylight. Most trains made several stops on their way into Spire Station, but this was an express. Nearly everyone on it was in uniform.

Training fields and barracks passed by her window; the distant spires drew nearer, and the train sank underground before coming to a halt at the end of its line. Everyone in the car rose as the doors whooshed open, and Ekatya let them go, waiting until the car was clear before stepping onto the platform. Hundreds of Fleeters jostled ahead of her, exuding a sense of importance and urgency as they rushed toward the hub at the center of the five train lines. She watched them clear the platform, then craned her neck and gazed at the arched rock ceiling high above. The architects had done a good job of making a utilitarian transport hub with no natural light seem spacious and airy. She wondered how many of the people rushing into the hub ever noticed.

Not that she had paid attention herself, back when she felt the same urgency.

Well. Time to move her feet and find out if she still had an ally in Admiral Tsao.

She walked into the hub, enjoying the myriad and delicious scents wafting from the ring of food shops, and crossed to the nearest row of tube lifts. Most of the passengers on her train had already been whisked away, leaving so many lifts open that she had no need to use the officers' lift on the end. At the nearest open tube, she lifted her palm to the scanning pad. Eye scan at one end, palm scan at the other—no one got into the Spires without passing redundant security protocols.

"Captain Ekatya Serrado, confirmed," the computer said. "Destination, please."

Ekatya held on to the circular rail with both hands. "Spire Two, level sixty-three, Admiral Tsao."

The rails were merely a precaution. Most of the time, the lift tubes operated so smoothly that she never felt any movement, let alone the gravity and centrifugal forces she should have as her tube sped through lateral and vertical chutes. A graphic on the tube's wall showed her progress through the complex, from the underground hub of the train station up to the trunk tubes at the surface, then a kilometer to the north to reach Spire Two, up through the central core of the spire, and out again to the tube bank nearest Admiral Tsao's office.

She had entered the tube in a noisy, echoing underground space perfumed by exotic foods. She exited onto thick carpeting in a nearly silent corridor, the air so perfectly filtered and recycled that the very absence of odor registered as a scent.

Settling her shoulders beneath her jacket, she walked down the familiar corridor to the admiral's door. The adjutant looked up from his desk and smiled as she entered.

"Captain Serrado, welcome back! It's good to see you after so many weeks of wondering if we could even get you off that planet. May I get you a cup of coffee?"

For a moment she was bewildered by his friendliness. "That would be lovely. Do you have the Allendohan blend?" She had developed a preference for the flavor from Lhyn's home planet.

"We certainly do. Let me get that for you." He bustled around the counter at the back of the room, speaking as he input the order. "Admiral Tsao is wrapping up a call. I'll tell her you're here, and I'm sure she'll be with you in just a few minutes." He crossed the plush carpet, holding out a dainty cup and saucer.

"Thank you." Ekatya sat in one of the comfortable chairs against the wall and sipped her coffee. She had only gotten through half of it when the interior door slid open and Admiral Tsao appeared.

"Captain Serrado. Please come in."

The adjutant was magically at her side, taking the cup and saucer from her hand before she managed two steps. She followed the admiral into her luxurious office, where the carpet seemed even thicker and a sinuously curved desk sat on the inside corner. One thing she had always liked about Tsao was the admiral's priority of aesthetics over power. While most of the brass put their desks facing the door, Tsao preferred not to have her back to the spectacular view. Her guests did instead.

Ekatya stood beside a visitor's chair while Tsao settled herself. The admiral was taller than she, with a full head of gray hair kept in a severe pulled-back style. She was slim in build, narrow of face, and bore a scar through her left eyebrow, a souvenir from her time on the front lines when the Voloth war was hot. Her blue eyes had not faded with age and still managed to look right through a person. Today, however, they seemed friendly.

"I'm so glad we got that nonsense with the debriefings over with," she said, then frowned at Ekatya's hands. "What happened to your coffee? Sit down."

"Your adjutant is very efficient, but I was done anyway," Ekatya said as she sat. "And I'm somewhat surprised at your characterization of the debriefings."

Tsao leaned back in her chair and sighed. "I know. I wish I could have supported you more openly, but half of that panel was waiting to jump on my back if I did. The only way I could help you was by making a show of impartiality. Otherwise my opinion at the final conference would have meant nothing."

That would have been nice to know two weeks ago. But Ekatya had played these games as well and understood the position Tsao was in. "It's good to hear that I didn't lose your support," she said carefully. "And apparently carried half the panel, since they set me free."

Tsao frowned. "Yes, that house arrest was…unnecessary. And embarrassing. I did lodge a formal protest against that, because regardless of how the debriefings went, we simply do not treat decorated officers that way. Or any officers who haven't broken the law. You did disobey orders and break several regulations, but the fact that you were awarded a new Pulsar-class ship should have put that in your rear sensors."

"So why was I given the special treatment?"

"You're not going to like the answer."

Ekatya waited.

"You attracted the attention of Director Sholokhov. He's the one who ordered your confinement to quarters."

"The head of Protectorate Security? I didn't know he could overrule admirals."

"He can overrule anyone, with the possible exception of the Assembly Leader and the President, and even then I'm not certain he couldn't arrange something behind the curtain." Tsao leaned forward, crossing her forearms on her desk. "Sholokhov is a very dangerous man. No one wants to be in his line of sight, not even me. I probably burned a few fingers even filing that protest against his confinement order, though it's entirely possible that he just laughed at it. He does love to demonstrate his power."

"Then I'm guessing he's the reason that debriefing panel was stacked with admirals who have never liked me."

"Yes. And now you see why my open support would have done you no good."

Suddenly, Ekatya felt much better about being in this building. "I do. Can I assume that panel did not reflect general Fleet consensus, then?"

"Don't imagine for a moment that there aren't a number of admirals wishing they could strip you down to ensign. You took the word maverick and put your own image on it. Had you been wrong in your assessment, your actions would have damaged the Protectorate to such a degree that it would have taken years to recover."

Ekatya did not react, and Tsao eventually nodded. "But your assessment was correct, and you saved us from a devastating shift in the balance of power. It would have taken more than mere years to recover from the Voloth gaining control of Alsea's nanoscrubbers. It might have taken half a century. They could have confined us to just a few planetary systems."

Again Ekatya waited. She was used to Tsao's style.

"So yes, those admirals are the minority. Most of us know exactly what you saved us from, and I personally believe your actions are worthy of a Presidential Medal of Galactic Service." She smiled for the first time. "Finally broke that mask of yours. I'll mark this as an accomplishment."

Ekatya was almost too shocked to hear her last words. "You… Galactic Service? But that's for—"

"Acts of such valor, distinction, or importance that they impact the course of history, yes. And that is exactly what you did." Tsao gave one brisk nod. "Unfortunately, in the course of doing that, you also got up the asses of some very powerful people. One of them is Director Sholokhov."

Still floating on the idea of a Medal of Galactic Service, Ekatya said, "But I've been cleared, so what can he do? I just need to keep my head down for the next year or so until I get my new ship, and then I'll be off his sensors."

Tsao looked at her pityingly. "It will be closer to a year and a half, according to the last estimate, and he can do anything he damn well wants. And what he wants is you."

"What?"

"You've been assigned to him, Captain. I received your new orders yesterday. Which was a surprise to me, since I thought I was the one who issued your orders."

Ekatya's jaw loosened. "I…wait. Fleet warship captains do not work for members of government. Not even directors."

"They do when they've been requested for temporary assignment in the absence of active shipboard duty."

"A temp assignment for a year and a half?" Ekatya's voice rose. "What happened to being the military liaison for the task force reviewing the Non-Interference Act?"

"Ironically, that's how Sholokhov maneuvered you into his clutches. You were already working with the government. He simply inserted himself as your reporting authority."

"So I'm still working with the task force, but reporting to him."

"Correct."

Ekatya closed her eyes and took a calming breath. "If he wanted me reporting to him, why put me through that hangman's debriefing? And the business with the confinement to quarters? It doesn't make sense."

"It does to him. He was proving a point."

"What, that he has power over my career?" The anger of the last two weeks was surging back.

"No. That he has power over your *life*. Captain…" Tsao paused. "Ekatya. Please listen carefully. I can't protect you from this. You are officially no longer under my authority. You are under the authority of a man who thinks nothing of destroying people's lives if they cross him, or if their destruction will gain him some tiny step forward in any of the thousand ops he's currently running. He sees people as strategic assets, nothing more. And now he sees you as a strategic asset. I don't know how he intends to use you, but he surely has something in mind, and just as surely, you won't like it. But I strongly advise you to do whatever you have to, short of breaking the law, and even then I wouldn't worry too much about the lesser laws."

Ekatya stared at her. She had never heard Tsao sound so concerned.

"I want you to come back to me when you've fulfilled your temp time with him," Tsao continued. "I want you in that new ship. But first you need to get through this, and that means staying on his good side." She frowned. "That might not be the right term; I'm not sure he has a good side. Just make sure he has no reason to punish you."

Tsao sent the new orders to her pad, offered a few more words of advice—most of which boiled down to *don't give him a reason to strike*—and wished her luck. When Ekatya stepped back into the lift tube, the knot in her stomach had nothing to do with dropping sixty-three stories back to ground level. How was she supposed to avoid angering a man she had already angered? Sholokhov had put her through Tartarus for two weeks simply to prove his power over her. And he had denied her the most basic right of communication, which should not have been possible. For Shipper's sake, convicted criminals had the right to communication!

On the train back to Lhyn's hotel, she did a records search for Sholokhov, filtered out all mainstream news sources—which she assumed he had some control over—and began reading the news from small outfits and independent writers. The stories were not flattering. One in particular made her queasy.

Sholokhov had been on a firing range with knock-down targets, practicing with two friends. They were using pulse pistols, civilian weapons which lacked the precision of hand phasers but had the advantage of a larger point of impact. Pulse projectiles were also prone to ricochets.

The three friends had emptied their charge caps, knocking down most of the targets, but Sholokhov had missed one. His two friends called out an on-range warning, after which no shooting could be allowed. Then they walked out to reset their targets.

Ignoring the most basic rule of shooting ranges, Sholokhov had put a new charge cap on his pulse pistol and attempted to down his last target. The pulse projectile hit the left edge of the target and ricocheted through the thigh of one of his friends, nicking the femoral artery. The only reason the man did not bleed out was that the range was close to a hospital.

The shooting was entirely Sholokhov's fault. Even raw Fleet recruits knew to never shoot downrange after an on-range warning was called. Failure to abide by one of the most basic rules of weapons handling resulted in heavy penalties up to and including discharge from Fleet.

Sholokhov admitted no fault. To the contrary, he was so angry at his friends for going on-range while he was still trying to down his final target that he forced the injured man to apologize for getting in his way.

Ekatya dropped the pad in her lap and stared out the window. Sholokhov had nearly killed his friend and made him apologize for it.

If that was how he treated friends, how was she going to get through the next year and a half?

CHAPTER 7
Memories

"Brings back memories, doesn't it?" Lhyn looked over with a sunny smile as they walked into the hotel lobby.

Ekatya stopped, then turned back to the door they had just come through. "I never came in this way. I had no idea this was the same hotel. You sneak!"

Lhyn's open laughter turned heads in the lobby. "So much for your observation skills, Fleeter. This is why you leave anthropology to the professionals. There are four entrances to this hotel, and you only ever used two."

"I might have used more had I stayed with my original intent of exploring Gov Dome after my lectures. Somehow I never seemed to see anything besides the inside of my room."

"Not my fault," Lhyn said as they crossed to the bank of check-in units. She bent down for a retinal scan.

"Entirely your fault. I came here with very professional intentions. It was a conference, after all."

Lhyn held up her pad to the unit, waited for the key transfer, then checked it. "I came for a conference, too. Just not the one I stumbled into."

Ekatya held up her own pad and received the key code. "You never stumbled."

She felt a haunting sense of familiarity as they entered the lift together, and when Lhyn pushed her against the back wall and kissed her, the familiarity took root in her bones. They had done this every time, unable to wait even for the twenty seconds it would take to get to her floor.

The lift door opened and Lhyn pulled back, her hand sliding down from Ekatya's shoulder and tangling their fingers together. "I remember being quite irritated that the idiot clerk pointed me to the wrong conference room. Do I look like a merchant marine?"

"How do you succeed in your field if you think in stereotypical terms like that?" Ekatya let herself be led down the quiet corridor. "Just because you're gorgeous doesn't mean you couldn't be a merchant marine attending my lecture series."

"Oh, that comment gets a reward." They arrived at their door, where Lhyn held her pad to the scanner. As soon as the door slid open, she pulled Ekatya inside and kissed her again, this time with less urgency and more depth.

"It's the truth," Ekatya said when they pulled apart. "Thank you, by the way."

"For what?"

"For bringing us here. I've been dreading coming to Gov Dome, and I'm dreading tomorrow's meeting, but this…" She looked around the elegant space. "You even got us the same room."

"Well, I certainly wasn't going to get us my old room. The Institute put me up in a closet. Captains get much better accommodation."

Ekatya went to the window and looked out over the busy landscape of Gov Dome. From the nineteenth floor she had an excellent view of the imposing buildings at the heart of the complex: the Presidential Palace, the Hall of Assembly, the Hall of Justice, and the Hall of Records. The four cornerstones of the Protectorate government lined the sides of a vast grassy square, anchored at its center by a pool full of water jets which never stopped their graceful dance, no matter the time of day or night. She had often stood at this window on her last visit, watching the jets play, and had never seen them repeat a pattern.

Lhyn's arms came around her waist and settled over her stomach. "I have such good memories of that view. And this room."

Ekatya leaned back against her. "Me too. It was so out of character for me, letting a stranger pick me up after my lecture."

"Maybe some part of you knew even then. We may not have the empathic centers of Alseans, but if we're tyrees, then *something* had to connect. I know I was drawn to you the moment I walked in the conference room and saw you up on the stage. You were practically glowing in the lights, and you had total command of the room. Those merchant marines were hanging on your words."

"Were you?" Ekatya's gaze was still on the view, but she wasn't seeing it anymore. She was seeing a tall figure at the back of that conference room, striding down the aisle as the audience was rising and filing out. The stranger had smiled as if she knew her, and Ekatya had simply stopped what she was doing and waited.

"Hanging on your words? No. I was focused on your tone of voice…and your body language…" Lhyn slid her hands up Ekatya's sides. "…and the way you used your hands." She brought her hands around and interlaced their fingers. "My experience with Fleet captains was that they were all business all the time—and usually exasperated with me and my teams. You should have been the last person I was attracted to." Resting her chin on Ekatya's shoulder, she added, "But I do remember that you were telling them something about what to do in the event of capture. It's hard to imagine a lifestyle where getting held up by pirates is an occupational hazard."

"Some of those shipping routes are ridiculously hazardous, and the most dangerous ones pay the best wages. Merchant marines aren't known for playing it slow and safe."

As she nosed into the hollow beneath Ekatya's ear, Lhyn whispered, "Slow and safe does not describe what we did that night."

"Or any of the next four nights." Ekatya turned and slid her hands up Lhyn's chest. "I don't want to think about tomorrow. Do you suppose we could relive one of those nights instead?"

"I thought you'd never ask."

CHAPTER 8
Sholokhov

Ekatya's good mood lasted through breakfast and continued to buoy her as she walked through the streets, across the park, and into the Presidential Palace. It even held up when she passed through security and her appointment was confirmed. It began to slip in the dark-paneled corridors with their ostentatious artwork, fell a bit further when Sholokhov's assistant ignored her greeting and pointed her to an uncomfortable chair, and died altogether after half an hour of waiting. She had arrived precisely on time for an appointment Sholokhov had made. It was clear that the power games had already begun.

Forty-five minutes after her appointment, the assistant stood up and opened the inner door. "Captain Serrado, Director Sholokhov will see you now."

She did not offer a thank-you as she walked past him. If power games were what Sholokhov wanted, then she would not put herself into a position of weakness by thanking an assistant who had, probably by order, treated her rudely.

The office oozed luxury, from the handwoven Galay Imperial carpet to the unique art in individually lit niches along the walls. It had the same dark wood paneling as the corridors, and Sholokhov's desk matched in both color and style, its massive bulk taking up the entire space in front of the wall of windows.

Sholokhov did not look up. He was sitting at an angle to his desk, reading an old-fashioned paper document, the ornate windows behind him lighting his features. His wiry, graying hair was closely cropped and ended at a bald spot atop his head. Though his body was slender, his face was rounded, with shaggy eyebrows shadowing the blue eyes that stood out vividly against his black skin. It was an unusual color combination, and one that Ekatya normally found attractive. On this man, it was unsettling.

As she had expected, his suit was expensive and perfectly tailored. The purple scarf of office was tied into an expert knot at the front of his throat, its ends draping gracefully over his shoulders. Each hand bore a heavy gold signet ring.

He said nothing, and she waited in silence. Eventually, he swiveled his chair back to his desk, signed the paper, folded and sealed it with a bit of putty, and pressed one ring into the seal. Then he set the stamped packet aside, picked up another paper, swiveled his chair around, and began reading.

Ekatya rolled her eyes. This was beyond petty. And who used signet rings in this age? Or paper?

She stood through three more signings and stampings, noting that he used the left ring for one of them and the right for all the others. She remained motionless as the assistant entered the room, silently accepted the four packets, and left again.

Fifteen minutes after she had walked in this room and one hour after her appointment, Sholokhov looked up at her. "Sit down."

"I would rather stand," she said. "I've been sitting for most of the past two weeks."

His gaze grew sharper, if that was possible. Her reference to the confinement he had arranged had hit its mark.

"I suppose you're feeling ill-used about that."

"Mostly just bored with the game playing." In her head she heard Tsao's voice saying *Don't give him a reason to strike*, but what was the point? This man was a torquat with an ego that would never be sufficiently stroked, and she might as well be honest since satisfying him was out of the question.

"Says the woman playing her own game." He leaned back in his chair and tapped one forefinger on the scrolled wooden armrest. "The interesting part is that you have a reputation as a straight shooter. I'm almost impressed by how well you've covered your real agenda."

Did he really think she was going to ask the question he wanted?

He tapped his finger a few more times, then abruptly let his chair come forward and rested his hands on his desk. "Sit down, Captain. I'm not going to get a crick in my neck."

She sat. Her point had been made.

"Did Tsao tell you the vote tally on the court-martial panel?"

"Admiral Tsao," she said, putting emphasis on the rank, "would never share information that I am not authorized to know."

"Good for her. I will. The panel voted four to three." He paused, then added, "In favor."

She had expected his first salvo to be unpleasant, but this slipped right past her shields. "Then why was I called back for a debrief instead of a court-martial?"

"That's a very good question. One I've been asking myself for several weeks. Imagine my surprise to find out that the vote for your court-martial was overruled by order of the President. She does not get involved in Fleet decisions, but for some reason she took an interest in the case of the captain who disobeyed orders and lost her ship to a pack of barbaric aliens who don't even have shield technology. I understand they still use *swords*."

Ekatya clenched her jaw but said nothing. He wanted her to defend his characterization of the Alseans. She needed to understand his game.

He waited, then gave her a slight smile. "It was a mystery, and I love a good mystery. So I put a few words in the right ears. Do you know what I learned? I learned that the order saving you from court-martial was tied to the order putting you into another Pulsar-class ship. And both orders came from an agreement between the President and the Lancer of Alsea."

Though startled to learn that she owed Andira even more than she had realized, she kept her face still.

"The President acted on a flawed recommendation from the negotiation team," he continued. "Which neglected to consult this office before issuing it."

You were cut out of the loop and your ass is burning, Ekatya translated. She was beginning to see how she had earned the enmity of a man she had never met.

"You, Captain Serrado, have an alien patron. A patron who somehow found herself in possession of something highly dangerous to us and used it to hold us hostage. The concessions that woman wrung out of us are beyond belief. We gave the Alseans everything but my underwear, and in exchange, we can't even land a trade ship there until two years from now."

Ekatya resisted the urge to point out the obvious. No trade or transport company in the Protectorate had ships that could land on Alsea, thanks to the nanoscrubbers. New ones would have to be built, and the negotiating team had calculated that no ships would be ready earlier than eighteen months from now. The condition that Alsea be allowed time to recover from the invasion and prepare for off-world trade had been a minor one as far as the Protectorate was concerned.

But not for Sholokhov, apparently.

"Fusion reactors, surf engines, base space tech, matter printers…not to mention a top-of-the-line warship left behind for them to pick over, including its entire contingent of fighters. I suppose we should be grateful you managed to get the shuttles away. And then you sat on their side of the negotiation table and *helped* that woman steal our credit chits and the rings off our fingers. So I am quite understandably concerned about where your loyalties lie." He brushed one finger over an ornament on his desk, which she now saw was a crystalline carving of the Protectorate emblem.

"I left Alsea," she said. "I believe it's obvious where my loyalties lie."

"Don't insult my intelligence!" he barked. "You could do nothing more for your patron while trapped on that backwater planet. You needed to get here. Now, I'm going to give you one chance to do this the easy way. What did Lancer Tal ask from you in exchange for getting you another ship?"

"She asked me to stay on Alsea."

The unexpected answer made him pause, then scowl. "This is not a joke."

"And I'm not joking. She wanted me to stay and work for her government, but she didn't want that to be a decision I made because I had no other options. So she gave me an option. I chose to return." And she was regretting that decision more and more every day.

"Why? What are you doing for her here?"

She stared at him for several seconds in silence. At last she said, "Director, you work in a world of shadows where no one says what they truly believe or intend. I think you don't know how to recognize it when someone is being forthright. I am telling you the truth. Lancer Tal is not my patron, but she is my friend. What she did for me is what one friend does for another. She didn't put any conditions on her gesture."

"Your friend," he scoffed. "Planetary leaders don't make friends, and if that's what you truly think, then you're not as smart as I thought you were. Nor are you a player. You're something far worse: naive."

"I certainly have been naive," she shot back. "I was naive to believe it when I was told that the Protectorate's sale of Alsea to the Voloth was a difficult but ultimately beneficial exchange. I stopped being naive when I found out that the five civilizations we were supposedly saving didn't exist, and the Alseans were being destroyed for profit. I didn't help them for the sake of a patron or even a friend. It was just the right thing to do."

"You're not only naive. You're an *idealist*." He spoke the word as if it tasted foul in his mouth.

"And you're a person who is so far down the sewer, you no longer recognize that some ideals are worth fighting for."

"How dare you!"

She was all the way in now, with no option but to play it out and hope for the best. "How long has it been since someone was honest with you? Who spoke and acted without a hidden agenda? Doesn't it get tiring having people trip over themselves to tell you what they think you want to hear?"

"Are you seriously trying to convince me that I should value being insulted for the sheer novelty of it?"

"That wasn't an insult. It was an observation that the nature of your job has, by necessity, altered your perceptions. You do difficult work, and I and everyone in the Protectorate who has benefitted from your vigilance appreciate that you do it. But there is a personal cost to what you do. I am not your enemy, and I am not an enemy of the Protectorate. I *am* an enemy of those who would defile the ideals of the Protectorate—whether they're Voloth or our own people. I swore to uphold those ideals, just the same as you. We're fighting on the same side."

He glared, speechless, and she guessed that no one had spoken to him that way in a long time.

Then his face went blank, the anger gone as if it had never existed. "Very well, Captain. If we're fighting on the same side, then you'll have no issues with my assignment for you."

"You're altering my orders," she said in resignation. Of course he was.

"Only slightly. You'll still be working with Minister Staruin on his task force, and I believe that you bring some useful skills to that table. But I don't believe that Staruin is prioritizing the security of the Protectorate. He has his own agenda. You will find out what that is, then report on the activities and possible agendas of the other members of the task force."

"You want me to spy for you?"

"If that's what you want to call it. I call it observing and reporting."

She hesitated, trying to find the right words. "Director, I'm not trained in infiltration. That's a specialist skill."

"True, but regrettably, you're what I have to work with."

He was enjoying this. She hated to twist on his hook, but she had to at least try to convince him.

"Wouldn't you have a better chance of success if you replaced me on the task force? Surely you've already seen that I'm not good at dissembling—or holding my tongue. You need someone who can play a role."

"I do," he said in an alarmingly cheerful tone. "And while I've definitely seen that you can't hold your tongue, I'm not so certain about the role playing."

"Director—"

His cheer vanished as he stared at her with cold eyes. "You're not doing a good job of convincing me of your loyalty, Captain."

"I didn't know I still had to," she snapped before she could stop herself. "I thought that was what the two-week inquisition was for."

"No, that was to convince Fleet of your loyalties. I'm not as naive." He opened a drawer in his desk and pulled out a pad. "Let's dispense with our little games, shall we? I need you to perform a task. You're trying to wriggle out of it, and I can't have that. So this is the part where we get down to the deal making."

He slid the pad across to her, and she saw at a glance that the file on it was an arrest warrant. How predictable, the little slime. He couldn't get at her through military justice, so he was going to the civilian justice system.

She picked up the pad and scrolled down, curious to see what the charges would be, and nearly dropped it when she read the name on the warrant.

"Ah, you've reached the meat of it, I see." Sholokhov was practically glowing with pleasure. "I had you figured out long ago, Captain. I did entertain the tiny possibility that I could be wrong, but obviously…I wasn't."

She took a breath, trying to wrestle down her rage. "There is no reason to bring her into this."

"There is every reason. I need you to do a job, and I can't trust you to do it. So I need leverage. It's a straightforward exchange—surely you can appreciate how forthright I'm being?"

"How can you possibly expect these charges to hold?"

He leaned back and crossed his hands over his stomach in a relaxed pose. "Let's see. The head of an anthropology expedition discovers that one of her team has betrayed her research to the Voloth, thereby destroying nearly a year of her work. She calls for help, but before help can arrive, the man selling her research is mysteriously tossed out an airlock. Who would have had the most incentive to kill him? And spacing…it's the sort of murder that doesn't require anything other than the ability to shove someone through a door and slam it shut behind them. Even a skinny academic could do it. Of course, there's always the ship's security footage, which could have cleared Dr. Rivers of any suspicion—but sadly, that footage was tampered with. Almost as if Dr. Rivers didn't want anyone to see what was on it."

Ekatya clenched her fists in her lap where he couldn't see. "Dr. Rivers was never under investigation. She cooperated fully with her captain at the time and with the investigators on our way back here. There is no evidence tying her to that murder, and anyone who knows her knows that she could never have done it."

"Do you know how many murderers are convicted after a dozen character witnesses swear up and down that so-and-so could *never* have done such a thing?"

"You have no evidence!"

He smiled at her. "You are betraying your naiveté. I don't need evidence. I just need a good story. And a lead scientist killing someone who sold off her work is an excellent story."

She threw the pad on his desk. "You're so bent on proving your power that you won't even consider the fact that I'm not the best person for this job. You would be far better served with someone trained in infiltration, but that's not your real concern, is it?"

He didn't move. "Do we have a deal, Captain?"

As if she had any choice. It didn't matter that Lhyn would never be convicted; all Sholokhov had to do was make certain she went to trial and then arrange for her to be denied bail. With his connections, he could keep her locked up for years until the system ground through its gears and spat her out the other end.

"I'll do your dirty work," she said in disgust. "But I want a guarantee that you will bury these ridiculous charges and make sure no one ever brings them up again."

"Ah, see? Now that's how I determine loyalties. You won't do what I ask for the sake of the Protectorate, but you'll do it for your lover. You've told me a lot today, but not with your words. And not with your *honesty*." He put the pad back in the drawer. "You can have your guarantee."

"And this assignment does not exceed the construction time of my new ship."

"I can't imagine it would."

"In writing."

"Of course. It will be in your office by the end of the day. Your new assistant is waiting outside; he'll show you to it. You're dismissed, Captain."

She stood up, seething at his usage of military authority when he had none. But there was nothing she could do.

The small chuckle that followed her out the door haunted her for months afterward.

CHAPTER 9
Revelations

Alsea, present day

It was dark outside when Ekatya paused to sip some water. After a long and enjoyable day spent walking the island trails, lounging on the black sand beach, and nibbling on any number of tasty treats, they had all returned to the central cabin for evenmeal and conversation. She had waited until after Jaros had gone to bed to tell this part of her story, and now her throat was dry from the constant use of her voice.

It hadn't been a nonstop tale, of course. Everyone had questions about Command Dome and Gov Dome, and there were even more about how she and Lhyn had met. Andira had a few things to say about her gift of choice being misinterpreted by Sholokhov, which led to a discussion of different cultures and how the inability to verify honesty could lead to paranoia as a lifestyle. Colonel Micah wanted to know more about an entire department of government being devoted to spy activities.

Now Andira rose and said, "I'm sorry, but I've just remembered something Aldirk needed me to do. I'm afraid I'll have to excuse myself from our conversation. It's a fascinating story, Ekatya—I look forward to hearing more tomorrow. Sleep well, everyone." She dropped a kiss on Salomen's cheek and was out the door before anyone could react. A few murmurs of "good night" and "sleep well" followed her, but Ekatya didn't think she heard any of them.

She glanced at Lhyn, who was gazing at the open doorway with a slight frown. So she wasn't the only one who thought this was out of character. Salomen's expression indicated concern and bafflement, and nearby, Lanaril merely looked troubled.

But not confused.

Yet Salomen was the one who had full access to Andira's emotions, so what could Lanaril know that she didn't?

It hit her like a shuttle then, and she was out of her seat instantly. Stupid, stupid, what had she been thinking? She should have known.

"I'm a little tired myself," she told the group. "Must have been all that sunlight—we don't get much of that in space. I think I'll head out as well. Good night."

Colonel Micah smiled at her and took up the conversation, effortlessly redirecting the others as Ekatya made her way to the door. She didn't think for a minute that he was unaware, but he was smooth enough to cover for her. Or, more likely, to cover for Andira.

She escaped onto the deck and was enveloped in warm, perfumed darkness. The owners of the resort prized their night sky and had minimized lights, setting up a system in which tiny, hooded ground lights along each path were activated only when a person set foot on it. Andira's route was obvious since it was the only one lit, and Ekatya could just make her out, walking briskly toward the Bonding Bower.

She set off in pursuit, but Andira was moving fast. By the time Ekatya reached the trunk of the giant delwyn tree, her friend was already on the deck.

The wooden steps winding around the trunk also conserved light, with three steps lit at a time. The next step lit up as her foot left the last one, creating a moving unit of light that led her upward.

When she emerged onto the deck, Andira was coming out of the cabin with a bottle in one hand and two glasses in the other. She did not say a word as she crossed to the table, sat down, and poured grain spirits into the glasses.

Taking the silent invitation, Ekatya sat perpendicular to her. Andira nudged over one glass, picked up her own, and tossed it back in one swallow. Ekatya followed suit, humming as the familiar burn worked its way down her throat. It had been nearly two years since she had tasted Alsean grain spirits, but that particular flame was memorable.

She refilled their glasses and watched Andira stare at Pica Mahal, its brooding mass interrupting the silver moon path that Eusaltin made on the water. At the moment, she thought, Andira and that volcano had a few things in common.

"You are nothing like him," she said.

Andira shook her head. "I am exactly like him." She drank off half the glass and resumed her contemplation of the volcano.

"I wouldn't be here if that were true."

"Then tell me how we differ!" Fury flared in her eyes when she turned. "I would have used your tyree bond to force you to do what I wanted. He used it for the same thing."

"Not the same thing at all. Your whole world depended on you, and how many options did you have? Sholokhov's little game—the only thing at stake was his ego. He had so many options, an entire spy organization at his fingertips, hundreds of people who would have been better at that job than I was. It wasn't a last resort for him. It was a power play to prove his superiority."

"Ah, so it's all a matter of degree."

She ignored the sarcasm. "Of course it's a matter of degree. Your legal system is a matter of degrees; so is mine. Commit this act and you pay a fine; commit that related act and you go to prison. Societies are built on those slopes."

Andira raised her glass in a mocking salute and drained it, but Ekatya noted that she wasn't refuting the point.

"It's also a matter of intent," she said. "Sholokhov took pleasure in using Lhyn as an axe over my neck. He didn't even know she's my tyree; he thought she was just a lover. If I hadn't had Lhyn, he probably would have dug up something on my grandparents and used that, and he would have enjoyed it just as much. Did you enjoy it?" She put a hand on top of the bottle as Andira reached for it. "Because it looks like you still feel so guilty that you walked out on the family party you've waited half your life for. How drunk do you plan to get?"

Andira pulled the bottle out from beneath her hand. "Drunk enough to not feel anything when Salomen turns me away tonight."

"You still haven't told her."

"No. But I'll have to now, because she'll want to know why I'm feeling this way. She would have followed me out if you hadn't. Fahla, what a day." She set the bottle down and picked up her glass. "I also had to tell her about my first tyree bond today. Might as well get all the secrets out at once, eh? By the way, thank you for that bad advice about waiting to tell her."

"What? I didn't tell you to wait until after your damned bonding ceremony!"

"Perhaps you should have been a little more specific, then."

"Stop," Ekatya said sharply. "I know you don't mean that."

Andira went still, then closed her eyes and shook her head. "No, I don't."

She didn't seem inclined to say anything more, so Ekatya tried to lighten the mood. "You're not Sholokhov. With a single exception, I never followed that asshead out of a room by choice."

That got a faint reaction. "I would, but only to teach him a lesson."

"I'd pay to watch it." She spent a moment fantasizing.

"I can feel that, you know."

"I'm well aware. It's not as if I couldn't dump him on his flat ass myself, but it would be so much better coming from a woman he's convinced is barbaric."

"Wouldn't that reinforce his belief?"

"Yes, but he loves being proved right. So it would be satisfaction all the way around."

Andira's expression relaxed, a hint of a smile playing about her mouth. "Thank you for that."

"Making you feel better? That's what a friend does. Especially after I made you feel bad in the first place."

"It wasn't your fault." She looked back to the volcano.

"I rather think it was. I got caught up in the story and forgot the implications." After a pause, Ekatya added, "Lhyn has a story that ties into this. It's not a good one."

"Is that why Lanaril keeps looking at her like she wants to give her a warmron?"

Ekatya nodded. "Speaking of that…I noticed that she knew why you left, even though Salomen didn't."

"She knows." Andira sipped her drink.

"I'm glad you've had someone else to talk to."

The silence that followed felt…off, somehow, and Ekatya's senses sharpened. She watched Andira, so focused on a volcano that could barely be seen, and that niggle at the back of her mind raced to the front and blew itself into full, bright color.

"Stars and Shippers," she whispered. "She was the one."

She knew that Andira had delegated the job of empathically forcing Lhyn but had never really thought about who the task had fallen to. Some faceless high empath, a warrior involved in the war effort.

But of *course* it would have been Lanaril.

"That first Sharing," she said. "In the temple. It was going to be then."

Andira nodded jerkily, refusing to turn her head.

"Oh, that fucking—" She shoved her chair back, walked to the rail, and leaned over it to catch her breath. The canopy of trees beneath her rustled slightly in the breeze, a soothing sound that only served to highlight the tension in her body.

Lanaril had always been there. Lhyn's first real friend on Alsea, the one she had kept in touch with while they were gone. The one she couldn't wait to see when they landed again.

The one she trusted.

The more she thought about it, the more Ekatya realized that some part of her had known. No matter how much Lhyn wanted them to be friends, she had always been wary of that woman. Now she knew why.

She was so upset over this revelation that it took several minutes to realize how Andira must be reading her reaction.

"Shek," she said softly. Then she tilted her head back, took a deep breath, and turned around. "I don't know how to explain to you that it's different, but it is."

Andira held up her glass. "Well, if you can't explain it, I certainly cannot." She emptied the glass, slammed it on the table, and rose from her chair. "Go back to your cabin, Ekatya. I have a hard conversation coming up, and you shouldn't be here for it."

Voices rang out in the clearing, and Ekatya looked down to see Salomen stepping off the main cabin's deck. The path to the Bonding Bower lit up as she walked toward them.

"No," she said. "I'm not leaving. I can't trust you to not make yourself look as bad as possible."

"This is between my bondmate and me."

"No, it's not! But do you know who *should* be here? Lanaril. That's why it's different. Because you told me the truth, right from the beginning, and she never has."

Andira watched Salomen's approach. "When would she have done that?" she asked in a weary tone. "When you and Lhyn had midmeal with her? During any of the quantum com calls that you never had? She has been Lhyn's friend, not yours."

"And that's not likely to change now."

"Has it occurred to you that perhaps that's the reason she's not your friend?"

Actually…no, it had not. But then why was she Lhyn's friend?

Salomen reached the tree and began climbing the steps at a rapid clip. No words were spoken on the deck until she stepped onto it, her worried gaze moving across both of them.

"I thought you were resolving whatever this was," she said. "But it suddenly became much worse. I cannot stay down there when you're feeling like this." She glanced at the table and then lifted the bottle. "Good Fahla. This was full when we left. What happened?"

Andira looked at Ekatya, who crossed her arms over her chest and leaned against the rail. "I'm staying."

"I don't want you to."

"Well, I do," Salomen said. "Both of you sit down. Now."

It wasn't until Ekatya was in the chair that she realized she had responded to that order as if it had come from an admiral. She looked at Salomen with new respect.

Salomen waited until they were both settled before taking her own chair and fixing Ekatya with a questioning look. "Something about your story upset Andira, and you knew what it was."

Startled to be the first one asked, Ekatya said, "She thought—mistakenly, may I add—that Sholokhov's threat against Lhyn was similar to what she did before the Battle of Alsea."

"You threatened Lhyn?" Salomen looked at Andira in surprise. "You were going to tell me about this. You mentioned it in the transport—something you did to make sure Ekatya stayed to help in the battle."

Andira closed her eyes. "Ekatya. Please leave."

There was a desperation in her tone that made Ekatya more determined than ever to stay.

"I think I need to tell this story," she said. "Here's the simple version: Andira asked for my help in the battle, but I had orders to destroy my ship to keep it out of Voloth hands and then abandon Alsea to the Voloth. And I was going to do it."

Salomen sat in stunned silence. Ekatya could hardly look at her.

"Those orders were terrible and I tried everything I could to avoid them, but the weight of Protectorate politics was too much. Nothing I said, nothing Lhyn said changed their minds. We convinced Fleet, but not the Assembly—not the people in charge of treaties. They were prepared to sell Alsea to the Voloth in exchange for an agreement on borders between our two territories, as well as five other civilizations that were in danger of being enslaved or destroyed. When Lhyn realized that I planned to obey my orders and she couldn't talk me out of it, she…left me."

She poured a new drink, needing the delay. It heated a pleasant path to her stomach and fortified her for the rest of the story.

"I only saw her once over the next three days, and it ended with a big fight. The next time I saw her, I was leaving with my crew and she refused to go. I had to leave her behind, on a planet I was abandoning to war and slavery." She gave a short, unamused laugh. "I didn't get very far. Right before giving the final order to destroy my ship, I came to my senses and cancelled the ship's self-destruct. Then I found out that it wouldn't have mattered anyway, because Andira had used empathic force on Commander Kameha and he had disabled the self-destruct. It was never going to work."

Salomen looked at Andira with wide eyes. "I had no idea."

"It gets better," Andira muttered.

"Then we learned that our shuttle wouldn't even make it to orbit. It was the nanoscrubbers, but none of us knew it then. I thought Andira had set me up in that, too. And when we landed in Blacksun, she informed me that she had warrants for using empathic force on my entire crew. Which in my mind explained why Lhyn had left me. That's why we fought that challenge."

"Because you empathically forced Lhyn?" Salomen asked slowly. "To leave her tyree?"

"No," Ekatya said before Andira could respond. She could hear the horror in Salomen's voice and just knew Andira would make it worse. "She didn't force her. Lhyn really did leave me. She knew I was doing the wrong thing, that giving up Alsea was a catastrophe that could not be allowed, and she was willing to die for her beliefs. She hoped that if she stayed, I would too."

"Of course you would. She's your tyree; there was never a chance you would abandon her to the Voloth."

"I didn't know that. Neither did Lhyn. And I really did try to leave. I just changed my mind partway through."

"You didn't change your mind," Salomen said with certainty. "It simply took you that long to understand yourself." She frowned. "This does fill in some holes about what happened then, but not about what's happening now."

"I didn't know Lhyn would stay," Andira said. "But I needed her to. She was the leverage I had to keep Ekatya here and make her willingly fight for us. So I procured a warrant, and I planned to do exactly what you thought a moment ago: empathically force her to leave her tyree."

"Great Mother of us all." Salomen slumped back in her chair with a shocked expression.

"And you know what kind of force that would have taken," Andira finished bitterly. She poured one more drink, tossed it down her throat, and shoved her chair back. "Go ahead and talk all night if you wish, but I'm done." She stalked into the cabin and slid the glass door shut behind her.

Salomen stared after her, then back at Ekatya. "And you knew this."

"Yes. We, er, talked about it during our fight."

"Then how—?" Salomen shook her head and sat forward with her hands on the table. "Do you understand the implications of what she was planning to do?"

"I think so. It may have been legal, but it would have meant taking away Lhyn's consent and her will. I know it tore Andira apart, and she still feels guilty now, even though she didn't do it. I know she believed she would never Return if she went through with it—that Fahla would not accept her."

Salomen inhaled sharply. "How do the three of you have such a bond with that between you?"

"Lhyn doesn't know. She can never know. I need your promise that you won't tell her."

"Do you not think—"

"No, I don't!" Ekatya leaned over the table. "She needs to feel safe here. I won't allow anything to ruin that for her."

Salomen had drawn back slightly, but now a small smile touched her lips. "Indeed you are tyree. You could power half of Blacksun with that much emotional strength."

"Good to know, but I haven't heard a promise." She was beginning to worry.

"I promise. I'm not fond of secrets, but I do understand why this one should stay buried."

Reassured, Ekatya slouched back in her chair. "Thank you."

"But I'm still astonished at your bond. Andira should have been the last person you would befriend."

"I did try to kill her first," she said with a shrug.

After a startled pause, Salomen smiled and shook her head. "And that's how I know you for a warrior, even though you have no castes." She sobered. "Please tell me one thing. Lhyn doesn't know, so she cannot forgive, but have you forgiven Andira?"

"I don't need to. She didn't do it."

"That was not my question."

"There's nothing to forgive, but I would if she needed it."

"And if she had done it?"

"I'd still forgive her."

"That was a very quick answer." Salomen did not look convinced.

"Not when you consider how much time I've had to think about it. Yes, it's easier to forgive what never happened, but I know her. I know what it would have done to her. I've thought about what I would do in a similar situation. How dirty would I get my own hands if it meant saving my world?" Ekatya hesitated, realizing that she had never said this out loud. "The closest thing we have to that kind of empathic force is rape. So I've—"

"That kind of empathic force *is* rape," Salomen interrupted. "It's a violation. Holding a warrant doesn't change that. It only changes the legality of it."

This was not at all what she expected from Andira's tyree. "If you're trying to defend her, you're not doing a very good job."

"I'm trying to understand whether you know what you're forgiving."

She needed another drink for this conversation. Refilling her glass, she said, "Andira told me about these arguments." She held the bottle over Andira's abandoned glass and lifted her eyebrows in question.

Salomen tapped a fingernail against it, halfway to its top. "She never wins them. But I'm not arguing with you."

"I know." Ekatya poured again, then set the bottle aside and lifted her glass. "You're asking a question I can't answer. We don't have that kind of rape. We only have the physical kind. And there sure as Hades isn't a way to legally rape someone."

Salomen made a face as she tried her own drink. "You have physical violation without the mental? Is that common for you?"

"More common than I'd like. It's not here?"

"No. The power, the control... I don't think the kind of person who needs that would get it from just compelling someone physically." Her forehead furrowed in thought, making her ridges stand out. "And how would a smaller person physically force someone larger? Unless they're like Andira and trained all their life for that kind of fighting. There has to be empathic force."

Ekatya stared at her, startled by the realization of just how different Alseans were. "Our rapists don't have that option. That's why most of them are male and most of their victims are female."

She watched the horrified understanding dawn on Salomen's face.

"Great Mother. I cannot imagine."

"I wish I could say that. For Gaians, the violation is physical. But the mental trauma—it takes a very long time to recover. Some people never do, not fully."

"It's the same with us. Empathic rape leaves very deep scars."

"Wait. First you say empathic force, then empathic rape...are they the same?"

Salomen gave her a slight frown, as if she were a child asking a simple question. "No. One is mental, and the other is both mental and physical."

Ah. Of course.

"Empathic rape is the only crime worse than illegal empathic force," Salomen added. "Thank Fahla, it's very rare."

Ekatya had been about to speak, but now she stopped as an unbidden memory surfaced: the moment right after their challenge fight, when she had asked Andira why she planned to force Lhyn if she hadn't meant to keep her as a lover. Once again she saw Andira folding in on herself, shocked beyond words at what Ekatya thought her capable of.

Not until this moment had she understood just how terrible an accusation that was.

"It's a severe crime for us, too," she said slowly. "Unthinkable, for any civilized person. And the best analogue I have. So I've thought about Andira's choice in those terms. Could I rape an innocent person to save half a billion others?"

Lifting her head, she met Salomen's steady gaze. "It's an impossible moral dilemma. If I refuse, I save a single individual and my own sense of morality. But I condemn everyone else, which makes it a terrible and cowardly act. How could I live with the consequences? All of those deaths and destroyed lives on my hands? Yet not refusing would make me a rapist, and I'm not certain I could live with that, either. Even imagining myself doing that to someone…"

She drank off the remainder of her glass and rolled it in her hand as she swallowed. "The only way out of that dilemma is to never get into it. That's why I can forgive her. Because I'm the one who put her in the impossible position of having to choose."

Salomen looked at her in silent sympathy. "You *have* thought about it."

"A few times, yes."

"The warrior penchant for understatement." Salomen leaned back in her chair, and though nothing changed in her expression, Ekatya felt as if she had just passed a test. "Thank you for telling me, despite your discomfort. I imagine you never thought you'd be discussing this with me."

"Not with anyone," Ekatya muttered.

A quick smile crossed Salomen's face. "No, but you've had the advantage of time. I haven't. Hearing you, feeling you…it helps a great deal."

"Then I'm glad."

"I have one more question, if you don't mind. Andira said that what she did put a strain on your bond with Lhyn, but if she didn't do it…" She trailed off when Ekatya sighed.

"We strained our bond all by ourselves. Andira helped us rebuild it—without mentioning that it might hurt her," she added with a trace of annoyance. "Your tyree has a habit of taking on burdens that don't belong to her."

Salomen's lips twitched. "I think she might share that trait with her best friend." She picked up the bottle and rose. "Take this, please. Andira won't need it tonight, and I would rather it go to better use elsewhere."

Ekatya knew when she was being dismissed. "Thank you. You'll be all right?"

"We will. Good night."

She got as far as the first step before turning back. "Salomen, wait." As Salomen looked over, one hand on the door handle, Ekatya closed the distance between them. Too aware of Andira's presence just beyond the door, she spoke softly. "I don't know what you're planning to tell her, but there's one thing she needs more than anything else. She needs to know that you still feel safe with her."

Salomen let go of the handle and turned, clearly caught off guard. "You really do know her." She stood still for a moment, then rested her hand on Ekatya's chest. "Your bond with her no longer surprises me. You have a good heart, Ekatya. The real tragedy here is that none of Andira's pain was necessary, because you would never have left Alsea. Your heart would not have allowed it."

She was through the door of the cabin before Ekatya could recover.

CHAPTER 10
Absolution

Tal stood at the far side of the dark cabin, her arms hanging limply at her sides as she watched the breeze move through the treetops below. Feeling Salomen's horror at the very thought of her forcing Lhyn had used up her tolerance for the evening; the shock and confusion that followed made her long for a drug-induced coma. For the first time since she and Salomen had sealed their bond, she wished she could block her tyree's emotions.

In a way, she could. By focusing on her own disgust and anger, she was able to push her sense of Salomen out to the periphery. And there was plenty of anger to keep her attention.

When the door opened, she wrapped her arms around herself and dropped her head, staring at the tiled floor as she waited.

Familiar footsteps crossed the room, bringing a warm presence with them, and a moment later she was pulled around into a warmron.

"You have extremely good taste in women," Salomen said. "If we weren't bonded, and Ekatya wasn't bonded, I'd ask her how she feels about interspecies relations."

Tal lifted her head, startled not just by the words but also by the inexplicable absence of anything she had expected to sense. Where was the judgment? The fear?

"She has put a great deal of thought into that situation. Her emotions have a depth and grounding that speak of maturity—she has not come to her conclusions recently or lightly. It's a complicated web you three have woven, but the most tangled threads are between the two of you. The very things that should drive you apart are what pull you together."

Salomen's gaze was unflinching as she continued, "I'm neither a warrior nor a philosopher. I cannot pretend to understand the reality of planning a war strategy or weighing the moral costs. But I am your tyree, and I know the truth of who you are. Ekatya said you needed to hear one thing, and I think she's right, so here it is." She tightened her arms and spoke softly. "I am still safe in your hands."

Tal choked, her breath expanding in her throat and refusing to move in or out. She had no chance to stop the tears; by the time she was even aware of them rising, they had already escaped.

Salomen smiled as she wiped away the moisture. "It's been a memorable first day of our bonding break, hasn't it? What do you have planned for tomorrow?"

Tal's laugh was a rasping sound, very close to a sob, but full of wonder and joy. "I do have excellent taste in women," she said. "The very best, and you prove it every day."

"True words," Salomen agreed. "Please remember them the next time we have a fight."

"I promise." She would have promised anything then. "I never meant for you to find out this way, today of all days…" She trailed off as Salomen shook her head.

"The truth about your bond with Ekatya? And those Sharings? That, you should have told me about. But this…it has nothing to do with me or our bond. It's a part of your past that I would hope you felt able to share at some point, when you were ready, but you never owed it to me. I'm somewhat uncomfortable knowing now, when Lhyn does not. I didn't want to keep any more secrets." She held up a hand. "And do *not* apologize for burdening me with another secret; that's not what I meant."

"I won't, then." Tal looked into her eyes and was suddenly desperate for the very thing she had wished away five ticks ago. "I need to feel you," she whispered, sliding her hands into position. "Will you…?"

Instead of answering verbally, Salomen slipped a hand around the back of her neck, cupped her jaw, and brought their foreheads together.

The sudden explosion of awareness still rocked them, even after so many Sharings, but they had fine-tuned their abilities with practice. This night, they had no interest in the minds around them. Pulling their senses into a tight, close net, they dove into each other, and no walls stood between them.

CHAPTER 11
Watching

THE NEXT DAY, EKATYA DID not let Lhyn out of her sight. They were all still interacting as a group, which meant Lanaril was always nearby, and she did not trust that woman around Lhyn.

She knew it was ridiculous. Lanaril was hardly going to pop out from behind a tree, grab Lhyn, and empathically force her. She was harboring an indefensible double standard, forgiving Andira while keeping a wary eye on Lanaril.

Unfortunately, intellectual understanding had no impact on her emotions, and the very casualness of their situation somehow made it worse. If Lanaril were still in her Lead Templar garb, cloaked in the solemnity of her office, Ekatya might have felt better about it. But to see her walking around barefoot, in a thin, sleeveless top with a colorful bit of fabric wrapped around her hips—the incongruity of it chafed. Someone that dangerous should not be dressing and acting as if she hadn't a care in the world.

She remembered her first view of Lanaril, at the memorial after the battle with the first ground pounder, and how impressed she had been both by the woman's calm beauty and her easy command of an audience of fifty thousand. The audience was gone, as were her formal clothes, but she seemed even more beautiful here than in the stadium. The sun brought out blue highlights in her wavy black hair, and when she laughed, her dark eyes sparkled and her white teeth made a sharp contrast with her olive skin. Worst of all, she carried the same serenity that Ekatya remembered. It showed in her walk, the way she spoke, and especially her slow, easy smile, which seemed to say that she was entirely at peace and wished only to make those around her feel the same way. Every time she turned that serene smile on Lhyn, Ekatya tensed.

She spent half the day tensing.

A side effect of following Lhyn everywhere was that she saw firsthand how her tyree was indeed turning this bonding break into a field study, despite all protestations to the contrary. Lhyn had an unending supply of questions, and the others seemed happy to oblige, probably because her interest in their answers was always genuine.

"Why do you still call her Tal?" Lhyn asked Colonel Micah as they sunned themselves on the beach. "She's nearly your daughter. Why not Andira?"

"Because she is not Andira to me. Not any longer." Micah tested the dryness of his skin—he had only recently come back from playing in the surf—and pulled on a pair of short pants that ended at mid-thigh.

Ekatya tried not to be relieved, but she really could not get used to seeing Alsean men naked. It was easier with the women, since their lack of Gaian genitalia was not immediately apparent. But seeing a smooth, curving ridge where the penis and testicles should be… She had to work not to stare.

"What do you mean, not any longer?"

He turned onto his side, the motion surprisingly nimble for a man as large and well-muscled as he, and propped himself up on his elbow. "When she was a child, she was always Andira. When she chose her caste and entered her warrior training, she became Tal. After that, the only time she was Andira again was when she and her father were in the same house, because he was Tal then. Once he Returned, that became her name at all times."

"Then she changed her name?"

"Changed it?" He looked blank.

"On the caste rolls."

"Ah, I understand. No, her full name has never changed since she chose her caste. Neither has mine. But we've used different parts of our names at different times in our lives. Most warriors have, though it's not limited to our caste. It's just more common for us."

"That is fascinating." Lhyn's fingers twitched, and Ekatya knew she was wishing she had a pad to record this. "Then do you think of yourself as Micah or Corozen? I mean, if I do something stupid, I'll think, 'Lhyn, you idiot.' Which name would you use then?"

"Micah," he said immediately.

"Even when you're around family who call you Corozen?"

His smile creased his cheeks, making his cheekbone ridges stand out. "That's a very new experience for me. I'm still getting used to it. But yes, even then."

"What about Andira? Salomen doesn't call her Tal. No one in our cabin circle does, except you and Jaros."

"You'll have to ask her, but I'd guess she thinks of herself as Tal. Her father did." He hesitated. "To be exact, which I think is what you want, I do call her Andira under certain circumstances, just as I called her father Andorin from time to time. But those are unusual occasions."

A shadow moved past Ekatya, and Lanaril walked to a spot near Lhyn. She sat in the sand as if it were a throne and said, "I overheard the last part of your conversation. If I may add to it?"

"Of course." Lhyn shifted to give her room.

"I counsel warriors more often than I used to. One thing I've learned is that they feel freer to speak of private things if I use their first names. When addressed by their family names, they tend to stay in a warrior mentality, but hearing their first name seems to break them out of a set of self-expectations. It certainly enhances the type of communication they seek with me."

"So you use names to tame them." Micah grinned at her.

"When necessary," she said in an amused tone. "Some warriors do need a bit of taming."

"Is that what you did with Andira?" Lhyn was the picture of innocence. "You've always called her by her first name."

"I have nothing to say about any taming of our Lancer, and if you were really my friend, you would not be trying to get me in trouble." She shook her head at Lhyn, whose laugh proved the truth of the accusation, and added, "I did ask her for that privilege. She was shocked by the request but allowed it nevertheless. Of course, she took it away the very next time I spoke with her, but I got it back."

They all turned when a shout came from near the water. "Don't you dare! Don't you—Andira!" Salomen let out a shriek as Andira tackled her right into a wave. After what appeared to be a significant battle involving a great deal of splashing, both women staggered onto the beach, laughing as they wrung water out of their hair and clothing. Ekatya watched with relief, delighted to see that the previous night had ended well.

"Why did she take away your privilege?" Lhyn asked.

"Hm?" Lanaril was still watching Andira and Salomen, but then her head turned sharply. The expression on her face was nothing Ekatya had seen before, as if she had been caught doing something wrong. "Ah…I didn't do something I had promised to do. She was not happy with me. It worked out for the best, though."

"Hard to imagine you breaking a promise." Lhyn was smiling, oblivious to the undertones, but Ekatya had her suspicions.

"Sometimes promises are made for the wrong reasons," Lanaril said, her answering smile serene once more. "Despite the warrior belief in honor at all costs, there are times when breaking a promise is the most honorable thing to do." She met Ekatya's gaze and held it.

Ekatya suddenly remembered Salomen's stunned reaction upon learning that she had intended to obey her orders and leave Alsea to the Voloth. As the shame swept over her, she looked away, unable to face the knowledge in those dark eyes.

In the end, she hadn't done it. Neither had Lanaril. What was she doing now, following Lhyn everywhere to protect her from a threat that didn't exist?

Making an asshead of herself, it seemed. And worst of all, Lanaril knew it.

"I believe I just heard a scholar impugning the honor of warriors." Micah let out an exaggerated huff. "As if we're too dense to know the difference between good promises and bad."

"If the description fits, Colonel."

Ekatya dared a glance up to find Lanaril's attention back on Micah.

"It occurs to me that you're the only scholar on an island packed with warriors, Lead Templar. Perhaps you might reconsider those words."

"I object to that," Lhyn said. "There are two scholars here, thank you very much. Don't worry, Lanaril, I'm here to back you up."

Ekatya could not remain. Making an excuse that she would not remember two minutes later, she stood up and walked into the forest, losing herself in the quiet gloom beneath the trees.

CHAPTER 12
Simplicity

ANDIRA HAD SAID THE TRAIL around the island was thirteen lengths. Lanaril thought she might have walked half that by now, putting her on the opposite side of the island from most of the others.

The track she was following hugged the island's edge, always in view of the water as it rose up a series of low ridges and descended back to sea level. Now she stood at a fork in the trail, deciding whether to continue ahead or take the narrow path that led down to a small cove.

She turned downhill.

The path was steep, skipping between rocks and tree roots and bending back on itself before depositing her onto smooth, black sand. She stood still, scanning the cove from one side to the other. It was tiny, easily missed by anyone not paying attention to the trail. And it was empty.

Perfect.

Shells were piled up along the wrack line, and bits of color poked out of the sand all the way to where she stood at the base of the cliff. The waves came up this far, then, probably during storms. She bent down to where a crescent of purple winked near her feet and carefully pulled out a round, flat shell the size of her palm, rough on one side and so smooth as to be reflective on the other. She ran her fingers over the smooth side, then set it back on the sand. Her sandals were soon sitting next to it.

Walking on this beach required more effort than on the swimming beach, where larger waves and guest traffic had removed most of the shells. Here they were so abundant that she had to pick her way between them, partly to save her feet and partly because she couldn't bear to break them.

Wave movement and a scattered layer of foam hid them once she reached the water. When she felt a shell crunch beneath her heel, she decided she had gone far enough. Standing shin-deep in the water, with the wavelets reaching to her knees, she stared out at Pica Mahal.

It was a relief to be alone, free of the emotions running rampant on the other side of the island. Andira and Salomen mostly kept their fronts up, but the others had very weak fronts. Micah was a low empath, Jaros was a child, and then there were Ekatya and Lhyn, pouring out their emotions like a pair of erupting volcanoes.

She was not used to such unending exposure. At the temple, where she dealt with varying levels of emotions all day long, she could always retreat to her study or her quarters when she needed a rest. Here there was no retreat, not during the first day when everyone was expected to remain in the group.

She had not thought to need a retreat today, but something had shifted in Ekatya overnight. The distrust and outright dislike, all aimed directly at Lanaril, had been bewildering and intense. For half a day she had kept to the periphery, trying to stay out of Ekatya's field of view, but after that she had snapped. Enough was enough; she did not deserve this and she would not tolerate it. So she had deliberately inserted herself into the conversation.

But she was not at the top of her game. The bombardment from Ekatya at such close range breached even her blocks, distracting her, and she had nearly let slip a secret that should never have reached her lips. Ekatya's suspicion had stabbed into her with such strength that she reacted on instinct, reminding the captain just how much reason she had given every Alsean on this planet to distrust her.

It had been spectacularly effective. The shame slammed into Lanaril's senses, hot and red, and Ekatya had vanished into the forest a few ticks later.

"Well done, Lanaril," she said aloud. "Striking out to avoid being hurt—quite worthy of a Lead Templar." Her own shame had eventually driven her onto the trail, but six lengths of walking had not diminished it.

Movement out to sea caught her eye, and she gasped when a great silver shape leaped out of the water, hung suspended for a piptick, and crashed back with a spectacular splash.

A wingfish! She stood in shock, wondering if that had truly just happened. All doubt fled when the wingfish leaped again—and then a third time. She thrust her fists up in the air and whooped.

She waited and hoped, her vigil rewarded when the wingfish reappeared to the east and leaped once, twice, and three times more. This time Lanaril did a little dance in place, shouting her glee. Again she waited, but when five ticks had passed and it did not reappear, she accepted that it was gone. With a silent thank-you to Fahla for the joy of such a gift, she turned toward the cliff.

Back where she had left her shoes, she stopped to brush the wet sand off her feet and paused at the sight of the house-sized boulder near the cliff. She had paid little attention when passing it earlier, but it looked easy to climb. The view from the top might lead to more wingfish sightings.

In a moment she was scrambling up, finding convenient handholds and footholds. The very top was the most difficult, with the last foothold a little too far down. She planted her hands on the smooth surface and hoisted herself up, swinging her foot to the edge and finally rolling onto the top. Victory achieved, she stood and dusted herself off.

"You made it," a voice said.

Lanaril let out an undignified shriek and jumped back, her heel slipping over the edge.

"Hoi, hold on!" Movement blurred in her vision, and someone grabbed her wrist, jerking her forward again. "Fahla, I'm sorry about that. I didn't mean to make you leap off again."

She looked up into a familiar face, though at the moment she could not put a name to it. Given the height of the woman who was still holding her, this could only be Andira's new Lead Guard. Her hair, as black as Lanaril's but longer, was unbound and draped around her face, hiding much of it.

The woman let go of Lanaril's wrist and pushed her hair back over her shoulders, revealing high cheekbones set off by beautifully narrow ridges, a generous mouth, and wide-set, dark blue eyes. "Glad I caught you," she said. "I don't think Lancer Tal would be impressed if I had to report that I broke one of her friends."

"What…? How long have you been here?" Lanaril had recovered neither poise nor manners.

"Long enough to see Blacksun's Lead Templar getting very excited about jumping wingfish."

Lanaril flushed. "Lovely," she muttered. "I thought I was alone."

"Obviously." The woman laughed at her discomfort, then held up a palm. "Well met, Lead Templar. I'm Vellmar."

Lanaril met her palm automatically, pausing when she felt the raw attraction. She did not often experience that; her rank and office tended to interfere. She glanced up, saw the emotion reflected in smiling eyes, and made a quick decision.

"Well met, Vellmar. Please, call me Lanaril."

Vellmar's eyebrows lifted. "I'm honored to do so."

"I'm not quite dressed like a Lead Templar. Or acting like one," Lanaril added.

Vellmar had an unguarded laugh. "No, but you might try that when you return. I'd bet you would gain quite a few new converts."

"For all the wrong reasons, yes. That sort of piety generally doesn't last long." Lanaril looked around the top of the rock for the first time. "Ah. That's why I didn't see you."

A light jacket lay next to a shallow depression in the stone. Anyone sitting there would be blocked from view by a fin of rock jutting up from the side.

"Yes, it's very private up here. If you had turned around and looked while you were standing in the water, you would have seen me. But you seemed very focused."

Lanaril nodded, realizing for the first time that Vellmar had a perfect front—the other reason she had been able to remain undetected. After a day and a half of withstanding emotional bombardment from the bonding party—and especially from Ekatya—being alone with a powerful high empath was a relief.

It occurred to her then that Vellmar was probably seeking the same solitude.

"I'm sorry; I've intruded on your peace," she said, turning away. "I'll just—"

"No, please don't." Vellmar caught her hand. "I told myself that if you walked back to the trail without seeing me, I would never mention having been here. But since you didn't, I wonder if you might like to come back to my cabin for a drink."

"Just a drink?"

"Anything else depends on you." Her smile was as unguarded as her laugh. "I'm sure you get offers like this all the time, and I would never have dared to ask before, but…right now you seem less like a Lead Templar and more like a very beautiful woman. Who dances at the sight of a wingfish. And I still have two days of leave, and you're on a bonding break, and the air is full of promise."

Lanaril could do nothing but smile back at her. "I cannot be a Lead Templar and a beautiful woman at the same time?" Good Fahla, she didn't even recognize the tone of her voice.

"You can and you are; I've seen it. But I would never have found the courage to ask that version of you back to my cabin."

"Not to mention you don't have a cabin back in Blacksun."

"Not like this. I'm in the Bonding Bower; it's breathtaking. And going entirely to waste."

She was smooth, Lanaril had to admit, with enough sincerity to make it charming.

"Then perhaps we shouldn't waste it," she said.

Vellmar's cabin circle was not far from the cove. It looked like the one Lanaril was in, with the Bonding Bower in another giant delwyn tree, though this one had four spreading branches rather than three. For the first time, Lanaril realized that the resort owners must have planned the entire island layout around the delwyns.

The view from inside was just as Vellmar had said: breathtaking. They were above the tree canopy, looking down onto a sea of green, and Lanaril was reminded of her first trip to Mahaite. The main island filled up the west view, while to the northeast, Pica Mahal collected clouds around its peak.

They sat at the table against the east wall of glass and shared a bottle of spirits while chatting about their families, their mutual experiences at Whitemoon Sensoral Institute, and the one person they had in common. Lanaril was fascinated to hear about the initial Sharing search for Herot Opah; Andira's version had been rather simplified compared to this. Of course, Vellmar had seen it from a very different point of view, and her awe at having been given such an unprecedented access was a pleasure to experience.

Her youth was another unexpected pleasure—she was surprisingly guileless given her rank and current assignment. Lanaril guessed she might be fifteen cycles younger, yet her lack of life experience manifested not as immaturity but rather as an endearing innocence and joy in life.

It took some time to understand what it was about Vellmar that put her so at ease: she listened more than she spoke. Lanaril was startled to realize how much she had told this virtual stranger about herself, but Vellmar seemed to draw it out of her. It was a role reversal that almost made her laugh. But it also made her realize how much of her life was spent listening, and how seldom she had someone looking at her with such intensity, listening as if every word she said was being heard, weighed, and understood.

After the emotional stress of the day, being with Vellmar felt like walking from a construction zone into a quiet garden. The sheer contrast enhanced Lanaril's appreciation of her company, and she did not front it. She watched the recognition grow in Vellmar's eyes, felt it whenever they touched hands, and was more than happy to let this go wherever it took them.

They reached the bottom of the bottle, and when Lanaril commented on how rapidly they had drunk it, Vellmar pointed across the cabin to the sun, low on the western horizon. They had been talking for nearly two hanticks.

She wandered over to the north wall, taking in the view of Pica Mahal, while Vellmar opened a second bottle. Behind her, she heard the tab being pulled and spirits splashing into glasses. The bottle thunked onto the table, and then…nothing.

"I think we should come back to the spirits later," Vellmar said. "After we've had time to absorb the first bottle."

Lanaril nodded but stayed where she was, her gaze on the volcano. She waited as the footsteps came up behind her.

"The privacy glass is active." Vellmar's voice was right next to her ear.

"Good." Still she did not turn.

Vellmar rested large hands on her waist as she nosed into her neck. "I'm so glad you climbed my boulder."

"I'm glad you caught me dancing at the sight of a wingfish." Lanaril leaned back into her, enjoying her strength and solidity. "Even though I was mortified at first."

"You don't feel mortified now." Vellmar's hands slid up her sides and around to her front.

"You haven't told me your name," Lanaril said as she linked their hands together. Their skin tones made a pleasing contrast, shannel mixed with cream.

"Yes, I have."

She reached back with one hand and pulled Vellmar's head down as she turned her own. Their lips met in a slow, exploratory kiss, tasting of spirits and sea salt and anticipation. She curled her fingers in the thick hair, giving a gentle tug to signal her withdrawal, but could not resist sliding her tongue along Vellmar's lower lip as they pulled apart. The shiver that ran through the body behind her made her smile.

Facing forward once more, she said, "I am not joining with a warrior. I'm joining with you. What is your name?"

"It really is Vellmar."

"It's really not. Or shall I call you Lead Guard?"

Vellmar began kissing a line down the side of her neck. "You…are much too accustomed…to being the one…in control." She sucked on the soft spot at the juncture of neck and shoulder.

"I worked all my life for that control. But I don't need it here." Lanaril pulled away and turned around, looking into her eyes. "I just don't want to call you the same name that all of your Guards do."

Vellmar hesitated, then shook her head with a smile. "Fianna. My first name is Fianna. And nobody uses it except my mothers. Even my brother calls me VC."

"VC?"

"Childhood nickname. I'm not nearly drunk enough to tell you what it means."

"Hm, a challenge. Are you truly telling me that all of your lovers have called you Vellmar?"

"They've all been warriors."

"Then I shall be your first lover to call you Fianna. Unless you prefer VC."

"What a choice. Fianna it is, then."

"Fianna," Lanaril murmured, running her fingertips along those wonderfully narrow cheek ridges. "Thank you for giving me the peace I needed today." She kissed the place where her fingers had been, then worked her way around Fianna's jaw, down her neck, and back up to her mouth.

This kiss was deeper than the first one, growing in heat as their hands began to explore. Lanaril was fascinated by the planes and muscles beneath Fianna's shirt and soon had it off altogether, her eyes widening at the athletic body in her arms. She had little experience with warriors and none at all with Guards, but this woman was exquisite.

She shivered as Fianna's hands moved up her thighs, lifting her wrap skirt as they slid higher. Gentle caresses grew more insistent, and then her skirt was gone, her shirt following soon after. Fianna paused long enough to strip away her own short pants, then pressed into Lanaril and pushed her against the glass.

Lanaril reflected that it had been many cycles since she had joined with someone against a wall…and then she stopped thinking about anything except the way they fit together, the sensations rippling through her body, and the way Fianna's voice grew husky as their passion rose.

Later, she had a vague concern that if her legs didn't stop shaking, she might fall.

Fianna did not let her.

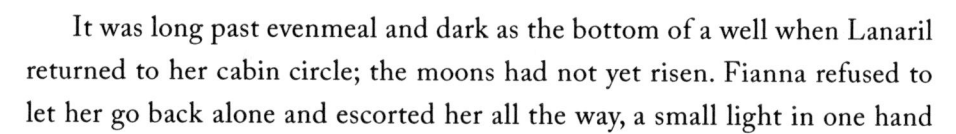

It was long past evenmeal and dark as the bottom of a well when Lanaril returned to her cabin circle; the moons had not yet risen. Fianna refused to let her go back alone and escorted her all the way, a small light in one hand and Lanaril's fingers in the other. The constant, reassuring touch felt safe.

She was even more grateful for the escort upon realizing that Vellmar knew the paths crossing the island, saving considerable time. She had not been looking forward to walking six lengths in the dark on legs that even now were not back to full strength.

Strains of music filled the air as they approached another cabin circle, and Lanaril drew them to a stop to watch the impromptu performance. Five Guards in casual dress were sitting on the deck of their main cabin, skillfully playing an old ballad on a ten-string, windpipes, and two small drums. Lanaril found herself tapping out the rhythm on her thigh, and when they swung into the refrain, she began to hum along.

Too soon, the song ended. The players grinned at each other as they set down their instruments and spoke back and forth, a peaceful rumble of conversation that flowed over her and brought back old memories of lying in bed at night, listening to her fathers downstairs.

"My birthfather used to sing that to me when I was a child," she said. "But not with such lovely musical accompaniment."

Fianna smiled down at her, and for a moment she wished she could always be surrounded by such peace and safety, rather than the ever-present needs of Blacksun Temple and those it served. She wished she could be cared for by someone like Fianna, whose protective instincts showed in every gesture and thoughtful act.

But this was not her world, and she had chosen her path a long time ago. With a tug on Fianna's hand, she indicated her readiness to resume their walk.

When they arrived at the edge of her circle, Fianna thumbed off the light, pocketed it, and drew Lanaril into a warmron. "Thank you for a wonderful evening," she said quietly. "And for accepting my offer."

"You were wrong about that, you know." Lanaril kissed the corner of her mouth, enjoying the scent of freshly showered skin. "I don't get offers like that all the time."

"Is everyone in Blacksun blind?"

"Would you have asked me in Blacksun?"

"Probably not."

"Then there is your answer."

Fianna nuzzled her throat, then sucked lightly on her jaw. "May I ask you again?"

She had two more days of leave, Lanaril remembered. And the air was full of promise. This might not be her world, but that didn't mean she couldn't luxuriate in it for as long as it lasted.

"If you don't, I will."

Fianna's smile was bright in the darkness. "Good night, Lanaril." Their arms stretched between them as she stepped back. Then their fingertips slipped apart, and a moment later Lanaril was alone.

She walked into the central cabin to find the conversation circle under full power. Jaros was in bed, a fact for which she was grateful when Andira took one look at her and said, "Did you fall into a thicket? Your neck seems rather scratched."

"Must have been that treecat on the transport," Micah said in his amused rumble. "I never did hear about anyone catching it. It's still on the loose."

"I suppose I deserve that." Lanaril had to smile at them, united in their easy teasing. "The treecat gallantly walked me home, and I may be visiting it again later. So far, I'm enjoying your bonding break very much."

She slipped past them before they could say anything else and shocked Ekatya by taking the empty seat next to her. "I hope I haven't missed any of your story."

"You haven't. I was just getting started." Ekatya had apparently found some peace of her own. The suspicion and dislike were absent, though a low level of unease and shame still lurked in the background.

By the time she finished her story, Lanaril understood those emotions a great deal better.

CHAPTER 13
Data jack

Gov Dome, Tashar, 16 stellar months earlier (11.5 Alsean moons)

After six months in Gov Dome, Ekatya was certain that when she left this place, she would never come back. The people here did not live in the real galaxy. They lived in a construct of their collective consciousness, an alternative existence in which their personal importance was enormously inflated while the consequences of their decisions were magically deflated. People became numbers and numbers became abstract, and the artificiality was further enhanced by the shield over their heads. It was a daily reminder of how special they were, how vital to the Protectorate and thus deserving of the most technologically advanced defense system in existence.

It was easy to make decisions impacting the health and safety of others when your own were never in danger.

Command Dome had the same shield system, but despite the bad taste her two-week incarceration had left in her mouth, Ekatya would return in a heartbeat given the choice. For many of the people working there, protection was only temporary until they shipped out. And she had a better understanding of her so-called debriefing now that she understood the man who had ordered it.

Sholokhov was the single most suspicious, paranoid, and judgmental person she had ever met. He was also brilliant and utterly ruthless, just as Admiral Tsao had warned. What Tsao had not said, but had become clear in Ekatya's conversations with him, was that Sholokhov divided people into three categories: threats, resources, and idiots. The first he neutralized as soon as possible, through any means necessary. The second he either used immediately or banked for future use. The third he ignored—unless they were a potential resource or became a threat through their own stupidity and poor decision-making.

He had no concept of friends or allies, viewing them instead as current or potential resources. Nor did he believe that resources could be counted on to remain trustworthy or useful. In Sholokhov's world, everyone acted in their own self-interest. It was only when their interests aligned with his that he trusted in the outcome.

Once Ekatya had figured out Sholokhov's categorization system, the story she had read about him shooting his friend made sense. Since he had no friends, the victim had been either a resource or a potential resource. But his entry onto the range when Sholokhov wanted to finish shooting at his target instantly shifted him into the idiot category. Idiots were owed nothing.

His treatment of her also made sense. He could not fathom Andira's real reason in negotiating a new ship for her, since he would never believe such a grand gesture could be made without an ulterior motive. Therefore, Ekatya must owe Andira something. That made her a threat, and Sholokhov neutralized threats. He had brought her to Gov Dome to control her.

But Sholokhov's system allowed for some individuals to occupy multiple categories, thus she could be a resource as long as her threat potential was properly contained. He had tied her up in a neat package. As much as she detested the man and his worldview, she had to admire his skill.

In truth, she was more qualified for her new job than she had initially thought. While a covert agent could have learned more than she did, what Sholokhov really wanted was her skill in reading people. So she went to the task force meetings, watched and listened, and took back her impressions for Sholokhov's review. It felt slimy and underhanded, but she never let Sholokhov see her discomfort. He would have enjoyed it too much.

Minister Staruin, she quickly realized, was not a threat. His agenda was refreshingly aboveboard: he truly believed that bringing less-developed worlds into the Protectorate would benefit both sides. His sincerity was not surprising given his leadership of the Reform Party, which had never held more than ten percent of the seats in the Assembly. If he were after power, he would be in one of the three parties that fought for majority governance, not in the party that had no chance of being anything more than a coalition member. What Sholokhov really wanted to know was whether Staruin was a resource or an idiot who might become a threat. She hated to categorize him as a resource, because that put him on the list with everyone else Sholokhov thought he could use. But he was certainly not an idiot.

Two of the ministers on the task force were, however. Ekatya had no idea how they had convinced a gullible public to elect them; their combined brain power would not threaten a microbe. Two others did have their own agendas but were similarly lacking in intelligence. Someone else must be pulling their strings.

Four were true believers like Staruin, and the last three were definite threats. They had their own agendas and were smart enough to do something about it. She just didn't know what those agendas were.

The saving grace of her time in Gov Dome was Lhyn. She had found their housing, introduced Ekatya to the best coffee houses and restaurants, dragged her to museums and parks, and most importantly, been there when Ekatya returned home after yet another day of dealing with inflated egos and idiots. Lhyn had a way of puncturing through it all, turning Ekatya's frustration into reluctant laughter.

For Lhyn, their location was fortuitous. Every major news agency in the Protectorate had their headquarters here, enabling her to dispatch her interviews with relative ease. Of course, she complained about every one of them, particularly the way the hosts insisted on simplistic questions when the reality of a culture built around a sixth sense could not be distilled into quick answers and catchy conclusions. She felt she was never given enough time to get her points across.

Ekatya thought she was the best advocate the Alseans could have asked for. When sympathetic interviewers waxed poetic about the empathic aliens, Lhyn brought them back to the ground with facts and scientific observations, reminding viewers that the Alseans were real, complex people and not mythical manifestations of the Seeders. When antagonistic interviewers tried to paint them as a menace to the Protectorate, Lhyn countered with personal stories that illustrated the compassion and kindness with which she and the *Caphenon* crew had been treated, despite the danger they had brought with them. Her description of Sharing with Blacksun's Lead Templar had been replayed so many times that it had acquired a legendary flavor. Then again, that might just be Ekatya's own perception, skewed by the Gov Dome inflationary ego field.

One thing was indisputable: Lhyn was now famous, the one true expert on a culture that everyone wanted to know more about. The only other person close to an expert was Ekatya herself, and she had been muzzled by Fleet, which classified her activities on Alsea. Lhyn was not subject to the same limitations.

Since their arrival on Tashar, Lhyn had worked tirelessly to speak for Alsea. Now she declared herself done with the ship travel and appearances. She was ready to hole up in their apartment for the next year, pulling together all of her research and writing the book on Alsea she had been itching to start.

Ekatya wished she could throw herself into work the same way. She missed her ship and especially her crew, all of whom had dispersed to other assignments or were snapped up by captains poaching her best officers, which was how she thought of it during her lower moments. She had worked hard to build such a capable and well-oiled team. Losing them to the four corners of the galaxy sometimes felt like a punishment rivaling the one she was serving with Sholokhov.

Because no matter how Lhyn or Admiral Tsao tried to spin this as a choice she had made or a path she needed to walk to find her new Pulsar-class ship at the other end, it felt like a punishment. She hated the Presidential Palace, hated reporting to Sholokhov, and hated the fact that even her assistant was a Sholokhov plant.

Ensign Bellows was fresh out of the academy, a slightly round, owlish young man with large golden eyes and a slow blink that irritated Ekatya to no end. She had run a check on him and found that his mother's wealth was responsible for his placement in the Presidential Palace, far from any potential harm. He had been raised in Gov Dome and had gone to school with the children of ministers and Protectorate power players, making him a perfect lackey for Sholokhov.

Being spied on by a coddled scion of wealth was bad enough. Worse was Bellows's choice of a cover: that of a hero worshipper. He met Ekatya on her first day with over-the-top awed shyness and never deviated from his act no matter how coolly she treated him. She frequently wondered if Sholokhov had specified the cover as a direct contrast to his own treatment of her, simply to keep her off balance.

Still, she was a professional. She knew how to utilize her resources, and for all of his poor acting and hidden agendas, Ensign Bellows was an excellent resource. His knowledge of the Gov Dome elite seemed endless, and he had an innate talent for data collection and management. He kept her schedule in perfect order, made sure she was prepared for her meetings and evening social functions, and proved adept at finding links and connections that would have escaped her.

It was just such a connection that had her in Sholokhov's office now. After six months of mostly useless discussion, the task force had finally agreed on a list of worlds to examine for possible first contact and eventual Protectorate membership. This was what she had been waiting for, an actual goal to research and work toward.

She had already recommended against the inclusion of the two planets in the Lexihari system, which had ended their interplanetary war just thirty stellar years ago. In her opinion, that was too recent to imagine that these cultures could handle advanced technology without turning it toward violence. But her concerns had been overruled.

"And we've found a likely reason why," she told Sholokhov. "Ensign Bellows has been running deep background checks on the three task force members who were the most vocal supporters of these planets. They all have something in common: recent campaign donations from Elin Frank."

Sholokhov had been sitting with his back to her, looking out of his window while she gave her report, but at this he swung back around. "Really. Our illustrious former ambassador to Alsea?"

"Yes."

"And you believe he is attempting to maneuver into a similar position on one of these planets."

"I have no basis on which to form a belief." She had learned that it was best to be very specific with Sholokhov, lest he make even more assumptions than he already did. "But given that he tried to take the emerging markets on Alsea and failed, it makes sense that he may be trying a different tactic here. Buy the politicians instead of being one."

"How do you know he tried to take the markets on Alsea? Something your patron told you?"

"Lancer Tal mentioned it when we discussed the new ambassador." She would not take the bait.

"As I said, your patron." He leaned back in his chair. "Someday you're going to tell me what you're doing for her." When she didn't respond—and she never did—he let his chair spring forward again. "Very well. It's an interesting assumption, but I need more than a guess. I need facts. Get me proof of Frank's connection with these planets, and I don't mean campaign contributions."

"That would be difficult to do given my position. At this point, you need a covert agent."

"Captain Serrado, you disappoint me. Must I remind you of our agreement? Find a way to copy the data from his personal gear. If he's working on something, there will be a digital path to follow, most likely in his home system. I doubt he'd keep those kinds of records and correspondences in his workplace."

For a moment she was at a loss. He couldn't really expect her to do that, could he? This wasn't reading people. This was breaking in and jacking data.

He picked up a file and swiveled around again, facing the windows. "You're dismissed, Captain."

Upon reaching her office, she was so furious about Sholokhov's insistence on power games and his delight in using military authority that she could no longer keep up any pretense with Ensign Bellows.

"In my office, now," she snapped as she strode past his desk. By the time she had entered her office and circled around her own desk, he was there, blinking owlishly at her.

"What can I do for—"

"Your superior," she interrupted, "has just ordered me to break into Elin Frank's home system and find evidence of his real agenda with the Lexihari planets. Since I have zero skills in that area, while you are quite comfortable with data systems, I can only assume it's really an order for you."

He blinked again. "My superior... I don't understand. I work for you."

"Can you drop the act for once? I'm well aware that you report to Sholokhov."

"But I don't—"

"Shut it!" she growled. "I don't need the lies, and I really don't need the hero worship. Even if that were real, it would have worn off after six months of...this." She gestured at her office and its constant reminder of what she currently was not doing. "Let's just agree that we both need to bring Sholokhov what he wants, and what he wants is something I can't give him. But you can."

"But—" Her glare stopped him. He did a remarkably good impression of a hurt child, then straightened his spine. "Director Sholokhov actually ordered you to break into Elin Frank's home system?"

"He ordered me to copy any relevant data from Frank's personal gear and strongly suggested we would find that data in his home system."

Bellows absently rubbed his shoulder, his gaze on the floor. "So he essentially told you to break the law."

"Surely this does not surprise you."

"Um…a little, yes." When he looked up again, his golden eyes seemed lighter than usual. "What happens if you refuse?"

That was the last question she had expected from him. But since she had demanded that he drop his act, perhaps she should drop hers as well. "To me, nothing. Someone else will pay the price instead."

He gaped at her. "Sholokhov is blackmailing you?"

"Again, I don't know why this would surprise you. Isn't that the standard cost of business around here?"

"Everything is surprising me today," he mumbled, and dropped into her visitor chair without waiting for permission. "Captain Serrado…I might be able to do what he wants."

"I presumed as much. Do you need me for this operation, or will you be using other personnel?" For all she knew, Sholokhov had a whole team of people who did nothing but this type of illegal data dump.

He hesitated. "I went to school with Sumiko Frank. She's one of the nicer ones in that group. I think I could get an invitation to her father's fundraiser next weekend."

"For Tzatis?" The election for the next mayor of Gov Dome was coming up, and Tzatis was one of the front-runners.

"Yes. We can't get into the banquet; that's for the really big players. But there's a mixer afterwards where everything is much less organized. There will probably be two hundred people there. I can get an invitation from Sumiko, because even if I'm not a player, you are. I mean, you're not really a player, but everyone knows you. You could get in, and I could get in with you, and then I could jack the data."

That was the least confident she had ever heard him sound, and yet he seemed oddly hopeful as well. She frowned at him. "I take it your performance is linked to mine?"

He started to say something, stopped, and then said, "I work for you."

"Of course you do." She gave up. "Fine. Get the invitation."

CHAPTER 14
Covert agents

THE ODD THING WAS THAT it worked so easily. On the night of the fundraiser, Ekatya had a driver pick up Bellows first, then her, and twenty minutes later they were standing in front of the guarded gate of the Frank residence. Amid the crowd of expensively dressed people gathered at the entry, they stood out in their dress uniforms—especially Ekatya, with her captain's bars and her chest full of medals. The burly man checking invitations took hers, looked her over carefully, and then gestured at a white-jacketed man behind the gate. White Jacket swung open the gate and smiled at them. They were in.

"Well done, Ensign," Ekatya said as they walked up the path to the three-story mansion with its colonnaded exterior. "Shippers, what a place. I can't imagine what it must cost to own this kind of property in Gov Dome."

Even with her very generous stipend, she and Lhyn were living in an apartment near the edge of the shield. Real estate prices near the center of the dome were outrageous, and a home this size, right here? It was a physical advertisement of Frank's wealth and influence.

"I don't think even the President could afford a place like this," Bellows said. "My mom says she wouldn't live in this neighborhood even if we could afford it, because it's such a target-rich environment for thieves."

"Meaning Frank has galaxy-class alarm systems?"

"Everyone here does. Why?"

"How will you get around it?" He hadn't brought any gear that she could see.

"I'm hoping I won't need to. They can't have the system turned on when two hundred people are coming and going."

"You're ho—" She stopped when a silver-haired couple walked too close. Grabbing Bellows by his upper arm, she hustled him off the path to a decorative bench and lowered her voice. "You're *hoping*? What are you playing at? You're supposed to be the professional here; I'm just getting you in. Please tell me you have a plan."

"I have a plan," he said, frowning. "I've been in this house before. I know where his office is. You just need to circulate and be seen and draw attention. I'll do the rest."

She focused in, looking for the lie or at least the weakness, but he stood straight under her examination. With a sigh, she turned back to the path. "Let's just get this done."

The fundraiser was exactly as dull as she anticipated. After six months in Gov Dome, she had far too much experience with political gatherings and knew what was expected of her. So she wandered through the crowds scattered throughout several rooms on two floors, told sterilized war stories, and chuckled at jokes that were not remotely amusing. Occasionally she would stumble upon a guest who could make witty conversation, and there she would stay for as long as she could, until another call of "Captain Serrado!" rang out and she was forced to turn and smile at someone else.

Upon moving into a secondary parlor, she was intrigued to find a display case of weaponry covering the entire width of the back wall. One of Elin Frank's companies manufactured weapons, often contracting with Fleet, but it appeared his interest ran deeper than mere production. The display housed a museum-quality collection dating back centuries. It even included an ancient leadslinger, along with eight of the original ammunition cartridges. That weapon alone was probably worth six months of her salary.

In between inane conversations, she worked her way along the length of the display, marveling at the quality of the pieces and the beauty of their presentation. Whomever Frank had hired to put this together was an artist. There was even a sword at the far end, elegantly held by transparent—

She stopped. That was an Alsean sword. A very fancy one, with a jewel-encrusted grip and an intricately etched blade, clearly not meant for actual use. But it was a thing of beauty and made the weapon next to it—a squat, bulky blaster-style gun she had never seen before—look crude and slightly repellent by comparison.

"I see you've found my Alsean souvenir," said a voice next to her. Elin Frank held out his hand. "Welcome to my home, Captain Serrado. It's a pleasure to meet the only other person in Gov Dome who understands the difficulties of working with overly sensitive aliens."

What an asshead. She was going to remember that introduction so she could quote it to Andira on their next quantum com call.

"They certainly don't share our values, do they?" she asked guilelessly. "I found myself having to be far more honest than normal."

He paused for a moment, his thin eyebrows doing a short dance on his high forehead. "I found that they took offense quite easily."

"Really? That's surprising. I shouted at the war council, lectured them even, and was informed afterwards that they respected me more for it. I could only conclude that they don't take offense at the way information is conveyed so much as whether that information is true or not." She sipped her lime fizz to keep her smile contained. It was her standard drink at events like this, easily passed off as alcoholic.

"You lectured their war council? And they didn't find that arrogant?"

"Lancer Tal said that arrogance itself is not an issue as long as it comes from genuine ability." This was both a lie and shameless name-dropping, but she couldn't help herself. Besides, she could see Andira saying something like that.

"Ah, yes, Lancer Tal," he said, swirling his drink. "An interesting woman, quite advanced for her culture. We spoke frequently, of course."

Name-dropping met and raised, Ekatya thought. And also a lie. At least her lie had been believable.

"A very interesting woman," she said. "I learned a great deal from her during my short stay. Did she give you a tour of the State House?"

"Ah…no, I believe she wished to but was called away. The Prime Scholar took me around. Lovely craftwork in that building; reminded me of some of the older houses of worship in the Galay Empire."

"Oh, I'm sorry you weren't able to get the personal tour. We were fascinated by all of the stories she told. It was hard to believe we spent over two hours simply wandering around the building with her."

One of his eyebrows tried to escape the other. "She's a capable politician. It was a smart move, ingratiating herself with you to get your cooperation."

"You might think that, and I certainly expected that sort of manipulation, because it's the sort of thing we would do, isn't it? But the Alseans aren't us. That tour was really between Lancer Tal and Dr. Rivers. I just hung about on the edges while Dr. Rivers took notes and asked about everything from the tapestries to the wood carvings to the age of the benches in the Council chamber. I thought Lancer Tal would surely run out of answers or at least patience, but she seemed to have a limitless supply of both."

"Patience, hm." He sipped his drink. "I suppose she had more time when you were there, before the treaty was signed and she had so much more on her desk."

"You mean while she was planning an all-out war to save her planet? She had no time at all. To this day I can't think of any reason but one for the courtesy she extended us. She was fascinated by the first aliens to reach her planet and wanted to learn all she could about us. I'm sure she was equally forthcoming with you."

She really had to stop this. Their conversation was barely rising to the maturity level of teenagers, and she was enjoying it far too much. Turning to the display case, she said, "It's a beautiful sword. Did you collect it for the artistry of the grip or the engineering of the blade assembly?"

That led to a discussion of Alsean weapons and engineering, after which Frank pointed to the ugly blaster and said with visible pride, "This is my latest. We based it on the Alsean molecular disruptors. They may have been primitive, but they had extremely impressive stopping power. Fleet rejected it, though. Said it was too limited." He looked at her hopefully. "Would you like to take one to the range and try it out? With your recommendation, I might get Fleet to reconsider."

"I don't have anything to do with procurement, Mr. Frank. My opinion would only be a personal one, and these days I'm not certain even that is worth much."

"Surely you underestimate the prestige your name brings, Captain. I know not everyone was pleased with your actions at Alsea, but you're still a hero to a great number of people."

Not the right people, she thought as she deflected both his praise and his request. The last thing she wanted to do was take an Alsean-inspired blaster onto a shooting range. Sholokhov would probably learn about it in four minutes flat and have her in his office one minute after that.

"Ah, well. Can't blame a businessman for trying to conduct business even at a fundraiser." Frank gave her an apologetic smile. "Your lovely Dr. Rivers is making quite a name for herself as well. It seems one can't turn around without seeing her in another interview. I must say I enjoyed that round table discussion with Minister Gazenfar last week. I half-expected the two of them to set the table on fire with the looks they were giving each other."

"Gazenfar always sounds like he wants to set things on fire. His party is built on xenophobia; it's not a surprise that he's beating the drum of paranoia about the Alseans. He beats that drum about anyone not born and raised in the core worlds."

"But these days his drum is being heard. Last year, the Defenders of the Protectorate were a joke. Today they have nearly forty seats in the Assembly. They're a growing power. It would be a mistake not to take them seriously."

"Forty seats is still less than five percent. They'll have to grow a lot more before they qualify as anything other than an extremist fringe party." And Lhyn had destroyed Gazenfar in their debate; the headlines had all been in agreement the next day.

"I think they have the potential to do just that." Frank took a healthy swallow from his glass and smacked his lips appreciatively. "Gazenfar might have found his issue this time. You and I know the truth about the Alseans, and Dr. Rivers is doing her best, but the average citizen is, shall we say, data-challenged. They don't want to learn about cultural nuances and Alsean law. What they know is that the Alseans massacred the Voloth with their minds and now they're going to be integrating into the Protectorate. That scares people."

"I agree, but those are the same people who kick up the dirt every time we bring a new planet into the Protectorate. There will always be people who don't want to share."

"Mm." He drained the remainder of his drink and set the glass on a passing waiter's tray. "The question is how many voters will listen to those people. Seems to me that Gazenfar and the DOP are capturing far more ears these days."

Another guest bent on gaining Frank's ear gave Ekatya the excuse to bow out. She slipped away, wondering where Bellows had gotten off to and how long it could possibly take to jack the data from a computer system. But they had agreed on gray mode until he contacted her, so she refrained from calling.

It took another hour of circulating and drinking far too many lime fizzes before she finally heard a soft double-click in her head. An incoming voice call was being routed from her pad to her internal com and now waited for acknowledgment. The pad's feminine voice—with an accent from Allendohan, Lhyn's little joke gift—informed her that the caller was Ensign Bellows.

"Serrado," she said.

"Captain." Ensign Bellows was whispering. *"I've run into a little problem."*

Ekatya began walking toward a corner that was momentarily free of people. "What is it?"

"Well, I got the data…but, um…I'm locked in the office."

She stopped walking. "You're what? How in all the purple planets—" With a glance around, she lowered her voice and infused it with all of her annoyance. "What happened?"

"Frank came in. Thank the Seeders he was talking to someone before he opened the door, or I would have been sitting there in plain sight."

"So you hid…"

"Yes, behind the sofa by the window. For twenty minutes." His tone made it clear that those twenty minutes had actually been a year and a half. *"And then he turned out the lights and left…and he locked the door."*

Ekatya pinched the bridge of her nose. "Why are you not simply overriding the lock from inside?"

"Because it doesn't work! I tried, believe me! The panel inside isn't the same as the one outside; it doesn't have the access ports."

He was highly stressed and more than a little frightened. Ekatya frowned. This didn't sound like the product of training in covert ops. It sounded like a fresh ensign getting in over his head.

"Captain, please. I don't know how I'm going to get out. If Frank finds me in here…" His breathing was becoming rapid.

"Ensign Bellows," Ekatya said in the quietest tone she could manage. "I need you to calm down and give me information. Where exactly is the office?"

"It's, um…" He swallowed. *"Third floor. North and east corner."*

"How many windows?"

"Ah…" She heard the sound of shuffling. *"Big one here behind the sofa. Another one on the north wall. Doors, actually. Sliding glass doors."*

"I assume the big one is on the east wall, then." She looked around, checking her space, and saw no one within hearing range. This would be so much easier in a private place, but at a party this size, there was no chance that she could lock herself in a bathroom.

"Yes, sorry, east wall."

She had been in a room on the second floor's northeast corner. Part of the party crowd was up there. There was a balcony, as she recalled, looking out over the beautifully landscaped backyard. It had a low lip and an ornate metal railing, which had been crowded by people leaning on it as they conversed.

"Is there a balcony outside of either window?"

More shuffling.

"Yes. Both of them. A big one on the east and a smaller one on the north."

"Wait. And keep the com open."

"I will."

His breathing was in her ear as she walked out of the crowded room, careful to keep her pace to a party stroll. With smiles and nods to various people she passed, she made her way up the stairs and into the second-floor corner room, then got caught in a short conversation before she could edge over to the north window. It was half the size of the east windows and had not been opened for party attendees to enjoy its small balcony. Nevertheless, there was a couple out on it, taking advantage of the privacy afforded by the location and the sheer curtain somewhat blocking the view from the room.

She sighed, edged into an open space away from anyone who could overhear, and murmured, "You're going to have to climb down onto the second-floor balcony. North side."

"I'm what? I can't do that!"

"Your alternative is waiting until Frank lets you out in the morning."

Panicked breathing.

"Ensign Bellows, you've been through academy training. You are physically capable of doing this. It's no harder than the obstacle course. You will simply climb over the railing, let yourself down so you're hanging by your hands from the bottom, and then swing in so that when you let go, you land on the balcony below. I will clear that balcony for you and I will be waiting to assist. Do you understand?"

All she heard was his breathing. She was about to say something else when he finally swallowed and managed a quiet *yes*.

"Good. Give me a moment. Keep the com open."

She sipped her drink, then tugged her pad out of her sleeve, held it up in front of her face as if to ascertain the video caller, and shook her head. Setting her drink on the nearest table, she made a beeline for the north window, this time in her full captain-on-the-bridge stride. Without pausing, she yanked open the door.

The couple on the balcony sprang apart. Older woman, younger man, almost certainly an affair. Perfect.

"I'm sorry to disturb you," she said, offering a smile as she held the pad near her chest. "But I must take this call; it's very important. And classified. If you wouldn't mind…?"

They couldn't get off the balcony quickly enough, muttering that it was fine and they were just enjoying the view. She nearly laughed as she slid the door shut behind them.

"We're as private as we're going to get, Ensign. Now is the time."

"Seeders save me," Bellows said softly.

She heard the door above her open. It didn't close again.

"Ensign. Don't forget the door."

"Shit! I mean…" The door slid shut. *"Sorry, Captain."*

"Don't worry, I've heard it before. Just get down here."

She held out her pad and began pacing back and forth in front of the window, making it look as if she were on a call in case anyone peeked out. Rustles of fabric and a few metallic clangs kept her informed of Bellows's progress.

"I'm on the outside of the railing," he whispered. *"But…"*

"No buts. Obstacle course, Ensign. Now."

One booted leg dropped into view. For several seconds, nothing else happened.

Ekatya was just about to order him again when he grunted and let himself hang by his hands. At full extension, his feet were still half a meter above and outside the top of her railing. He looked down at her, his eyes wide with terror.

She cut the call and put away her pad. "You're very close," she said in a normal tone of voice. "Give yourself a little momentum, then swing in and let go. I'll help if you need it."

"Okay," he gasped, and looked up at his hands. With a little grunt, he swung slightly inward, then out again, his legs dangling over a twelve-meter drop. Another swing inward and he let go.

His legs would land inside the railing, but his body was angled too far. Ekatya caught him around the hips and pulled back with all her strength, providing just enough power to bounce his spine off the top of the railing and land them both in a heap on the balcony.

"Oh, fuck," he groaned, curling into a fetal position. "Oh, fuck, that hurt."

He must be in pain, she thought. He wasn't even apologizing for the language.

"I'm sorry," she said, crouching next to him. "I lied about the obstacle course."

He groaned again. "Fantastic."

"If I hadn't, you wouldn't have made the jump." She laid a hand on his shoulder. "And you did a fine job. Can you stand?"

"Tomorrow, sure."

She smiled. "You don't work for Sholokhov, do you?"

He finally uncurled enough to look at her. "I told you that."

"You did, but truth and honesty are not exactly common currency in that building. I apologize, Ensign. I didn't believe you."

"Do you believe me now?"

"Either you're telling me the truth, or you were willing to risk significant injury just to convince me of something that's not very important. So yes, I believe you now."

He blinked at her, then managed a smile. "And the hero worship?"

"We'll talk about that later. Can you stand up?"

It took a few tries, but he managed to stand and, after bending back and forth a few times, was even able to walk somewhat normally.

Ekatya brushed off his uniform and straightened his jacket, then did the same for herself. When they were presentable, she slid the door open and they walked back into the room. No one noticed.

The data, once Bellows managed to break the encryption and parse through it all, did indeed provide evidence that Frank was buying favors from three members of the task force. Sholokhov was pleased.

So was Ekatya. For the next year, she grew to depend heavily on Ensign Bellows, whose competence was now twice as valuable because she trusted him. It changed everything, having someone in this building she could depend on.

When her ship was finally finished, she took Bellows with her. It was a smart, sensible staffing decision—and one she would come to regret.

CHAPTER 15
The gift

Alsea, present day

Ekatya was in her chair on the bridge of the *Caphenon*, looking at the readout on Lieutenant Candini's panel right below her and wondering why it made so little sense. They had already crashed on Alsea; how could it be saying that they were currently in orbit over Whitemoon? And what was that obnoxious banging sound? Was something else on her ship falling apart?

"Lieutenant Candini, stop that noise," she said.

"I'm not doing it," Candini said without looking around.

"Yes, you are," Ekatya insisted, and woke up.

She shook her head, momentarily suspended between the dream and reality. Judging by the light coming through the cloth walls of their cabin, it was just past dawn.

Someone knocked, five short raps on the corner log at the far end of the room.

Ekatya glanced at Lhyn, who was facing her and dead to the world. She had not slept this well for weeks, not until they had arrived on Alsea. If their visitor woke her with this infernal banging, Ekatya was going to boot them into orbit.

She pushed aside the covers, grabbed her shin-length robe off the foot of the bed, and held down the switch that controlled the cloth wall on her side. Her bare feet made little noise on the tiled floor as she walked to the other end of the room and peered through the newly made opening.

Andira was leaning against the corner log, dressed more warmly than usual in a long-sleeved shirt belted at the waist and long pants tucked into black boots. Her smile was bright.

"Good morning! Ready to start your day?"

"Shh!" Ekatya stepped out onto the deck. "Lhyn is still sleeping. As I would be, if you hadn't woken me up. This had better be good; I'm on vacation."

"Really? Me, too. Isn't it gorgeous today? We should go out and enjoy it."

She held her robe closed at the neck, sealing out the surprisingly cool air. "Why aren't you in bed with Salomen, like a normal newlywed?"

"A what?"

"A newly bonded person. Which you are. Which is why you should be in bed."

"You think we can only join in the mornings?"

With a quiet groan, Ekatya said, "I need a shannel before this conversation."

Andira laughed. "You need shannel twenty times a day. Go have a cup and then get dressed. Full coverage. You'll need it where we're going."

"Which is where, exactly?"

"It's a surprise." She lifted a hand, forestalling the next protest. "Let me say this. I'm here to take you to something that quite a few people have worked on for many moons now, and I guarantee it will make you smile. And I think you need a happy surprise, so please wake up and come with me."

Ekatya covered a yawn with her hand. "A happy surprise sounds nice, but did it have to be this early?"

"This is when the air is calm." Andira walked over to one of the deck chairs and sat down. "I'll be here when you're ready. Don't wake Lhyn, and don't dawdle."

"For the love of…" Ekatya spun on her heel and walked back inside, smiling despite herself at Andira's eagerness.

Lhyn slept on, oblivious to their guest. She did not wake up at the whoosh of the shannel dispenser, nor when Ekatya moved around the room, getting dressed and brushing her teeth. But when Ekatya leaned over to kiss her temple, her eyelids fluttered open.

"Going somewhere?" she asked in a gravelly voice.

"Somewhere, yes. I don't know where. Andira isn't telling."

"Oh. Well, if you're with Andira, you're safe."

Ekatya had to appreciate that faith. "Don't get into trouble while I'm gone."

"I won't." Lhyn closed her eyes again, and Ekatya wondered if she would even remember this conversation.

"Sleep well," she whispered, and tiptoed out.

Andira was standing at the top stair, looking at her wristcom. "Not bad for a spoiled ship captain."

"Says the spoiled Lancer who rents out an entire island for her bonding break. Now tell me why you woke me at the crack of dawn."

"Not yet. It would ruin the surprise." Andira bounced down the steps and set off toward the trail that led to the bridge.

Ekatya hustled after her. "You do know I hate surprises, right?"

"You won't hate this one."

"I'm up too early, my tyree is still sleeping, I'm being annoyed by a friend who thinks testing my patience is a good idea, and I don't know where I'm going."

"To the landing pad." They walked into the gloom beneath the trees and followed the pale path of the trail as it wound between the dark trunks.

"You're enjoying this too much."

Andira stopped and turned, her expression suddenly solemn. "What I want is for you to enjoy this. Those stories you've been telling—I had no idea how hard it had been for you. And you haven't let go. I see you guarding Lhyn even though she's perfectly safe here."

Despite the flush infusing her cheeks, Ekatya refused to look away.

"As your host, it's my job to make certain you're benefiting from this bonding break. You're relaxing, yes, but you're not relaxed. I'm hoping to speed up that process." Andira reached out to grip her shoulder. "Does that help?"

Ekatya inhaled deeply, the cool, moist scent of early morning in the forest filling her nostrils and clearing her head. "Yes. It helps." She patted the hand on her shoulder. "Let's go see your surprise."

The bright smile returned. "Speedy."

Their footsteps made no noise on the spongy path, with its covering of decayed leaves and bits of bark. Ekatya looked around with more interest, noting the difference in light and the many delicate, floral scents in the air.

"It doesn't smell this good at mornmeal," she said. "And I hardly smell anything but ocean by midmeal."

"It's the tropics. Once the sun gets past a certain point, everything closes up and saves itself for the cooler temperatures at night."

The flowers lining the path did seem to be more open than she remembered. "There's a desert planet in the Protectorate," she said as they skirted around the massive trunk of a tree. "It never had a large population, and now it's mostly settled by miners, but no one does anything during the day. They have a saying that the day is a cruel spouse, wearing you out with her demands, while the night welcomes you with the gentle arms of a lover."

Andira glanced over, her eyes crinkled in amusement. "That seems to say more about the culture than the environment."

"Now you sound like Lhyn."

"I'd take that as an honor. I enjoyed her story last night. She's never spoken of her family before. Seven siblings!"

Ekatya could well imagine how astonishing such a large family would be to the Alseans, whose near-perfect natural reproductive control had kept their population small for millennia. "Allendohan is a relatively new planet in terms of settlement. It was only terraformed a few generations ago, so big families are still the norm. Leaving is not."

"It did sound as if she defied a few expectations. Not that any of us were surprised. But does she never want to return?"

"She asked you, then. After I went to bed last night?"

"She was sitting out on your deck when Salomen and I came back from a…late swim."

"Right. You weren't swimming."

"That wasn't a euphemism. It just wasn't a complete description of our activities." Andira's smirk shifted into something more serious. "The three of us had a very nice talk. And she is welcome to make her home here for the rest of her life, as are you. I would love nothing more."

Though she had never doubted what the answer would be, Ekatya still felt a profound sense of relief. Andira's permission had been the only missing piece. "Thank you," she said. "You don't know what that means to her yet. But she needed it so much."

"That was obvious." Andira stopped again. "I won't ask until she's ready, but Salomen and I both wondered. She has a home and a large family, yet this is where she wants to be."

For Andira, who was only now creating a family of her own, Lhyn's priorities must have seemed baffling.

"A lot of that has to do with the story she needs to tell you. But even before that, Lhyn didn't often go back. Her home culture is still young enough that xenoanthropology isn't a valued vocation. At all."

"Ah, I see. And for her, it's a life calling."

Ekatya nodded. "She couldn't study for it on Allendohan, and when she did go back, she couldn't talk about it because no one really cared. They listened for the sake of being polite, but…"

"Passion has no patience for politeness."

"Exactly. She always felt like she was playing a role. She loves her family, but they don't know who she is."

"How is that possible? Her words match her emotions. Even a sonsales can read her."

"But you listen."

"And her family doesn't?" Andira frowned. "Lhyn is unique. Were she Alsean, she would rarely need a front. It would take willful ignorance to not know who she is."

"Or the kind of blindness that comes with a large family competing for attention." She and Lhyn had often discussed this, given their nearly opposite upbringings. As an orphaned child raised by her grandparents, Ekatya had never had to compete. She had not imagined that being raised with siblings and both parents could be worse, in some ways, than being raised with neither. But when she took personal leave during their time in Gov Dome, it was not Allendohan they went to. They visited her grandparents instead.

"She wants you to be her family, Andira. You and Salomen and Colonel Micah and the Opahs. This bonding break…it's doing more for her than I can tell you."

Andira watched her with a gaze so steady that Ekatya found it difficult to hold. She suspected she was revealing more than she meant to.

"I'm glad," Andira said at last. "Let's see what it can do for you now."

"It's already been educational," Ekatya said lightly as they resumed their walk. "Listening to Shikal's story about giving birth to Nikin—I think that fried some of my neurons." She saw Andira smile out of the corner of her eye and added, "Hearing about him breast-feeding his son fried most of the rest."

Now Andira laughed. "Lhyn's neurons seemed to be functioning quite well."

"That's because she gets distracted by her need for details and facts. Sometimes I think she never stops long enough to sit back and marvel at how…different you are."

"Hm. I thought you were going to say 'advanced.' Or perhaps 'inspiring.' Or—" She easily blocked Ekatya's half-hearted punch. "No?"

"I was trying to find a more diplomatic word than 'annoying,' but if you insist…"

They spent the remainder of the walk teasing each other, and Ekatya's spirits rose with every step. When they emerged from the dim forest, she was dazzled by the shifting flashes of morning sunlight on the water. It was a relief to look at the bridge, which reflected the sun in only a few places on its railings as it stretched across to the main island. At the other end, the state transport still took up most of the landing pad, but what made her breath catch was the smaller craft crouching in front of it.

The shining white fighter had curved blue and gold markings on its wings and a shield of the same colors on the side, anchored with the black silhouette of a temple and edged with a single word in Alsean script. Though Ekatya had not yet learned to read Alsean, she recognized the name of the city they had left three days ago.

She also recognized the two-seater fighter model. After all, she had left it here on Alsea, along with every other fighter assigned to the *Caphenon*.

But when she had left them, they were not white. And they did not fly.

"Great galaxies, look at that." She sped up her pace, leading Andira onto the bridge. A flock of sailtails launched off the railings, complaining loudly about their rest being disturbed, but she hardly noticed in her excitement. "You took off the hullskin?"

"We did. Chief Kameha said there was no other way to make them flightworthy."

"But that means you rebuilt them from the landing gear up."

Given its semi-organic and cybernetic nature, hullskin could not simply be peeled off a craft and replaced with new external material. It was similar to peeling the skin off an animal—feasible, but only if the survival of the animal was not a desired outcome. The fighters had to be completely taken apart and rebuilt, including all new framing, which was why the Protectorate had decided to build new shuttles for the Alsean atmosphere. It was more cost-effective than rebuilding existing designs.

"How long did that take?" Ekatya stared avidly at the sleek fighter.

"More than a cycle to finish all sixty. We've been training our pilots on them since we had the first ten done. This one is part of a unit based at Whitemoon, brought over this morning just for you. We thought you might enjoy, er, taking it up for a twirl, I believe is the phrase."

Ekatya chuckled. "Taking it up for a spin."

"What is the difference?"

"Not much, now that you mention it. How did you train your pilots on a craft no Alseans knew how to fly?"

"Remember Tesseron? The pilot who flew with Candini to Port Calerna?"

"Oh, yes. He made quite an impression on her. She wanted to recruit him into Fleet. He learned enough from that flight to train other pilots?"

"He's our best, and the only one with any prior experience, but we had some long-distance assistance. Chief Kameha asked your Lieutenant Candini to help us."

"She's not my lieutenant." The flash of bitterness was familiar but felt less sharp this morning.

"I didn't mean—"

She shook her head. "I know, and you didn't. How did Candini help?"

Andira accepted the redirect without comment. "She provided training modules for the flight simulators on the *Caphenon* and then offered some extremely valuable live flying quantum com time. We had all of our pilots in the theater at Blacksun Base, watching Candini in her fighter and asking a blizzard of questions. I watched the vid afterward. Our pilots thought she was a gift from Fahla, and Candini didn't disabuse them of the notion."

Ekatya had to laugh. "No, she wouldn't."

They were nearing the end of the bridge, and every step closer made the rebuilt fighter look that much more beautiful. She had appreciated the aesthetics of this model before, but the gleaming white exterior and Alsean artistry gave the craft an entirely new look.

"I think I'm jealous," she said. "I have thirty more of these on the *Phoenix* and thirty of the single-seaters, but not one of them makes me want to run my hands over it."

"You can't have this one. But you can take it up for a twirl."

"Spin."

"I prefer twirl."

"Of course you do."

They stepped off the bridge and strode toward the fighter, now a few meters away. A figure moved out from its shadow and into the light, standing straight and thumping his fists against his sternum in the salute for the Lancer. Ekatya had only seen him once, nearly two stellar years ago, but she remembered his enthusiasm and the way his happy, toothy smile had stood out against his dark skin.

"Lead Guard Tesseron, well met," she said, holding up her palm.

He met her palm touch with that same toothy smile. "Well met, Captain Serrado! And it's First Pilot Tesseron now."

"Then congratulations. I'm certain that was a well-deserved promotion, especially considering what I've just been hearing about training up a whole new group of fighter pilots."

He ducked his head. "Thank you again. I keep wondering when I'll wake up from the dream, but somehow I keep finding myself flying these."

"Are you ready to let someone else fly it?" Andira asked.

"If that someone is Captain Serrado, then yes." His smile grew, and Ekatya had the feeling that she would somehow be doing him a favor by piloting this fighter.

Andira turned to her. "There you are, a flight pass from our expert. I hope you still remember how to buckle the restraint harness."

"I will get you for that," Ekatya said. "In fact, maybe you should come with me and I'll show you a thing or two about why those harnesses are necessary."

"Of course I'm coming with you. Surely you didn't think I went to all this trouble just to stand here and wave while you had all the fun?"

Caught short, Ekatya stared at her. "How long have you been planning this?"

"A while." Andira looked far too innocent. "Oh, and I forgot to mention something. Tesseron brought a guest. Come on out!" she called in a louder voice.

Before Ekatya could ask, an unmistakably short silhouette appeared at the tail of the fighter. She was moving without even being aware of it, her heart leaping at the sight of her old friend.

"Chief!" she cried. "Shippers, it's been too long!"

"About time you made it back." Chief Kameha grinned up at her. "I thought you'd never escape Tashartarus."

It was their private name for Tashar, a combination of the planet's name and Tartarus, and hearing it broke open something inside her. As a flood of happiness welled up, she barely stopped herself from grabbing him and pulling him into a hug. Instead she held out a hand to his, only to find him holding up a palm in the Alsean way. Quickly she raised her palm, just as he held out his hand for a shake. With a laugh, she gave up and went with her first impulse. They had never embraced before, but she had not seen him since leaving Alsea, and in the meantime she had lost her crew and spent over sixteen months trapped in the paranoid cesspool of Gov Dome. To Hades with expectations; she was too glad to see a real friend.

He went stiff for a moment, then laughed as well and squeezed her tightly. "You have no idea how much I miss this," he said. "The Alseans have been wonderful, but nobody hugs me."

"That's your own fault. All you had to do was find a lover, and from what I hear, you've had your pick."

He blushed. "My pick, sure, but who had the time?"

"It's true; we've been keeping him rather busy." Andira had joined them, along with Tesseron.

"Then if it's hugs you need, come back to the *Phoenix* with me. I'm still trying to teach my chief engineer to speak in normal sentences."

"Do *not* try to poach the man I poached from you, Captain."

Kameha looked back and forth between them. "So if I came back with you, I'd be in charge of that lovely Pulsar-class ship that just fell out of the dock?"

Ekatya nodded. "She still smells new. The plantings haven't overcome that yet."

"I see." Kameha leaned in. "Did you know that I'm building a space elevator?"

"Are you trying to tell me that tweaking the power flow of a surf engine isn't the same?"

"Not even close." He leaned back again, hooking his thumbs into the decorative chest chain that held his light blue half-cape in place. "Not to mention the fact that your crew wouldn't worship me the way the Alseans do. I've gotten used to that."

"And yet you still can't find time for a lover. I don't think you have a proper grasp of being worshipped."

Andira made a soft sound of amusement. "Since it seems my Chief of Advanced Technology is beyond temptation, I'll take advantage of Tesseron and get a tour of that fighter. Join us when you're ready, Ekatya."

She and Tesseron climbed into opposite sides of the fighter, leaving Ekatya alone with a smiling Kameha.

"That was polite of her," he said. "I do love it here, but sometimes I want to scream at the idea of spending one more hantick being careful about what I think and feel. She left us alone together so we can pretend that she can't sense us."

Ekatya glanced at the fighter's cockpit to see Andira in the copilot's seat, her gaze on the control panel as Tesseron explained something from the pilot's seat next to her. "I thought she left us alone so we could speak freely."

"That too, but to the Alseans, it's all a kind of hearing. They talk about listening to emotions."

"How do you deal with that?" she asked. "It makes my skin crawl sometimes, knowing that I have no privacy. Especially around people I don't trust."

He shrugged. "I guess I learned to trust. They might know everything I'm feeling, but that's in my head, yes? So they see it as private. It would be rude for them to mention what they sense if I haven't said or done anything to bring it out of my head and into the open. It's like…" He paused, tapping his forefinger against his chin in a familiar motion. "Say we have a section chief briefing on the *Caphenon* right after you get off the quantum com with some torquat back at Command Dome. Everyone knows you're so angry you could chew through the hull, but you don't say a word about it. Nobody else will, either."

"Nobody would say a word because I'm the captain," she said.

"Bad example. Rephrasing. I'm the one grumping and you don't say anything."

"But I would, if we weren't in a briefing. I'd say something in private."

"Ah!" He pointed at her. "Exactly. If they're a friend, they might say something. But a coworker? A builder touring me around the latest output from the seed cable manufacturing? They won't."

"So you're saying it's not much different in the end. In terms of actions."

"No, not really. What made it different was how I felt knowing they knew. Once I realized they wouldn't embarrass me, I relaxed."

"But what about the Alseans you don't like? How can you stand knowing they know?"

"I don't have much choice, do I?" He smiled at her expression. "It might be harder for a captain than for a chief of engineering. I never bothered to keep my feelings off my face."

"Shipper shit," she said. "You may not have cared as much as I do, but there were always things you kept off your face. Shall I list them?"

"You should emulate the Alseans and not be rude. I take your point."

"I thought being rude was something I was entitled to. As a friend." It felt so good, so easy, to fall into this familiar routine with him.

His grin said he felt the same way. "I missed this. It's not the same over the quantum com."

"No, it's not." She looked him up and down, taking a moment of joy in his physical presence. "I can't believe how long it's been."

"I know." He sobered. "I'm sorry about Lhyn. Is she better?"

Ekatya shot another glance at the fighter, where Andira was now gesturing at something as Tesseron watched. "She is. Thank you for asking. We...haven't told anyone else. Here, I mean."

"Do you plan to?"

"Yes, and I'm dreading it. I think I'm dreading it more than she is."

"She might look thin and fragile, but that woman is strong," he said. "And she has you looking out for her."

"Not when I should have been." She tried to ignore the twinge of guilt, but he looked at her knowingly.

"When it counted." His voice was quiet but firm. "When she needed you the most."

She ran a hand through her hair, glancing back once more at the fighter. Andira looked away, but not quickly enough.

"A topic for another time," she said. "Apparently, I'm supposed to be relaxing by taking this thing of beauty up for a flight."

"It *is* a thing of beauty, isn't it?" He led her toward the fighter and gave the gleaming white exterior a loving pat. "The builders really are a caste after my own heart. When I told them what it would take to make these fly, they didn't moan about cost and materials and labor. They talked about the vast potential of hands-on learning and how they could use the opportunity to train an entire labor force for producing more. I told them how much work it would be, and they acted like it was a Shipper-damned gift. Couldn't wait to tear them apart and put them back together again. And they did fine work."

She put her hand next to his. It was odd, not feeling the soft texture of hullskin. This exterior was cool and smooth to the touch, and she had a sudden vision of Kameha in a factory somewhere, humming over blueprints and material samples and having the time of his life.

"We're never getting you back, are we?" she asked.

He paused, then slowly shook his head. "Who knows what might happen ten cycles from now, but what I'm doing here—it's a life labor. And I'm helping to change an entire civilization. Can't really ask for more than that."

"You could ask for a lover."

He gave her a look of exasperated affection, then began to speak of the friends he had made, some she had already heard about and others whose names she did not recognize. She leaned a shoulder against the fighter, watching his expression grow more animated as he talked about a life he no longer shared with her, people they did not have in common, and goals they no longer worked toward together. The tang of loss was sharp in her throat.

"Can you stay?" she asked suddenly, interrupting him in mid-sentence. "There have to be other resorts around here. We could find you something if you have the time. It's just so good to see you, and I don't—"

"Lancer Tal already invited me."

"She did? On her bonding break?"

"She called yesterday. Said there are a couple of empty cabins in your ring. I'll be here tonight and tomorrow."

"That woman." She exhaled, feeling the tension leaving her shoulders, and was not surprised to find Andira's eyes on her when she looked up. Ekatya smiled and nodded in acknowledgment, enjoying the way Andira's face lit up, then turned back to Kameha. "In that case, I have a fighter to fly while you go find your cabin. Be sure to check out the bathroom; it's spectacular. Or at least I assume it is, given what ours looks like."

"I'm looking forward to it. But first I have to make sure you remember how to get this off the ground. Sixteen months in Gov Dome…" He clicked his tongue disapprovingly. "I'm surprised you could find your bridge chair after that."

"Which is why they made me requalify on all of the shuttle and fighter models before I took the *Phoenix* out of the dock. So if you want to let me blow what little hair you have left off the top of your head, stay right here."

As he huffed in pretended offense, she pushed off the hull and stepped around him. The sun was barely up, and this was already a great day. Now she was going to make it even better.

CHAPTER 16
Taking it for a twirl

Tesseron climbed down from the cockpit at Ekatya's approach and held up a flat, padded object, rectangular on the outside with an open ring in the center. "Put this over your head, please. This side in front."

She tugged it on and stood still as he arranged it to rest comfortably on her chest and upper back. "What is it?"

"A crash collar." He strapped it into place.

"Which we'd better not need," Andira called from the copilot's seat. She was already wearing one.

Ekatya rubbed her fingertips on the collar. It looked like cloth but felt like flexible metal. "Does it inflate on impact?"

"Half a piptick before that." Tesseron finished with her straps and stepped back. "It's really just insurance, given the pressure seats in these fighters. We're already incorporating those in our transports. That is some shiny technology." He gestured toward the pilot's seat. "Climb in, Captain."

She scrambled up the short ladder on the pilot's side, which was still in its landing position while the copilot's ladder was already resealed into the fighter's belly. As she settled into the familiar seat, a quick scan of the control panel proved that not everything was the same.

"Alsean script," she said, tracing her finger over the slender, curving characters. "Suddenly that part of the qualifying test seems far more practical."

"I didn't think about that." Andira's tone was worried. "Will you—"

"If you finish that sentence, I'm going to be insulted."

Andira snapped her mouth shut, amusement on her narrow features. "I sense a certain confidence."

"Fleet piloting certification is very thorough. Part of the test involves flying in a simulated cockpit without any labels on the controls, because in a combat situation we can't be reading labels to find the right one."

"And how often have you flown a fighter in a combat situation?"

"Never," Ekatya said, certain that Andira already knew that. "Which is why all captains complain vociferously about that part of the test. And a few other parts, too."

"Then I'm glad your instructors are so thorough. Tesseron tells me that nothing has changed from the fighter you're familiar with, except that the new exterior means it flies faster in atmospheric conditions without shielding."

"Faster, really?"

"Smoother airflow," Tesseron said from his position on the top step of the ladder. "Hullskin isn't as slick. So the controls will respond a little differently. Not much, but a little."

"And that's the only difference?"

"That, and ours is more beautiful." His enthusiasm was infectious.

"I can't argue with that," Ekatya said. "I can't even take offense." She flicked on the nav screen and blinked at the lack of information. "All right, first issue. Where is my flight path?"

"That way." Andira pointed east, toward the ocean.

"Er…we're usually slightly more specific than that."

Tesseron chuckled. "Not here. The only things in that direction are a few fishing boats and the Crooked Ridge port platform. There's a cargo flight and a passenger flight twice per nineday between Crooked Ridge and the mainland, and they're not today."

"There won't be anything out there but us," Andira added. "And the airspace over this part of the island is closed this morning."

Ekatya could not hold back the smile. They were handing her freedom on a plate, with a gorgeous fighter to get her there.

"What about communication?" She tapped the quantum com. "Is this in general use now?"

"Not yet," Andira said. "Mass production is on the list, but we've had other priorities. For now, we're still using headsets." She picked up a small collapsible headset from her lap, opened it with a few deft twists, and held it out. Ekatya marveled at the light weight as she set it over her ears. Andira quickly unfolded and donned a second one, tapped the side of it, then reached over and tapped Ekatya's.

"We're on a private channel at the moment," she said, her voice sounding as if it were coming from inside Ekatya's head. "These are operated by voice command, so if you need to contact anyone else, just say it, starting with the fighter's identification. Blue Seventeen to Whitemoon Base, com check."

"This is Whitemoon Base," said a male voice. *"Blue Seventeen confirmed at Mahaite Island, altitude sixteen paces. Do you want coordinates?"*

"Not necessary, thank you. Com, switch." She met Ekatya's eyes and added, "Saying 'switch' automatically changes this to your previously set channel."

"Short and easy; I like it. And the sound is impressive. It's no different from my com implant."

"With the advantage that it also blocks external noise."

"Not that there's much of that in these fighters," Tesseron added. "It's one of the best things about them, the quiet."

Ekatya could hear him clearly despite the headset covering her ears. "I assume this accounts for voices and doesn't block them?"

"Yes," they said simultaneously.

She shook her head at the sensation of two voices coming into her brain through different pathways.

"Let's not do that, please," she said. "One of you at a time. So I have coms, I know where I'm going, and all of the other controls are the same. Is there anything else I should know?"

"Just how to put on your harness," Andira said with a grin.

"I am going to wipe that off your face," she told the infuriating woman, then turned to catch Tesseron sporting a matching expression. "Thank you for your assistance, First Pilot. Am I clear to depart?"

"As soon as I drag the chief to a safe distance." He nodded at her, saluted Andira, and jumped down.

Ekatya went through her startup checks, snapped on her restraint harness, and fired the engines. A thrill fluttered through her stomach at the familiar sound. It took less than a minute to finish the preflight checks, and when she looked up through the cockpit bubble, Tesseron and Kameha were standing at the foot of the bridge.

A quick glance verified that Tesseron had shown Andira how to put on her own harness. "Ready?" she asked.

"For ages."

Ekatya shook her head. "You only invited Kameha yesterday. Are all Lancers this impatient?"

"Why are we still on the ground?"

Without bothering to reply, Ekatya pulled back the control stick. The fighter jumped straight up at a rate of speed guaranteed to leave a newbie's stomach on the landing pad.

Andira merely looked interested.

Ekatya brought the craft to a hover and reminded herself that Andira piloted her own transports, even if they were slow cruisers compared to this. It would take a little more to shake her up.

Perhaps she would start with a nice, high-speed turn.

"Shall we fly a tour around Pica Mahal?" she asked.

"I was hoping we would."

The massive volcano was too close for her to open up the fighter's engines. But when they reached it, naked of clouds this early in the morning, she flipped them into a forty-five-degree bank and flew a circuit so rapid and tight that the seats engaged their pressure form, flowing into a new shape to support her head and the parts of her body that were being flattened by the acceleration forces.

"Yes!" Andira sounded delighted as she peered up through the cockpit bubble at the volcano's rugged flanks. "Now this is flying!"

Smiling ruefully, Ekatya rolled out of the bank to level flight once more. She would have to try harder. "Can we go inside the caldera? Any emissions?"

"It's dead and perfectly safe. They fly tour groups into it in the high season."

"Then we're going in." They climbed up over the lip of the crater, revealing a cavernous interior at least six kilometers in diameter. There was room for half a squadron to maneuver, let alone a single craft. Without warning, Ekatya shoved the control stick forward and dropped them in. The sudden change in attitude made even her stomach tingle, and she was the one piloting. Andira should have felt her stomach rise halfway up her throat.

A whoop rang in her ears, followed by a burble of happy laughter, and Ekatya smiled despite herself. The dignified Lancer of Alsea sounded like a child on a thrill ride.

The caldera was deep, its bottom still locked in shadows in the early morning light. Ekatya let the fighter's nose lead them halfway down, then pulled out of the dive and flew nearly straight up, crushing them into their seats. She leveled out and put the fighter into a hover, then looked over to check on her passenger.

Andira was beaming. "This is the best idea I've had in a cycle."

"You'd better not tell Salomen that. I get the impression she thinks your bonding rates higher." Ekatya pushed half of the thrusters forward and the other half aft with a quick flick of forefinger and thumb. By default, the thrusters would always fire with matching force, but she decreased the aft thrusters by a hair. Slowly, the fighter revolved in place, leading with its tail.

The view was spectacular. The caldera walls filled their vision, looming up into the sky and descending far beneath them. Mats of brilliant green vegetation encrusted almost every square meter, the tropical growth jostling for position in this protected place. Ekatya felt as if she had dropped them into one of her childhood fairy tales, and the waterfall that slid into view a moment later only reinforced the thought.

"Oh, how beautiful," she said, bringing their slow turn to a halt.

"I've only seen this in images." Andira leaned forward, intent on the waterfall. "The rock on the top part of the volcano is porous, so rainwater filters down through it. Then it hits that band of denser rock there—see it?" She pointed unnecessarily; the dark stripe encircling the crater was obvious by its relative lack of vegetation. "And pools up and runs out in several places. But most are ephemeral; this is the only place where it never stops. After a good rainstorm, there are thirty waterfalls in here."

"I would love to see that."

"As would I. Let's hope for a rainstorm in the next nineday and a half."

Ekatya glanced over. "You might be the only newlywed I ever heard of who hoped for bad weather on her bonding break."

"That cannot be true. Trapped indoors by water pouring out of the sky; whatever could a newly bonded couple find to do in such a situation?"

"If we're talking about you, I'd probably find you on my porch five ticks after dawn, wanting to spar or something equally ridiculous."

"This was a special occasion. If it rains, you'll see so little of Salomen and me that you might forget what we look like." Andira's playful expression became more thoughtful as she looked back at the view. "But afterward, we'll come out here for the waterfalls."

They hovered in place, staring at the sheets of water as they fell in what looked like slow motion, tumbling gracefully down the sheer wall. Bare rock evidenced how wide the waterfall could get; right now it appeared to be at half of its top flow.

Ekatya activated the ventral sensors and sent them to the virtual screens hovering in front of them. A tap of the control set the sensors to the visual spectrum, and she angled them until they showed the base of the waterfall. It fell all the way to the jumbled rocks on the crater's floor, where it landed as a seemingly gentle spray of droplets. Based on the enormous circle of bare, smooth boulders, she guessed that spray had enough force to sterilize the area.

She tapped the groundfinder, sending a pulse straight down. It came back with a reading of six hundred and eighty-two strides to the floor. She remembered that strides were roughly analogous to meters, making this a damned high waterfall.

"Well, this was worth getting up for," she said.

Andira gave her a delighted smile. "It really was. Think you can show me anything else?" An eyebrow quirked as she added, "Such as how fast this can go?"

"You've been waiting for that, haven't you?"

"Since the day Candini flew off with Tesseron. I tried to trade places with him then, but he wouldn't accept my offer." She settled back into her seat with a sigh. "I'm ready. Make me two-dimensional."

Ekatya found herself laughing as she flew them back out of the caldera, and it occurred to her that she had done more of that this morning than in the previous…two months? Three? Shippers, when *had* she enjoyed herself this much?

"It's a bad sign when you can't remember," she mumbled, forgetting about her headset.

"Speak again?"

Ekatya shook her head, leveled the craft, and hit the jump control. The fighter leaped forward, compressing them against their seats. She kept her finger on the control and didn't need to look at the velocity indicator to know that their speed was continually climbing—the increasing pressure on her body did that. The seat flowed up and around the back of her head, anticipating any changes of direction.

When they hit three times the speed of sound, she rotated the fighter one hundred and eighty degrees, putting the ocean above them and the sky below.

Andira let out a whoop of sheer joy, then another when Ekatya brought them closer to the water.

At four times the speed of sound, Ekatya righted them and flew as low as she dared. Then she put the aft sensors on the virtual screen.

A long, white track of foaming water marked their passage across the ocean. Under their tail, the water was lifted into the air by the low pressure created from their passage, a continual fountain they pulled along with them.

"Great Mother, I've never seen that before!" Andira whooped again. "I only wish we could fly over the Crooked Ridge port platform. We'd break every window in the place."

"I already have the window-breaking reputation. Let's not make it worse." Ekatya dropped their speed, and when it was low enough for her to maneuver without killing them, she angled the fighter upward and threw them into a barrel roll. When that failed to elicit anything but happy sounds from Andira, she stopped the roll with one wing pointed to the ocean and the other straight up and proceeded to fly them in a level turn of three hundred and sixty degrees. The seat flowed up around her, and she increased the acceleration, watching the pressure indicator climb.

"Shekking—" Andira did not complete her sentence, a strained huff the most she could manage under the extreme pressure. Ekatya maintained the turn for three, four, five more seconds, then pulled out.

"Still conscious over there?" she asked.

"Goddess above." Andira wheezed a few times. "I think my shoulders just met my hips. You've been wanting to do that since I mentioned your harness."

"Yes, I have." Ekatya was smiling so widely that her cheeks hurt, and she put them into another barrel roll for the fun of it. "Why am I not surprised that it took seven acceleration forces to finally take your voice?"

"That was seven AFs? No wonder. I did go up with Tesseron a few times; he didn't dare push me past five. That's why I wanted to go with you. I knew you wouldn't treat me like a Filessian orchid."

Ekatya was startled by the laugh that exploded out of her chest with no warning. "Do you know why we use Filessian orchids in our ships? Because they're some of the toughest flowers in the whole damned Protectorate. They're practically impossible to kill. You *are* a Filessian orchid, Andira."

"If I am, you are as well."

"There's a label I'd wear proudly: as tough as Lancer Tal." Ekatya leveled out their flight and looked over at her friend as they began to decelerate. "You knew this would happen, didn't you?"

"That you would try to flatten me? Yes, but—"

"No. That if I got out here with no limitations and no rules and no *fucking* orders, I'd feel free for the first time since I left Alsea."

The cocky smile vanished from Andira's face. "I didn't know. But I hoped."

Ekatya held out her hand and waited for Andira to take it. "You could probably already feel it, but just in case…" She squeezed their hands together. "I want you to feel it through my skin. Thank you, Andira. This was a beautiful gift."

"Well, the last one I gave you didn't work out quite the way I planned." Andira shrugged. "I'm very glad this one has been better."

"I'm not sorry you got me the *Phoenix*. Don't blame yourself for Sholokhov." She let go and in a lighter voice asked, "Did Tesseron let you get your hands on the controls?"

"I thought you'd never ask." Andira took hold of the control stick on her side. "May I?"

"Let's get it under the speed of sound, shall we? I'd like a shot at saving us if you misjudge."

A few minutes later, Ekatya lifted her hands off the controls and watched Andira, who beamed as she nudged the control stick from side to side. The fighter's left wing came up; then it leveled out and the right wing came up.

"That's roll, yes, and this is pitch…"

Ekatya watched the horizon go up, then down.

"And here's yaw…"

The nose went right, then left.

"Ha, I remembered. And this is…acceleration."

The last word had hardly left Andira's mouth when the fighter leaped forward, shoving Ekatya in her seat with tremendous force.

"Andira." She was rather proud that her voice remained so calm. "That's a bit fast; pull back on the speed and—"

Her sentence ended in a gasp when Andira rolled the fighter a perfect ninety degrees. A second roll had them flying upside down, the ocean ripping past the cockpit bubble at speeds Ekatya did not want to contemplate.

Especially this close and with an untrained pilot at the controls. She made a grab for the control stick, but it was unresponsive.

"You locked me out?" There was no semblance of calm in her voice now. Lockouts were only used in the event of systems failures, usually battle-induced, when the controls of either the pilot or copilot were malfunctioning in a way that could affect the fighter's integrity.

"Must have touched something I didn't mean to. Sorry, I'll get us to a safer position."

The horizon rolled around them, and they were right side up again. The ocean receded as Andira put them into a steep climb, but she wasn't controlling the airspeed properly. The climb was taking too much power. It was very difficult to stall a craft meant to fly into orbit, but Andira was dangerously close to it. And while stall recovery was easy when they had plenty of altitude to lose, they were still too close to the ocean.

Ekatya's worst fears materialized when the wings began to rock, the airspeed no longer sufficient to hold them up.

"Andira! Push it forward, you have to reduce the angle of attack!"

The next thing she knew, her stomach tried to exit her mouth as she became momentarily weightless. It would not have affected her under normal circumstances, but she was not in control of this craft. That changed everything.

The fighter fell onto its left wing, dropping them straight toward the ocean.

In her panic, Ekatya grabbed the control stick again, her mind refusing to accept that she could not stop this disaster. They didn't even have time to eject the cockpit pod.

"Level it out, level it out!" she shouted as the ocean rushed up toward her.

At the last second, the water shifted away as Andira somehow regained control and leveled the fighter. A welcome rumble of engines hummed through the soles of Ekatya's feet, and she watched with a dry mouth as the velocity indicator once again climbed to reasonable numbers.

"Stars and Shippers!" she blurted. "What in all the purple planets did you think—"

"Relax. I told you I went up with Tesseron a few times."

"A few times!" Ekatya was about to instruct her on how to deactivate the control lockout when she paused and took a closer look. Andira was handling the controls with too much confidence. Come to think of it, that little maneuver she had pulled was far too difficult for an untrained pilot.

"Andira?"

"Yes?"

"Did you just play me?"

The full grin Andira turned on her answered that question. "I'm checked out on both the single-seater and this one. Salomen arranged it as a bonding gift last moon."

"You lying, scheming, underhanded—"

Andira burst into laughter. "I'll admit to the last two, but I never lied."

"By omission! Fuck!" Ekatya slapped the heels of her hands against her forehead. "Why do I never learn with you?"

Andira was laughing so hard now that she had to slow their flight.

After a few seconds, Ekatya gave up and laughed as well. It bubbled out of her, growing louder and more intense until she was gasping with it. She couldn't stop. Her lungs spasmed, wrenching what sounded like a sob from her throat, and then she laughed again. Every time she thought she had herself in hand, she remembered the panic in her voice as she had shouted at Andira. That set her off all over again, because she had started this flight with the intention of playing Andira. She had been beaten at her own game.

When her laughter finally fizzled out, she felt more relaxed than she had in a very long time. Her body was limp, and her shoulders seemed strangely loose.

"That was…astonishing," Andira said. "How have you been holding all of that inside?"

She should have been embarrassed, knowing that Andira had literally felt her break. The prank wasn't *that* funny, but she had needed something to crack the hard shell she had grown around herself. Somehow, Andira had managed to provide it.

Or perhaps she had simply provided the environment where Ekatya could allow the shell to crack.

"I don't know," she said. "I didn't want to. When I left Alsea, I thought things would be so different. And they were, between me and Lhyn. But everything else…" She lifted her hands, then dropped them back into her lap. "I hated who I turned into."

After a long silence, Andira said, "There's one more thing I'd like to see, but I'm not checked out for orbital flight. Will you show me the *Phoenix*?"

"With pleasure." Ekatya was not surprised to find that the controls had already been returned to her. A quick ping with the locator and she had the *Phoenix* on her nav screen. She turned the fighter, pulled it into the best angle for gaining altitude while conserving energy, and locked in the route.

The sky was shading from blue to black when Andira spoke again. "I did lie by omission about my flight training. But that was for fun. And I didn't tell you about our bond because…" She blew out a breath, keeping her gaze firmly ahead. "No one was ever supposed to know. And there was nothing you could have done about it. But I have never lied to you about anything else since we became friends. Fahla knows I haven't much practice at the kind of friendship we have, but I don't keep things from Micah and I don't keep them from you."

"But I kept so much from you." Ekatya sighed. "You don't have to say it."

"Why did you?"

She knew she would have to face this question. She had known it for nearly two years, the guilt and dread growing every time she spoke with Andira on the quantum com and said nothing about what was really happening.

"Would you believe it was to protect you?"

For a very long moment, there was no sound but the throbbing hum of the engines and the faint hiss of wind noise that penetrated her headset.

"I believe you believe it," Andira said. "What I don't understand is why you thought I needed protection. And from what?"

"Do you know how I felt, hearing that I couldn't talk to you because you were burned and unconscious in the healing center? You nearly died, and I was sixteen days away even if I could have gotten orders within the hantick. I wouldn't wish that kind of helplessness on anyone, least of all someone I care about."

Andira turned to face her. "No, I don't know how you felt. Because I can't sense you over a quantum com and you didn't *tell* me." Her voice rose. "Do you know how I feel when I can't sense you? Blind. Blind and halfway deaf and completely dependent on you to tell me what I cannot know any other way, but you chose not to."

She waited for an answer Ekatya didn't know how to give, then shook her head and faced forward again.

They were well past the last wisps of atmosphere and had the *Phoenix* in visual range before Ekatya could get her thoughts together.

"I've never had a friend like you. But we're not just friends, are we? That bond..." She took another breath and said what she had been afraid to. "I missed you every day, Andira. Every damned day. And I'd look back on the time I spent here, with you, and it felt like a fairy tale—"

"A what?"

"Er...a story we tell children. Full of magic and happy endings."

"Ah. I understand." Andira made an odd sound. "You thought the Battle of Alsea was full of magic and happy endings?"

"You know what I mean." Now that she had started this, she was impatient at the interruptions. "We accomplished so much. We changed the course of history! We were *magnificent*, and we won, and then there were all of those Sharings, and I know you don't see it that way, but to me? Those were the very definition of magic. And then I lost it all. I went home to an inquisition, and spent over sixteen months—almost one of your cycles—doing shitty little jobs for a man I hated, and every day I asked myself why. Why did I leave? Why didn't I throw it all in the air and come back? Lhyn would have come with me in a heartbeat. We both missed you, but it was easier for her because she was doing what she loved..." She stopped herself. "Andira, you were rebuilding your planet and holding your people together with glue and a few frayed strings. And when I finally got out from under Sholokhov, you were in the healing center and then you were dealing with betrayal and murder and losing half of your High Council. I didn't want to be one more burden on you."

"You grainbird," Andira snapped. She turned in her seat, fixing Ekatya with a heated glare. "One. You are not a burden to me. You never could be; you're my first tyree! For Fahla's sake, do you still have no idea what that means? We are *bonded*, Ekatya. I missed you every day, too. Salomen could feel it in me a cycle after you left."

Ekatya tried to ask, but Andira rolled right over her.

"Two. Don't tell me how I feel. You think I didn't see our Sharings as magic? I thought they were the closest I would ever get to touching the face of Fahla. And three, how do you think I feel now, knowing that I burdened you with everything that was going on in my life when you had your own set of problems that you weren't telling me about?" She faced forward again.

"Like a selfish dokker, that's how. Like I took one of the few good things in my life and broke it because I wasn't careful enough."

Ekatya waited a moment, then spoke cautiously. "May I say something now?"

Andira waved a hand without looking, but her head turned when Ekatya caught her hand and held it.

"I'm sorry. I'm not any more used to this kind of friendship than you are, but I'll try to do better. And for the love of flight, you didn't break anything."

If it were anyone else, she thought, she could have spent an hour trying to explain herself, to justify it, to convince the other person of her sincerity. It was hard to remember how much she hated the idea of her emotions being so easily read when that very ease was saving her from explanations she couldn't put into words.

Andira's grip tightened. "I'm sorry, too."

"Don't be. I'd rather have you angry at me."

"It's not you I'm angry with. Fahla, look at this." Andira let go of her hand and gestured at the view. They were high enough now to see the transparent curved line of Alsea's outer atmosphere, a fragile shell holding in the precious elements that kept the planet alive. "My first time up here in a craft I can see out of, and I'm spending it making you feel bad about trying to protect me."

They were her own words, yet something about them rang false. Perhaps it was hearing them from someone else that made their fallacy suddenly clear.

"What?" Andira asked. "I know how you feel. It's difficult not to; you're bombarding me with it."

"That's not—" Ekatya stopped and tore off her headset, watching as Andira followed suit. Here above the atmosphere there was no wind noise to block, and she wanted no more barriers.

"I just realized you're not the one I was protecting," she said. "At least, not until the last two moons. You have…an idea of me, an image that I lived up to when I was here. I didn't live up to it after I left."

"And you didn't want me to know."

Ekatya nodded and checked her course toward the *Phoenix*, a good excuse to keep her head down.

"Were you afraid I'd think less of you because you spent a cycle being punished for what you did to save Alsea? I think less of your Protectorate, yes, but not you."

She looked up to find Andira watching her intently.

"Of all the people on that planet," Andira said, pointing, "and on that ship, I might be the one person who understands what you just said. I know about images and myths better than anyone. But you're not my captain. You can try to project whatever image you want, but I won't see who you want me to. I see who you are."

"That might be the most frightening thing you've ever said to me." Ekatya tried for a light tone, but there was too much truth in her words. She forestalled any answer by flicking on the quantum com and calling the *Phoenix*, which had surely been tracking them from the moment they cleared the atmosphere.

"Captain Serrado to *Phoenix*. I'm piloting the craft you're tracking, so please keep a lockout on weapons."

The com screen activated, showing the round, cheerful face of Commander Lokomorra, her new first officer. "We assumed you were a friendly, Captain. Given the identifier on that fighter."

Ekatya frowned at Andira, who put on a too-innocent look.

"What identifier?"

Lokomorra's eyes were outlined in black, a tattoo common in the megacity where he had grown up. His hair follicles had been permanently destroyed in two bands that ran from his temples to the back of his head, while the rest of his black hair was cropped short. The designs, in combination with his thick, forked beard, should have made him look ferocious. Instead, his eyes twinkled with amusement and two deep dimples appeared as he smiled. "You're showing up on our display as Blue Seventeen, Whitemoon Base Squadron, Caphenon Wing. And that fighter model, which I have to say is prettier than ours, is called a Serrado. Do you think we can get Fleet to juice up our colors like that?"

"Stand by, Commander." She flipped off the com and glared at Andira. "I'm flying a Serrado? And you didn't think to mention this earlier?"

"That would have spoiled the surprise." Her expression grew more serious. "We didn't name it after an image."

Ekatya opened her mouth, then shut it again and cleared her throat. "And the single-seat model?"

"There was some debate about that. After all, there were two Gaian pilots flying those in the battle, and both of them saved thousands of Alseans when they stopped ground pounders from hitting towns and villages. But one of those pilots did try to blow up the *Caphenon*, so in the end, everyone agreed."

The warmth was expanding through her chest. "Does Candini know those fighters are named after her?"

Andira nodded. "She was remarkably enthusiastic about helping our pilots once she heard."

"Oh, that didn't help her goddess complex. We'll never shrink her ego down to size now! And Sholokhov will spit his brandy through his nose when he hears about Serrado fighters."

"I hope he does, and I hope it burns."

Ekatya wanted to hug her, but settled for flipping the com back on. "Commander, we're going to do a flyby of the *Phoenix*. Also, it occurs to me that I didn't get enough weapons training when I did my qualifying flights. Would you load a few target drones into the tubes?"

"Of course."

"And Commander, I'll be checking the logs when I get back on board. If I find this has been put up on the bridge display, you'll be in charge of the morning PT runs for the next two weeks."

"Wouldn't dream of it, Captain. Didn't even cross my mind."

"Glad to hear it. I'll call when we're ready."

Andira waited until the com was off before saying, "He's quite a change from Baldassar. Far more casual."

"I have different priorities for choosing officers now. It's amazing how nearly having a court-martial on my record makes me view others with a more open mind. Lokomorra has two reprimands in his file for unprofessional attitude, yet no record of any broken or even bent regulations. Which told me that he did his job perfectly well, but in a way his commanding officers didn't like. I called him in for an interview and asked him about it."

"And?"

"And I liked him. So I corroborated his side of the story with four other officers, and it all lined up. What his captains didn't like was his personality. He's very relaxed on the bridge. Too relaxed for some people's tastes. But that doesn't mean he's not professional or that he doesn't take his duties seriously. I'm finding him to be an extremely competent officer."

"That *is* different. You wouldn't have accepted him on the *Caphenon*."

"No, I wouldn't have. But Lokomorra would probably have been the first one to tell me that we couldn't leave Alsea to the Voloth. After Lhyn, that is."

"I like him already." Andira looked from the planet receding behind them to the ship growing larger in their front view. "Those images you showed me didn't do it justice. She's beautiful."

The *Phoenix* hung before them like a brilliant jewel in the darkness of space, reflecting the sunlight off her hullskin and the many outside viewports currently exposed. The top deck was fully uncovered, its beautifully landscaped garden basking in the light pouring through the transparent hull.

Ekatya remembered her own first look, from the observation deck of Quinton Shipyards. Her strongest emotion then had been sheer relief in the knowledge that she was done with Gov Dome and Sholokhov. Now she enjoyed the surge of pride and felt no shame for it. She had paid a high price for this ship; her pride was earned.

"She looks so different with a whole hullskin," Andira marveled.

"Not to mention the distinct lack of crash damage." They were coming up on the *Phoenix* from behind, where the dual surf engines were by far the most prominent feature. Ekatya had always thought that one of the best parts of the Pulsar design was the way the engines blended into the body of the ship, looking perfectly in proportion despite their size. It was difficult to visually comprehend their enormity without a proper comparator.

She reversed engines to bring them to a near standstill, then coasted right into the mouth of the starboard engine.

"Great Mother." Andira gazed wide-eyed at the cylindrical shaft taking up their entire field of view. "You could fit half a squadron in this. Are you certain this is the same design? It seems so much larger out here."

"I imagine you don't often fly a transport inside the *Caphenon*'s engines."

"Not ever. Can we fly underneath it? I've never done that with the *Caphenon*."

"It's a bit difficult when the ship is sitting on the ground." Ekatya pulled them away from the yawning cavern of the surf engine and dropped them beneath the ship. With a small tap on the stick, they began moving slowly along the ship's length, close enough that the shimmering brilliance of hullskin was all they could see from one side to the other. Upon reaching the area where the lower decks curved out of the flat aft section, she followed the graceful arc down, then back up again as they approached the bow.

"We're under the fighter bays now, yes?"

"Correct. Full of shiny, hullskinned fighters that I can't deploy in your atmosphere. I went toe to toe with Admiral Tsao about that. I didn't see why we couldn't have at least ten Alsea-capable fighters, given the fact that the *Phoenix* is tasked with protecting this whole sector in general and Alsea in particular."

"What was her reasoning?"

"It wasn't her reasoning, and it's not tactical. It's political. There are some asses still burning over the terms of the Alsea Treaty, not to mention the fact that you destroyed the Voloth without any real help."

"Without—" Andira sputtered. "What do they think you and your crew did, sit outside watching the fireworks?"

"Believe me, they know all about our involvement." She had recounted every detail at least ten times during her inquisition. "But any other pre-FTL planet would have needed half the Ground Warfare division to hold off the Voloth. You did it with a crashed ship and two Protectorate fighters. That scares some people."

Andira gave a single nod. "The Defenders of the Protectorate. Ambassador Solvassen has been keeping me informed. I didn't realize they had that much political clout."

"They didn't, before. But they grew a lot in the last cycle, and some of them would do anything to turn general concerns about Alsea into a tsunami of paranoia." Her rage rose, thick and fast, and Andira looked over with a startled expression. Ekatya shook her head. "Later. The point is, there's plenty of political support for preventing nanoscrubbers from getting into Voloth hands, but not for aiding Alsean warriors in any sort of fight on the planet."

"In other words, if any Voloth get past you, it's our problem and not yours."

"No, it would still be my problem. At that point, my job would be to prevent any Voloth from leaving the system." And she would be the public scapegoat if anything went wrong.

They had reached the bow; ahead was nothing but deep space and stars. She pulled the fighter up and around, savoring the view in spite of their conversation. The *Phoenix* stretched out before them in all her glory, from the graceful curves of the skirt to the garden at the top of the dome and on to the magnificent engine cradle. Just below them, in letters and numbers twice the length of her fighter, the ship proudly declared her name and identity code.

"SPF-PC12," Andira read. "Ship of the Protectorate Fleet, Pulsar class, twelfth off the line."

"You remember." It seemed a long time ago that Ekatya had sat in Andira's State House office, watching the raising of the *Caphenon* and explaining what the identity code meant.

"I would hardly forget. We were preparing for battle at the time, and I was sharing my office with the one person who gave me a hope of winning it." Andira turned in her seat. "I'm not surprised at your lack of Alsea-capable fighters. We didn't ask for that in the treaty, and we wouldn't."

Ekatya rolled her eyes. "I forgot about Alsean pride."

"Shantu may be dead, but his power base is still there, and they have a legitimate concern. We cannot depend on the aliens who abandoned us."

Squelching the guilt, Ekatya said, "Hence the Serrado and Candini fighters."

"Exactly. And stop feeling guilty; you didn't abandon us. If you had, you wouldn't have spent a cycle under Sholokhov's boot."

"Good point." Ekatya took a deep breath. "I'm ready for some target practice. How about you?"

She didn't need to be an empath to feel Andira's excitement.

"What do I do?"

Two taps brought up the virtual targeting screens in front of both their seats, and a third transferred weapons to Andira's side. Ekatya demonstrated how the flight controls had now been remapped to weapons on the copilot's control stick, leaving that side to focus on firing solutions while Ekatya would focus on flight.

"I'm ready." Andira's smile brightened the cockpit.

Ekatya turned the fighter away from the *Phoenix*, took it out of shield space, and called Lokomorra on the quantum com. "Fire a drone, Commander. Threat level one."

"One? Wait one moment, Captain, I already had them programmed for level three."

"I'm working with a new weapons specialist."

"Understood." He looked down at his panel, then back up again. "All set. Shield active and…firing now."

Ekatya could not see the tiny drone as it streaked through the *Phoenix*'s shield, but the fighter's sensors picked it up immediately. A green dot appeared on both of their targeting screens, tracking rapidly from right to left.

"Oh, that asshead, he shot it right across us." Ekatya threw the fighter into pursuit, narrowly avoiding the low-energy laser that bounced harmlessly off the massive ship shield behind them.

"I assume the drone has inactive weapons? That's just a light show, yes?" Andira was watching her screen closely, her hand around the control stick and her thumb poised over the firing button.

"It is. But our weapons are hot." Ekatya saw the drone lining up for another shot and dodged it, then pulled in directly behind the fleeing bit of hardware. "Get it!"

A brilliant white beam lanced across space, impacting the drone dead center and blowing it to shreds.

"Yes!" Andira threw her hands in the air and did a shimmy in her seat.

Ekatya laughed. "I've never seen your version of a victory dance."

"Let me kill another one and you can see it again. How many threat levels are there?"

"Twelve. I can handle them at level three, but I've never gotten past that. It's not something I prioritize, obviously. But pilots like Candini can shoot down multiple drones at level twelve. It's like watching a ballet."

"Multiple?"

Ekatya could almost see the gears turning in her head. With a smile tugging at the corners of her mouth, she called Lokomorra again. "Give me two drones this time, Commander. Level three."

CHAPTER 17
Unexpected guest

WARNIC PUT HIS HANDS ON his lower back and bent backward, trying to ease the ache in his spine. He had finished three bonding ceremonies and was about to begin his fourth, and standing for all of these hanticks was taking its toll. Still, this was what he had most looked forward to when Lead Templar Satran had left him in charge of Blacksun Temple. She enjoyed officiating and did it as often as she could, making a day like this a rarity. The last time he had officiated for a whole day was… He frowned in thought. Probably when she had taken time off in the summer to visit her sister.

The final couple of the day were new to him; he had not been the one providing their pre-bonding services. But the templar recording their story had done a fine job, and Warnic was well prepared for that part of the ceremony.

They had met when the crafter entered the merchant's shop, looking for a place to sell his wares. He had been bonded before, but lost his bondmate during the Battle of Alsea and subsequently moved to Blacksun to make a new start in life. The merchant, who was a little older, told the templar during their interview that she had long ago given up on love. But when the crafter came into her shop, they turned an inspection of wares into a long conversation, then an evenmeal…and within half a moon realized they were tyrees.

They were a living reminder that Fahla offered second chances. She could bring hope from the ashes.

The guests filed in, rustling and speaking in low tones while they found places to stand. There were only fifty or so when Warnic's aide gave him the signal. This would be a small, intimate ceremony, then—a nice contrast to the prior one, which had apparently involved half of Blacksun. No one in this group would have a bad view.

The hired musicians began the bonding ballad as the great doors of the temple opened, framing the bondmates. Warnic watched them approach, enjoying their wide grins and the excited delight that rolled off them. Times like these made his long cycles of study and practice worth it, when he was privileged to be part of such a momentous and joyful event.

The ceremony moved forward smoothly. Warnic particularly enjoyed telling the story of the bondmates, during which the smiles on fifty faces and the accompanying love, amusement, and happiness made his own heart swell. Like the bondmates, most of the guests were mid empaths and did not front their emotions during the ceremony. He felt as if he were bathing in light.

The time came for the Great Sharing, and the templars lined up the guests according to the pre-stated wishes of the bondmates. Once everyone was in place, Warnic slid his hand into the opening of the merchant's ceremonial robe. She smiled at him, her joy singing through her skin, and he gave himself an extra moment to bask in the brilliance of that smile before turning his head to the crafter.

The moment his other hand touched the crafter's chest, his spine snapped into a rigid line, throwing his head back. Power poured through his body, effortlessly holding him in its grip. The hairs on the back of his neck stood on end, and his eyes popped wide open, staring involuntarily at the tree limbs overhead. For a few terrifying moments he thought he would fall over backward, destroying the ceremony and making a scene that would haunt his career forever afterward.

At last he managed to close his eyes. The slow blink seemed to unlock his body, and he forced himself to relax bit by bit, muscle by muscle. He didn't know how much time had passed while he wrestled himself under control, but the guests were still smiling and the bondmates were only slightly quizzical. Thank Fahla, he had managed to hide it.

He gave himself another tick to adapt to this ferocious power, then said a silent prayer to the Goddess before sending it outward. If he had not sufficiently controlled it…

But he had. Sighs and murmurs were the only sounds as the gift traveled on, and no one seemed to realize how much power he was holding back. It surged through him, trying to escape, and he fought it for endless moments until finally, finally he could break the connection.

His forehead was embarrassingly sweaty. Looking down, he quickly wiped it with his sleeve before stepping forward to make the final pronouncements.

Rote memorization came to his rescue, allowing his tongue to form the proper words despite his brain being unable to recall them. At last he reached the end, sagging in relief as he said, "Let the celebration begin."

The bondmates grinned and enveloped each other in a blissful warmron, then walked up to the molwyn tree and rested their hands on its trunk.

Warnic missed the early stages, too occupied in wiping more sweat off his face now that no one was looking at him. But the gasps of the onlookers and the wave of collective shock hitting his senses brought up his head.

The tree was erupting in divine flames. Even as he watched, they raced along the branches and outlined every leaf, until their blazing glory outshone even the sunlight beaming down through the top of the dome.

He staggered back a step, then another, before dropping to his knees.

"Fahla," he whispered. "You're here."

CHAPTER 18
Different worlds

Lanaril felt them long before she arrived at the little cove. Her front came up without thought.

She had hoped to find Fianna alone again, but judging by the combative glee in the air, she was in hot competition with someone. A man, and one she trusted enough to drop her front for.

She stepped off the trail and onto the black sand, but the beach in front of her was empty. They must be on the other side of the cove, blocked from her view by the enormous boulder where she had met Fianna the day before.

After a moment's thought, she walked to the side of the rock and began climbing, a tingle of anticipation lending an extra spring to her movements. This time she made it to the top with a little more grace.

They were halfway between her rock and the cliff that enclosed the cove, in the dry sand just above the waterline. Both were in sleeveless shirts and short pants, and Fianna's long black hair was tightly bound in a braid. Her shorter opponent had red hair and bulging muscles, and though he was out of uniform, Lanaril recognized him as Ronlin, Salomen's Lead Guard. The two of them were locked in combat, bare feet thrashing through the sand and skin shining with sweat as they grappled with each other.

Ronlin found an advantage and threw Fianna onto her back, but before he could follow up, she bounced to her feet and launched a kick at him. He dodged successfully and called, "You'd need two more handspans of leg to connect from that distance!"

"Shekking sand!" Fianna swore.

"Yes, blame it on the sand—"

"As if you weren't doing exactly that one tick ago, you whining baby dokker."

"Come closer and see how hard this dokker kicks, Longlegs!"

They were laughing as they closed in again, trading strikes and blocks, oblivious to their audience.

Lanaril watched in fascination. They were like children on the playing field. Their entire beings were sunk into competition, yet there was none of the antagonism that she was accustomed to sensing at adult sporting events. Instead, she felt a wild joy from both of them. She could not understand how two people could derive so much pleasure from what appeared to be barely controlled violence.

Warriors really were a caste apart, she mused as the two combatants struggled and shouted at each other. She and Fianna had not Shared the previous night, but they had otherwise been as close as two people could be, and yet it seemed as if they were from two different worlds.

She thought about Ekatya Serrado, who really was from a different world, and wondered whether the Protectorate captain would find more in common with Fianna than she did. What a difficult life that woman lived, where paranoia reigned supreme and trust was given only when all suspicion was allayed. One day, she was going to ask Andira how she had earned Ekatya's trust so quickly—especially given her friendship with Lhyn.

Because that seemed to be the issue, Lanaril's friendship with Lhyn. It wasn't jealousy, which she could have understood. It was more an expectation of harm. Ekatya had been *guarding* Lhyn from her yesterday. And today…

She drew up her knees and wrapped her arms around them. Andira had brought Ekatya back from some morning adventure in a fighter, and the two of them were glowing with happiness. They had been so excited at midmeal, talking over each other about volcanoes and waterfalls and shooting down drones in space. Lanaril had been astonished to hear the captain laugh. She had never heard it before, nor sensed the giddy delight that went with it. This, she realized, was the Ekatya that Lhyn spoke of. Her emotions were those of a completely different woman. Lanaril had asked her a question—she couldn't even remember what it was now—and watched as the smile slid off her face and walls so thick they were nearly corporeal went up in her mind. A new smile appeared quickly, but it bore no resemblance to the one it had replaced.

It had been a very long time since Lanaril felt that ostracized. The sensation brought back unpleasant memories of her childhood, before the testers took her away to be with others of her empathic strength. She had excused herself as soon as she could and walked to the back side of the island in search of easier company.

Though perhaps she should redefine *easy*, she thought as she watched the two warriors brawl. When Fianna had taken that first bold step yesterday, Lanaril had welcomed the distraction, wanting nothing more from it than what she received: an evening of simple, mutual pleasure, nothing else asked and nothing given. But here she was, wanting more after all, because she didn't understand Ekatya and perhaps Fianna could.

Fianna tripped Ronlin and ducked away, laughing as he threw a handful of sand at her. Then her head lifted and a wash of recognition pulsed through the air when she saw Lanaril. She smiled brightly, raising a hand.

Lanaril returned the gesture, her own smile coming unbidden as she felt the warmth of Fianna's happiness. It wasn't often that she could be so certain of her own welcome, and it was especially pleasant to feel so very wanted now.

Ronlin asked something in a lower tone, and Fianna turned back to him. Lanaril would have given a great deal to hear which terms Fianna was choosing to explain her presence.

Ronlin nodded and waved, but Lanaril had barely raised her own hand before Fianna barreled into him.

With a wordless shout, Ronlin stumbled backward, and their combat began anew. It had a different flavor now, with faster movements and a more competitive edge. Lanaril knew nothing about fighting, but it seemed that Fianna was overwhelming Ronlin. She winced as he was flipped into the air and thudded to the ground.

Fianna landed on top of him, sand flying as she scrambled to immobilize his limbs. They thrashed for half a tick before everything went still. With a startling suddenness, the edge drained out of their emotions, leaving behind a sense of satisfaction, combined with pride from Fianna and amusement from Ronlin.

Fianna rose to her feet and extended a hand to help Ronlin up. Both of them brushed sand off their short pants and shirts, though Ronlin soon gave up and simply took off his shirt, exposing a broad torso rippling with so much muscle that it nearly hid his chest ridges. Lower down, the tops of his pelvic ridges were sharply defined.

"Good Fahla," Lanaril murmured. Had she not already chosen a lover for this trip, she might not have let Ronlin leave this cove without an invitation. Apparently, she had been missing some opportunities with these Guards.

Ronlin slapped Fianna's shoulder and trudged toward the other side of the cove. He looked up, offering a farewell wave, and Lanaril admired the play of muscles in his thighs as she waved back. Then she glanced over at Fianna and promptly forgot Ronlin and everyone else on the island.

Fianna had also given up on getting the sand out of her clothes and was in the process of taking them off.

All of them.

No power on Alsea could have budged Lanaril from her spot as Fianna wriggled out of her short pants, left them in a heap with her shirt, and calmly unbound her hair while facing out to sea. When her hair was once again a free, sweeping curtain of black, she ran into the water and dove under a wave. Her head popped up on the other side, and she tilted back, smiling into the sunlight with her eyes closed.

Lanaril discovered that she had not been breathing sufficiently and took a great inhale to balance it out.

Fianna ducked under twice more, then swam to the shallows and rose out of the water like the Goddess herself, slicking back her hair as rivulets ran down her creamy skin. Her gaze never left Lanaril's while she waded the last few paces and stepped onto the sand. She looked away only long enough to scoop up her clothing in one hand, then walked to the base of the boulder.

"I hate to feed your ego," Lanaril said, smiling down at her. "But you're the most magnificent sight on this island. I'm not certain I can safely get down from this rock now that half of my brain has switched off."

Fianna's laugh sent a jolt through her stomach. "I could get dressed, if that would help guarantee your safety."

Lanaril let her gaze rake over the strong, sleek body still dripping water. "That might be for the best."

She regretted her moment of pragmatism as soon as Fianna shook out her shirt and pulled it over her head.

"Please do feed my ego." Fianna flapped her short pants vigorously and put one leg through. "I can only benefit from it. And as long as we're confessing, I should admit that seeing you gave me an extra incentive to finish that fight. Ronlin said I cheated." She fastened the waistband and looked up again.

"Did you?"

"No, but I might have turned a friendly sparring session into something less friendly."

"Will you pay for that later?"

"If we end up sparring in front of Varsi or Thornlan, definitely. Then it would be Ronlin having something to prove."

"So you were proving something to me." Great Mother, she really *was* like a child. Lanaril studiously ignored the warmth moving through her lower abdomen, which had nothing to do with the idea of a warrior fighting for her.

"Let's just say that defeat is not an aphrodisiac."

"You're assuming a great deal."

"Am I? Why are you here, Lanaril? And why is your front still up? There's no one here but me."

This was always the tricky part of any new relationship: the negotiations around dropping a front. She hadn't even considered doing it last night. Fianna had been just as guarded, even when she had come undone beneath Lanaril's hands.

"Why isn't yours?" she asked. "Doesn't it give your opponent an advantage if you're fighting without a front?"

"Why don't you come down from there, and we'll discuss fighting philosophy on level ground."

Lanaril nodded, rose, and moved to the other side of the boulder while Fianna began walking around it. Going down was not as easy as coming up, but she was saved the last few steps when Fianna lifted her by the waist. Her feet had barely touched the sand before she was pulled back against a warm, damp body smelling of sun and salt.

"Much better," Fianna murmured as she brushed Lanaril's hair to one side.

Shivering at the touch of lips on her neck, Lanaril said, "I thought we were discussing fighting philosophy?"

"I thought you might have forgotten about that by now."

She pulled away and turned, meeting an unrepentant grin. "You have a low opinion of me if you think my attention span is that short. Or else you have a very high opinion of yourself, thinking you can drive all thoughts out of my head with one kiss."

"I think I demonstrated my high opinion of you yesterday."

"Ego it is, then. What am I doing with a warrior?" she asked with an exaggerated eye roll. She was only partially joking, but with her front up, Fianna could not know that.

"Accompanying her back to her cabin, I hope." Fianna frowned as she pulled her shirt away from her skin. "The swim helped, but I still have sand in places it doesn't belong. I want a shower and a tall glass of Jarnell's special fruit drink. Care to join me in either or both?"

"The drink, definitely." Lanaril turned to lead the way back to the trail. "The shower, probably not. But I'm happy to wait for you to finish yours. Now tell me about fighting without a front."

"Normally, we don't." Fianna stooped and pulled a pair of sandals from behind a small log. Balancing easily on one foot, she brushed the sand off the other as she said, "You're right, it would give an opponent too much of an advantage. But Ronlin and I can fight as friends." With the sandal in place, she switched legs, brushing sand and looking as if she could balance this way for a hantick.

"Is that so unusual, fighting as friends?"

Fianna shot her a startled glance before slipping on the other sandal. "Sometimes I forget how little the other castes know." She started up the trail.

"I'm rather glad your front is down, or I might have taken offense at that."

"Then I am, too, because that would be a bad way to begin our afternoon." Fianna reached the main trail and waited until they could walk side by side. "I meant that I don't have much practice at explaining things. Things that everyone I know just knows."

"And here I am, still waiting for the explanation."

"Right. Ah…it's all about rank. I spar with all of my Guards, but I'm also responsible for them, which means I can't be one of them. I don't drop my front around them."

"That's understandable." And very similar to her own experience. She never dropped her front in the temple; it simply wasn't possible when her duties meant she was responsible for everyone in the building.

"And my superiors don't drop their fronts around me for the same reason."

Lanaril stepped over a tree root. "And then there is Ronlin, holding the same rank."

"Exactly. And I like him. I respect him." Her emotions made it clear that the latter was more important than the former. "We have a lot in common, and we've become friends. It's a relief to have someone in Blacksun that I can just…be with. Someone I can fight without it being a lesson from me or to me."

"Then I'm glad you have him, and sorry you don't have more like him. We all need someone we can just be with." She cast a sideways look at the woman pacing beside her, damp clothing sticking to her skin, and thought it was a shame that she couldn't just be with her. Fianna was such a restful presence, but their differences made anything more than a vacation joining impossible.

Remembering what Fianna had said earlier, she asked, "You mentioned him having something to prove to…other Guards in your unit, I think? Is that allowed?"

"Only Varsi is in my unit. Thornlan reports directly to Head Guardian Gehrain. There's no conflict of interest or authority with either of them, since Ronlin is the Bondlancer's Lead Guard. He could never find a lover in his own unit, but he's free to choose from mine."

"Which gives him a much larger pool than it does you. And explains why you made me an offer."

Fianna stopped walking. "You cannot think we're here because I have limited choices. I have all of *Blacksun*, Lanaril."

"Not on this island, you don't. But it wouldn't matter either way. The result is the same, and I'm content with that."

"You're content." Fianna reached out to touch her bare arm, an uninvited emotional skim. "You really are. I'd have thought the Lead Templar would expect more."

"Don't believe the stereotype." Lanaril was a little startled at herself for allowing such a presumptuous act. "Not all templars abhor the thought of joining without Sharing. What I wanted, you gave me. I hope I did the same for you."

"That and more. I hope you're still in a giving mood."

She watched the woman who had stood naked before her a few ticks ago, who still had not raised her front, and wondered how far she would let that openness take her. Joining with a lover who kept up no blocks? It would be halfway to a Sharing, without any personal vulnerability.

"I will not drop my front," she said.

"Right." Fianna's front snapped into place, though not before Lanaril caught the shard of her disappointment.

"But as for the giving mood," she continued, hoping to smooth over this bump in their previously easy exchange, "I didn't walk all this way just to watch you fight."

Fianna's smile was as open as her emotions had been a moment ago. "That was an added bonus for you, then."

With a huff of laughter, Lanaril accepted the hand she held out. She could ask about Ekatya and the warrior culture later. For now, there were more urgent issues to be resolved.

Half a hantick before evenmeal, Lanaril dragged her tired legs up the steps to her cabin. She should have realized how much stamina would come with Fianna's youth and athletic body. It was a good thing she had returned early enough to take a quick nap, or she might fall asleep in her chair during the family storytelling tonight.

The late afternoon sun slanted through the open side of her cabin, setting the floor tiles aglow and sending a beam of reflected light to the wooden table where she had left her reader card. She looked more closely, then groaned. The rolled edge of the card was glowing green, indicating at least one message. She had left strict instructions with Warnic to forget she even had a reader card with her, unless the Voloth invaded again. "And even then, I'll learn of it from Lancer Tal," she had told him. Whatever this was, it had better be critically important.

"If you haven't personally seen Fahla in my study, I will have you filling oil racks for the next two moons," she grumbled, pulling the reader card from its pouch and giving it a tap. It unrolled, stiffened into a sheet, and activated, showing a single message. She called it up and began reading.

Two ticks later she was sprinting across the clearing, all tiredness forgotten.

CHAPTER 19
Brainstorm

"Are you certain there's no mistake?" Micah asked.

"Quite," Lanaril snapped. She lowered her head and held up a hand. "I'm sorry. I'm a little…defensive, I suppose. Of course disbelief will be everyone's first reaction, but we cannot close our eyes to this. This is a miracle, not a mistake. As all of us here know, it's rather difficult to misinterpret a molwyn tree catching fire."

Tal tapped her finger against the glass of fruit juice she had been drinking before Lanaril burst into the main cabin. She had been fortunate not to drop it, given the drama of Lanaril's entrance and her unprecedented lack of a front. She may not have known Lanaril for long, but it was certainly long enough to know that only the greatest shock could have knocked down her front. It was back up now, and for that Tal was grateful. It brought some much-needed normality to a decidedly abnormal situation.

"I understand, but we still have to verify," she said. "Is there no chance that Warnic didn't get a little too deep into the celebratory bottle before his fourth bonding ceremony of the day?"

Lanaril let out a huff of laughter. "Warnic? No chance at all. He believes spirits cloud the mind. I've never seen him drink, not even at the Feast of the Wandering King." She dropped into the armchair next to Micah with none of her usual grace. "I know how it sounds, and I'll be speaking to the tyrees myself, but I think we have to accept that we've just had our second miracle in four days. It's—" She laughed again, a sound of incredulous joy, and looked at Tal with brilliant eyes. "We are living in a new age. Fahla is *here*. After a thousand cycles of silence, she is giving the divine gift again."

"But I thought…" Jaros stopped as all of the adults looked at him.

"What, Jaros?" Salomen had moved up beside Tal's chair. Grateful for her proximity, Tal reached out to tangle their fingers together.

Jaros stared at their joined hands, then at Salomen. "I thought you were the only ones."

"We thought so, too." With her free hand, Salomen tugged a chair next to Tal's. "But I'm not sorry if Fahla wants to give her gift to others," she added as she sat down. "We'll just be the first ones rather than the only ones."

"This hasn't happened in a thousand cycles?" Ekatya asked. "Do you know why not?"

Lanaril shook her head. "It's one of our greatest mysteries. Though a rather esoteric one. Most Alseans aren't aware that divine tyrees ever existed."

"I wasn't," Tal interjected. "Not until Lanaril told me."

"I never even imagined it until Tal told me," Micah said. Shikal and Nikin murmured their agreement. Chief Kameha, who had joined them for evenmeal, remained silent.

Lhyn leaned forward, intrigue showing in every line of her body as she focused on Lanaril. "How often did it happen before it stopped?"

"I don't know. Based on my research, it was a regular if rare occurrence. Then at some point, the gift began to manifest less often, until it finally ceased altogether."

"A thousand cycles without and then twice in four days… What are the odds of that?" Kameha wondered.

"They didn't teach statistical analysis in my templar studies, Chief. Perhaps the same odds as having aliens drop out of our skies and crash a ship in Blacksun Basin?"

"You can't calculate probability with a data set of two," Lhyn said.

"No, but you can make some assumptions just for the fun of it." Kameha waggled his eyebrows. "I've heard how you love to grind your numbers."

"I'd be grinding these into a powder." But Lhyn was already tugging a pad from the ever-present sleeve pocket in Gaian clothing, her enthusiasm belying her words. "And pulling those assumptions right out of my—" She stopped, glancing guiltily at Jaros. "Um. So, just to have something to work with, what percentage of tyrees do you think were divine in the old days? Half a percent? Point zero five percent?" She looked expectantly at Lanaril.

"The latter, if anything. Though that's entirely conjectural."

"Speedy." Lhyn didn't seem to notice that she used Jaros's slang, but he grinned. "And I know your population has been relatively static, so that works out to…" Her fingers began dancing over the pad, while she muttered things like "independent events" and "that won't work; maybe if I…" After a few moments, her fingers stopped and she tilted her head at the screen. "No matter how I shift around the numbers, I get ridiculous outcomes. I mean, this is all an exercise in statistical nonsense anyway, but these numbers are decimal points followed by a lot of zeroes and I don't see how that would change even if we had a bigger data set—" She looked up when Ekatya put a hand on her arm.

"I think it's safe to say that this is not a coincidence," Ekatya said.

"That's what I just said." Lhyn frowned at her.

Micah choked back a laugh and disguised it as a cough. "I agree."

"Of course it's not a coincidence!" Lanaril looked at them as if they all had grown third eyes. "Do you think it was random chance that the first divine tyree bonds appeared after Fahla's covenant was broken? Or that the first pair to bear this bond included the woman who broke that covenant and saved us as a result? This is a *blessing*. This is Fahla telling us that in making the hard choice and thinking for ourselves, rather than letting our entire culture die, we have proven ourselves worthy to bear her gift once more."

"Aldirk is going to lose sleep tonight," Tal said. "When Salomen and I were the only ones, it made a perfect story. Now that the gift has been given elsewhere—and to mid empaths, no less—that story is altered beyond recognition."

"Andira Shaldone Tal," Micah said in a voice she hadn't heard for many cycles. "You're looking a miracle in the face and thinking of political optics?"

"If you don't think miracles are political, you need to read more history."

"I'm lost," Lhyn said as Micah scowled. "Why are you surprised that mid empaths would have this kind of bond? Your original divine tyrees were a producer and a crafter."

"Yes, but they were high empaths," Lanaril told her.

Lhyn's bafflement rattled against Tal's senses, along with an odd shiver of alarm. "What? Then there's a very large hole in my understanding of your castes."

"In the ancient times," Tal said, "before our written history, high empaths were in all castes. It was only later that they were shunted into the scholar and warrior castes."

"Are you kidding me? I wrote a book on your culture and I didn't know this tiny little fact with huge, *enormous* ramifications? I thought high empaths were always pushed into the scholar and warrior castes."

"No, they were not." Salomen's voice cut through the heightened emotions in the room. "And I for one do not think it's a coincidence that for her second divine tyree bond, Fahla chose two of the so-called lesser castes. Perhaps she is telling us to right an ancient wrong."

"Speaking of politicizing a miracle," Tal muttered. Salomen shot her a sharp glance, but Tal barely had time to notice before the fear exploded across her mind, a shuddering, despairing plunge that was only just being held back from full panic.

The source was Lhyn, who was staring at Ekatya. "I got it wrong," she whispered. "I made a mistake."

Ekatya was also emanating fear, though it was far more controlled and held an entirely different flavor. While Lhyn's was deeply rooted and instinctual, Ekatya's was focused on her tyree. Leaning forward, she grasped Lhyn's hands and looked into her eyes. "You didn't make a mistake. You just didn't have the data. There's a difference."

"What difference? It's foundational! Everything is built on this and I made a mistake!" She was tilting over the edge into panic, and Tal could not understand why.

"Lhyn, you're still the expert. You're better than anyone I know at putting together patterns. And not knowing something is not the same thing as making a mistake. It's part of learning. That's why you're here, right? Because you want to keep learning."

Lhyn nodded, but her breathing was growing rapid. The effort she was making to hold back the panic set Tal's teeth on edge.

"You're on Alsea, you're safe," Ekatya said urgently. "And I'm here with you. I'm *here*." She let go with one hand and rested it over Lhyn's heart. "I'm here."

Lhyn held on to that hand with a death grip, pressing it tightly against her chest. She stared into Ekatya's eyes, her breathing now labored.

"Just breathe with me, all right? Slow it down, breathe with me. You can feel my hand. It's real, and so am I. Breathe with me." Ekatya took exaggerated breaths, never breaking their eye contact.

"I'm trying…" Lhyn's breaths were not as deep, and she was struggling for every one of them.

Tal felt sick as she watched, remembering the one time in her life when she had been swamped by a similar terror. It had overwhelmed her in an instant. That Lhyn was able to fight it this way spoke of both an indomitable will and far too much practice.

Lanaril was suddenly kneeling beside them. "Lhyn, it's Lanaril. Can you hear me?"

Lhyn nodded without taking her eyes off Ekatya.

"Good. I can help you, if you'll allow my touch. May I touch your arm?"

Another nod.

Lanaril rested her hand on Lhyn's bare arm. The projection of calm floated into Tal's senses a moment later.

"Ekatya is here with you," Lanaril said softly. "So am I, so are your friends and family. You're surrounded by people who can protect you. You can feel Ekatya's touch; you can feel mine. These touches are real."

Lhyn's breathing was still too rapid, but the escalation had stopped. She had gained enough strength to fight it to a standstill.

"This fear is in a different room," Lanaril said. "You're looking at it from the outside. It is not anywhere near you. It cannot reach you."

It was an incremental change, but Tal thought Lhyn's breathing had grown easier.

"Look at that fear, Lhyn. You know it can't hurt you now. It's safe to look at it. Tell me what you see. Describe it to me."

"It's…" Lhyn licked her lips. "Silver. And big. Bigger than me. There are…lightning bolts."

Ekatya did not move a muscle, but her pain at the phrase *lightning bolts* made Tal's own chest hurt. She felt Salomen's hand slip into her own, clutching it tightly.

"Those bolts cannot touch you." Lanaril's voice was soothing as she increased her projection of calm. "You're in a doorway, looking at that fear inside the room, and there's something else in the doorway as well. Something for you to use. How would you make that lightning go away?"

"I don't…" Lhyn shook her head. "I don't know. It's too big."

"An EM cage," Ekatya said. "Lhyn, you've seen one on the *Phoenix*. Remember? You were asking about it. Put the lightning in an EM cage, and it's completely contained."

Though Lhyn did not lose eye contact with Ekatya, her head lifted as she straightened her spine. "An EM cage," she whispered. "It's here. I can see it. But I…can't go in there."

"Has she seen a grounded grip?" Kameha asked from across the room.

Ekatya gave a slight shake of her head. "You don't have to go in. There's something leaning against the doorway, next to the EM cage. A long pole with a handle on one end and a clamp on the other. You can push the EM cage in the room with it, then use it to clamp on to the lightning and put it in the cage."

Tal was not familiar with the equipment being described, but she had never heard of any way to simply hold lightning. Attract it, conduct it, ground it, yes, but hold it?

Then again, she thought as she sensed Lhyn's fear receding, perhaps practicality was not the point here.

"It's in the cage," Lhyn said breathlessly. "But it's angry."

Lanaril took over, boosting her projection yet again. "It's angry because you're taking control. It can only be big outside the cage, but you've contained it. It's shrinking now, getting smaller and smaller while you watch. Smaller and smaller. Do you see it?"

The silence seemed too large for the room, until a pulse of triumph broke it apart. "Yes. It is."

"Good. It's still shrinking, because you put it in a cage and it can't survive there. It's so small now that it's falling apart. It cannot maintain its shape. It's breaking up into tiny pieces. Can you see it?"

Lhyn was breathing normally now, and though she still did not look away from Ekatya, her panic had receded with Lanaril's words. "I see it."

"Now those tiny pieces are shrinking, too, until they just…disappear. Like ground mist when the sun comes out."

"This is amazing," Lhyn whispered. The last vestiges of her fear were evaporating, yet she was not entirely in the room with them.

"Are they gone?" Lanaril asked.

Lhyn nodded.

"Do you remember what happens when a storm clears up? The air smells fresh and clean. You destroyed a storm, Lhyn. The air is wonderful. Take a deep breath of it."

Lhyn's chest expanded, Ekatya's hand moving with it, and her eyes finally slid shut. She breathed again, letting her head fall back, and released a soft laugh. After several more breaths, she lifted her head and grinned at Ekatya. "Incredible."

Ekatya's relief showed in her dropped shoulders. "You're here."

"I'm here. Because you are. Thank you, tyrina." Lhyn leaned in for a quick kiss, then turned to Lanaril. "And thank you. That was—I don't even have words to describe how marvelous that was. It's never been that easy before. I had control of it. I could just put it in the cage and get rid of it, and stars, the fresh air after! You were projecting, weren't you?"

Lanaril nodded.

"You were in her mind?" Ekatya's sudden suspicion made Tal wince.

Looking dismayed, Lanaril said, "It's the approved method for—"

"It's fine, Ekatya. She asked permission, and I gave it to her."

"When did she do that?"

"When she asked if she could touch me."

"And that's the same thing as invading your mind?"

Tal thought it was time to intervene. "It's not an invasion if it's done with consent." She did not budge when Ekatya glared at her. "And yes, when we ask permission to make a physical bridge, that usually means we're requesting consent for a deeper empathic connection."

"Good to know," Ekatya said shortly, and Lanaril flinched.

Tal could only imagine what she was feeling in such close proximity; even over here the waves of suspicion and protective anger were raising the hair on the back of her neck.

"Ekatya, what—" Lhyn began, but Ekatya held up a hand and shook her head.

"Nothing, it's nothing. It's just…" She took a breath. "Different from how we usually deal with it." Turning to Lanaril, she added, "Thank you. I appreciate anything you can do to help Lhyn."

Lanaril nodded graciously and returned to her seat, showing no outward sign of distress despite the continuing power of Ekatya's negative emotions toward her.

After tonight's party dispersed, Tal was going to have a serious talk with Ekatya. This could not go on.

Of course it was Jaros who asked what everyone wanted to know. "What happened? Why couldn't you breathe?"

Ekatya looked at Lhyn, who closed her eyes briefly before turning to face the curious child.

"I'm recovering from an injury. It happened two moons ago, and I'm fine now. But as Lanaril can tell you, sometimes the emotional recovery takes longer than the physical one."

"Very true," Lanaril said, diverting Jaros's attention. "We're still counseling Battle of Alsea veterans a cycle and a half later. Most of them are recovered enough to only need a little help now and again, but some of them will need continued healing for the rest of their lives."

"That's why Lanaril knew what to do," Tal added. "And though I mourn the reason for her expertise, I'm very glad she was here now." She looked at Ekatya and raised an eyebrow.

It worked. Chagrin pushed the suspicion down to a low ebb, and Ekatya's sincerity was more believable when she turned to face Lanaril. "So am I."

"I'm glad I could be here," Lanaril said. "And very sorry if anything I said triggered it."

"You were talking about divine tyrees being mid empaths," Jaros said helpfully.

"Jaros!" Nikin scolded. "We need to *avoid* the trigger, not repeat it."

"How are we supposed to avoid it if we don't know what it is?"

"That's a reasonable question," Lhyn said, forestalling Nikin's response. "And Nikin…thank you."

"For what?"

"For saying *we*."

His expression smoothed out. "I would give that consideration to anyone, but you're not just anyone. You're family now."

Jaros hopped off his chair and walked up to Lhyn. Placing a hand on her arm, he said solemnly, "I'm sorry you were hurt."

Lhyn stared at him, an incredulous huff of air escaping her throat. Then she put her hand over his and asked, "Do you give warmrons?"

In answer, he threw his arms around her shoulders. The angle was awkward, given her position on the sofa, but she made the best of it with a smile that lit up the room.

"Thank you," she said when he pulled back. "That really helped. It doesn't hurt at all now."

He nodded and went back to his seat, trailing satisfaction and pride behind him.

Lhyn watched him go, her smile unabated, then looked around the room. "None of you said anything to set me off. I did it to myself. And I'm the one who needs to deal with it, so please don't worry. I've had a lovely warmron now, so I'm in perfect health. Can we get back to what we were talking about before I so rudely interrupted?"

Tal wasn't sure they should let it go so easily, but Lanaril spoke up. "Yes, we can. And I was thinking that we have a significant issue with our new divine tyrees: they'll have to be trained."

Lhyn's relief at the change of subject was almost tangible.

With a final squeeze to Tal's hand, Salomen sat up straight and said, "That should have been the first thing we thought of. Can you imagine how shocking that must have been for them?"

"What are they talking about?" Jaros asked Nikin.

"I don't know." Nikin turned to his sister. "Care to explain to the rest of us?"

"Remember what I told you about how our empathic senses are magnified when we Share?"

"Ah," said Nikin and Shikal together. Micah looked thoughtful, while Lanaril met Tal's eyes in shared understanding.

Jaros kicked his heel against his chair leg. "Nobody tells me anything."

"You're not alone in that," Kameha said. "I'm still in the dark."

"We did tell you, Jaros." Salomen turned to Kameha. "When Andira and I Share, we can sense other Alseans for hundreds of lengths. The divine bond acts as a magnifying lens for our abilities. It's how we found where Herot was being held."

"I did wonder. That explains a lot." He looked between Salomen and Tal. "So these new divine tyrees—they're experiencing something like I would if I suddenly became a mid empath. I'd have no idea how to handle that."

"Shippers," Lhyn said quietly. She and Ekatya shared a look that seemed to involve an entire conversation, their mutual realization washing through the room.

"I still don't understand," Jaros said. "They're already mid empaths."

Salomen nodded. "Yes, but when they Share, they're much stronger. Possibly stronger than any other high empaths except Andira and me. But they have no control of it."

"Oh! So someone has to train them like Lancer Tal trained you." He beamed at Tal, delighted to be on the same level as the adults. "Will you be doing it?"

"Not if she has any self-preservation instincts," Salomen said.

Tal looked down, stifling a smile, but no one else in the room bothered to hide their laughter.

"I don't see why that's so funny." Jaros did not appreciate being left out once again. Nikin leaned over and whispered into his ear, leading Jaros to jerk up his head and stare at Tal. "But you wouldn't—"

"Of course not. Besides, training Salomen was difficult enough. I haven't yet recovered." Tal dodged Salomen's flying elbow, then caught her wrist and pulled her close for a kiss. "I hope I never do," she murmured, too low for anyone else to hear.

"Golden tongue," Salomen responded with a warm smile. "One day, that's not going to work."

"But that day is not today." Tal forgot herself for a moment, lost in contemplation of Salomen's smile, until she registered the unease that was flowing from both Ekatya and Lhyn. "You two look as if you have something to say."

They turned their heads, but it was Lhyn who answered.

"Your sudden increase in divine tyrees isn't the only odd thing that's happened lately. And by odd, I mean without precedent. But we can't explain it until Ekatya tells you the rest of her story, and then I'll have to tell you mine." She looked over at Jaros. "And I'm sorry, Jaros, but neither of those are suitable for you to hear."

"Nobody tells me *anything*," he repeated in disgust. "You always save the good stories for after I'm in bed!"

Tal barely heard him, so focused was she on Lhyn and Ekatya. Their matching dread rolled off them and smothered her senses like thick, acrid smoke.

"Not all stories are good, Jaros," she said. "I wish they were."

"Words for Fahla," Lanaril murmured, her gaze on Lhyn.

CHAPTER 20
Family circle

They had all settled into their chairs, spirit glasses in hand, and Ekatya noted that each of them was in the same chair they had occupied the previous two nights. The need to create familiar patterns was universal, it seemed, even among aliens. The only person who had changed chairs was Lanaril, who had inexplicably taken the seat next to Ekatya last night. She was there again now, a little too close for comfort.

Footsteps sounded on the wooden deck, attracting everyone's attention as Salomen came through the door.

"Were there any problems settling our resident grump in bed?" Andira held out one of the two glasses in her hands.

Salomen accepted it and sat on the couch next to her. "Several. He even tried the birth anniversary claim, not that he got very far with it."

"When is his birth anniversary?" Lhyn asked from Ekatya's other side.

"In half a moon. He'll be ten. He argued that since he's nearly halfway to his Rite of Ascension, that's quite old enough to take part in adult conversations, especially at such a special time as my bonding break, which he will never get to experience again."

"He really did pull out every tactic," Nikin said. "Reminds me of someone else, now that I think about it."

"Nikin, I can and will toss you in the water tomorrow," Salomen warned.

"For being right?" Shikal's smile was mischievous. "You gave me a very similar argument at about the same age. It didn't work then, either."

"But it did work when I was twelve. That was when you let me stay up late to watch the final results of the Lancer's election."

"Really?" Apparently, Andira had not heard this story. "Was it worth it?"

"Fahla, no. It was the most tedious night of my short existence. I couldn't believe I'd wasted my argument on that." Salomen tipped her glass toward Shikal. "And you knew I'd be bored into a coma!"

"Of course I did. Why do you think you won?"

The best part of this bonding break, Ekatya thought, was watching Salomen with her family. She found their dynamics enchanting, all the more so because they had embraced Andira as one of their own. Andira had tried to tell her on their flight back from orbit that this was her family as well, but she could not make that leap. Not yet, anyway. Perhaps someday she could with the Opahs, but Lanaril—that was never going to happen. To see her flit in tonight and help Lhyn so effortlessly, when Ekatya had worked so hard to learn what she needed to do…

Of course, she thought uncharitably, helping was a lot simpler when you could just go inside someone's mind and *fix* them. And then there was Lhyn, blithely unconcerned about letting Lanaril in because she didn't know how dangerous that woman was.

Ekatya sighed and reminded herself of what mattered. Lhyn was all right. Lanaril had helped her avoid a full-scale panic attack, the kind where Lhyn could not handle touch, could not be reached, could only fight alone. Not only that, but she seemed to have given Lhyn a new tool to use. Lhyn had actually been excited about it afterward, wondering whether the same imagery would be as effective without Lanaril's projection and, if not, how much difference the projection made. She was practically ready to start experiments.

And Andira had made herself quite clear with that look. Whatever Ekatya felt about Lanaril, she was on her own with it and she was expected to deal with it. Soon.

She glanced over at Lanaril, who was smiling as she listened to Nikin needle his sister, and acknowledged the truth she had been pushing back for days. This had to come out in the open. It was the only way she could move past it. She needed to hear what Lanaril had to say for herself.

Turning back, she watched Lhyn watch the others, noting the relaxation in her face and the light in her eyes. Normally, she was drained after an attack, but whatever Lanaril had done seemed to have energized her.

Or perhaps she was energized by the family that surrounded her. Because Lhyn was doing what Ekatya could not, and the others seemed very willing to take her in. Shikal, Micah, and Nikin had passed hanticks in easy conversation with her, answering her thousand questions and asking quite a few of their own. Salomen had taken a protective stance after that first night, while Jaros saw her as a playmate and wanted her to speak in various languages for his entertainment. Lhyn obliged with endless patience, despite having no experience with children. She told Ekatya that she didn't think of Jaros as a child, but as a miniature Alsean with a related but separate set of behavioral responses to social situations compared to those of the adults.

Trust Lhyn to break down child's play into a scientific endeavor—and make it work.

"Are you sure you want to do this?" she murmured under cover of the joking about Salomen's argumentative youth.

"No, but I need to. Especially after having a panic attack in front of everyone. The Alseans have a saying that a secret shared is a burden divided, and I think they're right. Besides, I'm tired of—" Lhyn stopped and lifted her head.

Ekatya looked up as well, finding everyone in the room watching them expectantly. "We're ready, then?" she asked into the silence.

"If you are," Andira said.

Ekatya took a fortifying sip of her spirits and rested the glass on her thigh. "Then I suppose it's my turn. Remember our quantum com call when I first took command of the *Phoenix*?"

"Vividly. It was the day before I challenged Salomen." Andira reached over and laced her fingers with Salomen's without looking. "You were happier than I had seen you in a long time. I thought it was the joy of finally being back where you belonged, but now… You must have been so relieved to be free of Sholokhov."

"I thought I was free. After all those months of working for him, I shouldn't have been so naive. Lhyn came out for the launch ceremony—"

"In which they don't launch the ship," Lhyn interrupted.

"They don't?" Salomen asked.

Ekatya had to smile. Lhyn was still disgruntled about this.

"No, they don't! Well, I mean, they do; it does leave the space dock. But it's really just a stroll around the moon." Lhyn set her drink down and crossed her arms over her chest. "It's an excuse to take a million or so journalists and Assembly ministers and Fleet brass for a ride, so they can get photos and vids of themselves, the ship, and her." She pointed at Ekatya. "You would not believe how *necessary* it was for every single one of those blowflies to have a photo taken with her."

"Blowflies?" Andira repeated.

"Parasites. Ugly, hairy ones. Yes, go ahead and laugh, but it took me two days to get from Gov Dome to Quinton Shipyards, and do you know how much I saw Ekatya during the twenty-six hours I was on board her ship? About an hour's worth."

"That's not true," Ekatya said. "You spent the night with me."

"That does not count as seeing you. My eyes were shut."

"Not all the time," Ekatya muttered.

Lhyn's cheeks turned a faint pink as everyone in the room laughed. "Right, fine, there was that. Anyway," she said pointedly, "they launch, do a little parade around the moon, and then go right back into the space dock because they have to get all of those blowflies back off the ship again."

"Because we can't finish our final preparations with a ship full of… dignitaries," Ekatya said.

"Well said." Andira shot her a wink.

"I do have to be careful not to pick up her vocabulary." Ekatya leaned over to drop a kiss on Lhyn's cheek. "And I treasured every minute of that hour." Mostly, though, she appreciated Lhyn's ability to lighten this moment. The story seemed easier to tell now.

"You better have," Lhyn grumbled, but her smile gave her away. "Four days of travel time."

Ekatya clasped their hands and rubbed her thumb lightly over Lhyn's wrist. "The point I was starting to make was that Sholokhov didn't come out for the launch. I was convinced he would show up just to make a statement. When he didn't, I thought perhaps he was making another statement—that I wasn't worth his time any longer. But he was just waiting for the right moment. We were back in the space dock, getting our last supplies and crew on board, and I was running around like—what's your phrase here?"

"A yardbird with twenty chicks," Lhyn said before anyone else could.

"Yes, that. And in one of the few moments of quiet that I managed to get in my office, my com officer told me I had an incoming call, priority blue. That's our top priority, normally limited to flag officers and critical orders. I thought it had to be Admiral Tsao."

CHAPTER 21
New orders

Aboard the Phoenix, 5.5 stellar months earlier (4 Alsean moons)

EKATYA WAS ON HER WAY out of her office, her mind already clicking over the remaining items on her checklist before their departure from the shipyard in five hours. All of the systems had checked out, but she had a question about the last surf engine power graph. Once again she wished Commander Kameha were on board—he had always been so good at bypassing the details she didn't need and focusing on the answers she wanted. Her new chief of engineering had a stellar record, but he wasn't Kameha and had never met a sentence he couldn't make longer and more impenetrable. She was not looking forward to training him in how to speak to her.

"Captain Serrado, you have an incoming call, priority blue." The voice of her com officer cut the silence of her office and froze her in her tracks. She spun on her heel and walked back to her new desk, its surface still barren but for the transparent screen she had only just turned off.

"Received, thank you." She pulled out the chair and sat on the cushion that still held her body heat. A tap on the embedded deskpad activated the screen, revealing the priority blue emblem and a prompt for her com code. She entered it with a rapid press of fingers and waited the half-second it took for the system to corroborate her fingerprints with her code. The emblem shrank, making room for the caller's com ID.

"Shipper shit." She closed her eyes and braced her forehead on her hand. "Just wonderful. What does he want now?"

Taking a deep breath, she lifted her head, shook out her hands, and accepted the call. "Director Sholokhov," she said flatly. "What a pleasure."

Sholokhov chuckled. "Captain Serrado, you were at great pains to tell me how appreciative I should be that you never lied to me. Why start now, just when I've gotten used to it?"

"Professional courtesy."

He waved a hand in dismissal. "Courtesy has its place. I prefer business. As in, ours."

"We have no business. You don't write my orders now."

"But I do." His smile was predatory. "It's in our signed agreement."

Oh, she hated this man. "Our agreement was that I served you until the *Phoenix* was ready. It's ready. We're done."

"Perhaps you should have paid closer attention to the wording in that agreement. You serve me until your ship is in *active service*. You're about to leave on a shakedown cruise, are you not? With a skeleton crew. The *Phoenix* is not in active service just yet, Captain. You're still mine."

Her stomach sinking, she pulled her pad from its sleeve pocket and brought up the file.

"Why am I not surprised you would have that contract so close at hand?" he asked in an amused tone.

She ignored him as she scanned down for the relevant paragraph. Unfortunately, he was not bluffing. Taking her time, she replaced the pad and crossed her hands on the desk.

"Let me make one thing perfectly clear," she said. "You're correct about our agreement. But I am not now, nor will I ever be, yours. Not in your most vivid imaginings."

"You're very concerned with semantics."

"I'm concerned with the way you confuse service performed in duty with ownership."

His unsettling blue eyes crinkled at the corners. It almost looked friendly. "I never thought I would say this, but I do miss your presence in this office. I enjoyed our verbal sparring."

She remembered the pleasure he took in saying *You're dismissed, Captain* every single time she left his office, and doubted very much that their sparring was what he missed.

"Is there a point to this call besides nostalgia?" she asked.

He gave an exaggerated sigh. "Yes, there is. Your new orders should be arriving any moment."

"Very well." She tapped the control to check for data piggy-backed on the vid transmission.

"Captain, you misunderstand me. I do not send alpha-band classified orders on quantum com calls. Anyone can break into those."

Raising her eyebrows, she said, "If by *anyone*, you mean genius-level data jackers with inside information on Fleet encryption."

"In my business, one can never be too safe."

"Then how exactly are my orders supposed to arrive?"

"Perhaps you should ask your Commander Lokomorra that."

This time she didn't bother to hold back the eye roll. She was about to tap the deskpad to call for Lokomorra when it chimed at her.

"Ah. That will be your commander," Sholokhov said jovially.

She shot him a glare, then rose from her seat and stepped into the door's sensor range. It slid open, revealing Lokomorra's solid frame. He made to enter but stopped when she held a finger against her lips. Gently pushing him away from the door, she followed him onto the bridge and let the door close behind her.

The transition was jarring. Both the upper and lower bridge displays were active, transforming the entire room into virtual space. In place of the walls and the high, domed ceiling of the bridge, she saw the downward-curving ribs of the space dock and the gigantic structure of the shipyard to which her ship was still tethered. Instead of a floor beneath her feet, she saw the darkness of space and the silver curve of the moon, which housed a hundred factories, all dedicated to manufacturing materials for ship construction. Her tactile senses told her she was standing on a deck; her eyes told her she was floating in space. Though she had long adapted to the sensory dissonance, many of the bridge crew had come from smaller ships without the advanced display capabilities of the *Phoenix*. It was best to get them used to it now, in the static safety of the shipyard.

Commander Lokomorra waited patiently, a dock ferry appearing to pass behind his head on its way to the shuttle bay.

"Did Director Sholokhov contact you?" she asked.

"No." The beads holding the ends of his forked beard clacked faintly as he shook his head. "I've never spoken with him. But Dr. Wells just brought this. She said someone left it on her desk." He held up a very familiar packet made of folded paper and sealed with putty.

A chill ran down Ekatya's spine. For a moment she was loathe to take it from him. How many times had she seen Sholokhov sign and seal these little packets? He had never told her what they were for, and she had never asked.

Now she knew. Worse, she knew he had a spy on her ship. Was it her chief surgeon?

Plucking the packet from his fingers, she said, "Get the security logs from Dr. Wells's office and find out who left this."

"Yes, Captain. Anything else?"

"Not yet. But stay close; I have a feeling things are about to get interesting."

Back at her desk, she was preparing to break the seal when Sholokhov said, "Wait. Describe the seal to me, and be specific."

She looked more closely. "It's a crescent moon, with the occluded side on the left. One star above the moon and three stars below."

"Then it's correct. Open it."

So that was what he was doing with his signet rings—creating a very simple encryption key. Anyone wanting to forge a message from him would not only have to copy the exact paper, putty, signature, and seal, but they would have to guess the correct seal to use.

But only two rings? That gave a forger a fifty percent chance of guessing right.

"How many rings do you have?" she asked.

He smiled. "Well done, Captain. And I won't answer that question. Suffice to say, more than two, and each of them has two faces."

She nodded, impressed despite herself at his ingeniously low-tech system. Then she broke the seal and read the orders.

"Do not say it on this transmission." His voice cut through her rising rage. "I know what you're thinking, but the situation has changed. Keep reading."

Her temper had died a quick death by the time she finished the last paragraph. The words on this paper had galactic ramifications.

"Are your spies certain about this?" she asked.

"As certain as they can be without setting foot on the ground. As you can imagine, intelligence gathering is a bit difficult in this situation. Given your experience in this area, you're the best person for the job. You'll be acting with full authority as a representative of the Protectorate."

An actual compliment from Sholokhov; she might lose consciousness from the shock. And this was a mission she would gladly have accepted regardless of who assigned it. "But Bellows has no experience. I have a dozen excellent data systems analysts on board right now. Any of them would be a better choice."

"Fortunately, you're not making that choice. I am."

"Director, this kind of contact requires special training. He's had none of it. This is not a safe assignment, and he is—"

"A commissioned Fleet officer," Sholokhov interrupted. "Sworn to perform his duty, and this is his duty. Give him his assignment and get your course laid. I expect your preliminary report within twenty-four hours of arrival, and a full report as soon as you have any evidence."

"Yes, Director," she said through gritted teeth.

"Until then." His image vanished, replaced by the priority blue emblem.

"So much for our shakedown cruise," she muttered. They were being sent in the opposite direction of the original route, which had been a tour of five widely scattered space stations where nearly a third of her crew awaited transfer. All of those people would now have to travel to Quinton Shipyards, where housing would be found for them until the *Phoenix* could return. Their wait had just been extended by more than a month; Fleet would never pay for that much time on space stations. Housing at the shipyard was far cheaper.

She tapped her deskpad, opening up the ship's all-call. "Section chiefs, report to the briefing room immediately."

CHAPTER 22
Briefing

Though the *Phoenix* was a twin of the *Caphenon*, Ekatya kept finding little things here and there that reminded her of how much had changed. One was the new briefing room table with its built-in holodisplay—technology borrowed from the Alseans. The Protectorate's holotech had never mastered the means of displaying graphs, data points, numbers, text—all of which made regular appearances in Fleet briefings—in such a way as to be equally legible from all sides. While strategizing with the war council on Alsea, Ekatya had noticed the superiority of their holotech and mentioned it to Admiral Tsao. It had clearly made an impression, appearing as a line item in the treaty agreement and now in physical form on her ship.

While the table was fully populated, four of the officers were only there in a temporary capacity. Her chiefs of science, navigation, security, and weapons were among the crew waiting for pickup in the wrong direction, and the most senior officers in their sections were now nervously sitting in chairs they had not expected to fill.

Correction, Ekatya thought, three of them were nervous. In a stroke of good fortune, she had managed to get Warrant Officer Roris and her full weapons team back and had ordered her to take the role of acting section chief. As far as Ekatya was concerned, the only reason Roris wasn't a section chief in reality was because she lacked the rank. Someday, she was going to talk that woman into the officer field commission program.

She had recruited her chiefs of personnel, procurement, engineering, operations, data systems, crew services, and botanics long before there was a completed ship to house them in. It had been exhausting, working for Sholokhov by day and as captain of the *Phoenix* by night, and being trapped in Gov Dome only made it worse. At least most of the chiefs had been living in Quinton Shipyards, overseeing final construction and assembling the personnel for their sections.

Chief Surgeon Wells, head of the medical section, was the last recruit and had arrived only four days before Ekatya herself. It was not ideal, but

Ekatya had been willing to wait in order to entice one of Fleet's best doctors to leave her Core-class vessel when it returned from an exploration mission. Captain Chmielek was less than pleased with his loss, but Ekatya couldn't deny that she was enjoying a bit of revenge on him and several other captains who had pounced on her *Caphenon* crew. To now be forced into a position of suspecting Wells after working so hard to get her was unacceptable. Sholokhov had mired her in suspicion while she worked for him, and she did not appreciate finding herself in the same place on her own damned ship.

Wells, along with everyone else, was staring at the holoimage of the Lexihari system floating above the center of the table. "The medbay will be fine," she said in answer to Ekatya's query. "We're only at half strength, but unless you plan on landing us in a battle, that's more than enough to handle the current crew complement. But why are we going to a system that was ruled out of Protectorate membership?"

Ekatya shot her a sharp look at that odd choice of words. They could be interpreted several ways, the least of which was disrespectful.

"I have no plans to land us in a battle," she said, the slight emphasis on *land* letting Wells know that she had heard the unspoken message. "But if one finds us, I'll do my best to win it."

Wells was slouched in her chair, her posture of graceful indolence adding to the feline look of her slanted green eyes, high cheekbones, and long, narrow nose. She was older than most of the section chiefs, a point that would normally be in her favor—Ekatya could never trust young doctors—but right now she was exuding the judgment of an older and wiser officer on an impetuous young captain.

Ekatya might have had a temper, but she was not impetuous, and she hadn't been young since her first space battle. She held Wells's stare for a moment before looking around at the others. "What I am about to say is classified at the alpha-band level. If it leaves this room and I find out who spilled it, that indiscretion will result in brig time and loss of rank. Does everyone understand?"

Murmurs of "Yes, Captain," filled the room, and she was gratified to see Wells finally sit up straight.

"This is as much a surprise to me as to all of you," she said, easing up on her attitude. "I was looking forward to a nice, quiet shakedown cruise, and to picking up the rest of our crew, but our orders have changed and for good reason. The Voloth have approached the governments of both of these planets."

There was a collective intake of air as everyone's attention sharpened.

"Just to be clear, I am not using 'approached' as a euphemism for 'invaded.' They're experimenting with a new method of expanding their empire." She paused, then added, "They're emulating us."

"They're *inviting* planets to join?" Commander Lokomorra did not hide his disbelief. "Since when do the Voloth recruit?"

"Since they got their heads ripped off and handed to them at Alsea," said Roris.

Ekatya hid a smile at the blunt words, so out of place among these high-level officers. Roris stood out physically as well, not so much for her stocky, well-muscled build but for her aura of calm and deadly competence. Most of her section chiefs were career desk pilots. Roris was a soldier.

"Warrant Officer Roris is correct," she said. "Their defeat at Alsea was so damaging that their central government collapsed as a result. The new government wants to avoid any similar embarrassments. And somehow, their spies found out that we had considered and rejected these worlds for membership."

"So they're targeting them specifically for that reason." Commander Jevon Kenji, chief of data systems, picked up the thread. He had golden eyes and bronze skin, and his long black hair was held in a dizzying number of tiny braids. "Which could be extremely effective, not to mention a good way of turning new cultures against us."

"Precisely," said Ekatya. "If our intelligence is correct about this, then we may also have to reconsider our entrance requirements. It could push this war onto a whole new level as both sides scramble to bring in new worlds."

"I see so many problems with that scenario that I can't even begin to list them," Wells said.

Ekatya nodded. "Which is why we've been sent to the system. Our orders are first, to verify the intelligence, and second, to make a counteroffer if that intelligence is correct."

"And the Rules of First Contact?" Lokomorra asked.

"Still apply until we've established the accuracy of the intelligence. Except for the biggest one, of course. We have to make contact to carry out our first priority, and that will probably mean a landing team."

"Not a safe mission," Roris noted. "You're going to need people with experience in this sort of situation. I volunteer myself and my team."

"You're weapons, not security," Ekatya said. "I appreciate the offer, but I want you here in case the Voloth object to our meddling in their affairs."

"With respect, Captain, the Voloth won't be in any hurry to engage in an orbital battle with this ship. If their spies are any good at all, they know you're in command. They're not going to mess with you if they can avoid it. They'll be a lot less shy about messing with the landing team."

Ekatya considered it. She had spanked the Voloth hard in their last encounter, destroying all three ships of an invasion group, and then helped the Alseans destroy the entire inventory of a second group. Roris was right; they would not be eager to challenge her again. And they wouldn't know she was on the landing team.

Besides, with a crew this new, she would feel much more secure having people she trusted guarding her back. Roris and her three teammates had earned that trust.

"You have a point," she said. "I've been assigned to lead this mission due to my experience on Alsea. Given that we have no idea what might be waiting for us, we should keep it to a small group. Roris, I accept your offer, but I want two dedicated security personnel as well, with infiltration training. We may be doing some illicit…exploring." She glanced at the acting security chief, who nodded. Turning to the acting science chief, she added, "I also want someone who either knows these two cultures backward and forward right now, or can thoroughly learn it before we get there."

"Yes, Captain." The small, slender man bobbed his head, and she reminded herself to have Lokomorra follow up on that. Shippers, she was going on a mission without the chiefs of most of the sections involved. The timing could not have been worse.

"As for the rest," she finished, "it will be me for negotiations and Ensign Bellows for data systems."

"What?" Commander Kenji's voice was a little too loud. "Bellows is so new he's still wet behind the ears. He's the last person I would recommend for this. I'm a much better choice."

"You're not going, Commander. I need my section chief on board." He was one of the few section chiefs involved who wasn't a temporary fill-in.

"Fine, then if you don't want to risk me, I can give you ten other names who have the training and would be more capable than Bellows. You can't throw—"

"Commander!" She glared at him. "The decision has been made. End of discussion."

He wisely shut up. "Yes, Captain."

Half an hour later, they had hammered out the details and Ekatya dismissed the group. "Commander Kenji, please stay," she said as the others rose from their chairs. "Commander Lokomorra?"

"Yes?"

"Remember what we discussed right after you made that delivery? I want it done now."

"It was already in progress when you called the meeting. I'll make sure it's finished." He nodded, then followed the others out of the room.

Commander Kenji looked at her with an odd mixture of trepidation and anger. "I still believe taking Bellows is a mistake."

"And you are welcome to share your beliefs with me *in private*. Not by contradicting my orders in front of the entire executive staff of this ship. And even in private, don't ever tell me what I can't do. Explain your reservations, make alternative suggestions, tell me why something might not work. But don't give me orders. Do you understand?"

"Yes, Captain," he said in a subdued voice.

Her point made, she spoke more kindly. "As it happens, I agree with you."

His shoulders stiffened. "Then why—"

"Because even captains have to obey orders from above."

"You were *ordered* to take Bellows? But that doesn't make any sense."

"It does to the person who wrote the orders. I questioned them too, and I was shot down. There's nothing I can do."

He looked down at the table, then up again with a slight grimace. "Then I guess I'd better give Bellows an immersion session on the Rules of First Contact. Not to mention methods of bridging alien data systems."

"I think you'll find him to be an excellent student."

He nodded, his braids gleaming under the lights. He must oil them, she thought idly.

"I'm sorry, Captain. I didn't want to start off on the wrong foot with you."

"You haven't. I appreciate your instincts; I just need you to express them a little more carefully." She held his gaze for a moment, then added, "My orders only specified that Bellows should be on the team. They didn't say that he should be the only data systems analyst on it."

His expression sharpened. "But you said it should be a small team."

"Remember what else I said? Offer me alternatives."

To his credit, he didn't waste a moment. "Captain, I respectfully suggest you take a second data analyst. Someone with more experience bridging alien data systems. In the event that negotiations don't get you the answers you need, you may have to find them in their communications records."

"I agree. Do you have someone in mind?"

"I do."

"Excellent. Get that person prepped, and don't forget they'll need a language chip."

"Yes, Captain." He didn't smile, but his whole body telegraphed his relief.

"That's all, Commander. Dismissed."

Left alone in the briefing room, she leaned back in her chair and stared at the display taking up the entire far wall. Like the bridge display, its projection of visual data from the sensors was flawless, giving the very realistic impression that the wall was an enormous window. The curved ribs of the space dock framed the view of open space beyond, and a flurry of dock ferries, construction bots, and equipment sleds were zipping around in a complicated dance that always seemed one second away from disaster. In truth, collisions were vanishingly rare.

She watched two dock ferries pass each other, one bringing last-minute crew on board while the other, having discharged its passengers in her shuttle bay, went back for another load. It was always this way just before a new ship launched. No matter how far in advance the requests and travel arrangements were made, some crew could not make it until the last moment. And this really was the last moment: the personnel umbilical had already been pulled back, and the airlock was sealed. In four hours they would detach all remaining umbilicals and launch. It was a moment she had anticipated, dreamed of, and fantasized about for nearly seventeen months—the time when she was supposed to be free of Sholokhov.

Yet here he was, still influencing her. Besides the spy and the mission, that little chat with Commander Kenji would not have happened on the *Caphenon*. She would have slapped him down for questioning her, refused to admit that she herself was not in complete control of their orders, and never bothered to teach him how to approach her more effectively. She had always thought that was for her officers to figure out for themselves. After all, it was what she'd had to do with every single one of her superior officers, including Sholokhov.

She didn't want to be that person anymore. She didn't want any part of her command style, decisions, or way of thinking to have the remotest similarity to Sholokhov.

For some time she stared at the view, lost in thought, until the briefing room door slid open just in front of the display. Commander Lokomorra entered, pad in hand. With his forked beard, burned-in hair patterns, and tattooed eyeliner, he would not have looked out of place as a blaster-waving pirate. But his uniform was crisp, his posture straight, and she was coming to understand that beneath his sometimes casual speech and attitude, he was an even more capable officer than she had first believed.

"Captain? I have the results you wanted."

"That was quick," she said as he sat in the seat next to her.

"We've got some good people down there in data systems," he said, and she smiled at that *we*. "They'd already done most of the work while we were in our briefing."

He set the pad on the table, pulled up the virtual screen, and tapped the file. "You're not going to like this."

She watched the security footage of Dr. Wells's empty office, showing several totes that had yet to be unpacked, a few shelves full of what must be heirloom books, and a desk already messy with instruments and files.

"Did you see it?"

"See what?" She frowned. "Nothing happened."

"Yes, it did." He put his finger nearly in the projection, pointing to a corner of Wells's desk. "There's the packet. Watch it again."

He restarted the playback. One moment that corner of the desk was empty, the next, the packet was there. It had appeared out of nowhere.

"Someone altered the logs," she said.

He smoothed one hand over his beard, pulling the two halves together. "Yes. And the analyst who gave this to me said that would take some real juice. She's trying to find any digital crumbs that might have been left behind."

"Lovely. Not only do I have a spy on my ship, but he or she is a data jacker. That makes it so much better."

His hand stopped in its smoothing motion. "A spy?"

She looked at him, assessing her options. To trust or not to trust?

Don't be Sholokhov, she told herself. "Not a Voloth spy. Someone on our own side, but not necessarily working for the benefit of this ship. Whoever this is, they're working for Director Sholokhov."

His brows drew down, the tattoos suddenly making him look dangerous. "I don't think I like this Sholokhov person. We haven't even launched and someone is spying on us?"

Us, she marveled. *Us* and *we*. Shippers, it was nice to be part of a team again.

"Not necessarily on us," she said. "Probably just me. Though I can't be sure of that."

"Why does Sholokhov feel he needs to spy on you? Didn't you just spend a year and a half working for him?"

"Yes, and that's why. Though I wouldn't be surprised if he has a spy on every ship in Fleet." It had not occurred to her before now, but the moment she said it, she knew it was probably true. This wasn't just about her. Sholokhov's network was vast.

Lokomorra gave his beard a tug, then let go and deactivated his pad. "I hate to say this, but I have an idea of who it might be."

"Please don't say Dr. Wells."

His lips thinned. "She's visible in the medbay security logs for an hour before this time and an hour after. But the time period when this packet appears? She's nowhere to be seen."

"Shipper shit." Ekatya sighed.

CHAPTER 23
Transition in

The real launch of the *Phoenix* was so smooth as to be unremarkable. Without the heaving mass of dignitaries cluttering up her ship, Ekatya found it relaxing to sit in her chair at the top of the bridge dais, give the order for the release of all final umbilicals, and then say the words she had been dreaming of for a year and a half:

"Take her out, Lieutenant."

The only way this moment could have been improved was by the presence of Lieutenant Candini at the pilot's station right below her, but Lieutenant Scarp was an excellent pilot in his own right. He lacked Candini's attitude and probably her ego, but he had impressed Ekatya during his interview, and his prior experience looked like a plan designed specifically to land him on a Pulsar-class bridge.

"Yes, Captain." Scarp tapped his console, grasped the control stick to its right, and moved it so gently that Ekatya could not see it.

But she saw the result. Both the upper and lower displays were still active, and the sight of the space dock sliding past sent a tingle along her skin. Though Scarp made it look easy, she knew that maneuvering a ship seven hundred and fifty meters long out of a tight space like this took a steady hand and phenomenal skill. The Pulsars were the largest ships that could be built in existing Fleet facilities. If the ship design engineers came up with something bigger than this, they would have to build a new shipyard to go with it.

One by one, the downward-arching ribs of the space dock slipped behind them until the last one vanished and nothing but open space lay ahead. Below their feet, half of the moon shone brilliantly with reflected sunlight, while the other half was so dark she could make out no details.

"Well done, Lieutenant Scarp."

He turned halfway, enough to shoot her a quick smile before returning his focus to the readouts. "Thank you, Captain."

"Was it easier than yesterday?"

"*So* much easier," he said with more emphasis than he had probably intended. The tips of his ears turned pink. "I mean, it was a little stressful having all of…um, having an audience."

He was now so embarrassed that she could see his scalp blushing. Nervous young officers with light blond hair shouldn't cut it short, she thought with an internal smile.

"I think we can all agree that we're glad to be done with the preliminaries," she said. "And Quinton Shipyards sent us a message. They said, 'Farewell and good hunting.'"

It was a traditional good luck wish for any departing ship, dating back three generations to the beginning of the war with the Voloth. She wondered if there would ever come a time when a Fleet ship launched with a goal of pure exploration instead.

"I'm taking it as a good omen that we didn't scrape our sides on the way out," Commander Lokomorra said. "Either time. Nice flying, Lieutenant Scarp."

There went the scalp blush again. "Thank you, Commander."

"Let's try a little speed, shall we?" Ekatya swiveled her chair around to see the space dock looming behind them. "Orbital until we clear the buffer zone, then sub point five to the marker."

"Orbital, then point five, confirmed."

The dock slowly receded, exposing more of the structure behind it. Five other space docks held ships in various stages of completion, each at a corner of the gigantic central hexagon that housed offices, lodgings, storage bays, and a thousand other facilities, all making up the greatest shipyard in the Protectorate. As she watched it drop away from them, something in her chest loosened its hold, allowing her to breathe more easily than she had in a very long time.

"Buffer zone cleared," Scarp announced. "Going to sub point five."

The engine hum, barely distinguishable before, grew slightly louder as the shipyard seemed to leap away. Before the *Phoenix* had finished its acceleration, Quinton Shipyards had already vanished, leaving only the moon marking its location. At one hundred and fifty thousand kilometers per second—half the speed of light—even the moon was rapidly shrinking to a dot. Ekatya swiveled her chair forward again and waited.

One minute later, they had traversed nine million kilometers and were nearly on top of the marker. Scarp decelerated smoothly, bringing the ship to a full stop with the marker hanging directly in front of them. The buoy itself was nothing special, simply a sign that Fleet considered this a safe distance from the shipyard to leave normal space.

"Deactivating displays." Ekatya tapped her console. For the first time since she had set foot on her ship, the bridge ceased to look as if it were floating in space and became a large, comfortably closed, circular room with a domed ceiling.

"Oh, thank the Shippers," Lokomorra said. "You're not going to make us watch."

She shot him an evil grin. "Not on the way in, Commander. But I make no guarantees on the way out." She opened the all-call and spoke to her crew. "This is Captain Serrado. We are now preparing to enter base space. Brace for transition."

Normally, transition required more preparation time, but the ship had already been on lockdown before they left the space dock. Since the entrance to base space did not have the same physiological effect as the exit did, there was nothing left to do but give the order.

"Commander Yst, open the portal."

In the bottom ring of the bridge dais, Lieutenant Commander Yst tapped her engineering console. She was a silver-haired woman five years away from retirement, and Ekatya hoped to keep her for all of those five years.

"Initiating pikamet beam," Yst said.

Ekatya pulled up a view from the forward sensors on her console. At the moment, all she could see was the marker and the black nothingness of normal space. The pikamet beam was invisible on this side, but exiting would be a different story.

"Interspace portal at thirty percent," Yst reported.

And that was another difference, Ekatya thought. Opening the portal between space layers took much less time in this direction. She had already flipped her brace bars into position; now she wrapped her hands around them.

"Sixty percent. Seventy-five. Ninety." Yst waited a few seconds, her gaze focused on her console. "Interspace portal now open."

Ekatya checked the tension in her harness one last time, took a firmer grip on her brace bars, and rested her head against her seat. "Take us in, Lieutenant Scarp."

"Yes, Captain."

It started with barely detectable vibrations and soon grew to a shaking violent enough to rattle her teeth. If that was as bad as it got, she would consider this an easy transition. For a moment, she felt a spurt of fear at the thought that she had never taken this brand-new ship through a transition before. But the *Phoenix* had passed all field tests with excellent scores and had been through transition two dozen times. It had to be safe.

The ship gave a great leap, as if it had been slammed sideways by something extremely large, and only Ekatya's harness kept her in her seat. She tightened her grip on the brace bars and marveled at the fact that the Protectorate's largest warship could be tossed around by interspace turbulence like a single-seat fighter. The internal battle hull did not help—it was designed to absorb shocks from weapon strikes, not the immense forces of a portal between space layers.

Twice more they were jolted, the second time so violently that it broke her hold on the left grip bar. Swearing, she wrapped her hand back around it and pressed her head more firmly into the seat. This brought back memories of crashing the *Caphenon*, an image she did not need in her head right now.

The shaking diminished soon after, becoming mere vibrations and finally smoothing out completely. Even before the navigation officer announced it, Ekatya knew they had arrived. Her console was lit up with the shifting red mists of base space. With a quick tap she converted it to a section status display, watching as the confirmations rolled in.

"Hullskin at one hundred percent functionality," Yst reported. "No damage to internal frameworks. Internal radiation levels normal."

Ekatya nodded to herself as each section chief, or acting section chief, reported their section's successful transition and readiness to resume travel. They were now in a layer of space where distances were compressed by a factor of ten thousand while radiation levels were higher by the same amount. This was not a place for the slightest mistake.

"All right, Lieutenant Scarp," she said as the last confirmation appeared. "Let's see how the *Phoenix* moves in base space. Confirm our course, standard acceleration to sub point nine eight."

"Course confirmed," Scarp said a few seconds later. "Beginning acceleration to point nine eight."

The deep, barely discernible throb of the surf engines permeated the bridge, an element of space travel that Ekatya felt as much as she heard. That sound had been a constant in her life for years. Hearing it now felt like home.

Once they reached cruising speed, there was no longer any reason to stay in harness. She slid her brace bars back inside her armrests, opened the all-call, and informed her crew that transition lockdown was lifted. Then she gratefully rose from her chair and walked down the steps to the deck.

"Point nine eight, eh?" Commander Lokomorra had followed her to the midway point between the dais and the wall stations, where they could not easily be overheard. "That's pushing it right to the limit."

"No, L one would be the limit." Ekatya shot him a smile. "And I've done that, too."

He stared at her in feigned horror. "I thought you were a sane captain. That's why I transferred. Are you telling me I made a mistake?"

"I'm sane most of the time. But in that situation, we were under a severe time constraint. I was on my way to stop a Voloth invasion."

The tattooed eyeliner was accentuated when he raised his eyebrows. "Alsea. You flew the speed of light through base space to get to Alsea in time."

She nodded. "And not one meter per second faster."

"Well, I know *that*. If you had, you wouldn't be here now. You'd be vaporized."

Ekatya remembered a conversation in the private cabin of Andira's transport, when she had introduced a supposedly backward alien to the concept of base space travel. "A friend of mine has a theory about that. She suggested that when someone breaks the speed limit in base space, what it's really doing is breaking the barrier between layers. They're going into the second layer of base space."

He pursed his lips. "That's a compelling thought. But the end result would be equally ugly. Going into a radiation field one million times stronger than normal space with nothing but hullskin for protection…"

"Which would explain why we never heard from any of those probes. They would have been fried within seconds."

"Huh. Is your friend published?"

She laughed at the idea. "I don't think our scientific journals are ready for a submission from the Lancer of Alsea."

His forked beard twitched; then he laughed as well. "No, I wouldn't imagine so. That was Lancer Tal's theory, eh? So much for the barbaric Alseans and their swords."

"Why is it that the only thing anyone remembers from Lhyn's interviews is the part about the swords?"

He shrugged. "Because we all secretly wish we had one."

CHAPTER 24
Symptoms

Over the next five days, Ekatya lost track of how many times she wished she had an Alsean empath on board. It would have been so easy if Andira were here. She could have introduced her to Dr. Wells, asked a few questions about Sholokhov and spying, and known immediately whether her chief surgeon was involved.

Since Andira was not available, she had to do it the hard way. Lokomorra was working with the data systems analyst, looking for any other clues in both security and communication logs, but so far he had come up blank.

"It doesn't look good," he said at lunch one day. "We're not finding anything exculpatory, and the fact that she's not in the security logs at that time is pretty damning. Lieutenant Kitt says that the technological know-how needed to erase someone from a video log is already daunting. She thinks there might be five people in her section who could do it, including her. But inserting someone into an existing video log—the tech doesn't exist. It's too complex; nobody could do it in such a way that the insertion would stand up to scrutiny. So Dr. Wells couldn't cover her tracks by putting herself into the security logs at that time. All she could do was go to the medbay toilet to give herself an excuse for vanishing off the logs."

It was a smart move, Ekatya had to admit. Security cams only covered the handwashing stations and open areas of the toilets; by law, they could not record any activity in the stalls. Privacy advocates had fought for that law, and Ekatya fully endorsed it, but at the moment she was finding it most inconvenient.

On top of that, Wells herself was taking every opportunity to demonstrate her disdain for Ekatya. She was sarcastic to the point of insolence, and while Ekatya knew from her personnel file that her commanding officers had consistently found her "outspoken," this felt different and more personal. She could not understand why the doctor had accepted the post if she had such a distaste for the ship's captain—unless, of course, she had been ordered to take it.

The situation bothered her so much that she wasted most of a precious quantum com call with Lhyn talking about it. Lhyn listened patiently, asked for clarification on several points, and then made an observation that floored Ekatya with its simplicity.

"Seems to me that you're looking at the wrong end of this. The point isn't that it's impossible to insert a person into a video. It's that it's feasible to erase a person from a video."

"I can see your big brain whirring," Ekatya said. "But I don't know where it's going."

"Think about it. Isn't this a little too easy? Dr. Wells is suspected because she's the one who found the packet on her desk. And then it's discovered that she's magically missing from the security logs at that exact time. What if the same person who left the packet not only erased him or herself from the office logs, but also erased Dr. Wells from the medbay logs? And then rearranged things so that she was seen entering and leaving the toilet at the right time indexes?"

Ekatya stared at her. "I can't believe I didn't think of that."

Lhyn shrugged, a soft smile on her face. "You've been very busy, taking a floating city out in space."

"Not so busy that I shouldn't have been able to spot a frame job when I saw one."

"So why would Sholokhov want to frame her?"

"I don't know, but I'm going to find out." She rested her cheek on her fist. "Damn, I miss you."

"Because I keep solving your problems for you?"

"Amusing, you are. Don't you feel it, too? I'm beginning to understand why Andira was so shocked to learn that we spent most of our time apart. It's almost…physical."

Lhyn nodded. "I've felt it since the hour I walked off your ship. At first I told myself it was perfectly normal. We've lived together for eighteen months, including Alsea, and now you'll be gone for at least five weeks. Anyone in our situation would feel the same way, but…"

"But you don't think it's normal anymore."

"No, I don't. I'm not sleeping well, and you'd think that would make me tired, but it's like I'm buzzing with nervous energy that I can't get rid of. I've been going for walks, trying to burn it off—"

"But it only helps for a short while." Ekatya lifted her head, more alert now. "Are you having trouble concentrating?"

Lhyn gave a short, unamused laugh. "Shippers, yes. Remember how I said my book deadline would be an easy target? I thought I'd have the final chapters done early, so I could have at least two weeks to work on my keynote speech for the Anthropology Consortium meeting. But I have the attention span of a barn fly. At this rate, I might be making an apology call for missing my deadline."

"You never miss deadlines."

"I know! That's *really* how I know this is not normal. And my chest hurts. On the fucking left side, like every bad novelist's cliché of a broken heart. Not always, just—"

"Sometimes it feels a little too tight, like if you could rub it the right way, the muscles would loosen."

With a long exhale, Lhyn said, "We're feeling the same things, aren't we?"

Ekatya nodded.

"What are we going to do about it?"

"What we already planned. We survive this shakedown cruise, and then you come to Quinton Shipyards so we can make the most of the two weeks the engineers will spend checking every system on the ship."

"And then you go off on your original space station tour, and I go to the Anthropology Consortium meeting."

"And after that, you meet me at Erebderis Station, and I bring a new civilian consultant on board. Nothing has to change, Lhyn. We'll get through this."

"I know we'll get through it. Eventually. But…you know what this is, don't you?"

Ekatya wished she had thought to pour a drink before starting this conversation. "Not until one minute ago."

"I didn't think it was possible. We're not Alscan. Why didn't we have any symptoms before Alsea? We were apart for ten months."

"I think you know the answer to that." There was only one likely cause.

They stared at each other in shared amazement.

"Doesn't this bother you?" Lhyn asked.

"Yes," Ekatya said truthfully. "But I've only known about it for a few minutes. It hasn't sunk in yet. I might be more upset tomorrow."

With an uncertain smile, Lhyn said, "I'm actually…um…"

"You're excited about it. And probably taking notes for a new book. Or an addendum to the one you're writing."

The smile grew more assured. "You know me so well. Ekatya, we are *unique*. We're like hybrids, except we were produced by the sharing of emotions rather than chromosomes."

"Please choose a different word besides hybrids. I don't mind unique, but…ugh."

"Don't be so squeamish. Haven't you ever heard of hybrid vigor? We might represent the best of both races."

"Or the worst."

"Pessimist. I can't wait to talk to Lanaril about this. There's so much to think about! And we should have our symptoms measured and catalogued, so we can set a baseline and see if there are changes…"

Lhyn was off and running, energized by yet another new research project, but Ekatya didn't hear her next few sentences. She heard Sholokhov instead, explaining why he didn't send alpha-band classified orders over the quantum com. Sholokhov, who had a spy on her ship and almost certainly someone watching Lhyn, and who would no doubt be horrified by the idea of Protectorate citizens having their brains altered through contact with an Alsean. Especially when one of those citizens was commanding a warship.

"Stop," she blurted, interrupting Lhyn in mid-sentence. "Don't call Lanaril. Don't talk to anyone about this. And especially do not put it in your book."

Lhyn stared, her mouth half-open before she closed it and tilted her head. "Why?"

"Because it's not safe for either of us. Lhyn, please. We'll talk when we can see each other, but not like this. Do you understand?"

For a moment, as a familiar stubborn look appeared on Lhyn's face, she thought she would have to marshal a more specific argument. Then understanding dawned.

"I do," Lhyn said with a sigh. "He has his fingers everywhere, doesn't he?"

"Yes, but it's not just him. The political situation is worse than it used to be. We don't want to add any fuel to the fire."

They looked at each other in silence until Lhyn forced a smile. "On the positive side, the symptoms can't get much worse. Because I can't miss you any more than I do already."

"I know what you mean." Ekatya relaxed. "I keep feeling like I'm going the wrong direction."

"At least you have a ship to distract you."

"Right now, I'd trade you some of my distractions."

"You'll figure out what's going on with Dr. Wells," Lhyn said with complete assurance. "Tell me when you do?"

"I will."

They spoke a few minutes longer until Ekatya's quota of quantum com time ran out. As soon as they had said good-bye, she opened the intraship com and sent Lieutenant Kitt a message. Then she sat down on her couch with the drink she had missed earlier and let her head fall back.

"Phoenix, set my display to Alsea One. No, belay that, Alsea Three."

The large display taking up most of the opposite wall blinked to life, revealing a hauntingly familiar scene. Above a sea of trees rose the dome of Blacksun Temple, and beyond that was the skyline of Blacksun itself. It was the view from their suite in the State House, so sharp and realistic that she could almost convince herself that all she needed to do was open the window to smell that piney air or feel the breeze that was stirring the trees into motion. Lhyn had recorded it before their departure, along with several other Alsean locations.

Ekatya sipped her drink, thinking of all the times she and Lhyn had sat in their Gov Dome apartment, relaxing with scenes of Alsea on their much smaller display.

"I wish you were here now," she whispered, and rubbed the tight spot on the left side of her chest.

CHAPTER 25
Dr. Wells

By mid-morning the next day, Lieutenant Kitt had re-analyzed the security logs and confirmed their suspicions. There was indeed evidence of alteration in the time indexes.

Ekatya was in the medbay ten minutes later.

In her earlier career, she had been on ships where the medbay lived up to its name: a single bay, with a few beds separated by curtains. Privacy was nonexistent, and no one could avoid hearing the noises of patients who were sick or in pain.

On a Pulsar-class ship, the medbay was a hospital. It spanned four decks, with equipment and storage on the top level, surgical bays on the third, labs and offices on the second, and treatment rooms on the first. She stood inside the entrance on the first level, taking in the space.

The lobby was two decks high. Second-level offices looked down onto the open area, their windows right above a hanging garden that climbed the walls and draped into the space below. Small trees grew along the wall behind Ekatya, still too young to reach past the first level. In another year, with rapid growth assistance from the ship's botanists, they would attain full size and brush the ceiling. Somehow, the combination of plant species neutralized the antiseptic odors that normally filled a hospital. All that remained was a pleasant scent of greenery, with a faint floral note from the blooming Filessian orchids that dotted the hanging garden.

In the center of the lobby stood the intake station, normally staffed by three nurses around the clock, but currently housing only one. Fully enclosed and soundproofed treatment rooms lined three of the walls, each fronted with plexan, a transparent material that could be made opaque with the flick of a switch. Unused rooms were always open to the lobby, as were rooms in which the patient needed constant visual monitoring. But when privacy was required, it was easy to attain—a luxury Ekatya very much appreciated.

To her right and left were arched doorways, each leading to the U-shaped corridor that separated the interior treatment rooms from the larger, second set that could not be seen from the lobby. These were for the non-emergency cases, the long-term patients, or those who wished for extra privacy.

And just past the left doorway, leaning a shoulder against the clear plexan of an unused treatment room, was the person she had come to find. Dr. Wells was in deep conversation with another doctor, giving Ekatya the opportunity to observe how she interacted with someone else. Her expression was open and warm, and a quick smile crossed her face in response to something the other doctor said. Ekatya had never seen her look that way before. A few seconds later, she watched a more familiar expression appear as Wells caught sight of her. The smile dropped, her expression closed off, and she gave a tight nod of acknowledgment. She turned back to the doctor to end their conversation, smiled and touched him briefly on his shoulder, then walked over to Ekatya with distaste oozing from her pores. Hands in her jacket pockets, she stood rigidly erect, making the most of her slight height advantage.

"What can I do for you, Captain?"

Ekatya looked at her light brown hair, piled in a twist at the back of her head, and remembered the piece of evidence that Lieutenant Kitt had finally pulled out. There had been no digital traces of the time index switch, but when Wells appeared on the security logs prior to the packet showing up on her desk, her hairstyle had been neat, with nary a strand escaping. When she was seen entering and exiting the toilet, the twist had been loose, as if several hours had passed since she put it up. And on the logs after the packet appeared, her hair was neat once more.

A technologically untraceable frame job, defeated by a hairstyle. Ekatya had to appreciate the humor.

"May I speak with you in your office?" she asked.

Wells frowned and brushed past her, leading the way across the lobby. She bypassed the lift and trotted up the stairs without a word.

The chief surgeon's office was centered on the back wall of the lobby, overlooking the intake station and the front entrance. Wells stalked inside, then turned and leaned against the front of her desk. With her hands braced on the edge of the desk and her legs crossed at the ankles, she was sending a very clear message that Ekatya was not invited to sit down.

Her office was tidy now, the totes unpacked and put away. There were a few more books on the shelves, art scattered about the room, and an antique brass microscope holding pride of place in an illuminated display case in one corner. But the desk was still messy.

Ekatya closed the door. "I think we'll need the privacy shield for this."

For a moment, she thought she saw fear in the doctor's eyes. Then Wells twisted her upper body, reaching back to press a control on her deskpad. As the wall of plexan turned opaque, she crossed her arms over her chest and waited.

"Do you remember this?" Ekatya held up Sholokhov's packet, now folded back into its original shape.

Wells glanced at it. "Yes, it was on my desk the day we launched. I gave it to Commander Lokomorra to give to you."

"Do you know who it's from?"

She shook her head.

"Director Sholokhov." Ekatya watched her carefully but saw no signs of recognition. "Does that name mean anything to you?"

"No. Is there a point to this?"

"So you don't know who framed you."

"What?" Wells dropped her arms. "What are you talking about?"

With deliberate movements, Ekatya pulled out the guest chair she had not been offered and sat in it. "There is a spy on my ship, Doctor. Placed here by Director Sholokhov, the head of Protectorate Security. This packet can only have come from Sholokhov himself; he uses them to send his most secret orders. The fact that you delivered it put you under a cloud, and that cloud got darker when we checked the security logs and found two things. One, the logs had been tampered with so that this packet simply appeared on your desk, with no record of who entered your office to put it there. And two, you vanished off the medbay security logs at that exact time index."

Wells stared at her, then pushed off the desk, walked around it, and collapsed into her chair. "I am not a spy."

"I know."

"I don't—" She stopped and shook her head. "Why would anyone want to frame me?"

"To instill suspicion, is my guess. I think you and I might be victims of a sick little game. So I'm here to ask you for an honest answer. What do you have against me? Why did you accept this post if you dislike me so intensely?"

In the long pause that followed, Wells's face grew expressionless, then gradually hardened, as if she were holding back the words that pushed to escape.

"The fact that you can even ask that question tells me how few ethics you have left," she said at last. "Believe me, I wouldn't have come if I'd realized you were the one who signed that order. I didn't find out until it was too late."

"Which order?"

"The one I was nearly court-martialed for circumventing! Did you sign so many of them that you can't remember?"

Her sarcasm had no impact; Ekatya was too busy trying to understand. "Why don't you assume that I have no knowledge of what you're talking about," she said. "Which is the truth. There's nothing in your record about a court-martial. Walk me through this."

"I am not going to—"

"Dr. Wells!" Ekatya snapped. "I am giving you a direct order. Explain. What order did I sign that you circumvented?"

Wells glared across the desk. "The one directing my research into an antidote for sartasin fever."

Ekatya waited, and when nothing else was forthcoming, she gestured for more. "Keep going."

"How can you—"

Ekatya stood up, resting her knuckles on the edge of the desk. "Just *tell* me!"

Dr. Wells stood as well, matching Ekatya's stance and leaning forward. "I poured my heart and soul into that research," she said furiously. "It was everything I love about medicine. And then I found out that sartasin fever was not what I'd been told. It was not an illness that had been devastating the most populated continent of Elonisus Prime. It was not threatening to break out into a sector-wide epidemic." She lifted a hand, then slapped it back down. "It was a manufactured atrocity that existed nowhere but in the dark vaults of Fleet military ops. It was a *weapon*. One that couldn't be released until Fleet could guarantee its own people's safety from it. And don't tell me you didn't know."

Shocked, Ekatya pushed off from the desk. "I didn't. I had nothing to do with—"

"You signed the order!" Wells shouted. "You *used* me. I was just some faceless doctor to you, with a knack for putting together antidotes. Did it ever occur to you that some of us take our oaths seriously? That some of us might be *sickened* by the realization—" She stopped, making an odd choking noise, and dropped back into the chair.

Ekatya sat with little more grace. "Sartasin fever," she whispered to herself. There was something familiar about it. "Sartasin…no, it wasn't a fever."

Wells scowled. "You're damned right it wasn't."

"No…I remember now. That was back when I first started working for Sholokhov. He didn't call it a fever. He said it was a Voloth bioweapon under development. He had a team working on an antidote, but they weren't getting anywhere." Ekatya looked up, meeting a still-furious glare. "I signed an order directing the formation of a new team, four doctors from four different ships who had experience with infectious diseases."

"Yes, thank you very much for including me on your Death Team."

Ekatya ignored the dig, her mind going over the past year and a half. "But I never heard about it again. I forgot about it with everything else that was going on."

"You forgot?" Wells sputtered. "You nearly destroyed my career and you forgot?"

"It wasn't real," Ekatya said slowly, the horror crawling up the back of her throat. "It couldn't have been. There would have been follow-up. There was never any follow-up; that's why I didn't remember."

Wells was frowning. "Now you're the one not making sense."

"He used both of us. I was told it was a Voloth bioweapon; you were told it was an epidemic. We were both lied to. And his fingerprints didn't appear anywhere on it because I'm the one who signed the order." She dropped her head into her hands. How many other orders had she signed on his behalf, not realizing what they were really for? She could barely contemplate it.

Several seconds passed before she could bring herself to straighten and look Wells in the eye. "Dr. Wells, I am so sorry."

Wells watched her in silence, her gaze flicking from Ekatya's face to her throat and back again. At last she said, "You really didn't know."

"No, I didn't. I swear it."

"You don't have to." Wells pointed to the side of her own throat. "Your heart is beating so hard that the carotid pulse is visible. Your face is flushed and your breathing is too shallow. I know the signs of stress."

"Oh, I'm stressed all right." She had thought she was done with this. Damn that man and his long reach. Would she ever be free of him?

"Protectorate Security? That's who did this?"

"Director Sholokhov, yes."

"It's good to know the right name at last, so I can kill him when I get the chance."

Ekatya smiled in spite of the tension. "You didn't kill me."

"I hadn't had the chance yet." Wells gave no answering smile, but her eyes were slightly crinkled and far more friendly. "I think I might owe you an apology, Captain."

"I owe you a far bigger one." She should have suspected. She should have looked into it. A Voloth bioweapon that no one ever spoke of again; how could she not have realized? Sholokhov would never have let something like that go.

And yet Sholokhov was the reason Dr. Wells was on this ship. He had all the morals of a slave trafficker, but he knew how to find and use talent. Dr. Wells had been on the top of his list for that research team. Ekatya hadn't remembered how she knew of Wells's reputation, but her name had been the first she had thought of when she was short-listing candidates for her chief surgeon.

At least this time, she had given the doctor a choice.

"Actually," she said ruefully, "knowing now what I did to you, I have to commend you for your restraint. And your discretion—you could have spread that story far and wide."

"That wasn't discretion," Wells said. "That was a court order."

"The court-martial you avoided," Ekatya said with a groan. She wasn't sure she wanted to hear this. "What happened? How did you circumvent the order?"

Wells sighed, her posture finally relaxing. "When I found out what sartasin really was, I organized the rest of my team. We all stopped work at the same time, citing a violation of our oath. I was hauled in as the team leader and ordered to finish the job."

"I'm guessing that didn't go well."

"I refused. There may have been colorful language."

Ekatya could easily envision it.

"That's when they threatened court-martial. I told them to go right ahead, and I would blow their sordid little secret wide open. I already had a list of reporters. They eventually backed down and cleared my record, but slapped me with a suppression order, which I'm violating right now."

"No, you're not. If my name is on the order forming that team, then I already know about this. In theory."

"Good point. So I'm still in compliance, not that I care." Wells picked up a small metal rod from her desk and began twirling it between her fingers. "I went on a year-long deep space mission just to get myself back together. It turns out that being lied to and threatened with court-martial is a little stressful."

"I'm beginning to realize that you're a master of understatement."

Her mouth quirked up in a quick half-smile. "Then I was recruited by the captain who also defied Fleet, who did what she thought was right instead of what she'd been ordered to do. I thought things were turning around. I was thrilled to be serving with you." She dropped the rod back on the desk, the clang when it hit reverberating around the office. "Until one of my old teammates called me and said, 'Do you know who your captain is?' On fucking launch day. What a joke." She looked up, pinning Ekatya with her stare. "I didn't believe him. I couldn't imagine that you could be the same person who signed that order. So he sent me a copy, and I compared the signature with my transfer order."

Her expression told Ekatya exactly how she had felt when the signatures matched. Betrayed, trapped, furious—all the things she herself had felt when Sholokhov gave her the arrest warrant for Lhyn.

She took a deep breath. "I'm sorry to say that I'm both of those captains. The one who signed that order and the one who defied Fleet at Alsea. But I only did one of those things knowingly."

Wells let her head fall back on her chair. "This has been a sewage sump of a week. And now I'm apparently a spy." She gave a derisive laugh, then raised her head. "But at least I'm starting to believe you won't try to force me into bioweapons research."

"Never," Ekatya said firmly. "Dr. Wells, I recruited you because your record is stellar and your reputation is even better. I wanted the best, and that is precisely what I got. I didn't expect the attitude, but I'm hoping that might improve now."

"It depends." Wells picked up the rod again, focusing on it as she asked, "How could you work for that man?"

"Because he's better at coercion than the people who tried to force you back to your research."

Wells looked up sharply. "You're serious? What did he have on you? Wait, don't answer that. You must have given him a whole platter of threats to choose from after what you did at Alsea."

"He didn't need any of those. He has no problems destroying innocent lives to get what he wants." She ignored Wells's intake of breath and continued, "But that's not relevant at the moment. Sholokhov is not a man to be crossed, and he has a long memory and an even longer reach. You crossed him. I haven't made him entirely happy, either. He arranged his revenge on you by framing you as his spy, knowing it would tarnish you for as long as you served on this ship. And I wouldn't be surprised if he arranged for your teammate to find out who signed those orders on launch day. He wanted us to hate each other."

"But why? What was the point?"

"You said it yourself. You were thrilled to serve with me. He took that away from you. I was thrilled to think I was out of his reach, and he took that from me as well."

Wells shook her head. "It doesn't make sense. All of that for something so petty?"

"You don't know Sholokhov. Petty is not in his vocabulary. You cross him, you pay."

"I didn't even know he was the one I was crossing. And it was more than a year ago!"

"Long memory," Ekatya reminded her.

"Stars above," Wells said quietly. "I'm grateful you saw through it, then." She twirled the rod a few more times, then tossed it on the desk and held out her hand. "Captain Serrado? It's nice to meet you. I know all about your actions at Alsea, and I'm happy to be serving with you."

Ekatya shook her hand. "Thank you. And I've learned quite a bit about how seriously you take your oath. I'm delighted to have you as my chief surgeon. People like you make Fleet what it's meant to be."

Wells smiled at her for the first time since she had come aboard. It lit up her eyes and changed her entire demeanor. "Thank you."

"So you're only happy to be serving with me? Not thrilled?"

The smile dimmed. "It's been a hard few days. I'm not sure I can get that back."

Ekatya nodded her understanding as she rose, but halfway to the door she stopped and turned. "Don't let him take that away from you. At least one of us can still win."

She could feel Wells's gaze on her back as she walked out.

CHAPTER 26
Transition out

"Full stop," Ekatya said.

"Full stop," Lieutenant Scarp repeated, fingers dancing over his control panel.

The deep throb of the surf engines slowed, the alteration in frequency only now bringing the sound out of the background. Ekatya was so accustomed to the faint rumble of surf engines at normal power levels that she didn't hear it anymore—until it changed. Then she could hardly hear anything else.

"Activating upper display." She tapped the display control embedded in her armrest, then the ship's all-call. "All personnel, prepare to exit base space."

Most of the bridge crew looked up as the ivory ceiling and walls seemed to vanish, replaced by the ghostly mists of base space crowding in on them. In this layer beneath normal space, where distances were compressed by a factor of ten thousand, the expansive openness of space was replaced by a suffocating, pressing murk that glowed in baleful reds and oranges.

Though the undulation of the layers and streamers was too slow to be detected in normal time, Ekatya had the eerie sense that she could see them moving out of the corner of her eye. On her first trip through base space, her captain had kept the display on for the duration of the trip. She had spent two days jumping at shadows, always trying to turn her head quickly enough to catch the movement that she felt sure was there. It was a common reaction, and they had all been warned ahead of time, but intellectual understanding could not overcome instinct. Eventually, her brain adapted and stopped wasting energy on a startle response, but the sense of something just out of sight remained.

What unsettled newbies the most, however, was not the false movement but the light. Unlike normal space, where light had detectable sources and traveled in predictable ways, base space glowed in every direction. The staggering levels of radiation, ten thousand times higher than that of normal space, were most likely responsible due to their interaction with base space matter. But no one had ever been able to prove it. Base space matter defied all attempts at capture and containment, and too many lives had been lost in the effort. It could only be studied through passive observation, which yielded nominal results since most traditional physics did not apply outside of normal space.

There were no stars in base space, no planets or asteroids or even gases that they could detect. There was no means of establishing navigational routes other than the network of relay stations with quantum locator beacons. The *Phoenix* was stopped in front of one now, a silver cylinder half a kilometer tall, narrowed at one end while the other sat at the center of a two-layer ring bristling with instruments and antennae. On the bridge display, its position at the bow of the ship translated to a location directly above the engineering stations.

"Section chiefs, check in," Ekatya said. She watched the virtual screen hovering above her chair as the data came in. Medical was ready, so was botanics, engineering, weapons… This would take a few minutes, she knew, and crew services would be last. The barber shops, recreation centers, bars, restaurants, tailors, cleaners, and other service establishments could not lock themselves down as quickly as the rest of the ship.

She could easily imagine the scene outside the bridge right now, having experienced it many times before. It was controlled chaos out there as personnel shut down their equipment, dumped whatever meal they were eating, or ran to get into bed. Blue lights would be flashing in every room and corridor, a visual warning of what was about to occur. The exit from base space, just like the entrance into it, could be violent. And even when it went smoothly, it was still a physiological trauma.

With a tap to the left armrest, she sent her chair in a counter-clockwise turn, checking the readiness of her bridge officers. Below her, in the inside ring of the central dais, Commander Lokomorra sat at the executive officer's station. Lieutenant Scarp was beside him, his hand resting on the pilot control stick though the ship was not moving. Navigation was next, and the final station in the ring was main weapons control, currently staffed by Warrant Officer Roris.

Two steps below, the exterior ring held eight more critical stations. All of the other bridge stations lined the walls, leaving the floor entirely bare other than the central dais. The layout was dictated by necessity, given the function of the deck as the lower bridge display, but Ekatya secretly appreciated the aesthetics of it.

She completed her turn, satisfied that everyone on the dais had their harnesses attached. Another glance at her virtual screen showed that only crew services and operations had yet to check in. It was time, then. Nearly everyone else on the bridge had done it as soon as the navigation officer announced their arrival at the relay station.

She pulled the vial from her chest pocket, shook a tiny green bead into her hand, and placed it under her tongue. The fizzing sensation confirmed that a dose of foramine was now entering her bloodstream; within one minute it would attain full potency and shield her from the worst effects of exit transition. She was not fond of the side effects—a slight fuzziness in her thought processes, a small decrease in reaction time—so she always put it off until the last moment.

Three minutes later she received confirmation from the last two sections. Tapping the all-call, she said, "All sections report ready. Brace for transition." She closed the channel and spun her chair to look over the engineering station. "Commander Yst, initiate the pikamet beam."

"Initiating."

As in normal space, the pikamet beam was not visible. But its effect on base space matter certainly was. In a perfectly straight line reaching out from the bow of the *Phoenix*, the mists and streamers glowed a brilliant white. Soon they were so bright that the automatic display filter activated, preventing temporary blindness in the bridge crew.

And there it was. After all the time of feeling that she could see movement if she just turned quickly enough, now it was happening for real. The base space matter was shifting, slowly at first, then more and more rapidly until it roiled, the currents carrying it in all directions away from the pikamet beam. Utter darkness now marked the path of the beam, an emptiness that expanded as she watched.

"Interspace portal at twenty percent," Yst reported.

A fighter would have already gone through by now, but a ship the size of the *Phoenix* needed a much larger portal. Ekatya waited, listening to the updates and watching the emptiness grow. She had done this more times than she could count, but it still felt a little bit like magic.

At ninety percent, she pulled the brace bars out of her armrests and snapped them into their vertical position.

At one hundred percent, she wrapped her hands around the brace bars, rested her head against her seat, and said, "Take us in, Lieutenant Scarp."

Since her chair was facing the portal on the display, she had the experience of sliding feet first into the tunnel of emptiness. It was slightly masochistic on her part, but she could never resist.

The compression started at the wall of the bridge, where the display wrinkled, then crumpled, then was sucked down a tiny hole. Ekatya watched her engineering staff crumple and vanish next. The distortion raced across the deck straight toward her, taking the bridge with it, until only the central dais remained intact.

The outer ring crumpled, then the inner ring, and then her feet were sucked in. She kept her eyes open out of a stupid sense of pride—a captain should not look away from the fate of her ship—and felt the nausea rise as her legs cracked and twisted. When the yawning emptiness rushed over her head, she no longer knew whether her eyes were open or not. She wasn't even certain she existed. This moment, in the infinite and infinitesimal space between spaces, was a time and place that defied all understanding. It lasted half a second, it lasted a year, and then her body was stretched and peeled and spat out, and she was swallowing the bile that hovered in her throat.

The first time she went through an exit transition, she stubbornly refused the foramine. She had never done that again. Even with the medication, it was all she could do to keep from throwing up.

But they were through. The upper display, now whole again, showed the wondrous darkness of normal space punctuated by a million discrete points of light.

She relaxed her hands, which had been clenched so tightly around the brace bars that letting go was painful. Flexing her fingers to restore the circulation, she swallowed several more times until the nausea finally receded.

"Everyone still have all their molecules?" she called out.

Groans and a few chuckles filled the air. Lokomorra looked up from his station with a grin that deepened his dimples. "Feels like my big toe got stuck in my ear this time, but other than that, I'm good."

"Holy Seeders," Roris croaked from her other side. "It is so much worse on the bridge."

"It's a much larger space than a weapons room or your quarters," Ekatya said. "You have more time to see it coming. And the display makes it more visceral."

"No kidding. Why do you turn it on?"

"Count your blessings, Roris. I could have had the bottom display on, too."

She thought she heard a whispered *Oh, fuck* and clamped her mouth shut. Roris was tough and proud, and it would not help Ekatya in her goal to get the woman into officer training if she laughed at her in front of the entire bridge.

She unclipped her harness, slid the brace bars back into their armrests, and asked navigation for verification of their position. They had exited base space at the relay station closest to their destination, which meant they still had six days of travel in normal space.

"Set course for the Lexihari system," she said, rising from her chair and making her way down the steps to the bridge deck. "Standard cruising speed. Commander Lokomorra, I'm headed for the medbay. You have the bridge."

"Yes, Captain," he said as she crossed the deck. "I'll try to keep it in one piece."

Her steps nearly faltered. Commander Baldassar wouldn't have dreamed of making such a public quip on the bridge, and she was halfway to a reprimand before recalling the conscious decision she had made to accept Lokomorra because of, rather than in spite of, his relaxed attitude.

Don't be Sholokhov, she reminded herself.

"See that you do, Commander," she said mildly. "And perhaps you could polish the deck while you're at it?"

Several of the crew at the wall stations looked at each other and smiled. Their stances loosened, and Ekatya could feel the ease in the collective bridge mood.

She wasn't used to it. But she liked it.

CHAPTER 27
Language chip

Ensign Bellows was waiting in the medbay lobby. He still looked a little green around the edges, which did nothing for his complexion and made his round face seem even rounder.

"How was your first exit transition, Ensign?" Ekatya managed to not smile too broadly.

"It was, uh…all right." He swallowed.

"All right? That must be how they say 'nauseating' in Gov Dome these days."

His expression cleared. "Even you?"

"Me and just about everyone else. There are a few lucky souls who aren't bothered, but not many. You didn't refuse the foramine, did you?"

"Seeders, no. Commander Kenji said if I did that, I'd wish I had died during transition, rather than just thinking I did."

She laughed and clapped him on the shoulder. "Then you were smart. Someone gave me the same advice my first time, but I thought I was tough enough to be one of the lucky ones. I wasn't."

"I'm learning more about you all the time, Captain." Dr. Wells had arrived with a tall, very slender man at her side. Holding a medpad against her chest with one hand, she extended the other. "Ensign Bellows, yes? I'm Dr. Wells, chief surgeon. This is Dr. Tatyn. He'll be doing your surgery."

Bellows gave her an uncertain smile as he shook her hand. "It's nice to meet you, Dr. Wells. Dr. Tatyn?"

"You're in good hands here, Ensign." Dr. Tatyn gestured toward an open treatment room. "I promise it won't take long."

Bellows took a step, then stopped and turned to Ekatya. "Captain Serrado, I'm just curious, but…why now?"

"Because we're going to have headaches for the next two days," Ekatya said. "Possibly three. And nothing they can give us will help."

"And we need to be over that before we arrive in the Lexihari system," he said thoughtfully.

"Exactly. We didn't schedule it earlier because I didn't want either of us to be debilitated right after launch. And we both had a pile of reports to read."

"Okay. That makes sense." He turned to Dr. Tatyn. "I'm ready."

Ekatya watched them go.

"You look worried," Dr. Wells said.

"I am. He's never been in space before now, his training in first-contact protocols started the day we launched, and this is the first time he's even had a language chip replacement. That boy does not belong on this landing team."

"Then why is he on it?"

"Sholokhov assigned him."

"Why in all…?" Wells trailed off. "There has to be a reason."

"I think it might be about control. Bellows worked as my assistant in the Presidential Palace for sixteen months. Sholokhov knows him very well. He doesn't know anyone else in the data systems section." Though she wouldn't be surprised to learn that he had a full dossier on her entire crew.

"You mean he's sending a virtual child on a first-contact mission because he doesn't trust anyone else?"

"Possibly. Probably."

Wells's expression darkened. "What is *wrong* with that man?"

"Nothing a lobotomy couldn't fix." She knew better than to speak so openly, but on this topic, she felt safe with Dr. Wells. It was one of the few things she did feel confident about when it came to her chief surgeon. They had cleared the air, yes, but they were still on edge around each other, and she didn't know when or if that would change. It infuriated her to think Sholokhov had won this one, too, but there was little she could do about it.

"I would volunteer to perform that surgery." Wells shook her head, then looked at her medpad. "Your record says you speak Common organically, which puts you in a minority. Your current language chips are High Alsean and Terrahan. Which one do you want to replace?"

It had been a difficult decision. She hated to lose either one. If she gave up High Alsean, and they could not complete this mission before her next quantum com call with Andira, she would have to resort to a translator. Lhyn of course spoke fluent Common, but in their more intimate moments, they conversed in Terrahan, Lhyn's native language. For the woman whose life was built around learning and speaking the languages of others, to have someone speak her own was a revelation. Lhyn always said that when Ekatya had shown up for one of their rendezvous and whispered *I've been waiting for this* in her own language—that was the moment she had fallen in love.

"High Alsean," Ekatya said.

"Really? That's not the one I would have guessed."

"Then it seems you still have a few things to learn about me, Dr. Wells." She hadn't meant it to sound dismissive, but Wells took it that way.

"I'm sure it's only a matter of time," she said shortly. "Shall we?" Without waiting for an answer, she walked toward a treatment room.

"Shek," Ekatya muttered. Sometimes, the Alsean curse just fit better.

No other words passed between them as Ekatya awkwardly positioned herself on the treatment bed and turned her head to the side. She hated this part. Any work on her lingual implant involved someone else being uncomfortably close to her face.

Her vision was filled by a lab coat as Dr. Wells leaned over, brushing her hair back and clipping it out of the way to expose the area behind her ear. The coat had been recently cleaned, judging by the new laundry scent still clinging to it. When Wells reached over to pick up an injector, Ekatya let out a breath, relieved to be able to see the room again.

"Wait," she said before she could think better of it. "I just realized that you never accepted my apology."

Wells lowered the injector. "Are you worried?"

"No, but… I'd feel better if I knew for certain that you weren't holding a grudge."

"That's a little insulting. Don't concern yourself, Captain. You already know I take my oath seriously."

It wasn't the answer Ekatya wanted, but the injector stung her throat and she forgot what she had meant to say. As she sank into the darkness, her tunneling vision caught sight of an impossible but somehow unsurprising figure standing next to Dr. Wells.

"Lhyn," she murmured. Even that single word seemed too heavy to drag from her throat, but she needed Lhyn to know. "I kept Terrahan. I couldn't give up any part of you."

"I know, tyrina," Lhyn said. "Go to sleep."

CHAPTER 28
Lexihari

Ekatya had thoroughly studied the Lexihari system when the task force was considering it for first contact and possible Protectorate membership. The inhabited planets were the second and third in a five-planet system.

Halaama, closer to the sun, was warmer and had a vibrant agricultural base. It also boasted an egalitarian society with an excellent civil rights record, a fact that had been brought up over and over by certain members of the task force bent on bringing it into the Protectorate.

Nylak was a cooler planet with rich mineral resources and a culture locked into a gender-segregated system. Females had few rights and were valued largely for their ability to pleasure the males and produce children. Ekatya could not believe Nylak had even been proposed, but since it was impossible to bring in one planet without the other, the Halaama defenders had claimed that pulling Nylak up to civilized standards would represent a great social experiment that the Protectorate was almost obligated to perform. What better proof of the benefits of membership?

That had spawned endless debates, all of which Ekatya found exhausting. She was more cynical these days, and the list of mineral resources on Nylak looked far too similar to those on the five supposedly inhabited planets for which the Protectorate had sold Alsea. If the push to get membership for Nylak was truly about freeing half of the planetary population from the chains of cultural subjugation, she would eat her captain's bars.

The history of the two planets was studded with wars. They were evenly matched in terms of technology, both cultures driven by the need to keep up with the other, though of course neither had faster-than-light capabilities. Both kept sizable fleets of warships despite the current lack of overt hostilities. Trade was highly regulated, and interplanetary tourism was nonexistent.

Ekatya had not given two seconds of thought as to which planet she would target. The men of Nylak refused to conduct business or diplomacy with Halaama women and would never accept her as the commander of her ship and representative of her people. Going there would mean putting Commander Lokomorra up as her proxy and leading him from behind. He was even less fond of the idea than she was.

Fortunately, Nylak's current position in its orbit placed it more than a light-hour away from Halaama, allowing them to fly straight to the inner planet without coming anywhere near its sibling.

On their way in, Commander Kenji had his analysts monitoring the electromagnetic frequencies used for communications by the two civilizations. No mention had been made of the Voloth. By itself, this proved nothing—the visit could have been a stealthy one, kept secret by the governments involved—but Ekatya had her doubts. The Voloth didn't do anything quietly. If they could prove Sholokhov's intel wrong, she could avoid a landing altogether and make this a very short mission.

That hope was dashed the moment a Halaaman warship hailed them.

Ekatya took the call on her virtual screen. The rest of the bridge crew could look to the display, which showed the transmission in four locations and translated all conversation to Common. The translator had been loaded with the diplomatic languages of both Halaama and Nylak before they left base space.

The warship captain, a middle-aged man with a series of dark dots tattooed in lines on each side of his bald head, was already scowling. "You have entered Halaama space without permission. State your name, destination, and intent."

Lokomorra glanced up at Ekatya, his eyebrows raised. This was not the demeanor of a man who had never before seen an alien ship.

"My name is Captain Serrado, and we have come with peaceful intent. We hope to establish orbit around Halaama, where with perfect deference I request the honor of a meeting with the Great Leader."

The man's expression grew more open at her use of their formal diplomatic phrasing. "I am Defender Ceylayana, here to serve," he said. "You are certainly more polite than your predecessors. They were unaware of basic courtesies."

"I can't answer for any who came before. This is the first time my people have been in your system."

He frowned. "Who are your people? The last ones looked like you."

Not for the first time, Ekatya wished the Voloth had some sort of physical difference that set them apart. But they were all Gaians, separated only by a fundamental moral conflict—and the refusal of the Voloth to call themselves by a name they now disdained.

"My people are the Protectorate, a group of planets dedicated to peaceful coexistence and mutually beneficial trade. Who did the last ones say they represented?"

"They called themselves members of the Guild."

Baffled whispers rustled through the bridge.

"We're not familiar with this group," Ekatya said.

"Nor were they familiar with you. They never mentioned a Protectorate."

"Then it seems we both have a mystery to solve. I hereby reiterate my deferential request."

He nodded. "I will deliver your request. The Great Leader may need time to answer. You will not progress until he does."

It took a stiff spine to tell the captain of a ship ten times larger than his that she wasn't going anywhere. Ekatya had to admire the attitude.

The Great Leader was on a video link from Halaama within ten minutes. His head was also bald and tattooed, though the markings took the form of two lines curving over the top of his head with a row of dots marching between them.

"Welcome to Halaama, Captain Serrado of the Protectorate," he said in a rich baritone voice. "You have made a good impression with your courtesy."

"Thank you. I find that courtesy is rarely wasted." She had to wait a beat before responding, given the one-second delay. Light-speed communication was so primitive.

"Nevertheless, it is a welcome discovery in those we hope will become friends. In our own system, such courtesy is a rarity."

Either that was a subtle push to determine whether she had already spoken with the Nylakians, or he was airing his distaste for an entire culture.

"It can be a rarity where I come from as well. I hope you will not think me discourteous if I say that I came here for a purpose and wish to pursue it. I understand others have approached you before our arrival."

"Yes, the Guild."

"Did they offer a treaty?"

He gave her a measuring look. "We have no need of a treaty; we are not at war. The Guild had some goods on offer, and we made a trade that was beneficial to both sides."

If this was the Voloth, they had changed tactics so drastically as to be unrecognizable.

"My people may also be interested in a trade relationship," she said carefully. "Would it be possible to meet to discuss it?"

After that, it was simply a negotiation of terms for their meeting. They were given permission to enter low orbit, from which their shuttle would be escorted to the Governing Palace. Ekatya requested permission for six of her fighters to accompany the shuttle, was refused any at all, intimated that she could speak with the Nylakians if the Halaamans did not respect her needs, and ended up with approval for three fighters, which was what she had wanted in the first place. In exchange, she promised that none of her landing team would carry weapons. This was of course a blatant lie, but she was reasonably certain that her team's weapons would not be detected.

In the seventeen days between her orders from Sholokhov and their arrival at Halaama, Ekatya and her section chiefs had hammered out every detail and possibility they could think of as they prepared for this mission. When the landing team stepped out of their shuttle and into the pageantry of a diplomatic occasion, she felt confident that they were as ready as they could be.

But they had not taken into account the excessive formality of the Halaamans. After an extremely lengthy greeting ceremony, they were led with many apologies through a scanner—which pronounced them free of weaponry—escorted into the multi-towered Governing Palace, and taken on a long and mind-numbing tour. This gave her team the advantage of being able to surreptitiously map much of the palace from the inside, but they paid for it by listening to droning speeches about the importance of this artifact, that historical figure, and the symbolism of the four—or five, Ekatya lost count—different architectural ages represented in the building's construction.

When the tour finally ended, they were ushered to an ornately decorated banqueting room where somehow, given only nine hours since their initial contact, the Halaamans had put together an enormous party. The team was seated at the head table with the Great Leader and several dignitaries of both genders, all bald and tattooed, and all of whom deflected every one of Ekatya's attempts to find out more about the Guild. There was always another dance performance to watch, a food item to be described and tasted, a singer to listen to, or something else to be discussed. Never in her life had she been so politely and consistently repelled.

When she finally dropped all pretense at subtlety and asked to discuss what she had come for, the Great Leader said in loud and jovial tones, "There is plenty of time for business tomorrow! Tonight is for pleasure, for celebration! How often do we meet another peaceful and courteous race? We must savor this moment!"

All of the dignitaries at the table gave a shout of approval and began talking over each other about past celebrations.

Ekatya gave up.

She tried again when the guests were herded to the opulent library for after-dinner drinks and informal conversation, but had no better luck. Expertise at avoidance was apparently a Halaaman trait.

The event concluded with a thousand wordy farewells, after which a squad of palace guards arrived to escort the team to their lodgings. There was no question of deviating from their path; the guards were expressionless and armed with weapons holstered at their hips. Where the banquet attendees had exuded nothing but conviviality, the guards gave off an air of professional menace.

Their lodgings consisted of three suites high up in a distant wing of the palace. Ekatya had a suite to herself, as befitting a leader. Her six security escorts were given another, while her anthropologist and two data systems analysts were given a third. Most of the palace guards retreated once they were settled, but one remained posted outside each suite door—for their own security, they were told—and Ekatya had noted two more staying behind in the junction room at the end of their corridor.

She wasted no time gathering her team into the living area of her suite. Lieutenant Kitt, the analyst chosen by Commander Kenji, pulled a tiny jammer from her chest pocket and set it on a decorative table in the center of the room. Checking its readings on her pad, she announced, "There are three listening devices and one video logger transmitting from this suite. Or were. They're not hearing or seeing anything now."

"So much for our trusting hosts. You've limited the jammer range?"

"Yes, the guards outside still have their radios. There are video loggers in the hall, too. No surprise there."

Ekatya looked around the group. "I've just spent four hours eating more than I wanted to and learning absolutely nothing. Did anyone else have better luck?"

Nine heads shook a simultaneous no. She was surprised it didn't create a breeze.

"The food was great," Trooper Torado offered. He reminded her of Colonel Micah, with his intimidating size and bristling haircut.

Warrant Officer Roris elbowed him. "Not helpful, Torado."

Ekatya smiled at their easy camaraderie and wondered, not for the first time, whether she might do Roris a disservice by recommending her for field officer training. She had such a tight-knit weapons team with Troopers Torado, Ennserhofen, and Blunt. They had stuck together through thick and thin and were now on their third ship assignment together. If Roris became a commissioned officer, she would lose this.

"The food *was* good," she agreed. "But that's not what I'm looking for." Ignoring the second elbow shot Roris sent to Torado, she turned to the youngest member of their group. "Ensign Bellows, you're more accustomed than most to boring diplomatic affairs. What did you think?"

Put on the spot, Bellows grew even more owl-eyed than normal. He swallowed and said, "I think they worked pretty hard at saying nothing."

And that was why she liked him. He had summed up that entire banquet in one sentence.

"I agree," she said. "I asked six ways forward and twelve backward and always got the same non-answer. And given that these people just met advanced aliens for apparently for the second time in their history, they had surprisingly few questions."

"Yes, what was that about?" Roris asked. "I noticed that, too. They didn't ask us *anything*. They just wanted to talk about themselves and their art and music and Seeders know what else. That was the worst date I've ever been on."

Torado and Ennserhofen snorted with laughter, and even shy Trooper Blunt smiled. The two security officers, who had been paragons of professional behavior throughout, kept straight faces.

Lieutenant Gizobasan, the team's anthropologist, caught Ekatya's eye. "The reports led me to believe these people would be far more curious. And even barring that, their culture is built around equal treatment and courtesy. The way they treated us looked courteous on the surface, but by their own standards, it wasn't. True courtesy would have meant asking us about ourselves and our culture."

"So what are we saying here?" Roris asked. "Besides the fact that they're hiding something and they don't want to ask us questions because then we might expect answers from them?"

"They're stalling," Ekatya said.

Gizobasan nodded. "That makes sense. They're putting us off while they ask the Guild about us."

"And we'll get no answers until they hear back. Which means the answers we do get will be dictated by the Guild. It also means we could be waiting a long time; they use light-speed communication. So unless the Guild has a ship within a few light-hours…" Ekatya loosened the throat guard of her dress uniform jacket. "Does anyone think there's a remote chance the Guild could be the Voloth?"

One of the security officers shook his head silently; the other shrugged. "Seems unlikely, Captain," he said.

One by one, every member of the team added their agreement.

Ekatya sighed. It just figured this would turn out to be complicated. "Protectorate Security wants this resolved as quickly as possible. I already reported my suspicions that the Voloth haven't been here, but now they're concerned about a new player in galactic politics. We're ordered to find out who the Guild are, and asking nicely didn't work. Looking at it from the Great Leader's point of view, he's made some sort of deal that benefits him so tremendously that he's ignoring the presence of a warship and what we might be able to offer until he can hear from his trade partners."

"Oh, I see where you're going with this." Bellows was exuding the air of excitement he had so often shared with her in the Presidential Palace, when the two of them were the only people they could trust. "Whatever this Guild is, they can't have a ship the size of the *Phoenix* or we'd have heard of them before now. So they must be offering something that offsets our potential, and that means technology."

Roris crossed her arms over her chest. "Or weapons."

Trust a weapons specialist to think of that. "You're right. We have to consider both. Either one would upset the balance of power in this system, not to mention giving capabilities to this planet that the Protectorate might not be happy to see. So…" She turned to Kitt and Bellows, who was practically bouncing in place. "This is where you two come in. We need to get into their communication systems."

"I don't think we can do that from here, Captain." Kitt indicated the com panel on the far side of the room. "I could take that apart and do my best, but we already know this room has been tapped, so my guess is the com panel is, too. Even if it weren't, this is an outlying unit. I'd need to know their programming language to make it work for me."

Bellows nodded. "We have to do what we planned."

"I was afraid of that." Ekatya looked at Lieutenant Korelonn, her lead security officer. "How did the mapping efforts go during our tour?"

He pulled his pad from its sleeve pocket. "We know where *not* to go."

"That's for sure," Torado muttered.

Korelonn cracked a slight smile, which did little to lighten his overall demeanor. He had a similar build to Torado, but where Torado was open and sociable, Korelonn seemed to view the world in a constant state of suspicion. His square jaw was already darkened with beard growth, though he had been smooth-shaven when they first boarded the shuttle.

"We did map a hot spot behind that last art gallery on the sixth floor," he said. "It was too far from the banquet hall to be the kitchen and not hot enough to be their temperature regulation equipment. The radio activity was strong in that area as well. I think that's our best bet for their communication core."

"I trust your best bet. All right, everyone, we follow the plan as discussed. Lieutenant Kitt, Ensign Bellows, get your gear ready. Everyone else, assemble your weapons. We'll wait here until sixteen hundred hours ship time." In local time, that would be the middle of the night.

Kitt and Bellows immediately took off their jackets, sat on the nearest chairs, and began pulling tools and bits of equipment from their jacket linings. The others found places to sit as well, and were soon immersed in assembling their weapons.

Ekatya stepped away from the group, activated her internal com, and brought Commander Lokomorra up to date.

"Not what we hoped," he said.

"I know. But we can't wait until tomorrow. There's no guarantee that tomorrow will give us answers either, and we can't keep our fighter pilots in their cockpits that long."

"Well, we could, but they'd be so paralyzed by the morning that they wouldn't be able to fly. They were sorry to have missed the banquet, by the way."

"Tell them they missed about four hours of nothing. I wouldn't mind sending them back except that I have a bad feeling about whatever it is that this Guild has sold to our hosts, and I'm not sure we could negotiate passage for our fighters down here a second time. Get the *Phoenix* ready for a hot pickup, Commander. I'll call when it's time."

She sat down on the last available chair and removed the false heels from her boots. The two halves snapped together into a pistol grip, which she then loaded with both types of nonlethal ammunition secreted in her uniform jacket lining. One was a shock charge, the other a tiny, instant-acting sedative dart. The grip held enough for twenty shots of each.

She pulled two barrels from another part of her jacket lining, screwed them in place, and attached the front stabilizer and sight. After slipping the flat holster out of one of her pockets, she locked the latch into position, clipped it to the back of her belt, and slid the pistol inside. Finally, she unzipped two inside pouches and scooped out the stun beads, putting them into her side jacket pockets for easy access.

Between her and the rest of the landing team, they were equipped to take out half the guards in this palace. Nor were they defenseless against the probably lethal weapons those guards were carrying: the flexible armor in their uniform jackets would stop most projectiles and dissipate all but the strongest of phaser charges. Not for the first time, Ekatya was grateful for cautious Fleet uniform designers who insisted that "dress" should not mean "sitting target."

Now came the hardest part: waiting. They sat around in an uncomfortable silence, until Ekatya asked Roris to tell the story of their memorable shore leave at Erebderis Station. She complied with enthusiasm and the willing assistance of her teammates, all of whom had been involved. The tale drew the group together in laughter, even the always-serious Korelonn. Then Roris mentioned Ekatya's fight with Lancer Tal, a teaser that had everyone looking expectant. With a martyred sigh and a concession that it was only fair she should tell a story too, Ekatya launched into an abbreviated version of her challenge.

"By the time I yielded, I hardly remembered my own name," she finished. "And it was only later that I found out she went easy on me. Don't ever get in a fight with an Alsean warrior."

"It wasn't that she fought an Alsean warrior," Roris put in. "It was that she picked a fight with the leader of the entire warrior caste. Our captain sets her sights high."

"You never told me that," Bellows said. "I was your assistant for sixteen months and I'm only now hearing this?"

"It's not something I'm going to sing about in the Presidential Palace."

"Well…yes, of course, but still! You got in a *fight* with the Lancer of Alsea! That's so…"

"Stupid?" Ekatya suggested.

"No, amazing! I hope Dr. Rivers put that in her book."

"Not if she values our relationship, she didn't."

She listened to their laughter and remembered those first days on Alsea, when she had worked so hard to hide her ties with Lhyn. That was a part of her life she didn't miss at all.

"Now, see, if I were going to pick a fight with an Alsean warrior, I'd have picked Lead Guard Gehrain," Roris said.

Torado looked at her askance. "Is there rot in your brain? He was bigger than me! And they have much denser muscle mass. That man *carried* me out of our weapons room. He would have crushed your ass into the dirt." Too late, he remembered where he was. "Sorry, Captain."

She waved a hand. "I think we can consider ourselves off the record. Besides, I want to hear why Roris would have fought Gehrain."

"Because if I'm going to get my ass crushed into the dirt, I'd want to look up and see him." Roris made a fanning motion by her face. "Once you got over the facial ridges, he was a fine specimen."

Shy Trooper Blunt, who until now had not said one word that Ekatya had heard, now spoke up clearly. "Yes, he was. And he preferred men."

"Oho!" Torado whooped and held up his hand. With a smile, Blunt punched her small fist into his palm. Torado then turned and punched Roris in the shoulder. "From Blunt to you, ouch!"

Ekatya settled back and listened as her weapons team entertained the group with tales of Alsea. They had two hours to kill, and she couldn't think of a more enjoyable way to do it.

CHAPTER 29
Unexpected ties

When they had planned their raid back on the *Phoenix*, Ekatya's first thought had been to blow out any Halaaman surveillance equipment with an electromagnetic pulse. Kitt and Korelonn had suggested that a better strategy would be to temporarily jam the equipment in the area they were moving through. As Korelonn pointed out, if they wanted to move in a covert fashion, leaving a trail of permanently disabled equipment was not the way to go about it.

"Lieutenant Kitt, you have the second jammer ready?" Ekatya asked.

Kitt patted the chest pocket of her dress jacket. "Right here, ready to blind and deafen everything around us."

"Good. I'll see all of you out and wait until you get to your doors. My guard shouldn't find that unusual. Then I'll take out mine while you—"

"Oh, no," Korelonn said. "With respect, Captain, your safety is my responsibility. I'll stay here with you and take out your guard."

She decided it wasn't worth the argument. "Very well. Who is doing the others?"

They concluded that since Torado was the largest of the remaining five in their suite, while Kitt was the tallest in her group, they would take the jobs.

"But I'll need help catching mine," Kitt said. "That man is big. Bellows, stay close to me."

"I will."

"Drag them here when you're done," Ekatya said. "An empty hall will attract less notice than one full of sleeping guards. I'm just sorry all the guards have shaved heads. I was hoping we could use their uniforms."

"I'll do a lot for a mission," said Roris, running a hand through her short brown locks. "But I'd have to be desperate to do that."

"You and me both." Blunt gave her white ponytail a tug.

The chuckles told Ekatya that despite gearing up for their operation, this group was still relaxed. That boded well for their teamwork.

They all made one last check of their weapons, and Ekatya called Commander Lokomorra to tell him they were on the move. He would alert the shuttle and fighter pilots, who would prepare for an evacuation.

When they had all gathered at the door, Ekatya opened it and stood at the side opposite her guard. He glanced at her with a faint look of surprise before returning his gaze to the opposite wall.

"Well done, everyone," Ekatya said in a normal tone. "Try to get some sleep in what's left of the night."

They filed out with a chorus of goodnights, and she stood slightly back to give Korelonn room. When both groups had arrived at their doors, she held up a finger toward Korelonn and called out, "Oh, I forgot something. Lieutenant Kitt, Trooper Torado…go."

She dropped her finger as she spoke, and the hall turned into a flurry of silent activity. Korelonn leaned around the door frame and shot Ekatya's guard with a sedative dart, then stepped out and caught him under the armpits as he toppled forward. She moved out of the way, giving him space to drag the guard back into the room. The others were already coming toward her, Torado hefting his guard over his shoulders while Kitt and Bellows were hauling theirs by his arms and legs. Within one minute they had all three guards lined up on the floor of the suite, where the first jammer would keep them hidden until someone made a physical check of the room.

With this act, they had gone from diplomacy to armed incursion. They could not leave the Halaamans with their weapons.

Torado and the two security officers stripped the belts off the guards and buckled them around their own hips. Korelonn grunted as he pulled out his new weapon and looked it over. "They're still using leadslingers."

"I hope they don't try that in their ships," Ekatya said.

He nodded. "I haven't shot one of these since my second year of training, when we covered primitive weapons. All right, people, we're still operating in nonlethal mode, which rules these out. But if you have to use them, be aware that they kick, they're inaccurate unless you've had a lot of practice, and they're going to sound like the inside of a rail gun."

"So if we want to advertise our position, we should use it, is what you're saying." Torado jammed his back in its holster.

"Exactly." Korelonn looked around the group. "Let's go. We have two more in the junction room."

"I'll distract them." Ekatya shot him a quelling look. "I'll look less suspicious than any of the rest of you."

Roris came up beside her. "This is you and me, Korelonn."

The carpet absorbed their footsteps as they all moved to the end of the corridor. Ekatya strolled right past both guards, who were standing against the wall on either side of the junction room's entrance, and got halfway across before they recovered from their surprise.

"Captain, our sincere apologies, but you can't leave this area," one of them said.

"I can't?" She turned to find that they had both followed her to the center of the room and now stood with their backs to her team. Behind them, Roris and Korelonn were lining up their shots. "My sincere apologies in turn. I must have been mistaken."

"Where are your guards?" the second one asked. He began to turn but stopped in mid-motion when a dart appeared in his neck. The first guard toppled to the floor right after him.

"Nice shooting," Ekatya said quietly as the others came in. "Any more nearby?"

As Korelonn consulted his pad, which had a thermal readout laid over the map he had generated during their tour, Roris and Ennserhofen appropriated the weapon belts of the sleeping guards.

"Not for another forty meters." Korelonn turned his pad toward Ekatya, showing the other two corridors branching off this room and leading to opposite sides of the map. "There are two more guards at the next intersection. After that, we're clear as far as this can measure. My guess is that during the night shift, they only set internal guards on the residential area."

"Lucky for us they value people over machinery." Ekatya glanced around the room, which was barren of any closets or furniture large enough to hide the guards. "Looks like these need to go in my suite as well."

Korelonn pointed to his second and Torado, who soon vanished down the hall, bent under their burdens.

"We can't carry any more back," Kitt said. "My jammer won't reach far enough."

"Then we hope we can hide the next two." Ekatya looked back at Korelonn. "Same routine?"

He chewed on the inside of his lip for a moment. "I don't like it. But it works."

It worked on the next guards as well. Though they were more suspicious, Roris and Korelonn only needed a few seconds of distraction. There was no handy furniture in this area, either, but Bellows found a toilet not far away. Soon both guards were concealed inside, their weapon belts now on Bellows and Blunt.

They moved silently, looking for a way to get to the sixth floor without taking a lift that might be monitored for usage. Once again it was Bellows who located the door to a flight of stairs. He reached for the handle but was stopped by a glaring Korelonn. "Not until you know what's behind it," Korelonn whispered, holding out his pad.

The stairs were clear, as was the corridor they exited into. Cautiously, they crept through several more passages and small junction rooms, all of which were unguarded. It appeared that security really was limited to the residential area and not dispersed through areas considered less restricted.

Korelonn relaxed slightly, both from the lack of thermal signs on his map and because Kitt's pad, which was monitoring electrical activity and radio signals, confirmed that the room they had targeted was indeed the communication core.

But when they came in range, the thermal scanner showed someone sitting inside it.

"Stun bead?" Korelonn asked.

"No!" Kitt and Bellows whispered simultaneously.

"You could damage the equipment," Bellows explained.

"And it's too much noise." Ekatya caught Korelonn's eye. "We shouldn't use stun beads until we have no other choice."

"Well, we're not sending you in there."

"You don't need to. Only one signal? We haven't seen any guards working alone. It's probably some data analyst staying up late. This is a time to just walk in and shoot."

He nodded, looking relieved that she hadn't tried to volunteer, and tapped his second for backup. When they arrived at their destination, the others hung back while the two security officers walked to the door, yanked it open, and vanished inside.

Ekatya heard an unfamiliar voice, the *thwip* of a dart, and then nothing. Korelonn poked his head back out. "All clear."

Kitt and Bellows wasted no time exploring the room, talking together in excited tones. The hapless analyst who had been working there was now lying in a corner, her legs carefully pushed out of the way. Korelonn kept an eye on his thermal scanner, monitoring the corridor outside for any movement, and Ekatya watched her data analysts for signs of progress. This had gone a little too smoothly so far. She was expecting trouble any moment now.

Bellows peeled off and came straight toward Ekatya, a smile on his face. "Lieutenant Korelonn can stop staring at his pad. We found the security terminal. It routes everything somewhere else, probably to a dedicated security room, but the data comes in here first and there are small displays. He can watch the whole building."

Korelonn looked intrigued. "Show me."

Before long, both of the security officers were tracking movement within the palace while Kitt and Bellows settled in front of an information terminal. Ekatya didn't see any difference between that one and the twelve others in the room, but they did, and she was happy to leave them to it. Bellows held up his pad, the virtual screen activated, and used the translation program to transform the Halaaman characters into Common text while Kitt read it and began inputting instructions. They spoke back and forth in a language that occasionally sounded like Common, but was otherwise entirely foreign. Data analysts were a whole different species when they got into their equipment and code.

Roris and her team flanked the door, looking ready to take down anyone who might wander in. Ekatya suspected that, like her and Gizobasan, they were simply staying out of the way.

Fifteen minutes dragged by, broken only by her call to Lokomorra to tell him of their progress so far. She was calculating the amount of time they had remaining before the first guards came out of sedation when the quiet of the room was interrupted by a shocked and too-loud call. "Sucking Seeders! Captain!"

She jogged across to Bellows. "What is it?"

His eyes were rounder than she had ever seen them. "I recognize this encryption."

"You *recognize* it?" Kitt's eyes were nearly as wide. "In the Great Leader's communications?"

"I'd know this anywhere. I spent a week breaking it after we went to the fundraiser. These messages are from Elin Frank."

Ekatya sagged against the nearest console as understanding crashed through her brain.

Sholokhov had known. Or if he hadn't, he had at least strongly suspected. *This* was why he had wanted Bellows on the team.

Why in all the purple planets had he not told her?

"Can you bridge the systems and get copies of those messages?" she asked.

"Already working on it." Kitt indicated a bit of equipment attached to the terminal.

"Working on it, or doing it?"

"Working, but…" Kitt checked a readout on the equipment. "If you give us another five or ten, we'll have it. In the meantime, we're taking images of the code, so even if we can't get the full communication train, we'll have that."

The next eight minutes dragged on forever. Knowing they were this close to getting what they needed made Ekatya even more certain that something was going to go wrong, so she was not surprised when Korelonn said, "We're out of time. Guards are on the move."

"No!" Bellows protested. "We just need another minute."

"You don't have it. Get ready."

Ekatya moved over to Korelonn's station, where two displays showed squads of guards jogging down the corridors. "Those are different uniforms," she said.

He nodded. "And they're carrying different weapons. The grips aren't the same. If I had to guess, I'd say these are the Great Leader's personal troops."

"That does not sound good." Ekatya called Lokomorra. "The situation just went light-speed. We're going to the roof now."

"Confirmed. They'll be ready for your call."

"Serrado out." Raising her voice, she said, "All right, let's go."

All of the others moved to the door except Kitt and Bellows.

"Lieutenant, Ensign, now!"

"Got it!" Kitt crowed. She scrambled to disconnect various cables, while Bellows raced over to the security station.

"We can blind them. I already prepped it." He yanked the loosened cover off the terminal, exposing the equipment beneath, then took a small device from his pocket. A tiny red light began to blink on what Ekatya recognized as an electromagnetic pulse bomb. "Get back," he said.

Ekatya and Korelonn backed away, and Bellows pushed the bomb into the tangle of naked circuitry. He had barely turned around before streamers of sparks arced in all directions from the station. Every display and illuminated switch went dark, not only at that station, but the ones on either side of it as well.

Bellows grinned at Ekatya. "You had the right idea about blowing out their surveillance equipment. It was just more effective here."

She shook her head with a smile. "Well done. But next time, tell me what you're planning. Now let's get moving."

Korelonn checked his pad. "The hall is still clear, but it won't be for long."

They poured out into the dim, quiet corridor and ran. Though they were moving twice as fast, the distance to the stairs seemed four times longer. Ekatya ticked off the landmarks as they flashed past: short corridor, connecting room, longer corridor, connecting room, left turn, and another long corridor…until they rounded the last corner and the stairs were finally in sight.

But between them and the stairs were the lift doors, which were sliding open with an ominous sound.

Four soldiers stepped out, took one look, and pulled their weapons.

"Stop!" one of them bellowed.

Ekatya had known it was too easy. Three stun beads were already in her hand, and she shouted a warning even as she threw them. She let the follow-through spin her in place and dropped to the floor so quickly that she skidded on her knees. Folding into a ball with her chest resting on her thighs, she covered her ears, closed her eyes, and waited.

The percussive force pushed against her back, and when she straightened, the echoes of what had been a deafening blast were still reverberating.

"The other way!" Korelonn shouted. "Move, move!"

She risked a look back. The four soldiers were inert on the floor, but a dozen more were running toward them from much farther down the hall. They would not get to the roof that way.

"Tell me you have other stairs mapped," she said as they ran.

"No. But I have an idea." He was holding his pad, checking for thermal signatures. They rounded a corner, ducked through an intersection, turned another corner, and stopped in front of a door. When he found it locked, Korelonn pressed his pistol against the lock plate and activated a stun charge. At point-blank range, the charge made a dull thud, followed instantly by a higher, metallic sound of something breaking.

With a pained hiss, Korelonn dropped the pistol and shook out his hand. Then he pushed open the door, kicked the pistol inside, and motioned everyone in what appeared to be a conference room. They crowded into the dark room and watched in silence as he carefully closed the door behind them, pulled the nearest chair from the large table, tilted it on its ornate back legs, and jammed it under the handle.

"Clever," Ekatya whispered.

"Learned that in security training," he whispered back. "Works great for these old mechanisms." He picked up his pistol and holstered it, then opened the back pocket on his jacket and pulled out a thin coil of cable.

Ekatya recognized it immediately and looked toward the floor-to-ceiling window. Yes, there was a balcony.

"Ensign Bellows, you're going to love this," she murmured.

They all froze as voices sounded in the hall, muffled through the thick door.

"They didn't go this way! Come on!"

"We need the security cams! What's taking so long?"

"They destroyed the whole system. Nayalam said it won't be fixed tonight."

The voices faded as footsteps pounded away.

Ekatya tapped Korelonn on the arm. "Down, yes?" At his nod, she pulled the others aside and spoke quietly. "They know we're on this floor, but thanks to Ensign Bellows and a well-placed EMP bomb, they can't see us. And they were depending on their security system, so none of them are carrying thermal scanners. We'll go down to the next floor and try for the stairs from there while they're searching for us up here."

Bellows swiveled toward Korelonn, who was testing the window for an alarm. "Oh, no," he groaned.

Ekatya smiled at him. "Don't worry, this will be easier. This time you get a grapnel and a cable."

"We're six floors up!" Kitt stared at the window in horror.

"And in a few minutes we'll be five floors up," Ekatya said. "Lieutenant, you've done this in training. With the exact same equipment."

Gizobasan looked nearly as frightened as Kitt, but she squared her shoulders and gave a short nod. "We can do it."

"You can," Torado said. "There's nothing to it."

"It's easy," Blunt added in her soft voice. "The only hard part is at the very top. The rest is simple."

Korelonn joined them. "Looks like you blew out more than just their video logging system. Their external alarms must have been routed through that terminal as well. Nicely done. Now, listen: I'll go first and lock down the other end. All you have to do is lower yourself a few meters and I'll catch you."

"See?" Ekatya told Bellows. "No swinging this time."

"Thank the Seeders. It was a week before my back stopped hurting."

The balcony was large enough for all of them to look over the edge as Korelonn attached the grapnel to the bottom bar of the railing and tossed the cable down. Though the night was warm, there was enough of a breeze to rattle the cable against the railing below. The sound could not have been that loud, but to Ekatya's ears it seemed like a crash of cymbals advertising their location.

Korelonn climbed over the railing, crouched on the bottom bar, then gripped it with his hands and let his body dangle over the edge. He wrapped his ankles around the cable and let out a soft grunt as he held on to the railing with one hand and grabbed the cable with the other. Then he was fully on the cable, swaying gently back and forth.

Kitt gasped. It did look precarious, Ekatya had to admit. Korelonn was hanging over a six-story drop, and while the aggressively pruned trees below them had looked pleasing enough this afternoon, in the darkness they seemed spiky and menacing.

It felt as if half an hour passed as Korelonn lowered himself hand over hand to the next floor. At one point, he froze in place while a squad of guards raced through the garden below, but none of them looked up, and no spotlight flashed on to mark their balcony. In truth, Ekatya reminded herself, the palace was enormous and the troops had only a vague idea of where they were. Discovery would require sheer luck, and the vagaries of fortune worked both ways.

Kitt made another choked sound when Korelonn reached his destination and began swinging. Again and again he swung, farther out each time, until he let go and landed with a thump on the balcony below them.

Time sped up once more. Korelonn had the cable secured and was motioning Roris down when Ekatya thought of something they should have done earlier. She dashed back into the conference room and began opening cupboards and drawers.

Bellows joined her. "What are you looking for?"

"Something to go between our hands and the cable. Cloth napkins, table protectors, anything flexible but tough enough to withstand the friction. If we have that, we can slide. Otherwise we'll have to go hand over hand."

He started a search on the other side of the room, and Ekatya paused to watch him. He had changed so much from the nervous, starstruck young ensign she had met a year and a half ago.

"Ensign Bellows."

"Hm?" He did not look up from his efforts.

"Before we go back out there, I just want to say…I'm proud of you. You've done a tremendous job tonight. I look forward to seeing what you'll grow into, because I think you'll be a fine officer."

He straightened and turned around. She could not see him well in the darkness, but she thought he looked both surprised and very pleased. "Thank you, Captain. From you, that means everything."

"You're welcome. You've earned it."

They smiled at each other, then turned by unspoken agreement and resumed their search. Ekatya pulled open three more drawers before finding a stack of rectangular cloths that were too small to be napkins and too large to go under glasses. She didn't care what they were, only that they would work.

"Found them." She yanked out a handful and hurried to the balcony.

Roris was already down, and Blunt was just stepping over the railing.

"Trooper Blunt." Ekatya held up two cloths. "Let's speed things up, shall we?"

Blunt smiled at her. "Perfect. Thank you." She lowered herself to the bottom bar, dropped over the edge, and locked her ankles around the cable.

As she lifted one hand from the bottom railing, Ekatya pushed a cloth into it. Blunt wrapped the hand around the cable, adjusted her grip, and held up the other hand. Ekatya gave her another cloth, and a moment later Blunt was sliding. It took perhaps two seconds for her feet to hit the top of the railing below. She went into a crouch, then accepted the assistance of Roris and Korelonn as they pulled her forward and she hopped to the balcony floor.

"That went well," Torado remarked. "You're next, Captain."

"Not yet. Lieutenants Kitt and Gizobasan should go first."

"I was hoping you wouldn't say that." Kitt sighed but climbed over the railing with alacrity. For all her worry, she had little trouble with the descent, which gave Gizobasan more confidence.

A few seconds later, Ekatya was on the cable, sliding so quickly that she had no time to think about the six-story drop below her. Her feet hit the railing with a thump, and she let the momentum bend her knees, allowing her to push forward and make the assisted hop to the balcony.

"Thank you," she said. Roris grinned at her, while Korelonn was already looking up for the next one.

Someone had forced open the window, and the others were gathering inside. Ekatya dropped her cloths onto an armchair and looked around the room. It was an opulent office, with heavy wooden furniture and art covering almost every square centimeter of the walls. Though she could not see much, what she did see made her doubt the owner's taste.

At least it was large enough to house them all without being crowded. Before long, Korelonn shut the window and pushed the armchair in front of it to keep it closed despite the broken lock. He checked the corridor outside with his thermal scanner, and soon they were creeping back toward the approximate location of the stairs.

It was more difficult now. They had not been on this floor and had no idea of the layout. It had smaller rooms than the floor above, as evidenced by the greater number of doors, and many more intersecting corridors. Several times they had to stop and backtrack as corridors curved around and began leading them the wrong direction.

At least the entire floor was dim, quiet, and free of soldiers. Thermal scans continued to show no sign of them.

Korelonn halted at an intersection, facing the dual corridors that both angled toward where they thought the stairs were.

"This is taking too long," Ekatya whispered.

"I know." For the first time that evening, his voice sounded tense. "I think we should split up. One of these has to lead to the stairs. Whoever finds them sends a runner back. No one goes beyond the next intersection."

"Agreed. I'll take Roris, Torado, and Bellows. You take the rest."

"You're not going without security, Captain."

"Fine, I'll take him, too. Let's just do it." Their luck was eroding; she could feel it. They needed to get out now.

Ekatya took her team down the left corridor. With the other three keeping watch ahead and behind, she and Bellows focused on finding the stairs. Each of them walked down one side of the corridor while holding up their pads, using the translation program to decipher the signs on the doors. It was slow going, because of course the palace stairs couldn't have a glass door that made them easy to spot from a distance. Every door was solid wood.

Office…office…office…toilet…parsing room, what the Hades was that? She shook her head and kept walking. Office…office…

"Captain!" It was Bellows, slightly ahead of her. "I found them!"

When she turned, he was opening the door.

"Bellows, no!" She raced over, reaching out to stop him. "Not until you—"

His head vanished in a spray of red mist, the blood and brains spattering the side of her face as she instinctively turned away. She was so close that when his body toppled backward, she could not stop herself quickly enough. He crashed into her, taking her down to the floor beneath him.

A cacophony of noise was exploding overhead, but her world had narrowed down to the soft carpet under her back and the dead weight crushing her chest, trapping her in place. She had to tilt her head away from the arterial blood, which continued to spurt with astonishing force. It hissed against her neck and jaw in pulses, sickeningly warm, running down her skin and into her collar as she struggled to push Bellows off.

Someone shouted. Through her closed eyelids, screwed shut against the spraying blood, she saw a brilliant flash. An explosion roared through her head, leaving behind a stuffy silence broken only by an endless ringing tone.

A stun bead, she knew. Probably a whole handful of them. She hadn't understood the warning call, and even if she had, only one of her hands was free enough to cover her ear. Bellows's body must have protected her from the worst of it, since she was still conscious.

She had just pulled her other hand free when the weight on her chest lifted and friendly hands helped her into a sitting position. The change in angle sent fresh rivulets of blood under her collar and down her chest, where it soaked into her shirt. She shook her head, ridding herself of the excess, and wiped her face and neck. There was so much blood that her hands skated over her skin, sluicing through the fluid.

Finally daring to open her eyes, she saw Roris crouched in front of her, her lips moving. By the expression on her face, she was asking an urgent question.

"I can't hear you," Ekatya said. Or thought she did; it was hard to tell. "But if you're asking if I'm all right, I am."

Roris nodded, then pulled out her pad, spoke into it, and held it up.

The text on the screen read: *We can't use the stairs. There were four soldiers, and we got them all, but the whole building must have heard the fight. They'll have every stair exit blocked now.*

Ekatya looked at the stair door, which was now shut with three bodies piled against it. One of them had no head and wore a Fleet dress uniform. In a perfect example of field practicality, Roris and the others had used Bellows's body to buy them time.

Because they certainly could not take it with them.

"Did you get his insignia?" she asked.

Torado bent down beside Roris and held out his hand. An ensign's insignia gleamed in his palm. Inside the nearly indestructible symbol was a data chip with Bellows's identification and medical record. It was the one thing they always brought back, even if they could not bring the body.

Ekatya rose to her feet. She was slightly wobbly; her balance would be compromised until her hearing returned. "Call Commander Lokomorra. Tell him it's now a worst-case situation. We'll have to evacuate from a balcony on the front of the building, fifth floor. Tell him weapons hot, and that goes for our team as well. We are not losing anyone else."

With one last look at the headless body of Ensign Bellows, she turned and led her team back the way they had come.

CHAPTER 30
Evacuation

By the time the landing team had barricaded themselves inside a likely-looking room for evacuation—one far from the stairs, down a small side corridor they hoped would not attract any searchers just yet—Ekatya's hearing was beginning to return. This was a profound relief, given that evacuation would involve jumping from the balcony railing into the open cargo bay door of the shuttle. She had not been looking forward to attempting that with compromised balance.

Her mind was ticking over the details of what was about to happen and how she could keep the rest of her team safe. She could not think about the fact that she had already failed. The death of Ensign Bellows was in the past; her team's safe return was still in the future. She would not allow her mind to return to that terrible moment when she had been reaching for his shoulder and watched his head disappear.

If only she had been one second faster. Just one Shipper-damned second.

Roris stepped into her line of view, a concerned look on her face. "Captain? Can you hear me yet?"

Ekatya nodded. "You sound like you're at the other end of a tunnel, but yes. How long?"

"Three minutes. The shuttle and fighters are already coming under ground fire, but they've got nothing that can penetrate our shields. Their aerial support isn't here yet. I'm hoping we can get out before it arrives."

"Well, we're due a bit of luck, aren't we?" Ekatya didn't wait for an answer before going to the window.

The side corridor, it turned out, led to a spacious office occupying one of the palace's towers. That in itself was lucky; it meant the room and its balcony jutted out from the main facade of the building. The shuttle pilot would have more room to get into position, and the fighters would have an easier time blocking them in.

This balcony was three times the size of the one they had entered from, but the railing was the same. She eyed the narrow top bar and then turned to examine the room. It was full of ornate, heavy furniture that could not be easily moved, but in their case, heavy was a benefit. They had already upended the immense desk and used it as the main prop in their barricade, which now resembled something left behind by an earthquake.

But they had not used that table along the back wall, with its crystalline decanters and glasses. It was too slight for the barricade, but perfect for her purposes. She walked over and began moving decanters to the floor. "Help me clear this off," she said. "We'll carry it out to the railing and use it for a launch pad."

Lieutenant Gizobasan was at her side in a moment, and between the two of them, they cleared the table in seconds. Torado and Korelonn each took one end and carefully maneuvered it out to the balcony, while Ekatya held open the door.

She had judged accurately; the top of the table was only a few centimeters below the top of the railing. With a satisfied nod, she went back in the room and picked up a cloth-covered footstool that sat forlornly in a corner. The high-backed, overstuffed chair it belonged to was in the barricade.

Once she had positioned the footstool in front of the table, she backed up two steps and took a trial run. The stool was a little too soft to make the perfect springboard, but it was easier than scrambling up from the ground.

When she reentered the room, she said, "I want this to go off as quickly as possible. We're going to form a line right now. Wait only until the person before you has jumped, and then you run. That means when you land in the cargo bay, you get the Hades out of the way so the next person has landing room. Understood?"

They all nodded.

"Captain, I think you should—"

"I'll go first," she interrupted Korelonn. "That was what you were going to say, wasn't it?"

"I think we'll all feel better when you're in that shuttle."

"And it didn't occur to you that the first person has the greatest chance of a problem?" She smiled at his fallen expression. "Too late, I'm going first. I want you to bring up the rear, so you can respond to any threats that might come from that door." She indicated the barricaded door of the office. "Everyone else, choose your spots. Do it now."

She stood in front of the window, arms crossed as the other eight arranged themselves in a line. It didn't surprise her that Roris joined the two security officers at the rear, pushing the rest of her team in front of her. Right behind Ekatya were Kitt and Gizobasan.

Kitt looked at her with a nervous smile. "Can't be as hard as sliding down a cable, right?"

"No, it's much easier," Ekatya said. "And faster."

She heard a welcome sound then and blessed her functioning ears for the forewarning. The shuttle swung around the farthest corner of the palace and came toward them, flying in formation with the three fighters bracketing it above and on both sides. A single click in her head heralded an incoming call, one that did not wait for acknowledgment.

"Lieutenant Delafield to Captain Serrado. Can you hear me?"

"My hearing is fine," she said. "Com, open call to landing team, mute unless tapped." A soft chime confirmed that the others could now listen in, with an option to speak if they needed to. "Do you see our little party setup on the balcony?"

"I don't—ah, yes, I do. Good idea." The shuttle and its accompanying fighters came to a stop right in front of her and hovered as each craft smoothly turned in place to face outward. *"Captain, be warned that we've been taking fire from palace windows. They're following us. The fighters will do their best to shield you."*

"Understood."

"Opening doors now."

The cargo bay doors slid open, exposing the well-lit, empty bay. Slowly, the shuttle backed toward the balcony, maneuvering so that the cargo bay deck was slightly below the level of the railing. The fighters moved in synchrony with it, keeping themselves and their shields between the balcony and a possible attack.

"Dropping rear shield."

Close enough.

"I'm going," she announced. Moving at a fast trot, she crossed the balcony, sprang from the footstool to the tabletop, and jumped before she could focus on the empty space yawning between the railing and the edge of the cargo bay. She hit the deck hard and tucked into a roll, then bounced up and ran for the weapon rack next to the passenger compartment entry. "I'm in," she said as she yanked a pulse rifle from the rack.

"Captain, they're already here." That was Korelonn. "Some are trying to break our barricade, but I can hear others moving into the next rooms. Sounds like two squads at least."

"I'll provide cover fire. Change of plans, everyone. Nobody goes until I call it. Kitt, are you ready?" At the open bay door, she braced herself against the left edge and brought the rifle to her shoulder.

"Ready."

The shields of the fighters were phasing in and out of the visual spectrum, proof of the weaponry that was bouncing off them. The Halaamans were not giving up. Though the fighters could block anything from above and most things from the sides, the two closest offices were inside their shield coverage. Ekatya was all her team had.

She sent three shots into each office window, shattering them both.

"Kitt, go!"

Just as Kitt hit the table, Ekatya saw movement at the window to the right. She sighted in on what appeared to be a uniformed shoulder, waited half a second for the blur of Kitt to flash across her view, and fired.

Kitt thumped into the bay with a small scream. "Shit!"

"You're all right." Ekatya sent another burst of shots into each window and detected no movement. "Clear. Go!"

It was not Gizobasan who came next, but Blunt, her white ponytail streaming out behind her as she ran.

"Dammit!" A soldier had appeared in the left window, and Blunt was exposed. Ekatya didn't sight in; there was no time. She swung and fired instinctively, holding the trigger long enough to make sure everyone in that room got down and stayed down.

Paying no attention to the weapons fire, Blunt soared through the air and hit the deck. She had hardly landed before she joined Ekatya at the other edge of the door, pulse rifle in hand. Her colorless eyes held a fierce expression. "I'll get this side."

"Understood."

Relieved from the burden of covering both windows, Ekatya settled into hunting mode. Shooting defensively was not good enough; she needed these soldiers neutralized. She scanned the part of the room that she could see through the open window. "Clear on my side."

"Wait," Blunt said. She fired a moment later, then called, "Clear! Go!"

Now Gizobasan came, running with a fearful look on her face. A small cry indicated a bad landing, but that was better than being shot.

Without looking, Ekatya said, "Kitt, help her out of the way." She had barely spoken when three bald heads appeared in her magnified view. Her shot blew the center one backward; the other two dove to the sides. "Clear!"

Blunt fired twice. "Clear!"

"Go!" Ekatya called.

Ennserhofen raced across the balcony and hardly seemed to touch the table before he was arcing into the cargo bay.

"Need any more help?" he asked from behind them.

"No room. Help the others if they need it. Wait!" Ekatya called as a head slid into her view. The soldier was crawling on the floor toward the window, hoping to escape notice. She set her crosshairs directly on the tattooed spots of his head, exhaled, and pulled the trigger. The spots and most of the head vanished.

"That was for Bellows," she muttered, scanning the rest of the visible room. "Clear."

"Clear," Blunt echoed.

"Go!"

Torado came flying in. "Someone is screaming on Blunt's side," he said. "He sounds pretty scared."

"Good. Scared soldiers have bad aim." Ekatya saw no movement in her room but fired twice just in case. Beside her, Blunt did the same.

"Clear," they said simultaneously.

"Go!" Ekatya called.

Roris jumped so far that she was halfway into the cargo bay before she hit the deck. Ekatya heard her thump into the bulkhead as she rolled out.

"A little too enthusiastic there," Torado said.

"Shut it. I'm in, aren't I?"

"Wait," Ekatya said as another head popped into her view. "They're persistent, I'll give them that." She took a second to steady her aim, then pulled the trigger. The body dropped to the floor.

"Go!"

Either she had killed everyone in that room, or whoever was left had given up. Nothing stirred while the two security officers jumped in quick succession. The moment Korelonn was in, she hit the manual control for the door and breathed a sigh of relief as the two halves sealed themselves shut.

"Delafield, we're all in. Get us out of here."

"Confirmed. Hold on tight."

She wrapped her hand through the nearest grab strap just as the deck tilted under her feet. A growing engine throb filled her ears.

"Com, end open channel." She looked around the eight tired faces lining the bay. Some seemed shocked, others simply relieved. Gizobasan sat on the floor with one leg tucked up and the other out straight.

"Can I pass this back?" Blunt asked, holding out her rifle to Roris.

Ekatya had forgotten she was still holding hers. She passed it off to Korelonn and watched as both rifles made their way into the rack.

The deck suddenly went out from under their feet, sending everyone crashing against the bulkheads. Only their grab straps kept them from flying through the air. As the shuttle leveled and they all found their footing again, Delafield's voice came over the bay com.

"Sorry, everyone. One of those crazy torquats just tried to ram us. I guess they got tired of their ammunition bouncing off our shields. They really do not want us to leave."

"A suicide pilot?" Ekatya asked incredulously. "What the Hades is in those files?"

"I don't know." Kitt scowled. "But I'll work day and night until I find out. I owe that to Ensign Bellows. He could have decrypted these files in an hour; he'd already done it once. It'll probably take me a week. But I'll find out. I'll—" She stopped, her jaw tight and eyes shining with tears.

"I know," Ekatya said. "Lieutenant Kitt, decrypting those files is your top priority. You have no other duties until you finish that job. I'll inform Commander Kenji of your assignment."

Kitt looked at her gratefully. "Thank you, Captain."

A few minutes later, Delafield informed them that he had outpaced the chasing Halaaman fighters and they could release their grab straps. *"Since you're my cargo, I can save you a trip to the decon chamber,"* he added. *"If that's your preference, Captain?"*

"Yes, good idea." Ekatya spoke in a slightly louder tone to reach the bay coms. "Positions, everyone, and it looks like Lieutenant Gizobasan could use some assistance."

Torado helped Gizobasan back to her feet, and they all stood with legs spread, arms above their heads, and eyes closed.

"Ready," Ekatya called out.

"Activating decon now," Delafield said.

A warning klaxon sounded, followed by the shuttle computer's voice. "Commencing cargo bay biohazard decontamination in five seconds…four…three…two…one…begin."

Once again, light filtered through Ekatya's eyelids, but this was not the overwhelming flash of a stun bead. Instead, a faint blue glow came and went as the sterilizing beams moved through the cargo bay. She had watched it enough times from outside the decon chamber to know exactly how it looked: planes of deep blue light passing over everything in the room and from all directions. A direct hit on her face made her wince and screw her eyes shut even more tightly. They were all inoculated against the various forms of radiation in those beams, but direct exposure of sensitive eye tissues was never a good idea.

She had read stories of the early spacefaring days, when decon involved stripping to the skin and being scrubbed down by a team of specialists in tightly sealed suits. It was time-consuming and inefficient, given the number of biohazards that regularly seemed to survive the process—and not something she would ever want to participate in while surrounded by the crew she was commanding.

The blue glow died away; the computer announced the completion of the process, and they all filed into the passenger compartment. Ekatya took the copilot's seat, appreciating both the view and the cushion. "This is quite a bit more comfortable than banging around the cargo bay," she said.

Delafield glanced at her and then did a double take. "Captain Serrado, are you all right?"

"Yes, why?"

"You…" He gestured toward his own face, at a loss for words.

It was only then that Ekatya realized what she must look like. "It's not mine," she said shortly.

Her tone of voice must have warned him off. Other than mission updates and calls to the *Phoenix*, he did not speak again for the rest of their flight.

As planned, Commander Lokomorra had brought the *Phoenix* nearly into the stratosphere to cut down on their escape time. He called Ekatya and

Delafield on the quantum com, looking harassed. To his credit, he did not even raise his eyebrows upon seeing Ekatya's bloody face.

"We're under heavy fire from three warships, but their weapons can't penetrate our shields. I'm getting very irritated, Captain. They won't listen to reason. I'm starting to think about hitting one of them just to get their attention. At this rate, we won't be able to get you and the fighters into the bays."

"Tell them exactly that," Ekatya said. "Tell them that we only want to leave their space, but you will not hesitate to return fire on the next ship that fires on you. Say that you would prefer to leave peacefully, but the decision is up to them. And then act on it."

Five minutes passed before the com lit up again.

"They're moving to a safer distance," Lokomorra said. "It took some fireworks to make it happen. One of them is flying a little more slowly since we took out their starboard engine."

"Well done, Commander. Any contact from the Great Leader?"

"Yes, he's demanding that you return their stolen property and apologize for your grievous breach of courtesy, as well as face charges for multiple murders."

Ekatya's smile was cold. "I'd admit to the stolen property part, but we were the ones using nonlethal force until they were discourteous enough to try to kill our entire landing team. Are we clear for entry?"

"You are. Come home, Captain."

"With pleasure. Get us out of this system the moment we touch down."

When they reached the *Phoenix*, the Halaaman warships were far enough away to pose no threat. Which was not to say they didn't try. Each of them launched missiles, but their missile propulsion was slow and the *Phoenix* had no trouble neutralizing them before they got anywhere near the escapees.

The fighters peeled off for their bay on the port side, while Delafield flew directly over the surf engines to enter the shuttle bay at the ship's stern.

Ekatya watched the sides of the tunnel slide past, the guidance lights on its walls flashing a pattern that led them forward. They emerged into the cavernous shuttle bay, flew over a row of parked shuttles, and settled down in the one open space. As the engines spun down and the ground crew rushed to lock the landing clamps in place, Delafield informed Lokomorra of their safe arrival. It was all so very normal. Ekatya dropped her head back against the seat and breathed easily for the first time in what felt like days.

Home, Lokomorra had said. Home.

Exiting through the passenger door inspired a comment from Kitt that leaving was easier than boarding, but otherwise the group was quiet as they walked across the deck. Torado stepped up next to Ekatya and held out his hand. "Captain?"

A shining ensign's insignia sat in his palm. She picked it up and tucked it into her chest pocket. "Thank you, Trooper Torado."

He nodded and dropped back, letting her lead the group out. When they passed through the door into the comfortable quiet of the interior corridor, Ekatya stopped them.

"I know we're all weary and heartsick," she said. "Ensign Bellows was a good officer and a fine young man. But he gave his life for a purpose. We will make certain that it wasn't wasted."

She glanced at Lieutenant Kitt, who was nodding.

"You all have tomorrow off. Record your reports and then take some time for yourselves. Remember that there are people on this ship you can talk to. They understand, and they can help. I'll tell the chief surgeon what happened. She will inform her psychologists, and if you choose to speak with someone, they'll already know why you're there. You won't have to explain."

She looked around the group and gave a single nod. "Take care of yourselves, and take care of each other. Lieutenant Gizobasan, report to the medbay and get that ankle looked at."

"Yes, Captain."

"Well done, everyone. Dismissed."

She watched them walk away, then turned in the opposite direction.

It felt healing, walking through these corridors. She had always loved the Pulsar design, with its beautiful mix of artistic aesthetics and practicality. The ceilings were higher than on many ships, giving a sense of open space that enhanced the crew's mental health and productivity. The arched doorways were a nod toward pure aesthetics, but the plantings that adorned them were entirely practical, an efficient means of carbon scrubbing and oxygen production. Flowering plants stood in softly lit alcoves, mostly Filessian orchids but several other species as well. All of them had been chosen not just for hardiness but also for their specific blend of scents, which neutralized the often metallic, stale smell of machinery and recycled air. Ekatya took a deep breath, enjoying the unique Pulsar scent: woodsy, ever so slightly floral, always fresh.

Between the flower alcoves were mosaics of colored tiles, lit by recessed spotlights in the ceiling. Every Pulsar-class ship had different mosaics, created by artists who competed for the honor. Ekatya had spent years wandering the corridors of the *Caphenon*, getting acquainted with the hundreds of mosaics that graced it. Now she had new ones to learn.

She paused in front of one, its abstract pattern of blues and grays reminding her of the ocean back home on a rainy day. She lost track of time as she stood there until the soft click sounded in her head and she heard an unwelcome voice.

"Captain Serrado, this is Dr. Wells."

Wells sounded irritated, and she had not offered the courtesy of a double-click call. Ekatya would have appreciated being able to answer when she was ready. Or not at all.

She reminded herself that she was still on duty and thus subject to instant access calls. "Yes, Dr. Wells."

"May I ask where you're going? Because your locator shows that you're not on your way here."

"I'm going to my quarters, Doctor. To take a much-needed shower. Is there anything else about my personal plans that you need to know?"

"Captain, you've just returned from a mission in which you were injured. I didn't think I'd need to remind you of protocol."

"I'm perfectly aware of protocol, thank you. My injuries were minor. I think they can wait until I've showered."

"If I had a bar chit for every time I heard some variation of that, I'd be an alcoholic. Report to the medbay, Captain." She cut the call.

Ekatya clenched her jaw in sudden fury. "You picked the wrong day for that, Wells."

Her anger had not abated when she stormed into the medbay, finding Dr. Wells waiting for her at the entrance.

Wells took one look at her and nearly dropped her medpad. "Slight injuries? How are you even walking? Come on, let's get you treated." She reached for Ekatya's upper arm and began guiding her toward the nearest treatment room.

Ekatya yanked her arm up and away. "Do *not* touch me without permission," she snarled.

Wells frowned. "Captain, I need to—"

"You need to *think* before you speak to me, and especially in that tone of voice. I didn't get shot; Ensign Bellows did. I'm just the one who caught his body. This is his blood, and his brains are probably in my hair if you want to take a sample."

Wells stood frozen, her jaw slack. "Oh, stars. Captain Serrado—I'm sorry."

Ekatya spun on her heel and stalked into the treatment room. She was already sitting on the bed when Wells entered.

The doctor was silent while she shut the door and activated the privacy screen. As the transparent wall turned opaque, she said, "Please accept my apology."

"Why should I? You wouldn't accept mine."

Wells sighed. "And that was a mistake. I should have."

"What convenient timing."

"Look, Captain—"

"I would like you to finish my examination, as your precious protocol demands, and let me get back to my quarters so I can wash Ensign Bellows's blood and brains off of me. That's all I need, so if you would just get to it without any unnecessary conversation?"

Wells bowed her head. "I understand you were affected by a stun bead explosion."

"More like half a dozen of them, but since Ensign Bellows's dying act was to helpfully fall on top of me and shield me, I don't have any lasting effects."

"Oh, for the love of flight! Captain, stop, please!" Wells held up her hands, palms outward. "Truce. I call a truce. Please? This is… I just want to help you."

Ekatya's fury drained away, leaving her defenseless against the sympathy in the doctor's eyes.

"Fine," she muttered. It was the most she could manage through the constriction in her throat.

Dr. Wells opened a drawer and picked up a small probe. "I need to assess the possible damage to your ears. I'll have to touch you to do that. Do I have your permission?"

Ekatya nodded, then closed her eyes against the gentle press of hands on her head. Something pushed into her ear.

"Your eardrum looks fine," Wells said softly. "Please tell me if you can hear this."

A tone sounded, deep inside her head.

"I can hear it."

"Good. Tell me when you can't hear it anymore."

The tone rose in pitch, higher and higher, until it vanished.

"It's gone."

"Very good. You haven't lost anything on that side. I'm moving to your other ear now."

Ekatya hated the careful way Dr. Wells was treating her, as if she were fragile and on the verge of shattering. But she had asked for it—no, demanded it. Wells could hardly behave any other way.

Her other ear was pronounced in good shape. She held up her head and stared into a too-bright light as her vision was assessed, then demonstrated her ability to visually track an object.

Dr. Wells stepped back. "Did you lose consciousness?"

"No."

"Any dizziness, headache, nausea?"

She shook her head.

"All right. I need you to take off your jacket now."

It should have been easy. Just unfasten the six tabs holding it shut and pull it off. But her fingers had developed a pronounced tremble, as well as an appalling weakness, and she could not get the first tab open. She tried again and again, yanking at the throat guard and getting more upset with every passing second.

"Will you allow me to help?" Dr. Wells asked.

She wanted to refuse. She wanted to shout at her, to tell her not to treat her like a damned victim, but the words would not come. Instead, she nodded and dropped her hands to her sides.

Wells pulled the tabs with infuriating ease, her hands steady and strong. When she opened the jacket, her intake of breath was audible.

"It's not mine," Ekatya said. For some reason, this seemed to be an important point.

"Is it all right if I make sure of that?"

"How much is there?"

"There's…a lot."

"I felt it, you know. When they pulled me upright, I felt it going down my collar. But I didn't pay much attention, because I was trying to get it off my face. I couldn't even open my eyes—" A laugh tore out of her, and she clapped a hand over her mouth. "Shippers, it isn't funny. I didn't mean—"

Dr. Wells looked pained. "I understand."

"You can't possibly understand."

"I've had people die in my arms, too."

"He didn't. He died before that. They blew his head off. That's why there's so much blood, because his heart was pumping it out and it was all landing on me. But he died before I caught him. He died because I was one second too late. I tried, Dr. Wells. I tried to stop him. I *knew* something was going to go wrong, and when I saw him opening that door—" Her breath caught. "I tried."

"I know," Wells said. "I know you did."

Ekatya let her head fall back and took a shuddering breath. "Please finish this examination."

"I will. But first I think we need to get rid of this shirt. May I take it off?"

At Ekatya's silent nod, Wells untucked the shirt and pulled it over her head. It was only then that Ekatya realized it was still damp; the material felt slimy as it peeled off her skin. She took the white hand towel Wells offered and refused to look as she rubbed her chest dry and attempted to clean her face. The blood there had already dried, so she shrugged and held out the towel.

"There's a wet patch in your hair, if you don't mind my help with that."

Again Ekatya nodded. Her words had run dry.

She felt Dr. Wells dabbing at a spot on the side of her head and knew it was not blood she was removing. Wells threw the towel into the laundry chute in the corner of the room, pulled a medshirt out of a cupboard above it, and helped Ekatya put her arms through the sleeves.

"I'll close it when we're finished," she said.

She went through the remainder of the exam swiftly and with a gentleness that almost hurt, always explaining what she was going to do before she did it. True to her word, she sealed the shirt when she was done, then helped Ekatya put on her jacket and refastened the tabs. She had not even asked. Somehow she had known Ekatya would not want to walk through her ship in a medshirt, even when the only alternative was a blood-soaked jacket.

"We're done," she said, stepping back. "You can go take that shower now."

Ekatya could not meet her eyes. She pushed herself off the bed and walked out without a word.

CHAPTER 31
Iceflame

EVERY STITCH OF CLOTHING SHE had on went straight into the recycle chute. Ekatya paused only long enough to remove the ensign's insignia and leftover stun beads from her jacket pockets before stripping and throwing the whole bundle in. She would need to have another dress uniform tailored, but she would have paid for fifty new uniforms rather than wear that one ever again.

She started the shower with cool water, wondering if normal people knew that dried blood came off skin more easily in lower temperatures. When she stepped under the spray, the entire shower floor turned pink. The odor that rose from her hair and skin was so strong that she wasn't sure if she was smelling it or tasting it.

After the first rinse, she turned the temperature as hot as she could stand and scrubbed her skin raw. It took two applications of shampoo before the water ran clean, and she silently thanked Dr. Wells for making that part easier than it might have been.

Dressed once more in a standard uniform, she sat down at her desk and composed a report to Dr. Wells explaining what had happened and why she thought psychological services might be particularly necessary for two team members. A second report, focused on the chronological events and performance evaluations of each member, was logged with personnel and simultaneously added to her official log. She still needed to debrief with the team and suspected she would be awarding commendations to several of them. She had no idea what had happened during the firefight at the stair entrance, or how it had been decided that Trooper Blunt would be the one to stand at the cargo bay door, providing cover fire.

Next she notified Commander Kenji of Lieutenant Kitt's current task priority. A quick check of the ship's status confirmed that they were traveling back toward the base space relay at L five point five. Halaama was well behind them.

Her immediate duties done, she called up the forward sensors on her display and sat on her couch, watching the view. She needed to make her report to Sholokhov, but at the moment she did not see how she could do it without saying something that would destroy her career.

As she stared at the star field, her mind went back to the moment of Ensign Bellows's death. Again and again she watched herself reaching out, just before his head exploded. She had seen many things in her career, but never before had death been that close and that personal. Her skin was clean now, but she still felt the blood spraying.

The thought hit with such force that it brought her up straight. She wasted no time putting a call through to Warrant Officer Roris's quarters.

It was answered quickly. "Yes, Captain?"

"How did they kill Ensign Bellows?" She saw the confused expression and realized how that had sounded. "I mean, what weapon did they use? They had leadslingers. Unless their ammunition was the size of my big toe, it wouldn't do that."

Roris's face cleared. "No, it wasn't a leadslinger. Those soldiers were different. Different uniforms, different weapons. Torado and I took them from the ones we pulled through the door. Wait, I'll get it."

She vanished from the screen and reappeared a few seconds later. "Here it is. We figured they designed these for use in their ships. Though why they haven't distributed them to all of their guards, I don't know."

Ekatya stared at the ugly blaster in her hand. "I need you to bring that to my quarters."

"Do you want the other one, too? I can get it from Torado."

"No, one is fine."

Within ten minutes, she had the blaster on her desk and Sholokhov on her quantum com. As usual, he wasted no time on greetings or courtesy.

"Captain Serrado, what did you find out?"

"What you already knew. The Guild is Elin Frank."

He sat back in his office chair. "So it *was* him. I didn't know for certain, but as soon as you reported on the lack of Voloth presence, he was my first suspect. You have proof?"

"I have correspondence with the Great Leader, encrypted with Frank's system. We haven't decrypted it yet."

He leaned forward again. "That is your top priority. I expect a full report the moment you have that data in the clear."

She made no response, simply watching him for several seconds as he began to frown. At last she said, "You really don't know the first thing about Fleet operations, do you?"

"What?" His shaggy gray eyebrows drew together. "Captain, I am giving you an order."

"Yes, I heard your order. What I didn't hear was any indication that you know the protocol for a commanding officer. When you send a team on a mission and the team leader reports back, it is *customary*," she spat the word, "to inquire after the welfare of that team before asking for results."

"Ah. I presume from this that not everyone returned unharmed."

"You're not going to get those files decrypted as quickly as you want. The only member of my crew who knew Frank's encryption system was Ensign Bellows, and he's dead."

"I'm very sorry to hear that," he said in an approximation of sympathy. "But it's clear that he performed admirably before his death, since you know about Frank."

"You are something else." Ekatya suddenly felt weary beyond measure. "We're working on the files. It will take at least a week. In the meantime, I do have other proof." She held up the blaster. "Frank tried to sell these to Fleet, but we weren't buying. He has one on display in his personal collection, in his house. He bragged to me about its stopping power. I can attest to the truth of that brag, because I saw it in action. This is the weapon that a Halaaman soldier used to kill Ensign Bellows."

For once, Sholokhov showed a genuine emotion. "Frank has *already* sold weapons to the Halaamans? That...surprises me. Captain, you've done well. That blaster is all I need to get started. Send me a scan of it, and have it checked for atomic markers to establish its planetary provenance. If those are already out there, then another shipment may be on its way. I want you to hold position outside the Lexihari system while you decrypt those files, and we take care of business on our end. I may have another assignment for you."

"Wonderful, I can't wait," she said. "At least I don't have any more inexperienced ensigns you can send out to die."

He paused. "I understand you're upset, Captain, so I'll ignore that. But don't do it again."

The screen returned to the priority blue emblem. She stared at it, then set the blaster back on her desk.

"The galaxy would be a better place if it had been you," she muttered.

She passed the orders to Lokomorra and watched her wall display as the star field shifted, rolling to the left. When the stars ceased moving, she changed the display to the video Lhyn had taken from the east bank of the Fahlinor River. The broad river flowed in the foreground, while across the water lay the manicured lawns and landscaping of Blacksun's State Park. Beyond was a forest broken by the tops of eight buildings: the six caste houses, each with a domed roof of a different color, and the even larger domes of the State House and Blacksun Temple. Through some bit of data wizardry, she could not see the shift when the recording looped. The water flow was uninterrupted and always different. She had spent hours upon hours with this scene on her display, and other than the large purple bird that drifted down the river now and again, she never saw the same thing more than once.

Letting the sound of the river soothe her frayed nerves, she took advantage of one of the best perks given executive officers: her personal matter printer. Lower ranks and noncoms ate in one of the messes on board or bought meals in one of the restaurants, but she had the option of eating in her quarters. Rarely had she appreciated that more than today, when she could not bear the thought of interacting with one more person—other than Lhyn or Andira, both of whom she fervently wished were here. Lhyn would know that this was not a time for questions and would provide comfort merely by her presence. And Andira wouldn't need to ask. She would understand.

But Ekatya couldn't talk to either of them for another three days, and given the distances and number of base space relays involved, she would have to choose one or the other. Right now, she wanted comfort more than understanding.

After a dinner she hardly tasted, she sat on the couch with a glass of iceflame in her hand. It was cold going in, hot going down, and exactly what she needed.

"Phoenix, play Kyrie Razinfin, Flight of the Return. Volume level eight."

It seemed the best way she could honor Ensign Bellows. She had no body to take back to his parents. He had been too new for a memorial to have any real effect. She would give one, of course, but he had been aboard for less than three weeks. Ninety-eight percent of her crew had never heard his name.

But the Alseans could mourn the loss even of those they did not know. So she sat with her eyes closed and listened to Alsea's most famous vocalist sing the lament she had first heard in a stadium packed with fifty thousand people. When the tears began to flow, she did not try to hold them back.

"For Fahla and Alsea," she murmured when the song made its triumphant finish. "Or in your case, for the Seeders and the Protectorate. If I had a sword, I'd raise it for you. You deserved so much better."

The sound of the river rose again, filling her quarters with its soothing voice. It had almost lulled her to sleep when her entrance bell rang.

She startled upright and hoped enough time had passed to erase the signs of her weeping. Her self-consciousness only increased upon finding Dr. Wells at her door.

"I come in peace," Wells said before Ekatya could utter a word. "And bearing gifts." She held up a bottle of liquid, clear on the top half and red on the bottom.

Ekatya felt an unwilling smile crack her face. "Iceflame?"

"Good for special occasions." Wells was still in uniform, but her hair was out of its twist and draped halfway down her back. It was a careful statement, Ekatya thought: not quite casual, but not on duty either.

She stepped back and watched the doctor walk in. "Have a seat. I'll get another glass."

Wells set the bottle on the coffee table and sat on the couch. "That's beautiful," she said, indicating the display on the opposite wall. "Where is it?"

"Alsea." The short answer invited no questions; Ekatya was not in the mood. On her way to the kitchen, she stripped off her uniform jacket and hung it across the back of her desk chair.

"I know you've eaten," Wells said, "so I thought it was time for the next phase of treatment."

Of course she had monitored her matter printer usage. "Then this is an official visit?" she asked, pulling a glass from behind its polished wooden brace.

"Yes. I'm here to officially get us both drunk."

"And you think that will help?" Ekatya sat on the couch and offered the glass.

Wells looked her in the eye as she accepted it. "I think it's the only thing that will." She shook the bottle, blending the two liquors, then filled both glasses and held hers up. "To Ensign Bellows."

Ekatya clenched her jaw against the tears she had so recently shed. "To Ensign Bellows." She downed the drink in a gulp, shivering at the freeze in her mouth that turned into a roaring flame in her throat. The heat evaporated the tears, leaving her calmer and less afraid of looking vulnerable. Without a word, she held out her glass.

Wells shook the bottle and poured again.

"To fresh starts," Ekatya said.

Wells smiled. "To fresh starts."

On their third shot, Wells proposed a toast to "my idea of the afterlife: a place with no Sholokhovs, and where being right isn't a complete fuck."

Ekatya nearly inhaled the drink she had just brought to her lips. When she got over the burn of that one—three in a row really did increase the heat factor—she said, "I have never in my life wished so hard to be wrong."

"I believe you. You told me this would happen back when I changed your language chip."

"Yes, but even then I never dreamed it would happen like that. Fucking Hades, what a horror. He was so—" She paused, remembering. "He enjoyed that mission. I keep seeing him smiling. And I told him I was proud of him. Fifteen minutes before he died."

"Then he died happy and proud," Wells said gently. "I read your report. He never knew what hit him. He never had a chance to be afraid. It was completely painless. He had a good mission, he made his captain proud—he was cut down too soon, but Captain, I have seen a lot of people die. There is no kinder death than what happened to him. If I could choose my own death, I would choose something like that."

Ekatya had not thought of it that way. She swallowed hard and held out her glass.

"One more, and then we need to slow down." Wells refilled their glasses.

"I thought you came here to officially get us drunk?"

"I said slow down, not stop." She handed over Ekatya's glass, held up her own, and said, "To caring captains who make their crew proud. I'm thrilled to be serving with one."

Ekatya choked, then threw down the drink in a desperate effort not to cry.

Iceflame really was effective. By the time that one hit her stomach, the water in her eyes was from pain. "Shekking Mother," she gasped. "That hurt."

"My language chips didn't work for that." Wells looked amused. "But it sounded…emphatic."

"It's an Alsean curse. It worked its way into my vocabulary."

"Shekking," Wells repeated in an experimental tone.

Ekatya chuckled to hear her say it. "The second word means mother, which is a reference to their goddess. Shekking Mother is about as nasty as you can get. It's a religious and sexual profanity."

"Oh, those are the best."

"Aren't they? Almost makes me wish I were religious."

Wells's laugh was a little scratchy, most likely from the alcohol, and it set Ekatya at ease. She turned sideways on the couch, facing her guest with one bent leg resting on the cushion. "Thank you for coming. And that is not something I expected to say when I saw you at my door."

"I know. That's why I brought the iceflame." Wells turned and settled back as well, reminding Ekatya once again of a lounging cat with her slanted green eyes and high cheekbones. "Captain, I'd like to take this moment to officially accept your apology. If you're still offering it."

"It was always out there. And I accept yours as well. I was…not myself."

"No, you weren't. But you had a giant excuse, which I understood as soon as you told me where all that blood came from. I'm afraid I was trying to make a point when I called you. I just picked a terrible time to do it."

"Did you ever." Ekatya found that she could talk about it now without foaming at the mouth, something she would not have believed possible twenty minutes ago. "I knew you were making a point. That's why I was so angry. It's the same point Sholokhov keeps making with me, over and over—that I'm not the one with the power."

Wells shook her head. "No. No, what a sewage sump this whole thing has been. I wasn't trying to tell you that you didn't have any power. I was trying to assert the little bit that I can claim. I thought you were doing what so many of my captains have done—ignore the protocols they make everyone else follow and try to show me that I'm just one more member of the executive staff. Most captains hate the power of the chief surgeon. We're the only ones who can tell you what to do. And after what you said when I installed your language chip, about holding a grudge…" She shrugged. "I thought you didn't respect me. I misread you because I hadn't gotten past the sartasin fever order. And that's entirely on me."

Suddenly, Ekatya saw that conversation far more clearly. She had indeed been ignoring protocol, and if her relationship with her chief surgeon had been healthy, it would not have been an issue. They needed to fix this.

"No, it's not," she said. "It's on Sholokhov. He did this to both of us."

"Let me take responsibility for my own stupidity, all right?"

Ekatya looked at her seriously. "I don't recruit stupid officers. And it is on Sholokhov, because he poisoned the well we were both drinking from. It seems to have taken a bottle of that to counteract the poison." She pointed at the half-empty bottle. "You were the one smart enough to see that, and to bring it here in spite of our last interaction."

"I'm starting to understand why you have the reputation you do," Wells said. "I hope someday you'll tell me what you told Bellows."

Remembering her early days with Bellows, Ekatya had to smile. "You're getting there faster than he did. Poor Bellows. He spent his first six months tiptoeing around me because I thought he was a spy for Sholokhov and—oh, Shippers." She stared at Wells. "He's done this to me *twice*. Or I've done it to myself. I'm an idiot."

"Well, if I'm not stupid, you're certainly not an idiot."

A silence fell between them then, but it was not uncomfortable. The thrumming song of the Fahlinor River helped, and probably the iceflame, but Ekatya thought it might also have to do with the doctor who had braved the fire-breathing captain in her den.

"Do you know," she said, "for a while today, I thought I might have killed him."

Dr. Wells did not look surprised or horrified, nor did she immediately negate the statement. She simply tilted her head to one side and asked, "How?"

"When I told him I was proud of him, I thought maybe I made him overconfident; maybe I shouldn't have said anything until after the mission was over. But then I remembered—he made the same mistake earlier. He opened a door without checking for thermal signals behind it, and Lieutenant Korelonn called him on it. Less than an hour later, he did the exact same thing. He was just too inexperienced. Putting him on that team was like asking a first-year cadet to take the senior's practical exam. But right up to that moment, I would have given him an excellent grade." She shook her head. "What a loss. He would have been such a good officer. And I missed him by one second."

"Tell me about that second," Wells said. "You've mentioned it twice now."

"Because I can't stop seeing it. He was ahead of me in the hall, looking for the stairs, and when he found them he just…opened the door." She held her forefinger and thumb apart. "I was this close. Literally this close to catching his shoulder and pulling him back, but his head—"

She stopped. That was not something she would say out loud. In her report she had used clinical terms, but there was no clinical way to speak of what she had seen. Or felt.

"What would have happened if you had been one second faster? Would you both have died?"

"No, I—" Again she stopped, her mind going over the possibilities. One second faster and yes, she might have been beside Bellows as the door cracked open, exposing her instead of him. Two seconds faster and she could have kept the door shut, and what then?

She would have spotted the thermal signals and made an action plan. They could have retreated, or they could have opened the door and tossed in the stun beads—no, they wouldn't have done that preemptively. The stairwell would have carried the sound through the entire building and alerted every soldier in the place.

She imagined the retreat and only then, while thinking it through more logically, did she realize those soldiers had likely been waiting in ambush. They hadn't been there when Ekatya scanned the corridor before taking her team down it. Which meant they had arrived afterward and probably heard them moving down the hall. Had they heard their prey retreating, they might have attacked. They had Protectorate weaponry she hadn't known about and no compunction about shooting without warning. Ekatya's team had nonlethal weapons plus four leadslingers, one of which was carried by an ensign who had no idea how to use it.

It could have been a bloodbath, avoidable only if one of her team had seen the danger in time and thrown stun beads. The fact was, Ensign Bellows had blocked the door and kept her and the others safe. His death had bought their lives, and she would never know if it could have happened differently.

"I don't know," she said slowly. "Until now, I never got past that second."

Wells nodded. "May I tell you a story?"

"Please do. I'd appreciate thinking about something else."

Wells tipped her glass to her mouth, then held it out and looked at it as if it had offended her. "Thought I had some left." She set the glass on the table and made herself more comfortable. "I was an apprentice, my first time out in space, full of the confidence that only comes with holding a medical degree, being first in my class, and having no idea how little that really meant."

Ekatya smiled. "Sounds familiar so far."

"We all go through it, don't we? Anyway, our ship was hit by the Voloth. They got through our shields and breached the hull in four places. We managed to escape, but the injuries that poured into our tiny little medbay…" She paused. "That medbay would have fit into my lobby. One deck's worth of it. We had stretchers lined up head to toe in the corridor, and in my memory that line went on forever. The real doctors were up to their elbows in blood—one was doing the initial triage and the other the most demanding surgeries. I led a team that received the patients sent to us by the triage officer and ended up with two patients I couldn't prioritize. One had a terrible wound, but the surgery to repair it would be short. The other had a less critical wound that needed a longer surgery, but he was in slightly worse condition. I thought, I don't have to choose; I can do them both. I'll save the trooper with the quick surgery and still have time to save the other before he goes over the line."

"I'm guessing that didn't work out."

"The second one seized on my operating table, and I couldn't bring him back. I ran out of time. I kept telling myself that if I'd had one more minute, just one more minute, I could have saved them both."

"Or one more second," Ekatya said. "How long did that haunt you?"

"A while. It did wonders to puncture my ego." Wells ran a hand through her hair, looking somewhere into the middle distance as she said, "We had a team meeting afterward, and individual debriefs. My supervisor assured me that I did everything according to my training. But that didn't help. I lost my edge, was second-guessing everything…until he finally pulled me into his office and said he wanted his star apprentice back. He said we could go over the situation again, but we wouldn't find a procedural mistake, because my real mistake was in thinking I had the power to choose both of those patients. That was what set me up for failure." She turned her head and caught Ekatya's gaze. "You didn't have the power to choose, Captain. You can't do it all."

"Power and choice," Ekatya mused. "It always comes down to that, doesn't it? We want the power so we can make the choices. And then we get it and realize we still can't make them."

"Yes, we can. And we have. You and I have both made choices, big ones. We just can't make *all* of them." She leaned forward, took Ekatya's forgotten glass out of her hand, and set it on the table next to her own.

"I thought we were slowing down?" Ekatya asked as she watched her shake the bottle.

"Fuck slow. I have an injector of kastrophenol." Wells filled the glasses.

"I can respect a doctor who's prepared. What's the toast?"

"To the psychological services you'll never ask for."

Ekatya raised her eyebrows as she accepted her glass. "The ones you're here to provide?"

"Oh, I can't do that. Wrong degree. But I can dispense medication." Wells tapped the bottle.

"In that case, I propose a different toast. To the last excellent choice I made: bringing you on board."

Wells almost fumbled her glass, but her smile was brilliant. "And my choice to accept."

The iceflame was easier on her throat this time. As they set their glasses on the table, Wells said, "It was time for me to move on anyway. Captain Chmielek and I were always butting heads."

Ekatya coughed, then let go of a full-throated laugh. "I'm so glad I could give you a different experience."

CHAPTER 32
Decryption

THE MEMORIAL FOR ENSIGN BELLOWS was held in Deck Zero two days after his death. As Ekatya exited the lift, she remembered looking at the schematics for the *Caphenon* and how baffled she had been by the idea of a deck that had no number. The bridge was physically on the second deck of the ship, but it was designated as deck one. The top deck of Pulsar ships was entirely devoted to a park built around a hill in the center: a clever disguise of the domed ceiling and upper display of the bridge one deck below. But it was a sacrificial deck, outside the battle hull, and was given no deck number.

The transparent hull over the park was covered with retractable hullskin, which could be rolled back. It was usually kept retracted during travel in normal space, making the park by far the most airy and inviting place on the ship. With such a spectacular view, it would have felt that way had it been nothing more than a storage bay with a metal deck and crates stacked in rows. Instead, it was a beautifully landscaped garden, designed in such a way that a person walking through it could never see the whole thing at once. The paths meandered, changing sight lines constantly, offering a sense of space and privacy invaluable to a crew for whom both were precious resources. Though the deck it occupied was one of the smallest on the ship, the design made it seem much larger.

The official name for the park was the Pulsar Garden Module, but no one called it that. They called it Deck Zero.

As Ekatya had expected, the memorial was sparsely attended. Besides her section chiefs and the members of the landing team, only a dozen others came. Commander Kenji gave a touching eulogy, despite having known Bellows for three weeks, and every member of the landing team had something to say.

When Ekatya rose to give her own eulogy, she noted that the group had increased in size. Crew members who were relaxing in the garden wandered over to see what was happening and stayed out of respect. By the time the five-piece band played "Another Star Falling," the traditional lament for

Fleet memorials, the crowd numbered around seventy. The sight of all those heads bowed in respect as the last notes faded brought Ekatya closer to tears than she had been since the day he died.

Lieutenant Kitt broke Frank's decryption in five days. She seemed embarrassed to have beaten Ensign Bellows's time and hastened to explain that he probably had not been able to work on it to the exclusion of all other duties the way she had.

"I've watched all of the messages," she said, her mass of tight curls bobbing as she sat down in front of Ekatya's desk. "Elin Frank is in most of them. He didn't want the Great Leader to have real-time communication, but he did want him to be able to send messages faster than light. So he dumped a quantum com relay in high orbit and gave him a pad that routes messages to it. The relay stored the messages, and Frank checked them through the nearest base space relay."

"So the Great Leader could call, but he might not get an answer right away," Ekatya said.

"Exactly. We were right. He was stalling, waiting for his message to be received."

"How often did Frank check those messages?"

"About every other day. Which means that if the Great Leader hadn't talked to Frank the day before we arrived, he would have expected to hear from him that day or the next."

"Which would have made his stalling a perfectly reasonable tactic." Ekatya frowned. "But it also means that Frank has known about our arrival for five days."

"Not necessarily. Once I realized how those messages were being sent, I asked engineering to scan for the relay in Halaama's orbit. It's old tech. I guess it makes sense that Frank wouldn't use the expensive stuff for a disposable relay." She looked disapproving at the idea of using anything less than the best.

"You jacked it, didn't you?"

Kitt's expression became smug. "This morning. It wasn't hard. He spent a fortune on super-advanced encryption and cheaped out on a relay."

"And?" Ekatya prompted.

"Sorry, I was thinking about—never mind. Frank hasn't picked up the messages. Not since we arrived in the system."

Sholokhov. It had to be Sholokhov. He had probably jammed all non-Fleet access to the base space relay the moment she reported to him. And of course he hadn't told her.

She stifled a sigh. "I might be asking you to jam that orbital relay, depending on what I find out later today. In the meantime, give me the highlights of those messages."

"I can do better than that." Kitt slid a data wand across Ekatya's desk. "These are the most important ones. The one you really need to see is at the top of the list. I've cued it to the relevant part. And, um…I should warn you that you're about to be sick."

Ekatya paused in the act of picking up the wand. "How sick?"

"This is bad, Captain. Really bad. I let the Great Leader touch my cheek during that greeting ceremony, and now I feel like I should scrape off my first layer of skin."

Steeling herself, Ekatya inserted the end of the wand into her deskpad and tapped the first file that appeared.

Her monitor lit up with Elin Frank's round face. "I'm pleased to hear that my samples have met your expectations," he said. Though it was his voice, his mouth movements did not match the Halaaman words. She wondered how much he had paid to have a translator built with his own voice pattern. "Yes, we can handle your order, but at the moment we only have four thousand blasters in stock. We can manufacture the other six thousand in two of your tanaala."

Ekatya drew in a breath, but Kitt made a *keep going* motion.

"As for the bio-force missiles," Frank continued, "I'm sure you understand that an order of that size is not something we can produce in a few tanaala. It will take more time, but be assured that we *will* fill it. I'll be sending a representative to finalize our agreement, and look forward to a long partnership with the Halaamans."

Kitt sliced her hand through the air, and Ekatya paused the playback. They looked at each other in mutual horror.

"They're going to bomb the Nylakians into extinction," Ekatya said.

Kitt nodded soberly. "And that long partnership he mentioned? They agreed to mining rights once Nylak has no one left to claim them. The

Halaamans will do all the work, and Frank will take thirty percent. The Great Leader called it a small price to pay for the assured security of his people."

"Assured security," Ekatya repeated. "What a lovely euphemism for planetary genocide. I wonder how much of this is really about security, and how much is about getting their hands on Nylak's resources. They're a Voloth race in the making."

"Captain, we have to stop this."

"I suspect it's already being stopped. This is excellent work, Lieutenant. Thank you for making it happen so quickly. I'll take it from here."

She wasted no time calling Sholokhov.

CHAPTER 33
Meetings and greetings

Six days later, a cargo ship emerged from base space at the relay nearest the Lexihari system and ran straight into a Protectorate warship already firing shield breakers. The cargo crew were likely still recovering from exit transition nausea when they lost their shields and found themselves facing a coldly angry Fleet captain, who told them to evacuate their ship or she would blow it up with them inside.

Ekatya had planned this in advance with Lokomorra and Roris. After the loss of Ensign Bellows, none of them wanted to take the slightest risk in this interception. They ruled out a boarding party even if the cargo crew stood down, given their own skeleton crew and lack of opportunity for proper training drills. Instead they made use of the two best weapons they had: surprise and intimidation.

The cargo crew were soon floating a safe distance from their ship, corralled in an orbital delivery vehicle guarded by four fighters. Ten more fighters swarmed the ship, taking readings and determining its weapons status and the likelihood of any additional crew hiding inside.

Before sending over a security team, Ekatya called the cargo crew and informed them that if even one person had stayed behind for sabotage, the charges against the rest would go from illegal weapons sales—which already had a long minimum sentence—to attacking a Fleet warship while committing illegal weapons sales. The latter would land them in a maximum security asteroid prison for life.

The jowly crew leader, who Ekatya did not think deserved the title of captain, assured her that she had their full cooperation. In fact, he offered, perhaps they could strike a deal? He had information on their employer that she might find useful.

Ekatya cut the call, looked down from her bridge chair to meet Lokomorra's eyes, and smiled.

The *Phoenix* made quite a splash when it appeared at Quinton Shipyards with a captured ship at its side and a brig full of arms dealers. Ekatya's crew spilled off the ship flush with victory and unspent wages and proceeded to make a different sort of impression as they lorded their experience over the crew members who had been stuck at the shipyards, waiting for their return.

"Some shakedown cruise," Admiral Tsao said when Ekatya called her. "Sholokhov can't be anything but happy with you after this."

Ekatya held back her first reaction. "I won't presume to know what Director Sholokhov thinks. But I truly hope you can expedite our conversion to active status."

Tsao's eyes glinted. "I'll light their tailpipes on fire. But I'm afraid the inspections do take time."

"I know. I just want to minimize the bureaucratic aspects."

"Now that I can do."

Ekatya had asked Lhyn to time her arrival for the day after the *Phoenix* returned, knowing that her first day would be insanely busy. Between turning over the prisoners, meeting individually with her missing section chiefs, and going through the interminable bureaucratic shuffling necessary to get the inspectors on board and set up with the appropriate *Phoenix* crew members and stations, she hardly had two minutes to herself.

But when she stood in the shuttle bay the next morning and saw Lhyn for the first time in forty-two days, she nearly staggered with the sudden absence of the ache in her chest. In the doorway of the shuttle, Lhyn stopped and rubbed her own chest, her eyes wide as they stared at each other.

Then Lhyn dropped her bag and ran down the ramp, laughing as she thumped into Ekatya's arms. Their kiss went on so long that someone in the bay whistled, which seemed to give the other crew members courage. A chorus of whistles, whoops, and applause made them break apart with breathless laughter.

"I like this new thing of not having to hide our relationship from your crew." Lhyn's green eyes were bright and joyful, and Ekatya could not tear her gaze away from them.

"I forgot how beautiful you are," she said. "It's not the same over a quantum com."

"Shippers, no. Never the same." Lhyn pulled her back into a fierce hug. "We're not doing this again. Ever again, Ekatya, do you understand?"

"I do. That ache... I got so used to it that I feel strange now."

"Me too. But I want to feel this strange forever." Lhyn straightened, keeping her arms around Ekatya's waist. "I'm thinking about cancelling my keynote speech at the Anthropology Consortium meeting."

"Lhyn, no. You can't. You've planned that since they asked you last year. It's too important."

"I know, but the idea of leaving you again…"

"Just for two weeks. We survived forty-two days; fourteen will be easy compared to that."

Lhyn shook her head. "Not two weeks. I'll give the keynote, but I'm not staying for the whole meeting. Four extra days of missing you? No. The travel time will be bad enough."

Ekatya smoothed a hand over Lhyn's hair, for once out of its braid and flowing over her shoulders in a thick mass of silver-streaked chestnut. "If I were a good person, I'd try to talk you out of that."

"Oh, good, I'm finally having an effect on you. You're loosening your morals."

"Finally? You've had an effect on me since the day you walked into my conference room."

They collected Lhyn's bag, went straight to Ekatya's quarters, and spent most of that day relearning every millimeter of each other's bodies. The lovemaking was explosive at first, reminiscent of how it had been after their Sharings with Andira, when their bodies buzzed with the lingering effects and every sense seemed heightened. Ekatya could not get enough of Lhyn, frightening herself at times with how little control she had and how easy it would be to hurt her. But Lhyn was equally passionate, brushing aside any concerns and repeating, "Please, please don't hold back. I need it all."

It took them an hour to burn off the pent-up need and settle into a more leisurely pace, and hours more before sheer exhaustion finally dropped them into a deep, healing sleep. Ekatya was shocked when she checked her chronometer immediately after waking and realized she had slept for ten hours straight. Beside her, Lhyn stirred and mumbled, "Maybe now I can finally concentrate."

Ekatya laughed and kissed her. "Only you can make me laugh before I've even had my coffee."

"That's on my résumé," Lhyn said. "Right below 'can make the stern, proper Captain Serrado act like a wild woman on leave.' I'm very proud of my accomplishments."

"I don't know that I'm so proper anymore."

Lhyn's understanding shone in her eyes. "Maybe you're learning that you don't always have to be."

In the officers' mess, they ran into Dr. Wells, who looked at Ekatya and smiled in a way she never had before. "This must be Dr. Rivers," she said. "I heard about your arrival yesterday. You made quite an impression on the ground crew."

"Just Lhyn, please. I'm not Dr. Rivers when I'm not working."

"Oh, I envy you that. I'm Dr. Wells twenty-four hours a day, it seems. But please call me Alejandra."

While Ekatya was getting over the surprise of Wells offering Lhyn a first-name acquaintance within one minute, Lhyn was already digging into the lingual aspect. "Do you shorten that to Aleja? I have a colleague with the x variant of that name, and she goes by Alexa."

"Never," Wells said. "It was my paternal grandmother's name, and I want to honor it. She was a magnificent lady. Tell me, is Terrahan your native language?"

"It is," Lhyn said in a surprised tone. "How did you know?"

Wells turned that new smile on Ekatya again. "Something Captain Serrado said once. It makes more sense now."

"I chose to keep my Terrahan language chip," Ekatya explained. "When I had to have the Halaaman one installed, I gave up High Alsean instead." And she had been very glad to get it back. She hadn't wanted Halaama in her head for an hour longer than necessary.

Lhyn looked suddenly pale, though she explained it away as a need for food—they hadn't eaten since dinner the night before. Once alone, however, she leaned across the table. "I knew you kept Terrahan. I dreamed it."

"When?"

"A few days after our first quantum com call. Maybe five days later? Four?"

"Five," Ekatya said, her stomach constricting as a memory slammed into her. "Lhyn, I saw you. Right before Dr. Wells put me under, I saw you standing next to her, and I told you I couldn't give Terrahan up. I thought it was a hallucination from the anesthetic."

"It's changing," Lhyn whispered in awe. "Or maybe growing."

"Into what?"

"I don't know. We need to talk to Andira about it."

Five days later, Ekatya's personal quantum com quota refreshed and she called Andira. She had planned to bring Lhyn in on the conversation a little later, but that idea died a quick death when she learned that Andira was badly burned and unconscious in Blacksun Healing Center. She was prepared to throw every inspector off her ship and burn her engines all the way to Alsea, but Colonel Micah dissuaded her with a revelation that rocked her back in her seat.

Tyrees. She was Andira's first tyree. It explained so much about the way she missed her. Colonel Micah had called it a partial tyree bond and intimated that Andira had suffered after their departure from Alsea—he said she should have been under the care of a healer. Ekatya thought about how hard her separation from Lhyn had been, even knowing that it was temporary, and could not imagine how Andira must have felt. Andira, who had the empathic strength she and Lhyn lacked and who had probably experienced their symptoms times a factor of ten. And in all of their calls since then, she had never said a word.

"You idiot," she murmured when she ended the call. "Andira, what were you thinking?"

A week passed before Andira called her back, waking her in the middle of the night. Ekatya left Lhyn sleeping and carefully closed the bedroom door before sitting at her desk to accept the call. She had half a mind to dress Andira down both for her idiot self-sacrifice and her stubborn silence on the topic. Then Andira was apologizing for not checking the time converter and all Ekatya could think was how wonderful she looked, healthy and happy, because she had finally found her own tyree.

How could she bring up her situation with Lhyn after that? It would make Andira worry and probably feel guilty, and Ekatya could not do that to her now. Not when she had just healed from horrific burns, not the day after she had finally joined and Shared with the woman she loved, not while she was already worrying about Herot Opah and an assassination attempt.

She would tell her on their next call, when—hopefully—things were resolved on Alsea.

"Why am I always keeping secrets for someone else?" Andira asked at one point.

"Because sometimes that's what you have to do for the people you care about," Ekatya answered. The irony nearly blinded her.

CHAPTER 34
The right thing

WITHIN ONE HOUR OF ADMIRAL Tsao's confirmation that the *Phoenix* had been cleared for active service and Ekatya now reported to her, Ekatya cashed in five days of her personal leave and boarded a shuttle with Lhyn. They were in Gov Dome two days later. Lhyn went to their apartment to pack up a few last things and make final arrangements to terminate their residency, while Ekatya—pointedly wearing civilian clothing—walked into the Presidential Palace. She had an appointment to keep.

Sholokhov watched her enter his office with a small smile, his blue eyes shadowed beneath his bushy eyebrows. "This is not a pleasure I expected, Captain. To what do I owe the honor of this visit?"

She sat in one of his guest chairs, taking up a very familiar position. But this was the last time she would ever have to do it.

"I'm here to ask you to do the right thing."

"Oh, this should be good." He crossed his arms on his desk and leaned forward. "Tell me, what does the ever-righteous Captain Serrado think is the right thing?"

"Signing this." She pushed her pad across the desk, already set to the official request that she had filled out.

He glanced at it, then did a near double take and examined it more closely. "You must be joking."

"I do occasionally joke. But I've never once done it in this office."

"Why would I sign this?"

"Because you sent him to his death."

"Captain Serrado," he sighed, "let me explain something to you. You command a ship with a crew of one thousand, two hundred and sixty-four. Part of your job entails developing a protective relationship with your crew, and I must admit you are admirably skilled in that regard. I am never in doubt that you protect your own." He sat back in his chair. "I protect my own as well, but my crew is somewhat larger than yours. I'm responsible for the security of the Protectorate. Hundreds of *billions* of people. I think in numbers you can't even comprehend. I have to. So where you are emotionally shackled by the death of a single member of your crew, I look at the numbers and see that this single death helped to save billions of lives on Nylak."

"Don't pretend that you care about the Nylakians. You just wanted to take down Elin Frank."

"You're right," he said cheerfully. "Nylak is not a member of the Protectorate and therefore not my responsibility. I don't care about them." He leaned forward again. "But you do."

She clenched her fists in her lap and reminded herself that she had come here for a purpose. Keeping her tone even, she said, "So now you're telling me that you sacrificed Ensign Bellows for my benefit?"

"Don't be intentionally obtuse; it's not worthy of you. I'm telling you that I sacrificed him to the cause of keeping Protectorate weapons out of the hands of those who have no business holding them. Frank wouldn't have stopped with the Lexihari system. That success, and the wealth it brought him, would have fueled more of the same. He would have destabilized systems right and left, causing incalculable damage and danger to the Protectorate. And its representatives," he added. "After all, it was a Protectorate weapon that killed Ensign Bellows."

"I agree that Elin Frank needed to be taken down," she said. "But you didn't need to use Ensign Bellows to do it. You had other options. It was your choice not to use them."

He glanced down at the pad. "And you believe I should feel guilt for his loss, and that signing this request will…unburden me? I think you might be confusing your own sense of guilt for mine."

"It won't unburden anyone, least of all me. But it might bring some measure of comfort to two people who have lost their son for reasons they don't understand."

"Those two people groomed their son for Fleet. They understood exactly what the risks were."

"Of course they did," she said sarcastically. "That's why they used their connections to get him stationed here, out of all possible danger."

"And who took him out of here, hm? Not me."

That hit too close to home. Her fingernails dug into her palms as she said, "Director Sholokhov, signing that form will cost you nothing. But it will help a pair of grieving parents. I have done everything you asked of me for a year and a half and never asked one thing in return. I am asking you for this."

He tilted his head, looking down his nose at her. "Now that argument bears some weight. It's true that you were far more diligent and faithful than I expected, given what I knew of you at the start." He picked up the pad and began to read.

As the seconds ticked past, she consciously unclenched her fists and forced herself to relax. He was taking it seriously; that was a good sign. She just needed to keep her temper in check.

She was gazing at the flowering tree in full bloom outside his window when he set the pad down with a decisive click and said, "No."

It took three full seconds to get her throat unstuck. "Why? What objection can you possibly have?"

"I read your final report, Captain. It was very detailed; I had an excellent picture of exactly what happened on that mission. What you're asking for has very specific guidelines, and Ensign Bellows simply does not satisfy them. He didn't sacrifice himself. He made a mistake. He is responsible…"

She didn't hear the rest of it. The roar in her ears made it impossible. His words had torn the door off the room where she had shoved sixteen months of anger, plus the last month of rage. She stood up so abruptly that the heavy chair rocked on its legs.

"You do not get to blame him for his own death!" she shouted.

He stopped, his mouth open in surprise while she planted her hands on his desk and leaned over so that she was nearly nose to nose with him.

"He made a mistake because he was *inexperienced*," she spat. "And I *told* you that. I told you he was not a good choice. You had other options, but you didn't even consider them because this was never about Bellows; it was about you proving your power over me. It was about you proving a point that you didn't need to, because I conceded it the very first time I sat in that chair!" She pointed behind her. "I told you that first day that we were on the same side. Have I done *anything* to disprove that?"

He didn't answer, apparently still stunned by her effrontery.

"You should have told me about Frank. You made a strategic error by keeping me in the dark. If I'd known what to look for, I wouldn't have needed to take Ensign Bellows with me. We could have linked in with him on the ship. He could have viewed that code in real time while we looked at it on the planet. He would still have seen the encryption, still have done what you needed him to do, but from the safety of the ship. He didn't need to be there. But you were so bent on putting me down one last time that you never even considered that I might know my job better than you!"

"Don't you speak to me in that—"

"I will speak to you in the tone you have earned by your *childish* actions," she snapped. "I know you don't give a tiny ant's ass about Bellows. It's all numbers to you. So let me put this in terms you can understand. He was a resource, an extremely valuable resource. He was a genius-level data jacker—and one hundred percent loyal to the Protectorate. You could have used him as a resource until you retired, and your successor could have used him for two more decades after. You threw that away, denied yourself access to his talent, all out of *spite*. It was immature and unworthy, and it cost you decades of potential use. Now you tell me: Is that the fault of Ensign Bellows?"

There was no sound in the room but her labored breathing as she tried to get her rage under control.

Sholokhov looked up at her with an unreadable expression. At last he said, "You are one of a kind, Captain Serrado."

She pushed off his desk and crossed her arms over her chest. "Meaning what?"

"Meaning I can't recall the last time someone spoke to me that way, except for a certain captain almost eighteen months ago. And that was tame compared to this." He picked up the pad without breaking their eye contact. "I still don't find your brand of honesty as enjoyable as you seem to think I should, but I've come to realize that there is value in it." Holding up the pad, he added, "You know that Ensign Bellows does not satisfy the criteria. Speaking *honestly*, he doesn't deserve this."

She held her tongue, knowing there was more to come.

He set the pad on his desk and drummed his fingers beside it. "But you do," he said, and pressed his thumb to the pad.

She watched in astonishment as he picked up a pad pen and signed his name next to the thumbprint. When he handed the pad to her, she could barely find her voice.

"Thank you," she said faintly.

"Don't thank me. This isn't a favor. It's payment for services rendered. You're right, Captain—you never asked for anything until now. I consider us even."

Horrified by the tears that were pricking at the backs of her eyes, she bowed her head and said, "Understood."

She had her hand on the antique brass door handle when he spoke again. "Captain Serrado."

Her shoulders tensed as she waited for the hated *You're dismissed, Captain.* But if he needed the final victory, she would give it to him.

"Regardless of how you see the result of this mission, the fact remains that you saved another planet. And this time, you did it under orders. Take the win and leave the rest behind."

Though he had been unable to resist a final dig about Alsea, the rest almost sounded like well-meaning advice. She turned to face him, nodded once, and quietly closed the door behind her.

After picking up her clothing bag from Sholokhov's aide, Ekatya changed in one of the many private toilets sprinkled throughout the Presidential Palace. Then she found the nearest matter printer and held her signed form up to the scanner. Within two minutes she was walking toward the exit with a slim black box in her jacket pocket.

In another twenty minutes, she stood on the porch of a large white house just far enough from the center of Gov Dome to be outside the best neighborhoods. It was still more than she could have afforded even on an admiral's salary.

She pressed the visitor button and waited, her heart beating uncomfortably fast. It seemed to take a year for the door to open.

"Captain Serrado." Ensign Bellows's father stared at her with the depths of grief shadowing his eyes. His wife was a silent presence behind his shoulder. "To what do we owe the pleasure?"

She almost smiled, recognizing the well-bred manners she had seen so often in Ensign Bellows. The greeting was nearly the same as Sholokhov's, but what a difference in meaning and intent.

"I came to bring you something that belongs to your son," she said.

His wife stepped around him. "Fleet already sent us the only part of our son you could bring back. And his possessions. Did they miss something?"

"No. This didn't belong to him until now." She looked from one to the other. "I know you haven't been told much about how he died. And I'm afraid I can't add much to it, because everything is classified…for now. I'm hoping it will become public knowledge later. But I think you should know that your son gave his life for a purpose. Fleet has recognized that."

She took the small box from the pocket of her dress uniform, opened it, and held it out.

They both gasped.

"Is that…?"

"Oh, Seeders…"

Ensign Bellows's mother burst into tears, while his father reached out with trembling hands to take the box. "A White Star?" he breathed. "My son earned a White Star?"

"For sacrificing himself to save the lives of others, yes. And not just a few others. Billions of them. Your son helped to prevent a planetary genocide. He saved more than four billion people. I am so sorry that you lost him and that his life was so short. But he was a brilliant officer, and he gave his life for a cause so great that there are truly no words to express it. That medal is the closest Fleet can come to it."

He looked up at her with tears brimming in his eyes, and she felt her own throat tighten.

"You should be very, very proud of him," she said gently. "As his captain, I am extremely proud of his performance under pressure and his service to the best ideals of Fleet." She swallowed the lump in her throat, then finished, "And I will never forget him."

CHAPTER 35
Grace

Alsea, present day

When Ekatya finally went silent, Lanaril stared at her in wonder. She had related the tale in a matter-of-fact tone, distancing herself from the events she was describing. But her emotions told another story, filling in an entire tapestry between the threads she had spun with her words. There was a depth and richness here that Lanaril had never even suspected—though she should have. After all, this was Lhyn's tyree, and Fahla never gave that gift without reason.

The squeaking of a seat cushion caught her attention as Andira rose from the wide chair she shared with Salomen. She crossed the room, pulled Ekatya up, and enveloped her in a warmron in front of Fahla and everyone in the cabin.

Lanaril cast a nervous glance around. She knew the Gaians viewed warmrons differently, but still…!

Chief Kameha was looking on with respect and a slight sense of embarrassment. It was clear that he saw nothing wrong with the warmron but felt that he was intruding on the women's privacy by watching.

Colonel Micah and the Opah men shifted in their chairs with spikes of shock and discomfort. Nikin looked at his sister with an appalled expression, but Salomen watched her tyree in the arms of another with a perfectly calm face, her eyes betraying nothing and her front as impenetrable as always.

Lhyn radiated a complicated mixture of love and grief—and an inexplicable warmth of approval.

"I understand why you didn't tell me," Andira said quietly. "I wouldn't have said anything, either."

Ekatya buried her face in Andira's throat as relief came off her in waves. "Thank you."

"And I grieve that loss with you. It was so unnecessary."

Ekatya nodded, the sorrow which had accompanied her story growing so intense that Lanaril could hardly bear to be in the same room with it. But it was tempered by something else: a profound sense of belonging, as if she had been waiting for this moment for a very long time.

Andira put a hand on the back of Ekatya's head, holding it against her own as her eyes drifted shut. Her bright blonde hair contrasted sharply with Ekatya's black, and they looked the very picture of a bonded couple.

Lanaril glanced at Salomen, who still appeared perfectly calm, then back at the extraordinary scene before her.

Andira's eyes were open again, staring right into Lanaril's, and their ice-blue depths held an expression of fierce protectiveness. In that moment, Lanaril knew that Ekatya had not told the whole story. She had offered a perfectly reasonable explanation as to why she would have wanted to learn more about her tyree bond from the only Alsean she saw as a friend, but this was more than friendship. It was even more than the intimacy of lovers. It was…

No. It could not be that.

Salomen rose from her chair, walked to the embracing couple, and rested a hand on Andira's back. Andira released Ekatya, who took a step back and looked up at Salomen with guilt hanging heavy on her shoulders.

"I don't have Andira's experience with your customs," Salomen said. "But she told me once that the Gaians did one thing far better than we, and then she showed me what she meant. Of course, that did get us into a great deal of trouble."

Her quip alleviated some of the tightness in the air; by now everyone there had heard the story of how Andira and Salomen had started their bonding process prematurely.

"But I think I'm safe from creating a divine tyree bond with you, so… may I?" Salomen opened her arms, and Ekatya stepped into her without hesitation. Her guilt dropped away as she was enfolded in a second warmron.

With that single gesture, Salomen defused any remaining tension. Her father and brother were still startled, but their spiky discomfort now dissolved into a bemused acceptance. Colonel Micah relaxed completely, a small smile on his lips as he watched. Chief Kameha's embarrassment had vanished, and Lhyn's previous approval had morphed into outright gratitude.

When the two women stepped apart, Salomen reached for Andira's hand without looking. "You have honored us and our family with your story. You don't know our traditions, and we would certainly have understood had you held back from this one. But you didn't, and I'm grateful. Do you know why?"

Ekatya shook her head, then cleared her throat and spoke in a slightly hoarse voice. "Because you've learned more than you ever wanted to know about the pale underbelly of Protectorate politics?"

"No, that's me," Andira said. "I've learned more tonight than in a cycle of meetings with Ambassador Solvassen."

"And to think Elin Frank was our ambassador for a moon." Colonel Micah emptied his glass and set it on the side table. "I can hardly imagine how much damage he might have caused."

"Oh, he wouldn't have stayed long, even if we hadn't ejected him. The kind of wealth and connections Ekatya was describing? He couldn't manage that out here. He was just here to set up his network, and then he would have gone home." Andira was about to say more but quieted down when Ekatya looked at her with raised eyebrows.

Turning to Salomen, Ekatya said, "Why are you grateful?"

"You're much more polite than certain others in this room," Salomen said in a whisper designed to carry to every corner. In a normal voice she added, "Because you proved me right. And as any of my family will tell you, I love to be proven right." While her father and brother made sounds of amused agreement, she laid her other hand on the center of Ekatya's chest. "I said you had a good heart. But I think I understated it—you have a great heart."

"True words," Shikal said. "What you did for those poor grieving parents..." He trailed off, his gaze moving between his daughter and son.

"What you did showed the grace of Fahla herself." Lanaril rose from her chair and held up both palms.

Ekatya swung around, her startled gaze going to the gesture they had not yet shared.

"Creating new families is not always easy," Lanaril said. "But you would be a credit to any fortunate enough to have you."

Hesitantly, Ekatya brought up her hands.

As they interlaced their fingers, Lanaril continued, "You held one favor from a very powerful man. Favors are currency. You spent yours not on yourself, but to bring comfort to two people you did not even know. That was a beautiful act of grace, and I honor it."

"Well said." Andira smiled at them.

Ekatya was studying Lanaril, her expression calm while her emotions veered between doubt and a strong desire to believe, all flavored by the unease that stood between them. "Thank you," she said. "From the Lead Templar of Blacksun, that's a testament I will treasure."

So diplomatic.

"This is not the Lead Templar speaking to the Fleet captain. This is Lanaril speaking to Ekatya." She let go, sensing that she had pushed as far as she could.

Ekatya nodded, then turned to her tyree. "Should we finish this tomorrow?"

"Oh, no. I didn't sit here and watch you relive that just so I can go to bed and dread doing the same thing for a whole day." Lowering her voice to a whisper, Lhyn added, "If I don't do it now, I don't know when I will."

"Okay." Ekatya stooped down to drop a kiss on her forehead.

Lhyn held her in place with a hand around the back of her leg. "But…I don't think I can do it like you did. Not in front of everyone. I thought I could, but…"

"You're in control of your own story." Ekatya's voice was soft, keeping their exchange at this end of the room. "You decide what you want to do. Who you want to tell."

"Lanaril," Lhyn said immediately. "And Andira and Salomen."

Andira crouched in front of her. "Would you prefer to do this in our cabin? The view is beautiful when the moons are out."

Lanaril's heart nearly broke at the grateful relief pouring off Lhyn.

"That would be… Yes, I'd like that."

"Then that's what we'll do." Andira faced the others and spoke in a louder tone. "If we leave you here alone, can we trust that this place will still be standing tomorrow?"

"It will have to be," Colonel Micah said. "Aldirk paid an immense guarantee to reserve this resort. If we destroy a cabin, I'll never hear the end of the whining about the costs."

"I believe we might destroy a few bottles of spirits, however." Shikal's eyes were twinkling.

"You mean a few *more* bottles of spirits," said Nikin.

Chief Kameha was already making his way toward the cabinets, giving Ekatya a short nod as he went. She nodded back, and Lanaril marveled at the perfect understanding that existed between them. Those two nods had been a full communication, complete with emotions expressed and understood on both sides. Lhyn often spoke of the importance of what she called "body cues" and teased her about her dependence on empathy, but only now was she beginning to realize how much these sonsales aliens could share with each other despite their empathic blindness.

With a comment about leaving the men to their preferred method of destruction, Salomen led the way out. The night air was heavy with the scents of flowers that did not bloom during the day, and tonight a chorus of insects sang high up in the trees. Fianna had mentioned something about them earlier—a courtship that only occurred for a few ninedays each cycle.

Andira and Salomen stepped onto the path to the Bonding Bower, which obligingly lit up all the way to the base of the delwyn tree. Lanaril was right behind them, but Ekatya and Lhyn paused on the deck. Lhyn was looking back toward the door.

"Kameha will tell them," Ekatya said.

"He will? When did you ask him?"

"This afternoon."

"But how did you know?"

"I didn't. I wanted you to have options."

Lhyn made a soft sound in her throat. "You're perfect."

"Not yet." Ekatya smiled up at her. "But I keep trying."

"That's what makes you perfect." Lhyn caught her hand and tugged her down the steps.

The group was halfway across the clearing when Andira said, "I have a question, Ekatya."

"Missiles away."

Andira laughed. "That's one I haven't heard in quite some time. What a joy to hear it again."

"What, Fleet speak?" Lhyn's emotional balance was more stable now. "I thought you appreciated a higher level of language."

"Hey." Ekatya elbowed her gently. "You're supposed to appreciate the cultural richness of a distinct dialect. What is it, Andira?"

"It was only two days after I called you at Quinton Shipyards that Parser sprang his trap on me. That was the day he showed Elin Frank the vid of me nearly killing him in a holding cell. But based on what you've said, Frank was in custody by then. How did Parser talk to him?"

"Because Elin Frank has more money than all the Shippers and Seeders put together. People like that don't wait for their trials in prison the way others do. He was under house arrest. I'm sure one of his lawyers gave him access to a quantum com, even though he wasn't supposed to have it. He wouldn't have stopped running his empire just because he couldn't go anywhere."

Andira turned and walked backward as she said, "Fahla does have a sense of humor. Two of the biggest blindworms in the galaxy were talking to each other about their greatness while one was in custody and the other was about to be."

"It does work out sometimes," Lhyn said.

"It does." Ekatya wrapped an arm around her waist.

They climbed the winding steps around the great delwyn tree and crossed the wooden deck, their footsteps sounding like a small herd of winden. Salomen slid open the glass door and led them into the cabin, a space Lanaril found familiar given her two afternoons with Fianna.

While she and Salomen poured drinks, Andira and Ekatya rearranged the chairs, creating an intimate circle with three chairs facing the sofa and the low table between them. Before long, the table was covered with glasses and bottles, and Lhyn was snuggled up to Ekatya on the sofa. Lanaril, Andira, and Salomen took their places.

"Here it is at last." Lhyn's nervous smile was the tip of an iceberg of apprehension. "I've been looking forward to this and dreading it at the same time. I want you to know, but it's not an easy story."

"Tell it at your own pace," Lanaril said. The level of anxiety rolling off both Lhyn and Ekatya was making her own heart beat faster.

"Take all night if you need to," Andira added. "None of us are going anywhere."

Lhyn looked down into the depths of her glass. "Um. What I meant is that it won't be an easy story for you to hear. I'm through it, and I'm all right now—" She stopped. "Well, mostly all right. Given what you saw earlier this evening, you probably have your doubts. But it's much better than it used to be, and getting easier all the time. It got much easier the moment I set foot on Alsea. Just remember that."

CHAPTER 36
Question and answer

Qwonix, 2.75 stellar months earlier (2 Alsean moons)

As the applause swelled, Lhyn gratefully sipped the water that had been left for her at the podium. After an hour and a half of speaking, her throat was as dry as a desert planet. But her keynote speech had been well received, and the three thousand people packed into the auditorium—the largest by far at the conference center housing this year's Anthropology Consortium meeting—were showing no signs of leaving. Everyone seemed eager to stay for the question-and-answer period.

At last the applause died down enough for her to start the final part of her obligation. Twenty minutes of this, half an hour at most, and then she could enjoy a nice dinner with colleagues and retire to her hotel room to relax. Tomorrow she would be on the dawn shuttle to Tlahana Station, where she would transfer to a second shuttle, and three days after that she would be stepping onto the *Phoenix*.

She could not wait. Walking away from Ekatya after their two weeks together at Quinton Shipyards had been twice as hard as walking away from her the day before her shakedown cruise. Her career with the Institute was over; she could no longer tolerate year-long communications blackouts. The very idea of going that long without seeing Ekatya made her feel panicky.

Alsea was calling her with a lifetime's worth of learning, and Ekatya's new assignment was the final piece to the puzzle. Lhyn could live part-time on Alsea and part-time on the *Phoenix*, which was now tasked with protecting Alsea and the sector of space in which it was located.

All that stood between her and her new life was thirty minutes of questions.

There were many raised hands to choose from, and she pointed at random to a man by the center aisle. He stood up, prompting the mic controller to drop a microphone from the ceiling. It hovered just above and in front of his head.

"What were the effects of your immersion in the Alsean culture, both on the culture itself and your interpretations of it?"

She had bet herself that would be one of the first questions.

"It's true that my study of the Alsean culture was like no other, due to my complete access. But it's also true that the Alseans experienced a Pulsar-class ship crashing on their planet, a ground pounder murdering their citizenry, and a full Voloth invasion. Those were such dramatic events, with such far-reaching cultural consequences, that I believe my presence made no comparative difference. As to the effects on my interpretation…" She paused. "We've been debating the Non-Interference Act for a very long time, and it's no secret that I've always championed the ideal of open access."

Shouts of "Yes!" and a swell of applause swept the room. This had been a contentious subject for her entire career. Many attendees sat in their seats, silent and frowning while others applauded, but she had a new outlook on this topic and no patience left for what she strongly felt was the wrong side.

"I never believed that a culture could be fully explored from orbital distance," she said when the room had quieted. "We throttle science at the source and then convince ourselves that our conclusions are objective and complete. How can they be when we don't even know what we missed?"

Over the murmurs of agreement, she added, "It's valid to say that my immersion affected my interpretation, precisely because I was able to see the Alsean culture so clearly from the ground. Far more clearly than I had during my previous ten months in orbit. It also affected me personally. Contact with the Alsean people changed my way of thinking."

"How?" her questioner asked when she stopped for a sip of water.

I fell in love with an entire planet, she thought, but this was not the venue for a statement like that.

Setting down her glass, she said, "I came to realize that we do both ourselves and the cultures we study a grave disservice when we prejudge them for not having the technology to travel faster than light."

A rumble filled the room, hundreds of whispers and murmurs from anthropologists who were most likely taking that as an insult.

"Before Alsea, I would have been the first to say that I *never* prejudged a culture, and neither did my colleagues, because our entire lives are built around studying these cultures with as much intellectual dispassion and open-mindedness as possible."

The whispers quieted.

"I really believed that. But here's the proof of my self-deception: despite my suspicions and the mounting evidence, I didn't truly believe that the Alseans could be empathic until I walked among them and had it proven to me through personal experience. Without that, I would have come to this meeting and never breathed a word about the most profound discovery in our lifetimes—perhaps in all of Gaian history—because everyone knows empathy is impossible. Right?"

Now the room was silent.

"How many other impossible things have we walked away from? How many other cultures have depths we can't see into because we refuse to *really* study them? Because we hold ourselves apart from them, thinking we're more advanced? We tell ourselves that technological proficiency equals sociological advancement, but that is just not true. We're the ones who tried to sell an entire civilization for profit. The Alseans gave unquestioning aid and assistance to a crew of injured aliens. Alsea proved the lie of technology signaling advancement, and now I wonder how many other worlds out there prove it as well. How can we distinguish between the ones that do and the ones that don't while we float above them and refuse to immerse ourselves in their culture?"

"Speak it!" said someone in one of the front rows. A loud clap came from the same place, which quickly spread throughout the audience. Surprisingly, some of the attendees who had been frowning earlier were now applauding. Perhaps she had moved this debate a tiny distance toward resolution.

When the applause died down, she pointed toward an older woman on the left side of the room.

"Did any of the *Caphenon* crew have sexual relations with an Alsean? You were there for two stellar months. That's a long time for Fleet types."

Lhyn was amused at the idea of Fleet types. The crew she had met ran the gamut from Lieutenant Candini's stereotypical pilot-run-wild personality to Ekatya, who could not be paid to put a toe out of line.

"Not as far as I know," she said. "But I didn't send out a survey."

The next questioner was stuck on the topic. "Can female Alseans even have sex with Gaians?" he asked. "Their anatomy doesn't seem compatible. A larger-than-average penis wouldn't fit."

The woman next to him turned and said, loudly enough to reach the microphone, "Did you grow up on an all-male planet? You do know there are other ways to have sex besides using a penis."

"Obviously, but we're talking about reproductive sex—"

"But that's not what you said—"

It took a full minute to reestablish order.

"Well, I know which chapter of my book will be the one everybody reads," Lhyn said, eliciting a swell of laughter as she pointed toward a well-dressed man in the third row.

"Can you honestly say you have no concerns about unleashing empathic aliens on the citizens of the Protectorate?"

She was so tired of this question, yet it followed her wherever she went. "Yes, I can honestly say that," she said shortly, and pointed at the next person.

But the man grabbed the microphone, refusing to let it go. "Then you're deluding yourself and trying to delude us. The Alseans are dangerous, and you're painting them as some sort of enlightened species second only to the Seeders. You're as dangerous as they are."

"You're not an anthropologist," she said. "None of us would use the phrase *unleashing empathic aliens*. That's a tag phrase from the Defenders of the Protectorate—a ridiculous name, by the way, because you're not defending the Protectorate. You're defending your own prejudice and fear. This is a scientific meeting. Your politics don't belong here."

Murmurs of disapproval rose from the crowd, and the people nearest the man leaned away as if to disassociate themselves.

He stared at her, unaffected. "It's not politics. It's a question of security. And the Battle of Alsea proved it's a question of life and death. There are aliens on that world capable of killing with their minds, and you think they should walk among us."

Lhyn noted the security officers making their way down the center aisle and breathed a sigh of relief. By hijacking the microphone, this DOP plant had guaranteed his ejection.

Pointing toward the officers, she said, "There are people working for this conference center who are probably capable of killing with their bare hands. No one seems to have a problem with them walking among us."

"That's a facile argument, Dr. Rivers. Real Gaians can't kill without anyone else noticing. There are defenses against someone who wants to kill you with their hands or a weapon of some sort. It's physical. We can't defend against the mental."

"And if you paid the slightest attention to what I've been writing and saying for the last year and a half, instead of shouting inside your own political bubble, you'd know we don't *need* to defend against the mental. The Alsean culture is built around regulating empathic powers. Alseans who would commit the act you refer to are criminals, and they are punished."

"But what about the ones who aren't?" He shook off the hands of the security guards now surrounding him, only to be swarmed. "What about the ones who aren't, Dr. Rivers?" he shouted as they pulled him away and began marching him back up the aisle. "What about them?"

The auditorium was deathly silent when he was finally dragged out the doors. Lhyn eyed the reporters lining the back wall—something she had never seen at an anthropology meeting before—and knew she could not let this stand.

"Shall we get back to talking about interspecies sex?" she asked.

It earned a laugh, but she could feel the discomfort in the air.

"Given the increasingly visible activities of the DOP over the past year and a half," she said, "I suppose it was inevitable that they would install plants in our meeting. But I'm not sure what they were trying to accomplish. Their only weapon is fear. They're terrified of the unknown, just as children are. Children depend on their families and cultures to educate them on which fears are useful and which can be dismissed, but some reach adulthood without ever learning to distinguish. They fear anything they can't understand, and they don't *want* to understand. They revel in their childish terror because it's a cultural tie—it gives them a strong connection to their chosen tribe. The tribe of fear.

"But fear is not an effective weapon in this room. Fear shrivels in the face of knowledge, and every one of us has devoted our lives to the pursuit of knowledge. I can't think of an audience less receptive to what the DOP is trying to sell."

The room burst into applause. When it died down, she indicated the back wall and said, "But given the media attention this meeting has drawn, I think we were not the target audience for this intrusion. The DOP is hoping this will be broadly disseminated. So let's speak to that broader audience."

She took another sip of water and then faced the reporters.

"In answer to the question: yes, the Alseans can be trusted to use their empathic powers in an ethical manner. This is not merely my opinion. The job of an anthropologist is to study a culture in order to answer just such questions as that one. My research team gathered data from numerous sources—news, documentaries, entertainment programs, observation of political and court processes—the list goes on. And then I found myself on the planet with direct access to libraries and all of their historical texts, written laws, and popular literature. I conducted interviews with and observations of citizens from all walks of life.

"What I learned from this vast amount of data—far more than we have ever gathered on any pre-FTL culture—is that the Alseans have built their culture around the ethical use of their empathy. They have a formal system of laws that govern its use, they have institutions that train the more powerful empaths to control and lawfully use their skills, and they have guiding principles, values, and moral structures around both the use and misuse of empathy. Alsean families are deeply connected by their shared empathy. Alsean doctors use empathy to help others heal.

"Meanwhile, one of their greatest historical villains was a king who tried to seize power through the abuse of empathy. His punishment wiped out any legacy he hoped to leave. He was stripped of his name, erased from history, and is known today only as the Betrayer. The Alseans imposed that punishment because they never wanted an empathic abuser to profit from that abuse, even after death. There could never be *any* incentive for abuse.

"So while it's true that Alseans exist who break the law regulating the use of empathic powers, it's also true that they are punished severely. On my home planet of Allendohan, there are people who break the laws and hurt others. They are also punished. I would not want my world, my culture, to be judged by the actions of the tiny minority who don't represent us. If that were the criteria for being accepted into the Protectorate, I wouldn't be here. Neither would any of you."

A hum of approval swept the auditorium, but she had one final message to convey, and this might be her last opportunity.

"The DOP wants us to be afraid. Well, if I'm going to fear something, it won't be the aliens who saved my life despite the danger my research exposed them to. I'll fear the people who tried to sell a civilization into slavery and death for a set of mineral rights. I'll fear the greed and immorality of some Gaians and the willful ignorance of others. Because fear does have a purpose. It shows us what we need to fight against. So let's fight against the *right* thing."

As the applause began, she picked up her water and stepped back from the podium.

She was done.

CHAPTER 37
Mistake

Lhyn had hardly been in her hotel room for five minutes when the door chimed.

Her first thought, as she crossed the room she had only just entered, was an exasperated *what now?* She had spent the day either on stage or socializing with colleagues; all she wanted now was a quiet evening alone.

Her second thought, when she tapped the pad by the door and saw the large man standing in the corridor with a bouquet of flowers, was curiosity as to who would have sent them. Flowers were not Ekatya's style. Perhaps her former director, wishing her a happy new life even if it wasn't at the Institute? Or maybe the conference organizers thanking her for the keynote.

Her third thought, when she opened the door and was shoved backward so forcefully that she lost her balance and fell, was that she had just made a big mistake.

Her last thought, when the injector bit into her throat and her vision darkened, was that Ekatya would never have been so stupid.

CHAPTER 38
First lesson

She awoke in a bed, lying atop the covers in a dimly lit room. She sat up abruptly, then held her head in both hands and tried desperately not to vomit. The sudden motion was a very, very bad idea. Whatever sedative had been used on her was the type with nasty side effects.

When the intense pain in her head finally subsided, she opened her eyes and sighed with relief at the sight of her body. She was still fully clothed in the suit she had worn to the keynote speech. Even her dress boots were untouched. At least for the moment, sexual assault was not on the agenda.

As quietly as she could, she got off the bed and prowled the room. It looked like a high-quality hotel room that had been denuded of all decorations and furnishings other than the bed. On the opposite wall was an enormous plexan window, which probably looked onto a beautiful view when it wasn't opaque. She located the control for the window and tapped it.

Nothing happened.

She tried again. Nothing.

Venturing through the open doorway to the left of the bed, she found an expansive bathroom with richly tiled flooring. On the stone counter, in a neat pile beside the sink, was a single towel, a bar of soap, and a small, unbreakable jar of dentifrice. There was no toothbrush. The bar of soap was lined up to exactly match the edges of the folded towel.

A pale rectangle outlined by brackets showed where the mirror over the sink had been taken down.

The sight of the toilet reminded her to be practical. She used it, then reentered the bedroom and considered her options. The bathroom had no window, while the bedroom window was a solid sheet of plexan, the type put into temperature-regulated buildings. The only exit from this room was the closed door directly across from the bathroom. It would surely be locked.

She gave the lever a cursory tug and took a surprised inhale when it gave beneath her hand.

Slowly, she opened the door a crack and squinted against the too-bright light. When her eyes adjusted, she found a blank-walled room empty of any furniture save an expensive wooden table, a matching chair, and a second, high-backed chair made of a black composite material. It was studded with built-in restraints.

In the wooden chair sat a fit, handsome, well-dressed man, looking right at her. His blond hair was impeccably cut, his short beard and mustache were trimmed to perfection, and he wore a golden stud in one ear.

"Good morning, Dr. Rivers," he said in a calm, deep voice. "Did you sleep well?"

"Who are you?"

He smiled. "I can see that's the first thing I'll have to train out of you. You don't ask the questions here. I do. Your job is to answer them the way I want you to."

She glanced to the left, where another door offered possible escape.

"Oh, you'd like to leave? Go ahead. I won't stop you."

It was clearly a trap, but what could she do? If she didn't try, she would forever wonder if she could have saved herself by simply walking out. There was always a chance he was just insane.

He did not move other than to turn his head and watch as she walked to the door.

Like the first, it was not locked. With a burst of hope she swung it all the way open, getting a brief glimpse of an empty corridor with identical doors.

Then a man stepped into the doorway, filling nearly all of it. She recognized him as the one who had pushed his way into her hotel room. He tilted his squarish, close-shaven head and regarded her as one would regard an insect.

She would never have imagined that a man that large could move so quickly. Before she could take a single step back, he buried his massive fist in her stomach.

Pain exploded through her, doubling her over and dropping her to the floor in a fetal position. She couldn't breathe. She couldn't do anything except scrabble her feet weakly against the smooth wood floor, as if somehow the movement would unlock her lungs.

It did not. She was helpless, silently struggling, unable to lift a hand to defend herself should the man at the door choose to strike again.

At last her diaphragm released from its paralysis, and she took in a gasping breath, then another and another. Tears ran down her face, an involuntary physical reaction to the shock and lack of oxygen.

The well-dressed man knelt down in front of her. "I said I wouldn't stop you. I didn't say *he* wouldn't stop you. He saw the coverage of your speech and your insulting comments about the organization we work for. He was a little irritated by that, so I told him he could teach your first lesson. Which is, your choices have consequences. So do your words. Think about that, Dr. Rivers."

Once again, an injector stung her throat.

CHAPTER 39
Second lesson

Her second awakening was identical to the first, with two exceptions. One, she knew not to sit up too quickly. Two, she was naked and under the covers.

"No, no, no," she whispered. "Please, no."

She tried to sit up, but even her attempt to move slowly failed. Her stomach muscles ached so badly that she could not use them and had to push herself up with her arms instead. Her mouth was desperately dry and tasted acidic.

Bracing herself with one hand, she leaned over and tapped the wall control to increase the light. Then she threw the covers aside and looked down at herself.

The fist-sized bruise looked horrific, but that was the least of her concerns. She examined her inner thighs, finding no abrasions, no stickiness or dried fluids. She felt no vaginal pain, and when she carefully got out of bed and leaned down to inspect the sheet, she could find no stains.

Her legs buckled beneath her, and she dropped her forehead to the mattress, gulping in air. When she got herself under control and pushed up again, she found something new in the room: a suit rack, with her pants carefully folded over the bar and her jacket arranged perfectly on the hanger. Her belt hung from a tab on the side, while her boots were precisely lined up on the base. On the polished wood floor beside the rack were her shirt, socks, and underwear, folded and wrapped in the water soluble film that indicated they had been freshly laundered.

She had not been raped, but someone had handled her body, undressing her and putting her to bed. The idea of either of those two men doing that—or Shippers forbid, both of them—made her nauseous. And she had a sinking feeling it had been both. The fastidious arrangement of clothing was almost certainly done by the man in the chair, but he wasn't big enough to easily move her. Especially given that she would have been an unresponsive weight.

In the bathroom, she stopped only long enough to relieve herself before walking straight into the shower, turning it as hot as she could bear, and washing every millimeter of her skin and hair three times.

Putting her clothes back on was like donning a suit of armor. She immediately felt safer.

Back in the bathroom, she poured some of the dentifrice powder into the palm of one hand, added a little water, and stirred it into a paste. Using her forefinger, she brushed her teeth and tongue and followed that by drinking as much water as she could hold. Then she detached the dry comb from its slot, pulled it out on its cable, and ran it over her hair. It really must be a nice hotel, she thought incongruously. The dry comb only took three passes. Cheaper hotels used combs that took nine or ten.

With nothing left to do, she sat on the foot of the bed and assessed her options. In the end, she had only two: stay here until she was dragged out, as she would inevitably be, or go out there under her own power.

She was just proud enough to go on her own.

He sat in the same position, watching her. This time he was dressed in a different suit. On the table in front of him rested a flat silver case, about twenty-five centimeters on a side and only a few centimeters high.

"Good morning, Dr. Rivers. Did you have a good night's sleep?"

She leaned against the door frame and crossed her arms over her chest. "It's the same day." It had to be. She had not urinated enough for an entire day and night to have passed.

"No, it's not." He pulled a pad from the sleeve of his suit jacket, tapped it a few times, and turned the virtual screen toward her. It showed the headlines from the day's news, and all of them were dated two days after her keynote speech.

"You could have manufactured that."

"I could have, but I didn't." He indicated the outside door. "Would you like to try again?"

This was all a mindshek, as Ekatya would call it. He was toying with her. But if she didn't try the door, then she would prove to him that he had already won. That was not acceptable.

When she opened the door and found the same man standing outside, she flinched and covered her abdomen with one arm. It was an instinctive but useless gesture.

The massive man tilted his head just as he had before, watching her.

She closed the door and squeezed her eyes shut, trying not to cry.

"Sit down, Dr. Rivers."

Turning around, she eyed the high-backed chair, its built-in restraints open and waiting. "I'll stand."

His tone did not change as he said, "My assistant very much enjoyed taking part in your training yesterday. He would love to do it again today. I suggest you sit down."

Ekatya would have used some deadly combat move against that man-mountain outside the door and escaped by now. Ekatya would never sit in a chair designed for restraint just because she was afraid of being hurt.

Until now, Lhyn had never thought of herself as weak. She simply lived a different lifestyle, too busy with her research and writing to throw herself into physical training the way Ekatya did. And learning hand-to-hand combat had never even crossed her mind.

Now she despised herself for her weakness, which left her helpless in front of this man. She was ashamed of not living up to Ekatya's high opinion of her. But her fear of being hurt was stronger than her shame.

She crossed the room and sat in the chair.

The gold stud glinted in his ear as he smiled at her. "Very good. I knew you'd learn quickly. After all, you're the great Dr. Rivers, the galaxy's foremost authority on Alsea."

"This won't work," she said. "Whatever it is you're trying to do. There are people looking for me right now. If this is really the day you say it is, then I've missed two shuttles and a check-in."

"Do you know why you're here?" he asked.

Because you're an egotistical asshead was her first thought, but she kept silent, assuming he would answer the question himself.

He did.

"You're here because you're the best in your field. We need you to do something for us. And I'm here because I'm the best in *my* field. No one is looking for you. Your lover did call the night of your keynote speech, but she's not worried anymore. You called her back yesterday."

Placing the pad in the exact center of the table, he activated a file.

She started when she heard her own voice.

"Ekatya, I'm sorry I missed your call. And I wish I could see you, but the hotel was swamped with all of the attendees and apparently we blew out the video band on their quantum com. So it's just voice messages for now until they get it fixed.

"And, well…I know this isn't what we had planned, but I'm staying here for a little while longer. This hotel is so nice, and I have the peace and quiet I need to get these edits done. I'm already past deadline, and I want to have this out of the way before I meet you, so I can focus on being with you once I get there. I hope you'll understand. It's just for a few days.

"I love you. I'll see you soon."

He smiled at her shock as he replaced the pad in its pocket. "Voice patch technology. Elegant, isn't it? And you made it so easy for us with all of those interviews. We have enough samples from you to keep you 'talking' for weeks."

She opened her mouth to tell him that Ekatya would never believe that, but common sense grabbed her just in time. He knew too much about her, but he couldn't know the most important thing.

"And how long do you think the video band excuse will work?" she said instead.

"Long enough to get what we need from you." He rested his hands on top of the silver case, fingers intertwined, and she was not surprised to see that his nails were all an identical length and perfectly groomed. "Dr. Rivers, you're about to publish a book that is very problematic. Fortunately, we intercepted the manuscript, and we know you haven't yet delivered the final version. So there's still time to do the right thing. We simply need you to rewrite the concluding chapter."

She forgot her fear in the face of this ridiculous statement. "To match your bigoted views? Not in this lifetime or the next. The DOP are a bunch of tiny-minded cowards, and I would never compromise my academic integrity to lie for you. No one would believe it even if I did. I'm on record a hundred times, saying exactly what I know to be true. The Alseans aren't a danger to us. We're the danger to them, as we've already proven."

"Oh, you're not doing this for me," he said calmly. "You're doing it for the organization employing me. And yes, that is the Defenders of the Protectorate. They're enjoying quite a surge in popularity these days, thanks to your Alseans. The right person at the right time could break into real power, surfing that wave. They just need a nudge."

"They'll have to find it somewhere else."

He eyed her. "You're very brave all of a sudden."

"There are things worth being brave for. My academic reputation is one of them. So is my belief in the Alseans." If they had studied her enough to know her habits, her voice patterns, her word choices, and her planned schedule with Ekatya, then surely they also knew her reputation for never backing down on an academic question when she thought she was right.

He sighed. "I did tell them you would say that. Would you like to reconsider?"

His calm manner was making her skin crawl. But she had no choice.

"I won't."

"Very well."

He nudged up his pristine sleeve with a single finger and tapped a device on his wrist. It looked a bit like an Alsean wristcom.

The mountain-sized man entered the room from the outside corridor and stood with his arms hanging loose at his sides. "Yes?"

"Osambi, it's time for the second lesson."

Osambi looked at her, his expression as impassive as ever. Then he smiled.

It was the most frightening thing she had ever seen.

She was out of the chair before the thought even registered, backing away from him as he approached. But there was nowhere to go in the unfurnished room, and he was huge. She screamed when he lunged for her, then screamed again when he caught her and yanked her around. Before she could take another breath, he had a thick arm clamped around her throat and both of her arms immobilized. She tried to kick backward, remembering something Ekatya had said about targeting the kneecap, but it was like kicking a tree.

Her vision was tunneling from the lack of oxygen, and her focus switched from escape to survival. Desperately she clawed at his forearm.

He tightened the choke hold.

She was limp and on the verge of unconsciousness when he slammed her into the chair and snapped the restraints closed on her wrists and ankles. By the time her vision cleared, her head had been locked to the high back by bands around both her throat and her forehead. She was utterly trapped.

The blond man had not moved.

"Let me explain what's about to happen," he said pleasantly. He tapped an access code into the front of the silver case, then held his thumb to a scanner. The top silently folded itself to the sides, and a padded ring rose up on three telescoping legs. When it stopped its motion, he lifted a silver circlet from the ring and held it up for her to see. Small round tabs sprouted from one side of it at irregular intervals, like leaves hanging from a vine.

"This is my own invention. I'm as proud of it as you are of your research." He handed the circlet to Osambi, who took it and vanished behind her.

"And I'm as good at what I do as you are," the man continued. "We have something in common, you and I. We've both worked very hard on our reputations."

She wished she could fling a defiant curse at him or pretend a lack of concern, but she was so panicked that her entire body was trembling. When Osambi's thick fingers brushed her forehead, she let out an involuntary squeak.

The circlet was pressed onto her head, its tabs sliding through her hair as Osambi settled it into position.

"That is an interface between your brain and my decisions." The blond man took a small control from his chest pocket. "And this is where I input my decisions. With this, I can send commands to your nervous system, telling it to generate specific nerve impulses that will result in targeted muscular contractions." He smiled suddenly. "It's so rewarding to be able to explain this to someone who understands. Usually, I have to find simpler words for simpler minds. Your mind is a thing of beauty, Dr. Rivers. I've been looking forward to training it."

Fucking stars, he really was insane. But the worst kind of insane: an intelligent sadist.

"Do you know what nociceptors are?" He waited a moment. "No, I see you don't. They're sensory receptors, part of your nervous system. They evoke pain in response to injury. Muscles, the periosteum—that's the sheath around your bones—and the connections between ligaments or tendons and bones are particularly rich in nociceptors. That's why a broken bone hurts so very much, or a torn ligament or muscle. Are you beginning to understand?"

She closed her eyes, summoned up every bit of her courage, and whispered, "I won't do it."

"I know," he said. "Because you don't fully understand yet. But you will."

She kept her eyes closed, her trembling slowing as her body seemed to realize that what was about to happen was inevitable. But she could not watch. She heard a chair scrape, and then smaller, more nimble fingers touched her head. The circlet's tabs moved slightly, and after a pause, she felt more than heard a hum as the tabs clamped down. Though they were not sharp, she envisioned a monster closing its jaws on her head, its teeth poised to crunch through her skull. She was on the edge of something terrible, and just as helpless as if her vision were reality.

The chair scraped again.

"Here is the beauty of my system," the man said. "I can target any part of your body I want. I can cause very specific damage to muscles, tendons, or bones. Or all three. For instance, I could break the index finger on your left hand."

She tensed, her left hand digging into the chair arm.

"But I won't do that, because you need your hands to make those changes to your manuscript. Keep that in mind, Dr. Rivers. It's a few small changes. It doesn't even have to affect your overall conclusions."

She tried to shake her head, forgetting that it was impossible. He saw it anyway.

"Yes, yes, you won't do it. You won't do it *today*. And you might not do it tomorrow. But I have unlimited time, while you have limited resources. Now, I did say I wouldn't break your finger. But I'm going to break something else."

Her body was rigid with anticipation as she waited, suspended between his words and the pain that hovered just above her, waiting to close its jaws.

When it came, it did not bite. It seized her upper right chest in an inexorable grip and slowly ground her ribs to dust.

As an active twelve-year-old girl, Lhyn had once missed a step while jumping from rock to rock on a mountain hike with friends. She had fallen awkwardly between two boulders, landing chest down on the protruding tip of a buried rock. It had fractured one of her ribs.

She had long forgotten the pain of that moment, but she remembered it now. This was the same pain, slowed down to an infinite agony. It was the exact moment of landing on that rock, over and over and over again.

And over.

And over.

Again, and again, and again and again.

She didn't know she was screaming until the seizing of her chest finally stopped and the roar in her ears ceased enough for her to hear herself. She closed her mouth and coughed, then cried out because the cough sent a flame of agony through her chest.

"Open your eyes."

She gasped for air, unable to take a deep breath without activating that excruciating flame.

"Dr. Rivers, open your eyes or I will break another one."

Her eyes snapped open.

His expression was perfectly calm, as if he had just offered her a cup of tea rather than inflicting the most horrific pain she had ever experienced. Not even her broken arm in the *Caphenon* crash compared. She had been unconscious for that and too much in shock to feel the full pain when she woke.

"That was your second lesson," he said. "I fractured your fifth rib on the right side. I could have fractured a lower one, which would have been much easier for you. Lower ribs don't impact your breathing nearly as much. But you're too intelligent, so I'm afraid your lessons will have to be a bit more… harsh. Now, I want you to think about what I'm asking you to do. It's only a few words. Just change a few words in the last chapter of your manuscript, and you won't have to feel this ever again."

Shifting his gaze, he addressed the man who still stood behind her. She had forgotten he was there.

"Osambi, take her back to her room."

Her chin slumped to her chest when Osambi released her head and neck. The tabs loosened their grip on her head, and she was vaguely aware of the circlet being removed and handed over to the blond man.

Osambi freed her wrists and ankles, then scooped her up into his thick arms as if she weighed nothing. The movement jostled her rib, and she cried out again.

Please, please don't drop me on the bed, she thought.

He dropped her.

CHAPTER 40
Missing

Ekatya came awake with a startled intake of breath, her hand automatically going to rub the ache in her chest. It had started two days after Lhyn's departure, and she had developed an odd appreciation for it. In the calm of her quarters at the end of a long shift, she fancied that it was a little piece of Lhyn that was lodged in her heart, quietly missing its owner.

Not that she would ever say anything like that out loud.

She dropped her hand down to tap the pad by her bed, bringing up the automatic night shift illumination. Smoothly, the room shifted from pitch blackness to a soft, reddish light.

Swiveling in place, she brought her feet to the floor and then froze, staring at the control pad she had just tapped.

With her right hand, which had been rubbing the *right* side of her chest.

"What now?" she murmured. Yet another new aspect to their tyree bond? She didn't enjoy these things cropping up when Lhyn wasn't here to discuss them with her.

She picked up her robe from the foot of the bed and pulled it on as she walked through the open door. The automatic illumination, having been activated by the bedroom control pad, detected her movement and brought up soft lighting throughout the space. To her left, the living area seemed uncharacteristically boxed in. Without the large display creating a virtual window, the space looked as small as it really was.

She turned right, walking past her desk and into the kitchen area, where she pulled a glass from behind the wooden brace holding it on its shelf. With a quick tap at the sink she filled the glass with water, drank it down, then upended it and pressed it into the cleaning rack. The tabs snapped into place, locking the glass in position.

The motions were already automatic, trained into her from years of living aboard a starship, where it was never wise to leave things lying around. Space travel in a ship the size of the *Phoenix* was smooth as an oiled marble ninety-nine percent of the time, but that other one percent—usually during interspace transition—could make things very messy very quickly.

She and Lhyn had both laughed at how long it took her to break those habits, first on Alsea and then on Tashar. Eventually, she had taught herself to be a little careless. But she had fallen right back into her routines within one day of stepping aboard her new ship.

Now she sat at her desk and tapped on the day shift illumination, set to one-quarter strength. The reddish light turned to a warm yellow as she activated her desk screen and checked the time converter. It was still early in the morning on Qwonix, but Lhyn would be up and getting ready to catch her shuttle. She was a little surprised that Lhyn hadn't returned her call last night, but then again, she was in a hotel with a few thousand anthropologists. They had probably gone out to dinner and stayed up all night talking about esoteric cultural mores.

Before she could touch the quantum com control, a message light blinked at her. Smiling, she pulled it up and listened to the welcome sound of Lhyn's voice.

Half a minute later, the smile dropped away. Staying? For a few *days?*

She stared at the playback line on her screen and slowly shook her head. That made no sense.

When she called the hotel, there was indeed no video connection. A harassed-sounding clerk informed her that it would probably take half a day to restore the service and he was very sorry for the inconvenience. At her request, he connected her to Lhyn's room.

Her call was picked up immediately, but it was not Lhyn on the other end. Or at least not the real Lhyn.

"This is Dr. Rivers. I'm in writer's seclusion for the next four days, because I can't seem to get this project finished any other way. I won't be listening to messages, so please don't leave one. If it's urgent, call the front desk and they'll notify me. Otherwise, try me again in four days."

Ekatya disconnected, her stomach lurching. She called the hotel again and got the same clerk.

"This is an emergency," she said. "I need to speak with Dr. Rivers."

"If you'll tell me your message, I'll pass it to her when she checks." His tone intimated that he did not believe her for a second.

"I don't need you to pass her a message, I need you to walk up to her room and transfer this call personally."

"I can't do that. Our guests pay for their privacy. I have strict instructions from Dr. Rivers—"

"I don't *care* what instructions you think you have, this is a genuine emergency! Dr. Rivers may be in trouble. How do you think your hotel will look if—"

"Dr. Rivers was here not half an hour ago, checking for messages. I'm looking at the notification on my system right now. Stop trying to bother her." He cut the call.

She let out a wordless shout of rage and slammed her fist on her desk. Then she dropped her head into her hands, her mind racing. Think, she told herself. Think and plan.

Something was very wrong. Lhyn's message would seem perfectly reasonable to anyone who didn't know how hard their separation was for both of them—or that Lhyn might not even have gone there for the keynote speech had Ekatya not encouraged her. It had been manufactured somehow.

But it sounded exactly like her. Ekatya had nothing to prove otherwise except a gut feeling. And that would get her nowhere.

A gut feeling…

She sat up straight. "Oh, shek," she whispered. The right side. Her chest had been hurting on the *right* side.

She had Commander Kenji's quarters on the intraship com before remembering just in time that she was still in her robe. When he answered, she had switched the call to voice only.

"Commander, I'm sorry for the early hour. But I need your assistance."

Commander Kenji asked no questions and met Ekatya in his office ten minutes after her call.

"Before we start," she said as she sat in his guest chair, "I have to tell you that this isn't ship's business. It's personal."

He nodded slowly, his black braids gleaming in the too-bright light of his office. Outside, the corridors were still in night shift illumination. "Then it must be something serious."

Her relief at his acceptance nearly brought tears to her eyes. "Thank you. That means a great deal to me." She held up a data wand. "I received a message from Dr. Rivers that sounds just like her. It's her voice, it's her phrasing, but it's not her. And I can't explain how I know that, but I know. Is there any way that you can prove this message is fake?"

"Most likely." He took the wand and plugged it into his deskpad. "If it's fake, there will be minute inconsistencies in the vocal pattern. Those can be leveled out, but they can't be erased entirely. There may also be background sounds that can't be fully separated from the voice. Voice patch technology has come a long way, but some things are still impossible." He tapped at his deskpad, staring at his screen, then looked at her. "This will take some time, Captain. Why don't you have breakfast, and I'll call you when I have something?"

She almost smiled at the gentle dismissal. He didn't want her hovering.

"That's a good idea, I suppose." Not that she could eat a bite with her stomach clenched the way it was. But there was always coffee.

It took Kenji more than an hour to call her back. She was surprised she hadn't worn a hole in her living area carpet.

"It's a fake," he said, looking solemnly at her through the desk display. "I can give you all the technical explanations if you want a real report, but the short version is, this was a very expensive job done by someone who knows their work. If I didn't have access to the best military systems in the Protectorate, I wouldn't have been able to find the inconsistencies. At least not in less than a day."

Her heart was pounding so hard that she could feel it in her throat. "Thank you, Commander. I can't tell you how much I appreciate this."

"It was no trouble. But Captain…that's the sort of message a person produces when they want someone to disappear."

"I know." She had no idea how she was speaking coherently.

"Is there anything else I can do to help?"

"If I think of anything, I'll tell you. I have another call to make. Thank you again."

She activated the quantum com with trembling fingers. There was only one person who could help, and he had set the whole thing up. She just didn't understand why.

Director Sholokhov came on the screen looking exactly the same as always, despite her calling an hour before most people in Gov Dome were waking up. "Captain Serrado, what an unexpected—"

"Why?" she blurted. "Why would you do this? You said we were even. You agreed that I did everything you asked."

He frowned. "You're making no sense. What are you talking about?"

"Why would you take—" She stopped as the thought hit.

Sholokhov loved to play games with her, yes. But they were all power games. Games where he withheld information from her, never games where he pretended not to have information himself. That was antithetical to the image he liked to present.

"Captain, if you're going to call at such an uncivilized hour, would you do me the courtesy of speaking in whole sentences?"

"Lhyn has been kidnapped," she said. "I thought it was you, but it's not, is it?"

He stared at her. "That's impossible. I've had an—" He snapped his mouth shut.

"I knew you had someone watching her. I mean, I suspected. Are they still? Did they see anything?"

"Slow down, Captain. I've never seen you like this. It certainly does prove that I was right about which lever to pull with you. Now, tell me what you know."

She told him about the fake message, explained that the whole hotel had been taken off the visual quantum com band just to back it up, and reiterated Lhyn's planned schedule and how unlikely it was that she would deviate from it. Then she prepared herself to make an offer that would shackle her to him for the rest of her life.

"This is extremely disturbing," he said irritably. "There's a new player on the board, and I only hear about it from you? I'll get back to you." The screen went blank, leaving her staring at it in abbreviated shock.

It was a good thing they were in transit between space stations, because Ekatya was useless all morning. Had she been required to actually perform her job, it would not have gone well. She went through the motions on the bridge, retired to her office the first chance she had, and proceeded to drive herself insane imagining all of the possible ways Lhyn could be hurting right now.

Sholokhov finally called after lunch.

"She was taken immediately after returning from dinner," he said without preamble. "Right out from under my operative's nose, which I am not pleased about. We've traced her as far as the city shuttle station, where she was transferred to a ship in orbit. That ship filed a false flight plan. I'm having it tracked now, but it's painstaking work. The moment the ship left orbit, this became a far more difficult task."

She waited for him to inform her of the cost. Though he had not given her the chance to offer earlier, he would expect it. Sholokhov did nothing for free.

"The word on the wires is that Kane Muir picked up a new job," he said. "This might be it. Captain, I've wanted Muir for a very long time. He's had his fingers in some very nasty jobs and interfered with several projects of mine. I believe you and I might be able to help each other. If you hear anything, think of anything, you call me immediately. Do you understand?"

"Yes," she said faintly. She could hardly fathom her good fortune. Sholokhov had neither friends nor allies, but he did engage in temporary alliances when interests aligned. Right now, his interests aligned with hers.

In a stronger tone, she asked, "Who is Kane Muir?"

"He's a ghost. He's slipped through my net three times already, and he's cost me—well, never mind that. Muir is a freelance fixer, the best in the business. But this is the closest I've ever been to him, thanks to your warning. You did well, Captain."

He ended the call. She was still staring at the screen, the word *fixer* repeating in her head. She knew what that meant.

Her hand drifted up to the right side of her chest.

CHAPTER 41
Obedience

ONCE LHYN RECOVERED FROM THE agony of being dropped on the bed, she looked for a way to bind her chest and stabilize the injury. There was nothing in the room she could use, other than tearing a strip off the sheet. With her right arm pressed tightly against her side, such a vigorous physical motion was impossible.

But she had a towel.

Working slowly and with only one hand, she laid the towel on the bed and folded it twice lengthwise. Then she sat with her back to it, threaded one end under her right arm, and used her left hand to pull the other around her body. Gathering both ends in front of her sternum, she twisted them together until the towel was as tight as she could make it. Though not ideal, it did support her chest and provided some relief—for as long as she could hold the ends in her hand.

She had no idea how much time passed after that, but it felt like hours. Hours in which all she could focus on was breathing, because if she took anything more than a shallow breath, it set off a fresh flare of pain. Until now, she had never appreciated what a miracle a full, deep breath really was. She didn't think she would ever take that for granted again.

When the bedroom door finally opened, she jumped involuntarily and stifled her groan.

The blond man came in, carrying a bed tray.

She could smell the food from where she sat, propped up against the head of the bed, and her stomach growled in response.

He smiled at her. "Very clever, using the towel. I'm impressed. Though it's no more than I expected from you. Come in, Osambi."

As he set the tray on the floor, Osambi stepped in, a medkit dangling from one hand and a stack of clothes held in the other.

Lhyn pressed herself farther against the headboard at the sight of him.

"Thank you." The blond man put the clothing and kit on the foot of the bed. "Now, we need to get you undressed. You don't want to sleep in those clothes."

"No." The very idea of Osambi touching her made her cringe.

"I'm afraid no isn't one of your options. Don't fight, Dr. Rivers. It will only hurt you more."

"No, no…" She tried to scramble away, toward the other side of the bed, but Osambi wrapped his massive hand around the back of her neck and squeezed. His fingers and thumb bit in, immobilizing her.

He held her in place as he yanked away the towel and stripped off her suit jacket with no concern for the pain he was causing. When her right arm was pulled back, she barely managed to stifle a scream.

Her shirt and bra went next. If she had thought the idea of him undressing her was nauseating, the reality of it was ten times worse.

The blond man came around the side of the bed and examined her naked torso. His gaze lingered on her breasts, and when he looked up, he smiled. "It just occurred to me that I haven't introduced myself. My name is Kane Muir, but you can call me Kane."

She was positive it had not just occurred to him. He had made a deliberate point of telling her his name while she was held immobile and half-naked in front of him.

"Keep her still, Osambi." He shook out a pajama top and, with Osambi's one-handed assistance, put her arms through the sleeves and buttoned it up. They kept her hands from getting anywhere near Kane, a precaution she could only wish were necessary.

Kane opened the medkit and took out an injector. "I did warn you about fighting. Perhaps next time, we won't have to do this with you in a neck hold. I'm told it's quite unpleasant."

Her head jerked in an involuntary movement away from the threatening injector, but the resulting pain from Osambi's grip stopped her. She could swear that she had felt the bones in her neck grinding together.

When the injector's cold tip touched her skin, she closed her eyes and waited for the next terrible thing to happen.

Her pain faded to a tolerable level. He had given her an analgesic?

She opened her eyes to find him replacing the injector in the medkit.

"The towel was a good idea," he said, "but not sustainable. And you shouldn't restrict your breathing, because that could cause fluid buildup in the lungs." He clicked his tongue. "Nasty. It leads to complications, and I don't want that when I've taken such care to give you a nice, clean fracture. You have no displacement, and as long as you don't move around, you won't hurt too badly."

He took off her boots and began undoing her suit pants. Osambi's fingers dug into her neck even more tightly in a silent warning. She wondered how large these bruises would be.

"Dr. Rivers, I am going to ask Osambi to let you go. Then I want you to stand up. Will you obey and not fight, or do I put you back in the chair?"

She wanted so badly to resist, but she would do almost anything to avoid that chair.

"I won't fight," she whispered.

"Good. But that wasn't a complete answer. I also asked if you would obey. Will you?"

She knew exactly what he was doing. It didn't matter. "Yes."

"Ah, excellent. Osambi, let her go."

The pressure on her neck had lasted so long that its release hurt nearly as much as the original grip, even with the analgesic. She swallowed hard and used her left hand to push herself closer to the edge of the bed. Then she stood up.

Kane stripped her suit pants and underwear at the same time. She looked down at him, kneeling at her feet, and felt a wave of hot shame. Here she was, lifting one foot and then the other like a child being dressed by a parent, when Ekatya would have kicked Kane in the face and taken out Osambi somehow, or at least gone down trying.

As Kane pulled up the pajama pants and settled them around her hips, she closed her eyes again and sent out a silent apology.

Kane ordered her back on the bed, up against the headboard, and then set the bed tray across her lap.

"Eat everything. Neither I nor Osambi will be leaving this room until you do."

She obeyed. At least in this, she was doing something good for herself as well.

A few minutes after they took out the tray and left her in the closed room, she felt her head swimming and knew they had drugged the food.

CHAPTER 42
Third lesson

When she woke, the suit rack was gone, along with all of her clothes. She was now barefoot and dependent on Kane for clothing. It was so obvious, the path he was leading her down, but all of her intellectual understanding did her no good. In a way, it made it even worse.

Getting out of the bed was far harder than it had been last time. The analgesic had worn off, her stomach muscles still hurt from Osambi's fist, and now she couldn't use her right arm to help push herself up unless she wanted to suffer the pull on her broken rib. Standing erect felt like a victory. But the effort made her short of breath, and her victory nearly turned to a panic attack when she could not get enough air in her lungs. Desperately she took rapid, shallow breaths, but they weren't enough. She threw her head back, steeled herself, and breathed deeply several times. It hurt, but it was worth it. She no longer felt as if she were suffocating.

Her mouth tasted like wet fur from the drugs. Rubbing her teeth and tongue with the dentifrice felt like the most pleasant thing she had experienced in days. As she rinsed, she realized with dark amusement that it *was* the most pleasant thing she had experienced in days.

She skipped the shower since toweling off was now an impossibility. It wasn't just the broken rib that hurt, but also all of the muscles that had been brutalized in the process of breaking it. Her chest felt as if she had been hit by a shuttle.

After relieving herself, she took a sponge bath with the washcloth that had appeared next to a new, smaller towel, clearly for just this purpose. Then she walked out and sat on the foot of the bed.

The last time, she had gone out there of her own volition. She would not do that again. If the only control she had over this was to make them come and get her, then she would take it.

Her control did not last long. Perhaps two minutes after she had sat down, Osambi opened the door.

"Dr. Rivers!" Kane called from the other room. "It's time."

She sat for another ten seconds, until Osambi shifted his weight. Standing stiffly with her head high, she looked straight ahead and walked out the door.

Kane was waiting in his chair, dressed in yet another suit. The silver case sat on the table in front of him, along with two pads that were lined up perfectly with each other and the case. "Ah, there you are. Good morning."

She stopped next to the restraint chair. "It's not morning."

"Oh? What do you think it is?"

"It's… I don't know," she admitted. "But I know it hasn't been three days. You've only fed me one meal."

"And you were very hungry for that meal, weren't you? It has been three days, and it's time for your third lesson. Sit down."

She briefly closed her eyes, then sat in the hated chair.

"Your training is coming along nicely. Let's see how far we get today." He brought up the virtual screens on the pads. Pointing to the one on her left, he said, "This is your original manuscript. Over here are the few changes I'm asking you to make."

She reached out and angled the right pad slightly toward her.

He frowned and realigned it. "Read it as it is, please."

"I can't see it clearly."

She could see the battle being waged behind his eyes. This would undoubtedly cost her, but right now she didn't care. She would pay the price to take back a little of her power.

Gritting his teeth, he said, "Very well."

She angled the pad again, a hair more than the first time, and hid her smile at his intake of breath.

Her self-congratulations lasted exactly as long as it took to read the highlighted paragraphs. Straightening, she said, "I will not put my name on those words."

"Dr. Rivers, be reasonable. It's just a few words. All you're doing here is admitting to the *possibility* that some Alseans, once released from the regulatory influence of their culture, may pose a danger to us. You're not saying it will happen. You're saying it could happen."

"And your DOP employers will take those words and use them to negate everything else in my book. No. You're also not telling me how you expect anyone to believe this even if I did it. You can't erase the last year and a half."

"Ah, well…there is one other thing we're asking you to do. We need you on video, explaining that while you have a known tendency to throw yourself into your research and identify with your subjects, you examined your data more thoroughly while editing your manuscript and believe the situation calls for a little more nuance."

This time she did smile. "You can invent a recording with my voice on it, but you can't create my image and make it believable. You need me to do that voluntarily."

His expression hardened. "Yes, we do."

"You'll never get that, and do you know why? Because I understand what you're doing here. You're never going to let me go. You can't afford to, because you know I would go straight out and recant everything."

She had not thought it through to the obvious conclusion until now, but for the first time since her kidnapping, she was not afraid. Her head was clear and so was her fate.

"I do so enjoy the intelligent ones," he said. "And they are so unfortunately rare. You've been a joy to work with, Dr. Rivers. I particularly enjoyed listening to you tell me that you would obey me yesterday."

The shame welled up, swift and unwelcome, and she felt the heat in her skin. "That was yesterday." Too late, she realized her error. "I mean, that was before you drugged me."

"Don't second-guess yourself. That was indeed yesterday. Why not obey me today as well? You could save yourself so much…pain."

The way he said the word, caressing the syllable like a lover, made her shiver with dread.

In a last attempt at holding on to her self-esteem, she said, "You're going to kill me anyway. I'd rather die knowing that I stood up for the truth."

They stared at each other in silence. She could not read his expression until a smug smile appeared.

"Remember those words, Dr. Rivers. Because you're going to take them back, at the same time you take back these." He indicated the pad on the left. "Osambi."

She didn't try to run this time. There was no point to it, and Osambi took too much pleasure in hurting her. Nor did she close her eyes as her wrists and ankles were locked to the chair. But she had to when Osambi pushed his disgusting hand against her face, pressing her head back while he locked the band around her throat. He reeked of cologne.

The forehead band went next, then the circlet. As before, Kane stood up to check the circlet's placement and trigger the clamping of the tabs. Then he sat down again and pulled out the control unit.

"Are you ready?" he asked pleasantly. When she refused to answer, he sighed. "Dr. Rivers, that's such a simple question. If you'll recall, I told you in the beginning that your job was to answer questions the way I want you to. Let me make things a little more clear. If you answer me, I will only break a low rib. It won't impact your breathing nearly so much. If you don't answer me, I'll break another high rib."

She did not want to think about trying to breathe with two broken ribs in her upper chest.

"I'm ready," she said, hating every syllable.

"Good," he purred.

The pain seized her on the lower left side of her abdomen, a giant hand reaching in and slowly grinding her bones. She whimpered, trying with all her might not to scream, and she almost succeeded. But the pressure built and built and built, until it finally burst out of her in a wail.

The giant hand stopped squeezing, and she had just enough time to wonder whether Kane had simply waited for her to perform to his satisfaction.

Then the unthinkable happened.

"No!" she screamed when the hand slammed into her upper right chest. "No, no, no…"

Her screams devolved into cries of pure agony. This was a pain that she had never imagined existing. But neither had she imagined anyone intentionally and repeatedly wrenching a bone that had already been broken.

When the hand released her at last, her voice was hoarse. Lost in the lingering pain that throbbed through her entire torso, she barely registered Osambi pulling off the circlet and unlocking the restraints. Once again she was hoisted into his arms, carried into the bedroom, and dropped unceremoniously onto the bed.

Knowing it was coming did not make it any easier. Fire shot through her chest as she hit the mattress, and she wanted nothing more than to roll into a fetal position and sob. But she could not turn onto either side.

"Dr. Rivers, look at me."

Breathe, she told herself. Just breathe.

"I am addressing you, and I expect your obedience. Do you want to hurt even more than you already do?"

She peeled open her eyes and found Kane standing at the side of the bed, looking down at her.

"I need you to understand what just happened. I did not lie to you. I told you that if you obeyed, I would not break another high rib. And I did not."

Semantics. He was playing semantics while breaking her apart piece by piece.

"Had you not obeyed, however, I would indeed have broken a second high rib. You made a wise decision."

Then why didn't it feel that way?

"It's important that you understand that while I may phrase things carefully, I do not lie. I'll remind you of that the next time we speak."

He walked out and closed the door behind him.

CHAPTER 43
Cowardice

KANE BROUGHT IN ANOTHER MEAL. "Time for dinner," he announced.

She was almost certain that it had been morning just a few hours ago. "I'm not hungry."

"You should be. It's been hours. You need to keep up your strength if you're going to continue defying me."

"How am I supposed to keep up my strength with food you've drugged?"

"Ah. I do admit to drugging your last meal, but you needed the sleep. I haven't drugged this one."

She looked at him, then away.

"May I remind you that I do not lie?"

"I'm still not hungry."

"Osambi, would you come in, please?"

She flinched as the giant man entered the room, making it seem smaller just by standing there.

"Tell me," Kane asked him in a conversational tone, "how much did you enjoy striking Dr. Rivers in the stomach that first day? Would you like to do it again?"

Osambi turned a terrifying smile on her.

She ate.

When she had finished the meal, Osambi took out the tray while Kane sniffed the air with a grimace.

"You stink of sweat and fear," he said distastefully. "I can't abide uncleanliness. You need a bath."

Dreading where this was going, she said, "I'll take one."

"And how exactly are you going to do that? You can't reach all the places you need to wash, not with a broken rib on each side. You need help. It's not a weakness to admit that. Osambi!"

She closed her eyes in resignation and kept them closed while Osambi stripped her bare. At least this time it was easier, with only a button-up shirt and stretch-fabric pants to remove. But he still managed to hurt her by yanking the shirt down her arms.

By contrast, Kane was extraordinarily gentle. He was solicitous of her broken ribs, shifting her arms with great care as he wiped down her torso. She was mortified when he brushed the wet washcloth over her breasts, but he made no untoward moves.

Then he told her to spread her legs.

"I only needed help with my top half," she said desperately. "I can take it from here."

His expression turned stern. "Was that a no, Dr. Rivers? Did we not discuss your job here?" Leaning closer, he said quietly, "Obey me."

She stared at him, trying to think of a way out.

"Your next chair time isn't scheduled until tomorrow morning, but I can change that."

She spread her legs and closed her eyes, a tear leaking out as her torturer gently cleaned the parts of her body that he should never have seen, much less touched. When she imagined confessing her cowardice to Ekatya, she put a hand over her face and choked back a sob. How could she ever find the words to explain why she had given up without a fight?

Kane did not take advantage, simply moving on to her legs without a word. Then he dressed her in a fresh pair of pajama bottoms and put her arms through a clean top.

As he buttoned it, he murmured, "You're an attractive woman, Dr. Rivers. I do have my assignment, but perhaps you and I could make a deal."

Her eyes snapped open. "I would rather die."

She thought he would be angry, but he simply smiled. "As you've so astutely pointed out, you *are* going to die. The only question is how. I can make it easy for you, or I can make it more excruciating than you can even imagine."

He leaned down to the medkit on the floor and pulled out an injector. "Let me give you a sample of how easy I can make this for you."

She didn't flinch from the injector this time, and the reward was beyond price. He hadn't given her a mere analgesic. He had given her something that made her pain float away on a cloud of contentment. It had been such a constant for the last several days that she had forgotten what it was like to not feel it.

She remembered now. She gloried in her full, deep breaths, with no broken bones restricting the movement of her lungs, and smiled dreamily. "So nice," she murmured.

"Yes, it is. Good night, Dr. Rivers."

Before she drifted off to sleep, she thought he kissed her cheek.

CHAPTER 44
Hope

"Good morning, Dr. Rivers."

She had grown to detest that phrase. Last night's pain-free euphoria was a distant memory, and she was back to feeling the full impact of two broken ribs—on opposite sides of her body, just to make things as difficult as possible—all of the muscles used to break them, and the continuing ache in her stomach muscles from Osambi's fist. Her neck also hurt from the pinch he had put on her the first day they had stripped her. She could not move her body nor turn her head normally, and she could only take shallow breaths. Her entire existence was again focused on getting enough air and trying not to hurt more than she already did. She wanted another injection, despised herself for wanting it, and hated Kane for creating such opposing needs.

The intellectual side of her, still holding itself distant from the proceedings, saw very clearly how she was being psychologically manipulated. But that didn't stop her from feeling what she did. All it did was make her feel even more helpless.

"Isn't this the part where you tell me it's not morning?" Kane asked with a knowing look. He wore yet another new suit and was leaning forward on the table, his forearms resting on either side of the closed silver case.

"I don't know what time it is." She sat in the restraint chair without being told to. There was no point in resisting.

"Then I do believe we're making progress. If you'd like, you could end this right now by changing those few words in your manuscript and speaking into that recorder." He gestured.

She had not even seen the camera in the corner. Up until now, she had prided herself on noticing every detail of her captivity. She was slipping.

"I won't lie for you," she said tiredly. "I won't betray the Alseans, and I won't betray my own integrity. So let's just get this over with."

"As you wish. Osambi?"

She gave the huge man no reason to handle her roughly, but he still found a way. In what was becoming depressingly normal, she was soon immobilized.

"Are you ready, Dr. Rivers?"

Obey me, she heard him say, even though he had not spoken the words. If she refused to answer, he would make her hurt more than he was already planning to.

"I'm ready," she whispered.

"Oh, look at that. You're doing so well. I'm going to reward your obedience today. I promise you that I will not break any bones."

She perked up. That seemed unbelievably generous.

She changed her mind when the muscles of her stomach seized, in exactly the same place where Osambi had struck her the first day. Except that Osambi had only struck her once, while this felt like being struck again, and again, and again, and again…

The scream tore out of her throat despite her best efforts. But unlike yesterday, when Kane had stopped upon hearing her, today he kept her in the throes of agony.

"Stop!" she cried. "Please!"

It stopped.

She nearly sobbed with relief. Until this moment, she would not have believed that anything could rival the pain of slowly breaking her ribs, but she had underestimated the capabilities of Kane's interface.

"Did I hear you say you'll change your manuscript?"

Tears ran down her cheeks at the sheer hopelessness of it all. "No," she croaked, knowing that she was signing on for more suffering. The first day had been one rib. The second day had been two. Kane loved order, so today was going to be three sessions, and she still had two more to go. The only question was which area of her body he would target next.

"Very well."

He targeted the same place.

She howled as her battered muscles seized once more, the pain spreading to her lower ribs and back. Far off in a distant part of her mind, her intellectual self marveled at how much anguish could be inflicted without causing permanent damage. In a more visceral part of her mind, she saw Osambi in the doorway, lunging forward and burying his massive fist in her stomach.

Again, and again, and again…

When it stopped, she had no air left in her body. Her ribs were on fire once more; she must have taken deep breaths in between the screams.

She had barely adapted to the lower level of suffering when her muscles seized for the third time. Kane was not breaking bones, but he was tearing apart her abdominal muscles fiber by fiber. She honestly could not say which was worse.

After an eternity of pain, the seizure stopped and she gasped for air once more. Her whole torso throbbed, and even shallow breaths hurt. She thought she might never breathe normally again.

When Osambi dumped her on the bed and closed the door, she spent several minutes trying not to cry because she didn't have enough air to do so. She felt light-headed and dizzy, and when she saw Ekatya standing next to the bed in her regular uniform, she did not even question it.

"I'm sorry," she whispered.

Ekatya sat on the bed, her weight making no dent in the mattress. "Why are you sorry?"

"Because I'm not strong enough. He's going to kill me and I can't stop it. It hurts so much, and I'm starting to wonder how I can make him angry enough to just kill me and get it over with. I can't live this way."

Ekatya touched her cheek so gently that it made her eyes water. "You have to keep fighting. Remember the day we met?"

The smile felt foreign on her face. "You looked so good on that stage. All of those merchant marines, watching you like you were an oracle."

"And I was telling them the rules of capture. What is the first rule of capture, Lhyn?"

She closed her eyes, trying to remember, then opened them again because she couldn't bear not seeing Ekatya. "It wasn't really your words I was paying attention to."

"But you know. Even when you're not paying attention, you still pick up the details."

It was wonderful to have something to think about other than how much she hurt now and how much she was going to hurt soon. She let her mind go back to a far more pleasant time, when she had been directed to the wrong conference room and walked in on a Fleet captain giving a lecture. The captain had said…

"Survive. The first rule is just to survive. You told them to do whatever they had to, that there was no shame in…" She trailed off and stared up at the loving eyes watching her. "In…submitting when the alternative is injury or death for themselves or another."

"There is no shame," Ekatya repeated. "No shame in doing what you have to. You think you can't admit to me what you've had to do? You're doing *exactly* what I would do."

"But I'm not." She began to cry. Ekatya's presence had soothed her enough that she had sufficient air to let her tears go, and it was such a relief. "I'm not. You would never have gotten yourself into this mess in the first place. Even if you had, you would have escaped that very first morning. I can't do what you would do."

"And if I had two broken ribs? And was being put through a carefully designed program of drugs, psychological manipulation, and a disrupted circadian rhythm? I'm not a machine, Lhyn. He's *torturing* you. But you're standing up to him. You've already withstood three separate times in that chair. For the love of flight, you're an academic with no military training, and you're making him work for what he wants."

Her tears slowed. It sounded so much better the way Ekatya was saying it.

"If I survive this, and I tell you what happened, will you say this to me for real? Will you tell me I wasn't a coward?"

The tears seemed to have transferred to Ekatya, sliding silently down her cheeks. "I'll tell you that you are the most courageous person I've ever known. You're the person who was willing to die to save the Alseans. You're *still* the person willing to die to save them."

"Then I'll keep trying. I want to survive. I want to hear you say that."

"I will tell you again and again, tyrina."

Warmth flowed through her, easing the pain in her body. "You've never called me that before."

"Do you like it?"

"I love it."

"Good. You're so brave, tyrina. So brave. Sleep now. It won't hurt as much."

"Will you still be here when I wake up?"

"I'm always here." Ekatya reached out and touched her chest. "Always. Nothing he can do will ever dislodge me."

"I love you," Lhyn murmured sleepily. "I'm so glad you're here."

"I love you too. Sleep now."

CHAPTER 45
Plan of action

"Sleep now..."

Ekatya woke up hearing the words coming out of her mouth. For a moment she didn't know where she was. The dream had been so real.

As the last vestiges of sleep cleared and she felt the dull ache in her stomach, fresh tears washed down her cheeks.

"It *was* real," she whispered. "It was real."

Lhyn was suffering. She could hardly even think about the ways in which Lhyn was suffering, but at least she was alive. And somehow, they had connected.

She had to get back there.

She wiped her cheeks, rolled over, and attempted to force herself to sleep.

Ten minutes and six different positions later, she admitted the futility of that endeavor. She was not going to find Lhyn this way, not until she exhausted herself.

Or...

Until she *drugged* herself.

She threw back the covers so forcefully that they ended up on the floor, but she hardly noticed as she pulled on her uniform and commed a sleepy-sounding Dr. Wells.

Four minutes later she was in the medbay, pacing anxiously while she waited for the doctor, who had said she would be there in five. With her gaze fixed on the main doors, she was startled to hear Dr. Wells speak from behind her.

"Captain Serrado?"

Wells was walking toward her from the lift beside the stairs. The chief surgeon's quarters were above the top deck of the medbay. Her closest path in was straight down the lift, a fact Ekatya should have remembered.

"Dr. Wells, thank you for coming so quickly."

Wells covered a yawn with her hand. "Sorry. Of course I would come quickly, if only to find out what a 'non-medical personal emergency' is."

She still looked half asleep. Come to think of it, her quarters were much closer to the medbay than Ekatya's. She should have gotten there before her.

"I didn't check your schedule. What time did you get to sleep last night?"

"You mean this morning? About four hours ago. I'm all right, Captain. Tell me what's wrong."

"Not here." Ekatya tilted her head toward the nearest empty treatment room.

Inside, with the door shut and the privacy screen activated, she said, "I'm invoking doctor-patient confidentiality."

Wells sat in one of the chairs and gestured at the other. "I'm listening."

"How much do you know about the Alseans and their empathy?" Ekatya asked as she sat down.

"Ah…well, that's not where I expected this to go. I've read everything Dr. Rivers has written on the topic, along with most everyone else I know. Spit in a roomful of medical staff and you're guaranteed to hit someone who can quote her."

"So you know about tyrees."

"Who doesn't?"

"And how their connection is physiological as well as emotional."

"Yes, though I could argue that the emotional connection is physiological as well, since it's enabled by—" She stopped and looked more closely. "Why are you asking?"

Ekatya hesitated, then reminded herself that she had to trust or this would never work. "Lhyn and I are tyrees."

There was a moment of charged silence.

"That is *really* not where I expected this to go."

"It's the truth, Dr. Wells. I know it sounds impossible—"

"You're right, it does."

"I said the same thing when Lancer Tal told me we were tyrees. I didn't believe her until she proved it. Mind to mind."

The tiny intake of air sounded loud in the closed treatment room. "You went through an Alsean Sharing. You've let everyone think Dr. Rivers was the only one. Why isn't this in your medical record?"

"I disobeyed orders for the sake of Alsea and barely escaped court-martial. It didn't seem wise to volunteer that bit of information."

She saw that hit right where she had aimed it, reminding Wells of her own near miss with a court-martial.

"Still, you should be checked—"

"I'll sit through any exam you want. Just not now. Right now, I need you to believe what I'm telling you. We're not empaths and we don't have the emotional connection, but we're connected in other ways, ways that transcend distance. And we've recently learned that…that our bond can also include two-way communication."

Wells stared at her. "I'm going to take a wild scientific leap and guess that you don't mean two-way communication while you're in the same room."

"Do you remember when you changed out my High Alsean language chip?"

"Of course."

"Did I say something out loud, right before I went under the anesthesia?"

Her expression softened. "Yes, you did. It was…personal."

Ekatya's hands clenched in her lap. This was about to get far more personal, but she would do anything she had to. "I saw Lhyn standing next to you. That's why I said what I did. And when Lhyn came aboard after our shakedown cruise, she told me that she was really there. She thought it was a dream, but she knew I chose to keep my Terrahan chip."

After several long seconds of silence, Wells said, "All right. Let's suppose, hypothetically, that what you're saying is physically possible and—"

"It's not hypothetical!" Ekatya snapped. "He's torturing her, and he's going to kill her if we don't get her out of there!" She saw Wells draw back, envisioned a swift diagnosis of mental incompetence for duty, and held up a placating hand. "I'm sorry, I'm just… Dr. Wells, Lhyn has been kidnapped."

"*What?*"

"She's been kidnapped, and Sholokhov thinks—"

"Sholokhov is involved?"

"Yes, because the man who has Lhyn is…" She stopped, realizing in that moment that she knew it was Kane Muir who had Lhyn. Sholokhov was working on a supposition, but she *knew*.

She had to tell him.

But how could she explain her source?

"Who has Lhyn?" Wells asked urgently.

She refocused. "His name is Kane Muir. He's a fixer; he gets people to do whatever his employers need them to do. He's in the process of breaking Lhyn right now, and she's resisting with everything she has, but we're running out of time. He's ramping up the torture and if she breaks, if she gives him what he wants, he'll kill her."

Wells looked horrified. Then she straightened and said, "Tell me what you need me to do."

"I need you to *believe* me. Please, just set aside your scientific practicality and accept what I'm telling you. I can connect with her. I've done it twice now. I saw her twenty minutes ago."

"How?"

"The same way she saw me when you changed out my language chip. In a dream. But it was *real*, Dr. Wells. It was real. She was directing it, because I was saying things I couldn't have said otherwise—I knew things that only she knows. But everything I said, I would have said anyway…" She trailed off, realizing how utterly impossible this sounded. Wells was looking at her with skepticism written all over her face. "I don't know how it works. I just know that it does, and it's the only connection I have to her. It's the only thing that can possibly save her. No one knows where she is, and Kane Muir has escaped Sholokhov three times already. If he escapes again… Please, *please* believe me."

The skepticism did not fade, and the drive that had pushed Ekatya out of bed and out her door sputtered and died. She dropped her face into her hands. She was never going to convince Dr. Wells. She was probably going to be booted out of her bridge chair and that might be for the best anyway, because she couldn't concentrate, and Lhyn was going to die because she was failing in the very first step of her action plan. She was failing.

"Captain."

She shook her head. She did not want to hear these words.

"I don't know if I believe you. But two years ago I would never have believed empaths could exist, and here we are, with an entire planet of empathic aliens. So tell me what you need me to do."

Hope poured through her, giving her new strength. "I need you to drug me. Not enough to put me under, but enough to…I don't know, break through whatever walls keep us apart when we're conscious. Something enables us to connect when we're both not fully on the conscious plane. Or the unconscious one. Lhyn was awake, but she was half out of her mind with pain and shock, and Kane's been drugging her—" A sob crawled up her throat, but she pushed it back down with savage force. She had no time for that. "I need to control this somehow, so I'm really there. I can't help her unless I can really be there."

"You need to uncouple the ascendancy mechanism," Dr. Wells said.

"What?"

"Your brain trades off. The conscious side is ascendant when it needs to be, and when you sleep, the subconscious takes over. Each side accomplishes specific tasks, and neither one can accomplish those tasks if the other is still active. There's a mechanism that regulates the tradeoff. What you need to do is temporarily uncouple that mechanism, so both sides can be active at the same time."

"Yes," Ekatya breathed. "Yes, exactly. Can you do it?"

"I can, but it's tricky and I'll have to monitor you constantly. And you—"

"I'm ready." She began to strip off her uniform jacket.

"Wait. Captain, you might be ready, but I'm not. I need to calculate your dosage and think about contingencies and get everything set up before we start. I won't do this until I'm certain I can make the procedure safe for you."

"I don't *care* if it's safe—"

"But I do. I'll help you, but your safety is paramount. Those are my terms."

"She could die!"

Wells fixed her with a calm gaze and repeated, "Those are my terms."

"You're a hard woman, Dr. Wells." Ekatya was not calm at all.

"I'm a chief surgeon, and that means I make hard decisions. You do the same thing. I'm sickened by what's happening to Lhyn and I'll do anything I can to help her, but she is not my patient right now. You are. And you're asking me to take a leap of faith."

It took every bit of willpower Ekatya had to sit there, breathe deeply, and acknowledge that Wells was right. As much as she wanted to charge in and take action, this was a mission and missions had to be planned.

"I understand," she said at last. "When will you be ready?"

Wells looked upward, apparently making mental estimates. "About an hour."

"An hour!" She stopped herself. "Fine, an hour. I'll…I'll figure out some way to not die of a stress-induced heart attack before then."

"That sounded like a joke, but I'm wondering if I need to give you a sedative before we start. Which would complicate my dosage calculations considerably—"

"No, I'm fine. Don't do anything that would make this take longer than it already will." Ekatya stood up, then paused as an idea occurred. "I'll program a translator and send it over. I'll be speaking out loud, and I don't want Lhyn to say anything Kane might be able to understand."

Dr. Wells nodded. "You'll be speaking in Terrahan."

"No. If Kane is good enough to outwit Sholokhov, then he's done his research and he'll be ready for Lhyn to speak her native language under duress. But I doubt he'll expect her to speak High Alsean."

CHAPTER 46
Through the door

Dr. Wells met Ekatya in the medbay lobby an hour later and led her into the lift. At her look of surprise, she said, "You thought we'd be doing this in a treatment room?"

"Why aren't we?"

"Because I'm not going to inject you once and then sit down to read a book. I don't think you realize what you've asked for, Captain."

They stepped out on the third level and walked down the hall to an empty surgery bay. Ekatya stopped in the doorway, staring at all of the equipment that had been arranged around a bed. "What in all the purple planets is this?"

"This is what I need to make sure I can balance both sides of your consciousness, monitor your brain waves and vital signs, record the data, and regulate the dosage required to keep you there. And I am pushing the limits of both my abilities and my ethics doing this alone. At the first sign of trouble, I'll either yank you out or bring someone in to help. I need your permission for the latter."

"And if I don't give it, this is over before it starts?"

Wells nodded.

"Then I give it. But it had better be someone you trust implicitly, because if word of this gets out—"

"You have my personal guarantee it won't."

Ekatya nodded and pulled off her jacket as she walked to the bed.

Wells took it from her hand. "Your shirt, too. I need access to your inner elbow and your chest." She traded a medshirt for the uniform shirt and hung the clothes in a locker while Ekatya tried to get comfortable on the bed.

Before long, Ekatya had a cannula in her arm and data recorders taped to her chest and head. She couldn't remember the last time she had received medication through a cannula, but Dr. Wells explained that she would be titrating the combination of drugs necessary. "There's a certain bit of trial and error," she added, which did not fill Ekatya with confidence. But this was her only option. She had to trust.

When her head began to swim and she felt as if she were falling backward through a tunnel, her hopes rose. She closed her eyes, waiting to connect, waiting to see Lhyn and tell her she was there to help.

But she never found her. It was as though she hit a closed door and could not go through it.

When Dr. Wells brought her back to full consciousness, she panicked.

"No! I can't give up!"

"We're not giving up. But you said you both had to be in that space between conscious and subconscious. If Lhyn is fully awake, or fully asleep, you won't connect. We just need to wait and try again."

They tried every hour on the hour.

On the fourth attempt, the door was open.

Nothing Ekatya had imagined prepared her for what she saw when she went through it.

CHAPTER 47
Teamwork

Kane had sadistically targeted her stomach muscles three times now. On top of the torn and bruised tissues from the previous session, the pain was beyond excruciating. Lhyn had screamed herself hoarse. When the spasms finally stopped after the third time, her entire world had come down to a single goal: surviving the fourth assault. She only had to live through one more, and then she could rest.

Gasping, she opened her eyes and thought that Kane had gone too far and she really was dying. Because Ekatya stood on the other side of the table, her hands over her mouth and tears streaming down her face.

"I couldn't stop him." Ekatya could hardly get the words out, and she was speaking in High Alsean. "I'm so sorry. I tried, but my body isn't here."

Lhyn opened her mouth to tell her it was all right, but Ekatya held up her hand.

"Don't speak to me. Not yet. Don't let him know you see me. But I *am* here, Lhyn. This is not a hallucination. I'm really here, and you have to survive this so we can get you out."

"Dr. Rivers, would you like this to stop?"

Kane was watching her as calmly as ever, the hated control in his perfectly manicured hand.

"Yes," Lhyn croaked.

Kane's eyebrows rose. "Really? Then—"

"But your price is too high."

His eyes narrowed. "You should have stopped after 'yes.' This one will hurt."

And oh, Shippers, it did. He chose the lower rib on her right side, to match the lower left rib he had already broken. It seemed to take an hour for the giant fist to slowly, viciously tear her bone apart.

When it ended, she slumped in the chair, held upright only by the neck and forehead restraints. Her throat hurt from the screams, and she could not stop a cough. It sent such a wave of pain through her abdomen that she nearly passed out.

But she was done. She had survived four.

She opened her eyes, seeking Ekatya and finding her exactly where she had been before, anguish carved in every line of her face.

It's all right, I'm done, she wanted to say, but the words were torn from her brain along with every other rational thought when the seizure slammed into her upper left chest.

The sheer shock of it undid her completely. She didn't understand how she couldn't be done. Kane was obsessed with order; he had been torturing her in a linear progression. This went against everything she had observed in him. It didn't make sense.

Only now did she realize that being prepared for pain could make a difference in how it felt. She had not been prepared for this, and it was by far the worst. She no longer made any sound as she screamed.

After an eternity of agony, it stopped, but that hardly mattered anymore. She was terrified by the realization that she no longer knew what to expect. Not since this torture had begun had she been so close to giving up. She had no strength to open her eyes, not even to see Ekatya.

When Osambi began to remove the restraints, the relief sent tears coursing down her cheeks. It was over. He wasn't going to hurt her again. She could live for another few hours.

"Lhyn, I'm still here." Ekatya's voice trembled. "I'm still here, and I'm not going anywhere. Fucking Hades, I don't even know if you're conscious. What?"

"Gently, Osambi. At this point, she's rather fragile. I wouldn't want any internal organs to be punctured. She may want to die, but I can't let that happen just yet."

"Dr. Wells says you're still conscious, because if you weren't, I'd be thrown out of this connection. Listen to my voice. You're not alone. Not anymore."

She would never have guessed that Osambi knew how to be gentle, but the huge man somehow got her out of the chair and onto the bed without hurting her any more than necessary.

"I'm still here, Lhyn. It's over for now."

Breathing was nearly impossible. She had matching broken ribs on each side of her chest, both high and low, and abdominal muscles torn and strained beyond bearing. Being conscious was a torment all on its own, and she longed for the escape of sleep. Or drugs. She remembered the beautiful peace of the drug Kane had given her and wondered what it would cost her for another dose.

"Open your eyes, Dr. Rivers."

She really did not know if she could.

"Are you that easily broken? Just by a little surprise?"

"You despicable piece of shit." Ekatya spat out the words, her voice brimming with a hatred Lhyn had never heard before. "You're not worth the dirt under her feet. If I ever get my hands on you, you'll know what it means to be broken."

She might have been losing her mind, but this fantasy was far better than reality. If Ekatya were truly here, Kane would already be in pieces.

Simply envisioning it gave her strength, and she peeled open her eyes to find Ekatya standing next to Kane, glaring at him with a burning fury. Oblivious to the vengeful spirit beside him, he smiled down at Lhyn.

"Ah, there you are. You're very intelligent, but you can make mistakes. Sometimes you forget that, don't you? You're the best in your field, and you forget that you're not always right, not every time. You were wrong today. Do you understand how yet?"

She no longer understood anything, a fact he seemed all too aware of as he added, "Well, I'm sure you'll figure it out. After all, I did give you all the clues you needed. I numbered your lessons for you. Your mistake was forgetting the first one." He leaned forward. "Perhaps you also made a mistake about the Alseans. There's no shame in admitting it. And then this could all be over."

Straightening, he smiled more broadly, then turned and left. The door clicked shut.

Ekatya stepped to the bed, her silky black hair sliding over her uniformed shoulders. She looked so healthy, so *whole*.

"They're gone," she said. "But I'm still here. Tell me what happens next. How long do you have before they come back?"

Lhyn licked her lips and tried to find enough saliva to swallow. Her throat was so dry from the screaming that she was not sure she could speak.

"Say it in High Alsean."

Her eyes opened all the way, and she looked at Ekatya—really looked at her—for the first time.

The hallucinatory Ekatya would not ask her to speak in High Alsean. That was a strategic tactic, and strategy was Ekatya's specialty. Not hers.

"Is it really you?"

Ekatya's smile was breathtaking. "It's really me. My body is on the *Phoenix*, and Dr. Wells is taking good care of it. But the part of me that matters is here with you." She tilted her head, listening to something Lhyn could not hear. "Dr. Wells begs to differ and says my body matters, too. I suppose she has to say that; she's a chief surgeon."

Pain was malleable, it seemed. It was worse when she wasn't expecting it, and right now, with joy rushing through her veins, it was better. Ekatya was *here*. Just looking at her made it easier to breathe.

"Tell Dr. Wells thank you," she whispered. "If I don't survive, at least I'll die having seen you one more time."

"Oh, no. No no no. That's not what I'm here for. I'm here to get you out. Lhyn, listen. I can only connect as long as you're in this state. If Kane comes in here and drugs you again, I'll lose you. And if you fall asleep, I'll lose you. So we have to act now."

"How…" She swallowed, grateful to even be able to, and found that she could speak in a rasping voice. "How do you know he drugs me?"

"Because I was here before. That wasn't a hallucination. That was me. But I was dreaming; we did it by accident. This is on purpose."

It took a moment for the import of that to sink in. When it did, a whole new level of dread came with it.

"Then…you know?" she asked hesitantly. "About the rest?"

Ekatya reached out, her fingers hovering above Lhyn's cheek. "I wish I could touch you, like I did in that dream. Yes, I know. And you're still the most courageous person I've ever met."

The sheer relief loosened a tightness in her chest that had nothing to do with Kane's cruelty. Tears leaked out, sliding down her temples and into her hair. "You really were here. You know what that means to me."

"I do, tyrina." Ekatya smiled again, her beauty lighting up the room. She was like a comforting, golden glow in the dark and terrifying cave Lhyn had been living in. Her mere presence imparted strength.

Slowly, carefully, Lhyn pushed herself up and back to lean against the headboard. Moving hurt, but it was slightly easier to breathe in this position.

"They won't come back for a while. Kane's pattern is to hurt me, then throw me in here so I can think about how much it hurts and how I can make it stop. Then they come in and…make it hurt less."

She could not meet Ekatya's gaze.

"There is no shame in submitting," Ekatya said quietly. "It's no less true now than it was then. It doesn't change just because I'm really here this time."

She looked up to see Ekatya watching her with eyes full of love and not an atom of judgment. "Thank you," she whispered.

Ekatya nodded. "Let me tell you what's happening out here. It turns out that Kane Muir has a very powerful enemy. Sholokhov hates him. He hates him so much that he's helping me find you, and he's not even asking for lifetime slavery in return."

Lhyn managed a tiny smile. "That's a lot of hate."

"I know. So just think about what Sholokhov will do to Kane when he catches him. That man will not go to any prison we've ever heard of."

"Make sure he catches Osambi, too. He's a monster. I don't know which one is worse."

"Lhyn, I only know what you pushed in my head during that dream. Do you have any idea where you are?"

She shook her head. "It looks like an expensive hotel room. And I got a glimpse of the hall outside. That looks like a hotel, too. But I don't know where. I can't see out the window."

Ekatya glanced at it with a startled expression. "That is…very strange."

"What?"

"I couldn't see the window until you mentioned it. It's like I'm not seeing through my eyes *or* yours. More like I'm seeing through your memories, your thoughts. And I'm making some kind of visual composite out of them." She frowned. "So they've deactivated the window. We need to reactivate it."

"I don't know how to do that."

"I don't either, but you know what? I have a shipload of engineers here." She switched to Common. "Dr. Wells, call the chief engineer—no, wait, he'll take forever to explain and nobody will understand it. Do you know an engineer who can give clear, concise instructions on how to temporarily disable a plexan window? Lhyn's has been turned opaque and she can't see anything." She paused. "Perfect. Call him right now. Keep it on your internal com and don't let him come down here, just…tell him to walk you through disabling this one and then reactivating it again." Switching back to High Alsean, she said, "Dr. Wells knows someone. I thought she might. Doctors know everyone. She's going to practice on the window here in the surgery bay."

Lhyn could only look at her, marveling at her existence in this place.

"What?" Ekatya asked.

"It's really you. Not even in my most feverish dreams could I come up with the things you're saying. It's just so…you."

"It's really me, tyrina." She tilted her head. "And I am so proud of you. What I said in that dream—Kane is a professional. Sholokhov says he's the best in the business. And he can't break you. I think you're driving him insane with your resistance."

She didn't believe that. "I'm not resisting anymore. The last two times, I sat in that chair without him even asking."

"Hm." Ekatya pursed her lips. "What is the second rule of capture?"

She seized on the question just as she had in the dream, when having a pleasant memory had meant so much. "It's…to delay."

"You're incredible. You weren't even paying attention, and that was years ago. Yes, to delay. To say or do *anything* necessary to avoid acts that might debilitate you or make you unable to assist your own rescue, as long as what you do doesn't compromise your mission or your loyalties. Did sitting in that chair without being asked compromise the Alseans?"

"No."

"Did it keep you from being hurt even worse?"

"Yes."

"Then it was the right thing to do." She shifted her head. "Dr. Wells is back." For quite some time she was silent, giving Lhyn the space to think about what she had said.

She was looking at this from the perspective of a Fleet captain. And she approved of what Lhyn had done. She *knew* what had happened and she was…proud.

When Ekatya focused on her again, Lhyn was feeling far stronger and more herself. It was remarkable, she thought, how losing the burden of shame and guilt could have a physiological effect.

"Lhyn, I wish I could do this for you. But I can't interact with anything physical. I have to ask you to stand up and walk over to the control pad for the window."

She looked at the distance from the bed to the opposite wall. It seemed insurmountable.

"I can do it," she said. She had to.

"I know you can. Don't do it yet, though. I'm certain Kane has you under audio observation, but he may also be watching you. If he's watching, then you won't have much time. So let me talk you through it before you move."

Anything that let her rest longer was fine with her. "Okay."

"It might be very simple. Kane most likely assumed you wouldn't have any idea how to reactivate that window, so he probably didn't damage it. He just interrupted the circuit that powers the internal reaction."

"Simpler words, please. I don't speak engineering."

Ekatya smiled at her. "One of the very few languages you don't speak. First, you're going to take the cover off the control panel. They're made to be removed by hand, so get your fingernails in the slots at the top and jerk it toward you. It will drop down on a hidden hinge at the bottom. Understood?"

The familiar Fleet speak curled around her brain, bringing a breath of normality with it. "Understood."

"Once you get the cover off, look at the bottom right corner. You'll see a clear tab with circuitry showing through. It's probably on a flat cable, but if not, then look for a cable that's hanging loose. All you have to do is put that tab back where it belongs. The slot for it is in the same corner, on the right edge, facing left. Lhyn, you may only have seconds to do this. The moment you get that tab in, put the cover back on and hit the control. And then look."

"Understood."

She spent a few moments breathing, then began the slow and painful process of moving herself to the edge of the bed. When she tried to straighten, the pull on her abdominals as the muscles were forced to lengthen was excruciating. In the end, she could not stand erect but remained hunched over.

At least her legs still worked. Though her broken ribs jarred with every step, she had been through worse. And Ekatya was beside her every step of the way.

Pulling down the cover required the use of pectoral muscles that had been torn apart in the breaking of her upper ribs. She bit her lip to keep from crying out, but she got it open. The tab was exactly as Ekatya had described, and it was a matter of two seconds to slot it in. She flipped the cover back up, then put her fists on it and leaned her body weight forward. It snapped shut without requiring any muscular effort.

"Smart," Ekatya said approvingly. "Let's see where you are."

Lhyn tapped the control and gasped as the room was suddenly flooded with the red light of either sunrise or sunset. "Oh, my fucking stars," she breathed. It was the last view she had expected.

"I don't recognize it. Where are you?"

She pointed a shaking finger. "That's my conference center. I'm in the same city."

"That clever slime worm." Ekatya scowled. "He set a false trail. Sholokhov is looking for you all over the sector. Everywhere but here."

"What time is it?"

She seemed to hear the real question. "That's sunset."

Lhyn held on to this data point with fierce determination. It anchored a whole new reality. "The sun sets in the east on Qwonix. So I'm northwest of the conference center. And this floor is higher than the conference center roof."

"An expensive hotel tower taller than the conference center and northwest of it. There can't be too many buildings that fit that description. How far away? I can't see clearly."

"Maybe four kilometers? Between here and there I can see one large city park and two small ones." She rested her forehead against the window and looked down. "And there's a shorter building right next to this one with a shuttlecraft landing pad on top. It's a blue square with a red circle in the center."

Looking upward was more difficult without the ability to turn her neck. Instead, she shifted her body slightly, rolling on her forehead, and peered up as well as she could. "I think I'm on the top floor."

"Perfect. You did it. Now turn it back."

She shifted back and stared longingly at the view. It was like breathing air after nearly drowning. How could she trap herself in this windowless room again?

"He hasn't noticed yet, but you can't take—"

She hit the control and stifled a sob as the window turned opaque once more.

"I'm sorry, tyrina," Ekatya said softly. "But we have to keep you as safe as we can."

"I know. Why didn't he come running in here?"

"It's sunset. And as far as he knows, you're incapacitated. Maybe he's out getting something to eat."

She looked back at the window, then hung her head and shuffled to the bed. Sliding on was misery, but she felt better when she was braced against the headboard again.

"Lhyn…I have to go. Just for a few minutes."

Her head snapped up. "No!"

"I have to tell Sholokhov where you are."

"No! Don't leave me!" The idea of losing her, of being alone again in this nightmare, was more than she could bear. She wasn't courageous at all; she was terrified. Her breathing spiraled out of control.

"Lhyn, stop, stop, please! Dr. Wells!"

Tears of agony rolled down her face, but she couldn't change her breathing. It was an entity of its own, jerking her shattered ribs and sending molten lava through her chest in rapid, crashing waves. And it was only getting worse.

"I'll stay! Lhyn, I'm staying, I won't leave you, I'm right here. I'm right here." Ekatya was holding out her hands, as if she had tried to grip Lhyn's shoulders and failed. Her expression was frantic. "I'm not going anywhere. Please, please slow down."

Gradually, her breathing stabilized, but the tears still flowed. She hurt so much and she was so ashamed. "I'm sorry," she gasped. "I want to be brave, but I can't do this without you."

"You don't have to. I'll find a way. Just…let me talk to Dr. Wells for a moment."

Lhyn nodded, then rested her head against the headboard and closed her eyes. Ekatya carried on a one-way conversation in Common for several minutes, and she could imagine that she was back on the *Phoenix*, sitting on the sofa in their quarters with one of her Alsea programs on that wonderful display. In her mind's eye, she saw Ekatya at her desk, speaking on the intraship com in those same tones, strategizing and finding ways to make things happen.

What she wouldn't give to be there now.

The rise and fall of Ekatya's voice nearly put her to sleep until she changed back into High Alsean and said, "I'm calling Sholokhov from here. I've managed to talk Dr. Wells into taking the hardware off me so I can put my uniform shirt back on and appear mostly normal. We've had to move a few machines around. But I can make this work."

She looked so worried. Lhyn wanted to take that look away, but she was not strong enough to tell her to go. "I'm sorry. You shouldn't have to do that."

"Oh, Lhyn, this isn't your fault. I'm the one who's sorry. I should have planned better. All that time waiting—" She dropped her head and shook it once, then lifted it again. "Wish me luck."

"Good luck. Don't let him talk you into lifetime slavery."

Ekatya's surprised smile brightened her whole face. "You're feeling better."

"You're not leaving," Lhyn said simply.

"No. I'm not. Never again, if I can help it. But Dr. Wells does have to reduce my dosage a little, so I won't look like a janked-up addict when I call Sholokhov. I'll still be here, but…maybe not as solid. Are you all right with that?"

Lhyn passed her hand through Ekatya's arm, meeting nothing but air. "You're not solid now." She closed her eyes again. "I'll be fine as long as I can hear you."

"Good. Then you can listen to me tell more lies per minute than the day Grams caught me skipping school."

Only Ekatya could make her smile at a moment like this. "I haven't heard that story."

"The next time we call them, you should ask her. Dr. Wells is changing the dosage now. But I'm still here. Did I tell you about the time I had to take care of our third-grade class pet over the weekend? It was a horsehair snake, and it got out when I forgot to close the terrarium lid. I didn't tell Grams or Gramps, because I didn't want to get in trouble, but it backfired when Gramps put a shirt in the laundry chute. I never knew his voice could go that high."

Ekatya spun her tale, and Lhyn kept her eyes closed as she listened. She refused to look, afraid of seeing an empty room. When Ekatya's voice began to sound a little farther away, she told herself that she was simply in the bathroom, out of sight but still speaking. Still here.

"Dr. Wells says I'm ready," Ekatya said, interrupting the story she had just begun. "I'm going to call Sholokhov now. Start the lie counter."

Ekatya switched to Common and greeted Sholokhov. He must have immediately asked about her location, because she explained that she had been involved in a stun bead accident during a training drill and her chief surgeon wasn't letting her out of bed yet. It was an excellent cover, justifying not only her presence in the medbay but also any lack of mental acuity he might notice.

Sholokhov seemed to accept that, and Ekatya began telling him about Lhyn's location and Kane's false trail. The lie counter spiked when she explained how she had gotten the information.

"I don't know. Somehow, she got hold of a quantum com and called me. She had very little time; I wasn't able to ask any questions." Pause. "Well, I've learned never to be surprised by what Lhyn can do."

Lhyn found herself smiling.

"She sounded close to delirious. It may have been her one moment of lucidity between the drug doses and the torture sessions. I wouldn't be surprised if she doesn't remember what she did."

Her smile grew.

"Yes. No, I don't… How long? All right. Thank you. Yes, I will." Ekatya let out a long exhale, then switched back to High Alsean. "Help is on the way. And Dr. Wells is pouring the drugs back in."

Her tone carried vast relief, but Lhyn couldn't share the feeling. It seemed too good to be true. She had been through too much to believe that it could really be over.

"It's only a matter of six or seven hours now. Unfortunately, Sholokhov has to get some of his operatives back here before he can move on this place. The local law enforcement can't handle Kane and especially can't be trusted to keep you safe. So we have to wait."

"Then we wait. As long as you're here, I'm all right. Tell me about the second time the horsehair snake escaped." Ekatya had left her dangling, and she needed some way to pass the time before she would dare to open her eyes again.

"Oh, the second time was much worse. That was when I found out that our snake was female. And pregnant. Also, horsehair snakes are live-bearers, and they like to give birth in underwear drawers."

Lhyn chuckled. It hurt like holy Hades, but this was a pain she could welcome. "I'm guessing it was not your underwear drawer."

"No. Poor Grams. Gramps told me years later that she had to buy a whole new collection of underwear, because those little hairs get everywhere and no amount of laundering gets them back out. And they itch."

She knew better than to laugh, but she could easily envision the reaction. Ekatya's grandmother did not keep her feelings to herself, especially when she was irritated.

"But he also told me that Grams secretly thought the babies were the cutest things she'd ever seen. That's how I ended up with three of them as pets for the next five years. I thought I'd talked Grams into letting me keep them, but the truth was that Grams wanted them and manipulated me into being the one to take care of them."

"Your grandmother is smart. I'm not surprised you turned out the way you did."

"Grams is sharp as a sidian blade and my role model for how I want to be when I'm her age. And Gramps is my role model for how I want to be now."

Her voice was louder, and Lhyn risked opening her eyes. Ekatya was on the bed next to her, leaning against the headboard with their shoulders almost touching.

"You're here," Lhyn whispered. She didn't care so much about a rescue that might never happen. She cared that Ekatya had not left her alone. This was real and immediate, and the only thing that mattered.

"I'm here, tyrina. And you're going to be all right."

They sat in silence then. Lhyn suspected that while Ekatya was not saying it, she was recovering from her quick change in dosages and probably from her dual performances, for both Sholokhov and her. She wished that she could return the favor, letting Ekatya relax while she spun tales, but she did not have that in her.

After several minutes of quiet comfort, Ekatya asked, "What did Kane mean about you making a mistake?"

She had forgotten that. She didn't enjoy remembering. "I thought today would be four. Four impacts in that chair, I mean. The first day it was one, the second day it was two, the third day it was three. Kane is obsessed with order. Irrationally obsessed. In his appearance, in everything he touches—I really upset him just by moving a pad slightly out of alignment. So I knew today would be four. That's all I thought I could survive, and then he hit me with a fifth, and I was so shocked…I wasn't ready…"

"It's all right. I know. Don't think about it anymore. But it hasn't been four days. You were taken the night before last. It's been less than forty-eight stellar hours."

"Forty-eight hours!" Lhyn could barely grasp it. "I knew he was mindshekking me, but I didn't know it was that bad. He told me it was five days."

"I thought you said four."

"No, the first day he didn't—" She stopped, the horror of it flooding her body.

"What is it?"

Her breathing began to run out of her control, jerking at her chest wall and filling her torso with flame.

"Lhyn, stop, stop, I'm still here! Please!"

"He…fucking game…I was…so stupid…"

"Lhyn!"

"I won't survive it…I can't…Ekatya…"

She lost herself in a haze of pain, the edges of her vision blurring into darkness as Ekatya hovered in front of her, trying desperately to talk her down. None of the words penetrated, but the voice did, and she held on to it with everything she had. When her breathing finally slowed and she could see clearly again, Ekatya looked as if she had sprinted the length of her ship.

"You look worse than I feel," Lhyn rasped.

"I don't think that's possible. And I *hate* not being able to touch you."

She knew Ekatya would not ask. She had to say it.

"Ekatya."

"I'm here."

"It's not a linear progression. It's the spiral sequence. I didn't think of it because he didn't use the interface the first time; he used Osambi. But he made a point of telling me that was my first lesson. One blow to the stomach. And for my second lesson, one broken bone."

"Oh, shek." It was Ekatya's turn for the horrified realization. "And every number in the sequence is the sum of the preceding two."

"The third lesson was two bones. The fourth was three shuttles hitting my stomach. And this last one was a lovely assortment of five." Lhyn looked at the opaque window, mocking her with its emptiness. "The next one will be eight. I barely survived five. I won't live through eight. Not with my mind intact."

"You won't have to." Ekatya straddled her body, bringing her face between Lhyn and the window. "He's not going to put you in the chair again."

"You said it would take six or seven hours for them to get here. He'll have time."

"Second rule of capture, tyrina. Delay."

"How can I delay that long?"

"You agree."

Lhyn stared at her. "And then he'll kill me."

"No. You agree, but you don't do it right away. Because you need time to recover before you can do what he asks."

Her mind whirred away at the possibilities. "He wants me to appear in a video," she said. "I can't do that in the condition I'm in. I need sleep. And time to heal."

Ekatya smiled. "Exactly. He'll believe it, because he's an arrogant asshead and he thinks he's demoralized you by catching you in his little mathematical trap. Play it up. Play to his ego. Give him what he expects and buy yourself time. All you need is a little bit of time."

Time. She had thought she had so much of it, a lifetime ahead of her with Ekatya and the joys of learning more about the culture she had come to love. But Kane had taught her a new view of time, measured in minutes of agony and hours of pain.

"Ekatya, if something goes wrong—"

"Then we'll deal with it together."

"No, that's not what I meant. I don't know how much time I have to tell you this." She reached up as far as she could, her fingertips hovering over Ekatya's uniform jacket. "If something goes wrong, I want you to know that…that I don't have any regrets. I would rather have had a short life with you in it than a longer one without you."

Tears pooled in Ekatya's eyes. "I feel the same way. You know I do. But I don't want a short life with you. I want to see those silver streaks in your hair take over your whole head. You're going to be stunning."

"If we…" Lhyn licked her lips and tried again. "If I make it through this, then I want us to be official."

"Official what?" Ekatya drew back. "Is this…are you making a proposal?"

Lhyn nodded.

"You told me you didn't believe in that. You've studied too many cultures and seen too many variations on the same thing, and none of them change what's inside."

"I'm not the same person who told you that. And you're not the same person I said it to."

"That is the truth and a half." Ekatya's lips curved into the soft smile she never showed anyone else. "You certainly know how to make a proposal memorable. Where do you want to do it? I'll take you anywhere."

"Take me home. To Alsea."

She had lived and breathed Alsea for two and a half years now, first studying it from her research ship, then a glorious two months living there, then writing her articles and her book and doing the best she could to share the beauty of that culture with anyone who would listen. For the past year and a half, all she had wanted was to go back.

Now she *needed* to go back.

"I've never heard you call anyplace home before," Ekatya said.

Lhyn almost shrugged before thinking better of it. "I liked being a nomad. I always felt tied down in Allendohan, like I was stuck in the tiny back end of the universe. Once I got out, I stayed out. But…Alsea is different. I think I've been looking for it all my life."

"I think Alsea is fortunate you found it." Ekatya sat back on her heels, her thighs pressed weightlessly against Lhyn's legs. "I'll gladly take you home. Besides, if a pair of tyrees need to get bonded, there's really no other place to go, is there?"

They watched each other with silly smiles, and Lhyn had never breathed more easily. Then Ekatya cocked her head to listen. When she looked back, her eyes were sparkling.

"Dr. Wells says congratulations. And that she's delighted to be the first to know."

CHAPTER 48
Control

THEY HAD ANOTHER TWO AND a half hours together before Kane returned. Ekatya kept her apprised of the time, a power of knowledge that changed everything. She had control. She knew when she had been taken; she could extrapolate the average time between torture sessions; she could establish a mental chronology of everything that had happened and everything that would happen. Kane had broken her body only as a means of breaking her mind, but her mind was far out of his reach now.

When the door opened, she closed her eyes and waited.

"I'm right here next to you," Ekatya whispered.

"Dr. Rivers."

She did not respond.

"I know you're not asleep. Open your eyes."

He stood beside the bed, medkit in hand. She met his gaze, then closed her eyes again and let her head roll to the side.

"You seem to be missing some of that…spirit I've become accustomed to over the past five days. Could it be that you've realized your mistake?" He waited, and when he next spoke, it was with quiet authority. "Dr. Rivers, look at me and answer my question."

Slowly, she looked up at him. "Yes. You're using the spiral sequence."

"Ah, very good. Do you have any idea how few people even know what that is? I'm sorry that we're nearing the end of our time together. It will be a long time before I meet another mind like yours." He set the medkit on the floor and straightened. "Tomorrow will be your sixth lesson. How many times am I going to use the interface?"

"Eight," she said tonelessly.

"Very good. Three more than today. And the day after?"

"Thirteen."

"And the day after that?"

"Twenty-one."

"And…just as a hypothetical scenario, the day after that."

"Thirty-four."

"Tell me, Dr. Rivers, do you think you can withstand thirty-four commands from my interface?"

She shook her head.

"Can you withstand twenty-one? Use your voice."

"No."

"What about thirteen?"

"Maybe."

He paused. "Maybe? You were barely conscious when we took you out of the chair today, and that was only five. Just five, and you think you can withstand two and a half times that number?"

It was on the tip of her tongue to point out that thirteen was not two and a half times more than five, but she didn't need him to know how much spirit she really had.

"I won't do what you want me to do."

Beside her, Ekatya made a quiet sound of surprise.

Trust me, she thought. Kane didn't want her to give up. He wanted her to break.

"Oh, I see," Kane said. "You do love to organize your data, don't you? You think that because I've spent five days on your torso, I'll stay there. Eight more tomorrow, thirteen the day after that, and you'd be dead. Your torso would be a pulp, and it would be impossible to avoid a punctured lung or liver." He shook his head. "Another mistake; that's two in one day. You're slipping, Dr. Rivers."

She closed her eyes again.

"You will look at me when I'm speaking to you."

"I am…" She took a breath as she opened her eyes. "…having difficulty breathing. I don't know how long I can keep my eyes open."

He hummed thoughtfully. "It's true that I did work you particularly hard today. It was necessary to bring you to the place I needed you to be. Very well." He crouched down, rustled in the medkit, and stood up with an injector in hand. "This will not be as pleasant as the last one I gave you, because you haven't earned it. But I need you a little more lucid."

"If that's a stimulant, I might not be able to stay," Ekatya said. "Don't give him a reason to hurt you!"

The injector's bite had become welcome by now, and she sighed in relief as her pain washed back, a tide retreating from the shore. Though it remained in view, it was distant enough to make her feel almost giddy by comparison.

She risked a glance to the side. Ekatya was still there, watching with a worried look on her face.

"Better?" Kane asked as he put away the injector.

"Yes."

"Good." He straightened and looked down at her. "Then let's talk about your second mistake. You're trying to kill yourself, Dr. Rivers, and I have two problems with that. First, I can't let you do it. Second, I find it insulting that you believe I would not see your intent."

She looked down, letting her head fall. He reached beneath her chin and forced it back up. It was the first time he had touched her face, and his fingers tightened when she instinctively tried to pull back. She could smell the subtle scent of expensive skin cream.

"You still think you're the smartest person in this room, but you've walked into a trap yet again. I told you your first day in the chair that I could break the index finger on your left hand, yet you believe I would limit myself to damaging your torso." He let go and leaned down, bracing his hand on the bed. "Your injuries so far were only to get your attention. Now that I have it, let me tell you how long I can make you suffer. Do you know how many bones there are in your foot? Twenty-six. Tomorrow I can break eight bones in one foot. Or I can break four in each foot, and the next time you have to use the toilet, you will have to *crawl*."

A shiver racked her body. She had no doubt that he would do exactly as he described and enjoy watching the results.

"The next day I'd have thirteen to work with. I could break more bones in your feet, or perhaps snap your fibula. I can pull your patellae permanently out of place, and after that, even crawling would be something you could only dream about. I can make your vertebrae separate. I can turn your body into a sack of broken pieces and still leave enough intact for you to do what I need."

She stared at him in horror, wondering if he had truly done this to others.

"I see this hasn't occurred to you. Has it?"

"No," she whispered.

"Would you like to reconsider your answer to my question? Do you think you can withstand thirteen commands from my interface? And twenty-one the day after that?"

She shook her head, carefully and with a minimum of motion.

He bent lower, placing his mouth near her ear, and whispered in a sensual manner. "I can make it so easy for you. One injection and you'll go to sleep with a smile on your face, just like you did before. All you have to do is change a few words. Say a few things on the video. And then it will all be over."

His tone became harsh as he pulled back far enough to stare into her eyes. "Or I can make you wish I really was careless enough to kill you. Surely, *surely* that can't be worth it to you. What are you defending at such a horrific cost? A few aliens that by your own admission would be criminals on their world? You would suffer the worst death imaginable, a death that would take *weeks*. And for what?"

He pushed off the bed, picked up the medkit, and took a step back. "I'm done trying to convince you to save yourself. I am going to walk through that door, and once I do, you'll be in that chair tomorrow even if you've changed your mind. You have one chance left."

She watched him walk to the foot of her bed, then turn and stride across the room.

"Lhyn, what are you doing?"

Ekatya's tone was disbelieving, and Lhyn wanted nothing more than to touch her in reassurance. Without taking her eyes off Kane, she held her hand where Ekatya's thigh would be, then let it sink down to the bed.

Kane was reaching for the door lever when she said, "Wait!"

He stood facing the door, his shoulders lifting and falling as he took a large breath. When he turned around, the triumph shone in his expression. "Yes?"

"I…don't want to die that way."

"No, I don't believe you do." He came back around the bed. "Then you'll change the text I asked you to?"

She nodded.

"Use your voice, Dr. Rivers. It's such a pleasant one."

"Yes. I'll change it."

"And say what we tell you to on the video?"

"Yes, but I can't… No one will believe it if I look like this. I need rest. Rest without pain. I need that injection."

He looked at her silently, his expression giving away nothing, and she began to worry that she had played her hand too soon. Beside her, Ekatya shifted, her insubstantial body tensing for an attack she could never make.

Lhyn desperately wished that she could.

"You're quite smart enough to try this manipulation," Kane said at last.

Her heart sank.

"But I also think you're smart enough to realize what the consequences will be if you renege tomorrow," he continued. "So I'll choose to believe you, if you'll tell me two things." He leaned down, putting his face centimeters from hers, and lowered his voice. "Tell me you'll obey me."

Despite everything, she found it nearly impossible to say the words. And he knew it.

Slowly, she blinked, inhaled as deeply as she could, and did what she had to.

"I will…obey you."

A broad smile creased his face. "Very good. You're almost there. There's only one thing left between you and a peaceful night of sleep." He brought up a finger and ran it lightly along her jawline. "Tell me that you belong to me."

"Oh, what a *fucking* little torquat!" Ekatya burst out. She vanished from Lhyn's peripheral vision and reappeared just behind Kane, her head next to his. "You can't belong to him because you've already given yourself to me. You asked me to bond with you, and you are my tyree. I give myself to you, Lhyn. I belong to you. So you look at me and tell *me* who you belong to."

There could not have been two more contrasting faces in her vision: Kane, with his perfectly groomed exterior hiding a rotten, grasping core, and Ekatya, her blue eyes flashing as she spoke the words Lhyn knew she had never said to anyone before.

She barely remembered to speak in Common instead of High Alsean. Locking eyes with Ekatya, she said clearly, "I belong to you."

Both Ekatya and Kane smiled.

"You have just passed your training," Kane said. "We'll speak more about this later. But for now, you've earned your reward."

The injection sent her pain floating up, up, until she could no longer feel any part of it. Her lungs expanded with ease, and she took a breath of pure joy as her eyes fell shut.

"Good night, Dr. Rivers."

"I love you, tyrina. I'll see you on the other side."

When she woke, a deep hum was reverberating through her body. She recognized it even before becoming fully conscious: the sound of surf engines. She was on a ship.

Keeping her eyes closed, she listened for any clues about her situation. Her head felt startlingly clear, and she knew Ekatya would not be here. That had been a waking dream, induced through drugs and a fog of pain. It wasn't real.

And now Kane was transporting her somewhere else.

She could not think about what would happen when she broke her promise. There had to be a way to speed up her death. Maybe she could surprise him and grab his medkit. It wouldn't take long to overdose if she could just get her hands on—

"It's good to have you back with us, Dr. Rivers."

The voice, so close to her ear, jolted her out of her thoughts. It was deep, slightly nasal, and held the accent of a Tashar native who spoke Common organically.

Definitely not Kane.

She opened her eyes to find a low ceiling overhead, curving down to meld with the bulkhead next to her bed. Another bulkhead at the foot of the bed held a status display with what appeared to be her bio readouts. She tried to turn her head, but her neck muscles were not responding.

An older man appeared in her vision, leaning over with a kind smile. "You're safe now. We're taking you to Tlahana Station. For now, I have you on meds to reduce the inflammation and speed up the healing of your muscle fibers. You'll find it difficult to move, but that's the price for the faster healing. It will get easier. Are you in any pain?"

The question startled her. How could she not have noticed immediately upon waking?

"No," she said, amazed by the truth of it.

"Good. That's what we want."

She studied him, not trusting this apparent miracle. "Who are you?"

"One of the people sent to help you."

Not a real answer. "Where is Kane?"

His expression hardened. "Secured in the front of the shuttle. He'll never hurt you or anyone else again." He watched her for a moment, then shook his head. "You don't believe me. I understand. You've been through a trauma, and your system was clogged with a dozen different drugs. It's taken me half the trip to neutralize them. Right now, you don't know what's real and what isn't."

After all of Kane's psychological manipulations, the very fact that this man knew how she felt made her even more suspicious.

"Perhaps it will help if I pass on a message," he said, pulling a pad from his sleeve pocket. "Captain Serrado sent it through Director Sholokhov." He activated a file and held the pad in her line of sight.

The message was three sentences, written in High Alsean. Ekatya would have needed a translator program to produce the text, but she knew Lhyn could read it.

Lhyn, you're on the other side. It was not a dream.
You're still the bravest person I've ever met.

"I see that means something to you," the man said gently.

"Yes. It does," she managed. But her voice shook, and the trembling spread through her jaw, down her torso, out to her arms and legs.

He rested one hand on her shoulder. "Don't worry about the shaking. It's just your body realizing that it can finally let go. You *are* safe, Dr. Rivers."

Warmth radiated out from his hand, the first touch she had experienced in days that was neither painful nor meant to shame or manipulate. She focused on it, desperate for him to stay, to keep her grounded in reality, to not leave her alone again.

"Don't…"

"I'm not going anywhere," he said, seeming to read her mind. "You can let go."

He held her gaze, his hazel eyes full of understanding as she stared at him and shook. Gradually, the trembling slowed, then began to sputter, with longer and longer periods between bouts of shaking. After a final shiver, her body sank into the bed as if it suddenly weighed twice as much.

"Good," he said. "You should be able to sleep now. A nice, healing, natural sleep. No drugs."

She was already halfway there, falling into a lassitude of pain-free safety.

It was not a dream, Ekatya had said.

She closed her eyes and breathed.

CHAPTER 49
Breathing

With a little creative rearranging of dates, Ekatya was able to reroute the *Phoenix* to Tlahana Station and still remain on schedule for their five-station tour. An egregious abuse of her position disguised as a practical evaluation of their surf engines ensured that she arrived only one day after Lhyn.

The first test of her patience came during docking maneuvers, when she had to sit on the bridge and pretend that she cared about the myriad details of docking the Protectorate's newest and largest warship to a station that had been built before the Pulsar class existed. They were at the end of the longest pylon, the only place with enough room for them, and getting the umbilicals hooked up was nowhere near as clean and efficient as it had been at Quinton Shipyards.

Her second and bigger test of patience came during the waste of time known as diplomatic duty, when she and her section chiefs met the station commander and his staff for a formal dinner, followed by cocktails. But the ache in her chest had abated. Her body knew Lhyn was here. On the *Phoenix*, the ache hadn't ended until they saw each other. She wondered whether this was a natural progression of their bond, or if they had accelerated it with their mental connection.

The minute that it was remotely feasible to do so, she made her farewells, ducked out of the private dining room, and headed toward the central hub.

"Captain, wait!" Dr. Wells caught up to her. "May I accompany you? I feel a bit like she's my patient as well."

"And you're bored to death in that dining room."

"That too," Wells admitted. "But it's not even close to the main reason."

"Come on, then." Ekatya set off again, her boot heels clicking on the tiled floor.

Wells fell into step, and they walked in companionable silence through the post-dinner crowds that surged in and out of the retail shops on this level.

The ceilings here were more than twice as high as those in the administrative section, and the corridors were easily ten times wider. It was a vast open space compared to what Ekatya was accustomed to on her ship, and the noise and undisciplined crowds made her edgy. She just wanted to get through it and into the quiet confines of the medical section.

They left the retail shops behind, walked through a slightly less busy corridor of service shops, and entered the bulbous central hub. Viewports all around offered spectacular views of the station's pylons and the many ships currently docked, but Ekatya had eyes only for the signs directing them to Tlahana Medical.

"This way." Wells pointed ahead to an unmarked door on their left.

"But the signs—"

"Are for people who don't know their way around. I do."

"Oh. Yes, of course." She had forgotten that Wells had been stationed here earlier in her Fleet career.

The door opened onto a narrower corridor that enveloped them in a hushed calm. Wells moved through it with confidence, straight to a large data console on the wall that was clearly meant for staff. She tapped away at it.

"Are you authorized to be in here?" Ekatya asked.

Wells tapped twice more, then smiled as she pointed to a record. "Yes, because Lhyn authorized both of us."

Ekatya's heart jumped simply from seeing the name on the file. "She would think of that."

Wells loaded the medical record into her pad, then led the way around two corners and through another door. On the other side was a space much like the medbay lobby on the *Phoenix*, with treatment rooms arranged around a central nursing station.

"I'll wait here," she said. "She's in that one."

Ekatya followed her pointing finger to a treatment room with clear plexan—Lhyn's doctors wanted to keep her in view. A still figure lay on the bed.

She was inside the room without any memory of crossing the lobby. Slowly, she approached the bed.

Lhyn seemed to be asleep. Her face was pale and her throat was bruised, more on one side than the other. Ekatya had not seen those bruises when she was with her—possibly because Lhyn had already forgotten about them? Anything that had not been in her thoughts or active memories was invisible to Ekatya's vision there.

If bruises that painful didn't merit Lhyn's attention, she shuddered to think what did.

"Hello, tyrina," she said softly. "I'm here, and you're safe, and I don't know if I can ever let you out of my sight again."

Lhyn stirred, her eyes blinking open. A slow smile transformed her face. "Tyrina. I love that name. Please don't let anyone call me Dr. Rivers."

"You worked hard for that title. Don't let him take it away from you." She leaned down and pressed a soft kiss to Lhyn's temple. "It's so, so good to see you," she murmured before pulling away.

"It's good to be seen. And to breathe. I've spent my whole life breathing and never given a thought to what a miracle it really is."

"I think you might be a little happy on drugs."

"I'm a lot happy on drugs, and thank the Shippers for that." Lhyn looked up with luminous eyes. "Ekatya…there are no words—"

"Shh, you don't need them—"

"Yes, I do. You made me feel so safe. It was such a nightmare, but the moment I realized you were really there, I was…at peace with it. Whatever happened, I could get through it because you were there."

Ekatya could not speak. Seeing Lhyn with her own eyes, being able to touch her—it was too much, and she was fully occupied with keeping her tears back.

"Don't cry," Lhyn whispered. "I'm all right, thanks to you."

"Can't…" Ekatya shook her head, then bent over, buried her face in the clean sheet next to Lhyn's shoulder, and let it out. Lhyn combed her hair with gentle fingers, murmuring that she was all right, it was over, they were both safe, and all Ekatya could think was that she was supposed to be the strong one, the one who wasn't hurt, and Lhyn was having to take care of her. What a fine example she was setting.

She straightened, wiping her cheeks, and summoned up a watery smile. "It's not thanks to me. You're the one who fixed the control panel and figured out where you were. You even beat Kane at his own game in the end."

"And you're the one who found a way to get to me. I'm still not sure how you managed that."

"Oh, that was…" She turned to look out the clear wall of the room. Wells was reading her pad, but she seemed to feel Ekatya's gaze and looked up. "That was Dr. Wells taking a leap of faith."

Lhyn rolled her head too carefully and glanced out into the lobby. "I'd like to thank her."

Ekatya lifted a hand, and Wells gave a nod.

"Hello, Lhyn," she said as she entered the treatment room. "You're looking rather amazing considering what I just read."

"I hope that record doesn't include the images they took."

"It does. And I'm going to keep them as evidence of the astonishing feats of strength our bodies are capable of when given the right incentive. You should not have been able to get off that bed, much less save yourself the way you did."

"I didn't—"

"Oh, yes you did. I was there. I heard it."

"Don't argue with her, Lhyn. She's even more stubborn than me."

Lhyn looked back and forth between them. "Is that possible?"

Wells laughed. "Apparently so. I have something of a reputation. But I wanted to thank you."

"For what?"

"For renewing my belief in miracles. I stopped believing a little while back, but you and your tyree changed my mind."

Seeing Lhyn's look of alarm, Ekatya said, "I had to tell her. And even if I hadn't, she would have heard it while I was with you. It's under doctor-patient confidentiality."

"Your secret is safe with me," Wells assured her. "Really, I'm just angling for an invitation. I've never seen an Alsean bonding ceremony."

Lhyn lit up. "I haven't either. I mean, not in person. But I'm looking forward to seeing Andira's."

"Who is Andira?"

"Lancer Tal," Ekatya clarified.

Wells looked at her, then Lhyn. "You're on a first-name basis with the Lancer of Alsea?"

"I think Lhyn was half in love with her before they even met." Ekatya slid their hands together and reveled in the warm physicality of it.

"Only a quarter," Lhyn said. "It didn't go up to half until after I met her."

"You weren't kidding when you said I still had a few things to learn about you, Captain."

The next five minutes did more to calm Ekatya's fears than all the sedatives in her medbay. Lhyn smiled, occasionally chuckled, and seemed miraculously untouched by the horrors that had been inflicted on her. But she moved only with the greatest of care and never shifted her torso. When her eyelids began to droop, Ekatya kissed her forehead, told her to sleep, and led Wells out of the room.

"Let me see it," she said once they were in the lobby.

"See what?"

"Her record."

"Captain, I don't think—" Wells sighed when Ekatya stopped and held out her hand. "You will never be able to unsee it," she warned as she pulled the pad from her sleeve pocket.

"Do you think I'll ever be able to unsee Lhyn in that chair? I need facts, not nightmares." Ekatya took the pad and read through the clinical listing of Lhyn's injuries. Then she pulled up the images and stopped breathing.

"It's not—"

"Don't tell me it's not as bad as it looks," she snapped.

"No, it's exactly as bad as it looks. But it's not *permanent*. She will heal. The psychological injuries will take far longer than what you're looking at there."

Ekatya's vision blurred as she gazed at the image of Lhyn's torso, which was such an unending mass of hematomas and horrific swelling that she could not recognize it. Only a week ago, she had touched her lips to the soft, perfect skin just above that navel, and now—

The pad was gently removed from her unresisting fingers. "Don't do this to yourself," Wells said. "She's safe. You saved her."

"I told her to go to that meeting." Ekatya was staring straight ahead and seeing nothing. "She didn't want to. She was going to cancel her keynote speech. I told her to go."

"This is not your fault."

"I told her to leave Alsea, too. She didn't want to do that either. I said the Alseans needed her as an advocate, because some people—" She crossed her arms tightly over her chest and looked up at the ceiling, blinking back tears.

"The Alseans did need her as an advocate. And she has been the best one imaginable."

"And look at the price she paid!" Ekatya rounded on her, ready to pour out her anger and self-blame, but was brought up short by the sight of the man coming through the doors on the other side of the lobby. Tall, with a bald spot and blue eyes standing out against black skin, she would have recognized him in any crowd even without the purple scarf of office draped over his shoulders.

"Captain Serrado," he said as he walked up beside Wells. "It's a pleasure to see you again in person."

"Director Sholokhov, may I introduce my chief surgeon, Dr. Wells." She watched the recognition wash across Wells's face as they shook hands.

"Your reputation precedes you, Dr. Wells," he said.

"So does yours."

His shaggy gray eyebrows lifted. "I'll take that as a compliment."

Ekatya could almost see the *You shouldn't* forming on her chief surgeon's lips, but fortunately Wells had a sense of self-preservation. "You did a good thing yesterday," she said instead.

He glanced at the treatment room, then turned to face Ekatya more fully. "I've lost three operatives to Kane Muir. Two of them didn't make it past twenty-four hours. The third lasted just under forty. Dr. Rivers outlasted them all and somehow managed to learn where she was and get a message out. She should work for me."

Ekatya fought down the snarl that rose in her throat and only then saw the glint of humor in Sholokhov's eyes. He was baiting her.

"I think Dr. Rivers is happy with her current job," she said. "But I'll convey your offer."

"Please do. In the meantime, I wonder if you'd like to accompany me to station security?"

Her stomach froze into an icy knot. "You have him here?"

"He's awaiting transfer. I can give you some time if you wish to speak with him." His manner was calm, but the slight emphasis on *speak* told her that he was indeed making her an offer. It was unethical, illegal, and immoral—and she would take it with both hands.

"I very much wish to speak with him," she said.

"I thought you might. This way."

She strode out of the lobby at Sholokhov's side and didn't realize until much later that she had left Dr. Wells standing there.

CHAPTER 50
Gift-wrapped

Kane Muir was strapped to a chair in the center of an otherwise empty interrogation room. Ekatya had been to station security a few times in her career, usually to pick up—and dress down—young officers who had gotten themselves in trouble. She knew those rooms normally had two chairs and a table. The lack of furniture in this one was confirmation that she had not read Sholokhov wrong.

They stood at the modified plexan window, which allowed viewing only one way. There was no one else in the area. It seemed that all of station security had taken a simultaneous break period.

"The staff will be returning in fifteen minutes," Sholokhov said.

"That's more than enough time. Do you have a knife I can borrow?"

He raised his eyebrows.

"I'm not doing this with him strapped down." It wouldn't be nearly as satisfying.

"Ah. I understand." He pulled an expensive folding blade from somewhere beneath his jacket.

She accepted it and moved toward the door, her blood thrumming with anticipation.

"All I ask is that you leave him alive," Sholokhov said. "I'm still hoping to get answers from him."

She paused in the act of tapping the door control as the realization hit.

This wasn't a gift. It was a trap.

"Thank you," she said, and stepped through the door.

Kane looked unbearably clean and intact. Not a hair was out of place on his blond head, his beard and mustache were perfectly trimmed, and his inmate uniform was crisp and new. She thought about the wreck of Lhyn's torso and took a deep breath to tamp down her instincts.

"I'm Captain Ekatya Serrado," she said. "Lhyn Rivers is my bondmate."

"Bondmate?" He smirked. "Are you both Alsean?"

"No, but I almost wish we were. Because right now I'm ashamed to call myself the same species as you."

"You're here to exact revenge, then. I wouldn't expect that of a Fleet captain."

He put up a good front, but when she opened the knife, he looked slightly nervous. She made a show of inspecting the blade, her eyebrows rising when she realized it was a sidian knife—sharp as a straight razor and nearly impossible to dull.

She stepped up to him, pulled up a lock of his hair, and sliced it off.

"What are you doing?" His calm had already evaporated. That was easier than she had expected.

She dropped the hunk of hair to the floor in front of him and pulled up another.

"Stop this right now!"

"Stop whining. You need a haircut."

"That's not a haircut!"

She dropped another chunk of hair and went to work on a third. "I admit I haven't been trained in proper technique. This might be a little uneven."

He clamped his jaw shut and visibly trembled with rage. In two minutes the floor around him was covered with ragged hanks of blond hair.

She bent down and cut off his sleeves, taking care that one was left longer than the other. Then she did the same to his pants.

Standing back, she examined him with a critical eye. "One more thing," she decided. "You need a shave."

"Don't you dare!"

She grabbed him by the throat, curling her fingers around his laryngeal prominence and squeezing. He immediately stopped all efforts at speaking or moving, his eyes nearly popping out of his head from the pain. He had gone from angry to terrified in a heartbeat, and she couldn't deny the pleasure throbbing at her fingertips, nor the immense temptation to squeeze just a little harder. A vision of Lhyn's bruised throat floated before her mind's eye as she lifted the knife.

He began moaning as she cut away what she could of the left half of his mustache, and wound down to whimpers of distress when she reached across to the right side of his face and sliced off most of the beard.

Releasing her grip, she blew off the knife, pocketed it, and dusted the short hairs off her hands. "Ugh. Disgusting. You're so unclean. You should bathe once in a while."

He coughed, then twisted his head from one side to the other. "I am not unclean!" he cried, and coughed again.

"Tell that to my hands. I need to wash them now." She looked up at him and let a smile cross her face. Then she began to laugh, because he truly did look ridiculous. His hair looked as if one of her botanists had gone wild with the shears; he had half a mustache and half a beard, each on opposite sides of his face, and his clothes gave him the appearance of a stowaway who had been caught in the gears of the shuttle bay doors.

His face turned red as she laughed, then purple when she took out her pad and held it up. "Say hello," she said, still laughing. "Lhyn is going to love this."

"Lhyn," he spat. "I broke her in less than forty-eight hours. I *owned* her. You think she's your bondmate? She'll never truly be yours because she will never get me out of her head. She obeyed every one of my orders, including when I told her to spread her legs. She told me she *belonged* to me. To me! Not you."

She put away the pad. While her laughter had died, she still managed to keep a smile on her face. "You never broke her."

He smiled as well. "But I did. Easily. I'm only sorry I never got to the third day." His subtle hip movement told her exactly what he meant.

"Well, why didn't you? Could it be because she fooled you? Because she learned where you took her, got a message out to call for help, and got you captured? You avoided capture for years, and an untrained academic beat you at your own game and turned you in. That doesn't sound like a broken person to me. It also doesn't sound like someone who obeyed you very well." She shrugged. "I heard you were good, but I have no idea how you got that reputation. Really, an *academic*. I mean, I'd understand if you were beaten by a trained operative. But an anthropologist?"

His jaw clenched. "You should have been there. You should have seen her looking up at me and saying, 'I belong to you.' I know people; I know how their minds work. I've spent a lifetime studying and manipulating them. And I know that when she said that, she meant every word."

Ekatya nodded. "She did. Because she was talking to me."

Looking around with exaggerated movements, he said, "Did I somehow miss seeing you in the room?"

"I just spoke with her. She told me everything. The only way she could say those words was to imagine that she was saying them to me, that I was looking at her instead of you. So yes, you read her accurately. She did mean every word. She just didn't say them to you." She looked him up and down disdainfully. "She also said that you were irrationally obsessed with your appearance, and I can see why. No wonder you work so hard to keep it up. You're nothing without it. A pathetic little boy. A little boy with all his toys who still lost to an untrained academic. *She* manipulated *you*."

His face was red again when she pulled out the knife and cut the ties off his legs. "Little boys shouldn't be tied up. It makes them think they're dangerous. You're not dangerous at all. You're pathetic."

His wrist ties went next, and she pocketed the knife once more. Casting a glance around the floor, now littered with hair, scraps of clothing, and cut ties, she said, "There's not much of you left, is there? You thought I was here for revenge, but I'm a Fleet captain. I hunt much bigger prey than you. You're not worth my time."

She turned around and began to walk away, listening for movement behind her. When she heard the rustle of fabric, she smiled.

Adrenaline flowed through her veins, slowing time as every sense poured data into her brain.

One step forward, and there was the slight scrape of a chair being lifted from the floor.

Two steps forward, and rubber-soled shoes slapped the tiles behind her.

Three steps, and the air moved.

Four steps, and she dropped to a crouch. The chair whistled over her head from right to left. That meant Kane was just behind her and now off balance, his body rotated toward her as he swung the chair.

It also meant that his leg was in the perfect position.

She shot upright, pivoting toward him as she brought up her leg, then lashed out with a downward strike to the side of his knee. Her boot heel tore through every ligament, breaking all cohesion in the joint.

Kane barely had time to scream before she planted her boot on the floor and followed through with her spin, leading with her left elbow. It crashed into his jaw with stunning force. He was dropping, his broken knee going out from under him, but she was already unwinding her torso and using all of that force and speed to throw a right-handed punch. For a fraction of a second, she considered landing that punch in his throat, where it would crush his larynx and suffocate him.

But if she killed him, Sholokhov would have her where he wanted her. She was too well trained in hand-to-hand combat to claim that she had made a mistake or that she had felt lethal force was her only option.

Her punch smashed into the opposite side of his already fractured jaw, shattering the bone.

Kane landed on his back, his howl cut off as he gagged, unable to open his mouth or spit out the blood that now filled it.

She desperately wanted to break his other knee and destroy his testicles, but he was down and no longer a threat. She had no excuse. Instead, she stood over him and looked down as he rolled to the side, gurgling and moaning, tears mingling with the blood that dribbled out in strings.

"Look at you," she said, speaking loudly to be heard over his muffled wails. "Crying like an infant from two broken bones. You couldn't break Lhyn in forty-eight hours, and I broke you in less than ten minutes. You really are pathetic."

She walked out the door and closed it behind her, muting the sound of his agony.

Sholokhov was looking at her with a small, incredulous smile. She held out his knife and said, "Thank you for the loan."

He took it off her palm. "That was quite a performance, Captain."

Straightening the sleeves of her dress jacket, she said, "It was…cathartic. I appreciate your giving me the opportunity."

"You didn't take that opportunity in the way I expected."

"I know."

He stared at her for a moment, then broke into a low chuckle. "Well done, Captain Serrado. Well done. I'm sorry our agreement has been completed, because you really are a valuable resource."

"I'm a Fleet captain. I'm always a resource."

He offered his hand, and when she took it, he held the grip slightly longer than necessary. "Farewell and good hunting, Captain."

"To you as well." She let go and glanced through the window, where Kane was still gagging on his blood. Looking back at Sholokhov, she said, "Take him apart."

Now his smile was vicious. "I will."

CHAPTER 51
Home

Alsea, present day

NEVER IN HER LIFE HAD Tal felt such a homicidal rage toward a person she had never met. In the heat of her fury, she thought less of Ekatya for staying her hand. Surely no one deserved death more than the man who had hurt Lhyn so badly. How could Ekatya not avenge her tyree?

She kept her head down, staring into her empty drink glass. Ekatya had an uncanny ability to read her and had once said that her emotions were all in her eyes. She would not let her friend see her eyes now.

For a long moment, no one in the room spoke.

At last Salomen said, "We are honored that you felt safe enough to share this story. Thank you for trusting us with so much."

"This is the only place I do feel safe," Lhyn said. "Here and on the *Phoenix*. And sometimes not even there."

"Why not?" Lanaril asked.

"No windows. At least, not in our quarters or most of the ship. We have sophisticated displays that can fool our brains into thinking we're looking out of a window, but my brain isn't fooled. I spent a lot of time in Deck Zero. If I can't see outside, I…I can't breathe, sometimes. And today we found out that I don't handle intellectual surprises very well, either."

Tal tightened her hand around the glass and wondered if she could squeeze hard enough to break it.

"Does it help, knowing those men are in custody?" Lanaril's voice was soft.

"Osambi isn't in custody," Ekatya said. "He was killed in the raid. Sholokhov had no interest in him; he was a small fish. So he didn't risk any of his operatives trying to capture him."

"I didn't believe it until they showed me images," Lhyn said. "I couldn't. But seeing him really, truly dead—yes, it helped. What really helps is knowing that Kane Muir is miserable."

Surprise lifted Tal's head. "But surely he's healed by now."

"Yes, but when Ekatya did that to him, she gave Sholokhov a blueprint."

"Sholokhov recorded that from every angle," Ekatya said. "Which didn't surprise me once I found out. He heard every word I said, analyzed everything I did. And then he used it to design Kane's interrogation."

Lhyn let out a small laugh. "He's in a cell with crooked windows, a crooked door, and images permanently fixed to the wall in an off-center position."

"And crooked," Ekatya added. "Not too much—just enough to set him off."

"Plus they haven't let him cut his hair or shave. So it's still the way Ekatya left it, just longer."

"He cracked in days." Ekatya's satisfaction held a hard edge. "The first thing he spilled was who hired him for that job. It was one of the rising stars in the Defenders of the Protectorate, a protégé of the party leader. She was planning a little party shuffle: push out her boss, take over his job, and leverage the paranoia Lhyn's revised conclusion would have caused. The DOP could finally have taken enough seats in the Assembly to have a say in Protectorate policy, and who knows where it would have gone next?"

"She was a co-owner in that hotel," Lhyn said. "That's how they were able to get me in there with no one seeing. And they blocked off the top two floors, so no one was around to hear."

Ekatya reached for her hand. "I heard," she said quietly.

"I know."

For a moment it seemed they were the only two in the room. Then Ekatya squeezed her hand and turned toward the others. "She's not having much luck with that strategy now that she's in prison. And the DOP lost power."

"Oh, it lost more than that. It lost *legitimacy*." Lhyn sat up straighter, her emotions colored by anger for the first time since she had begun her tale. "I don't know Shipper shit about politics, but I know what it means when a party suddenly becomes invisible in Gov Dome. Every minister who ever allied with them now runs the other way when a DOP minister tries to say something. It's nothing official, because the trial hasn't started and the press doesn't have all the facts. My name hasn't been released."

"That's why you haven't heard anything from Ambassador Solvassen," Ekatya told Tal.

"Right, but the press knows the DOP's second-in-command was arrested for transactional instigation of kidnapping and torture, and it's no secret that I vanished off the scene the night of my keynote speech. The fact that a DOP plant made a big point of confronting me and calling me dangerous that night has worked against them. It's pretty clear that the word is out behind closed doors, and nobody wants to be associated with a ship that's about to explode."

"It's going to be a beautiful explosion," Ekatya said with a touch of pride. "Lhyn will make sure of it."

Lhyn's anger turned cold. "There's a downside to torturing the most publicly visible anthropologist in the Protectorate. I'll be a lot more visible when I testify. Even more so once the trial is over. They tried to put words in my mouth. I have plenty of words to say now."

"Will you have to go there to testify?" Salomen asked.

"No. I'll do it from here. I'll do everything from here, because I'm not leaving. Thank the Shippers for quantum coms."

"Good," Tal said shortly. "Because if you had to go back, I wouldn't let you leave without at least ten of my best warriors guarding you."

Lhyn's anger abruptly vanished under a thick, soft blanket of comfort and security. Her eyes reddened as she said, "That would make an impression."

Watching her reaction to the mere idea of feeling safe sent Tal's fury soaring again. She was grateful to Lanaril for asking the next question.

"How is the DOP losing power when it was only their second-in-command who was arrested? Our caste Prime would have to resign for the shame of having chosen a second so badly, but the caste itself would simply elect a new Prime and the Council would move on."

Ekatya shook her head. "That's not how it works in the Assembly. Your political system is stable; your numbers don't change. Six castes, thirty Councilors per caste."

"Plus the Primes," said Lhyn.

Tal almost smiled at her inability to let a factual omission go unremarked.

"The Assembly isn't stable?" Lanaril asked.

"Our parties are always fighting for more seats," Ekatya said. "And they change. New ones rise, old ones fall—the strongest ones have been around for a long time, but it's always in flux."

"It's predatory is what it is." Lhyn had recovered. "They eat each other at the first sign of weakness. And it wasn't just a second-in-command. It was the leader's protégé, the person he was training to eventually take over the party. They can't shake that off as bad blood at the top. It colors all of them. It's really going to color them when Kane testifies."

"Which he will. Sholokhov told me that Kane is singing every song he knows—"

"That doesn't translate," Lhyn said.

"Oh, right. I mean he's giving up answers to every question Sholokhov asks. He's a fountain of information because he's desperate to get back to a normal cell and get a haircut. It's driving him literally insane. Sholokhov just keeps finding new questions. I doubt he'll ever give Kane what he wants. Kane killed three of his operatives and made a fool out of him, and Sholokhov never forgets."

"Show them what Sholokhov sent you." Lhyn nudged her arm.

Ekatya reached into her sleeve pocket and brought out her pad. A few taps activated the virtual screen, and she rotated it to face outward.

Tal leaned forward, fascinated by what she was seeing.

The image had captured the moment just before Ekatya took Kane down. She was walking toward the cam while Kane was rushing up behind her, chair raised for a strike. His face was twisted with rage and hate.

But it was Ekatya's expression that held Tal spellbound. She was staring straight into the cam—and she was smiling.

It was not a smile Tal had ever seen on her, but she recognized it. That was the triumphant, almost feral smile of a warrior suffused with adrenaline and battle joy. Kane may have thought he was still fighting, but Ekatya had known the moment he lifted the chair that the fight was over. For her, the real battle had been in forcing him to react—and she had already won it.

"Sometimes I still wish I'd killed him outright," Ekatya was saying, but for Tal, it had all fallen into place.

"You couldn't have," she said with certainty. "Sholokhov is a brilliant strategist. He was playing to win both sides. You may have thought no one was in the area, but I'd bet a moon's wages that he had a team of healers around the corner, waiting for you to do what he thought you would."

Ekatya's head went back, the realization exploding like a starburst on Tal's senses. "Stars and Shippers. That would be just like him. Why didn't

I think of that? I thought the trap was to tempt me into killing Kane for him. He would have gotten rid of someone he hated without any personal risk, and then he would have had me forever. But this—he would have had everything. Me under his thumb *and* Kane still able to answer questions."

"He would have had it from me. I would have been too blinded by rage to see that trap." Tal looked at her in admiration. "You are a gifted warrior. And you…" She shifted her gaze to Lhyn. "Ekatya was right. Your courage is without measure. I hope you never doubt that."

"Thank you."

But Lhyn did doubt it, and it was more than Tal could bear.

"I have something for you." She crossed the room to the storage cupboards, pulled out a slim case, and returned to stand beside Lhyn. "I had planned to give these back to Ekatya, but now I understand that they belong to you. They have since the moment they were left here." She opened the case and offered it.

Ekatya's shocked recognition turned instantly to approval, and when Tal met her eyes, a wash of gratitude warmed her senses.

"These aren't mine," Lhyn said with a frown.

"Oh, yes they are." Ekatya pointed at the silver medal. "This is for extraordinary service performed for the Protectorate. You did that when you prevented the DOP from getting a foothold in the Assembly. And this one," she touched the red star, "is for courage under superior fire. It's easy to win when you have all the power in a situation, but if you're outnumbered and outgunned and you still refuse to be beaten—that's true courage. I won this medal while surrounded by two hundred thousand tons of protective armor called a ship. You did it with no protection at all. You deserve this far more than I do."

Lhyn turned the medal over and read the inscription on the back. "Ekatya, these have your name on them. They're yours."

"Not anymore. I left them for you on the *Caphenon* when I realized what you had been through in the crash. I was outside, being treated and told everything that was going on, while you were trapped in our quarters, alone—" She stopped. "I meant for them to be vaporized when we blew up the ship. But I'm glad Andira saved them, because they're yours."

Lhyn's confusion bordered on denial, a willful rejection that Tal suspected was based on the source. Ekatya would always support her tyree, therefore her praise could be dismissed as comforting words.

"Doctor Lhyn Rivers," Tal said in a tone that turned every head in the room. "Stand up, please."

Lhyn uncurled from her spot next to Ekatya and rose, towering over her.

Tal met her uncertain gaze and said, "I am Andira Shaldone Tal, Lancer of Alsea. I speak so that all may hear."

She watched Lhyn straighten at the ritual words and held back a smile. It was not surprising that she would recognize them.

"Courage has never been limited to the warrior caste," she said, "and those who make extraordinary sacrifices for Alsea are remembered in our history regardless of who they are. You have performed a service of incalculable value to my people. You risked your life and suffered unspeakably, and I am convinced you would have given your life had it been necessary. You did this for Alsea, for a people you cannot even claim as your own. I can offer nothing that would come close to proper payment for such a service, but I can give you a claim to our people and our home."

Lhyn raised a hand to her mouth, her eyes shining. A nascent understanding took root in her emotions, and now Tal did smile.

"As Lancer, I have certain executive powers. You are hereby named a citizen of Alsea, with all of the rights and responsibilities inherent therein. You will be remembered forever as the first alien to be recognized as Alsean. With your permission, we will record exactly why this honor was accorded to you, so all will know that it was not a political gift but a reward, more than earned."

As tears pooled in Lhyn's eyes, Tal added in a softer voice, "Of course, we'll have to decide on your caste. I presume you would accept the scholars?"

"Yes," Lhyn whispered. "Yes, please."

"Then it will be done. Alsea is proud to take you into her heart. And I'm proud of you as well." She opened her arms and was immediately swept into a warmron. For a moment she was afraid of hurting Lhyn's ribs, the story still too sharp in her mind. But Lhyn held her tightly.

"Was that last part still the Lancer?"

"No. That part was me. Please, Lhyn, never doubt your courage again. I can feel it when you do, and it hurts me, because you truly are extraordinary."

"You might be talking me into it." Lhyn held her a few pipticks longer, then released her with a shaky laugh. "How did you know? It's the one thing I wanted, but I didn't think I could ask. I didn't even know you had a mechanism in place for it."

"We didn't until recently. Prime Builder Eroles campaigned for it because she wants to offer citizenship to Chief Kameha. The Council agreed because the value of his services is self-evident and even they can't avoid seeing that we might benefit from more like him in the future. So we need to offer some sort of incentive besides wages and housing."

"Is the Prime Builder going to be angry with you for giving the first one to me?"

"Probably," Tal admitted.

"Almost certainly." Lanaril's smile was wide as she approached Lhyn and clasped their hands together. "But I'm delighted with her choice and proud to welcome you to my caste. You're a more than worthy addition to the scholars. If you'll accept me, I would be honored to be your sponsor, to help you learn what's expected of you. We'll go straight to the caste house as soon as we return to Blacksun and get you enrolled."

"I would love that."

It was when Ekatya pulled her into a warmron and murmured, "It really is your home now," that Lhyn lost her composure. Tal turned away, giving the two what privacy she could, and found Salomen smiling at her.

"That was very well done, tyrina." Salomen drew her toward the windows and spoke quietly. "For a moment, I thought I would have to hold you back. I've never felt you so angry."

"I can't recall the last time I've been that angry. Not even when I first heard about Herot, and I was under the influence of drugs then. I still don't understand how Ekatya kept herself from crushing his throat." She glanced back at the embracing couple. "But I admire her for it. That's a strength I can barely fathom."

"It does make her insistence on keeping your secret much more understandable."

"True words. It feels like some sort of lesson from Fahla, doesn't it? That Lhyn would feel safer here than anywhere else."

"Based on what we just heard, she *is* safer here than anywhere else." Salomen lowered her voice further. "You do realize that they're not just tyrees."

"They're not divine tyrees, either. They're something different. I don't know how Lhyn hasn't burst with questions about it before now."

"Because she couldn't ask until she told her story. And she couldn't do that until she was ready." Salomen looked across the room, where Lhyn was now wiping tears but smiling as she spoke with Lanaril. "Prepare for a blizzard of questions now, though."

"Oh, I am," Tal said as she watched Lhyn. "I'm just grateful she's here to ask them."

CHAPTER 52
Secrets

THEY TALKED LATE INTO THE night, long enough to see both of the moons rise from the ocean. Eusaltin raced ahead, reaching a point overhead before Sonalia made her appearance.

Everyone had questions and conjectures about their bond, especially Lhyn, who spilled them as though a dam had been breached. Which, Ekatya thought, was exactly what had happened.

Much discussion was expended on the fact that while Ekatya had been able to see and hear both sides, Lhyn had not. Ekatya shared Dr. Wells's hypothesis that since her participation in the connection had been carefully managed, with a perfect balance of conscious and subconscious, she was "in the doorway," as she put it. Lhyn had not been balanced and so was entirely on her side, able to hear and see Ekatya, but nothing else through the doorway.

Lhyn was eager to take part in an experiment testing the hypothesis, but Dr. Wells was adamantly against it until she had progressed further in her mental healing. It was an ongoing frustration for Lhyn, which she was eager to express to the sympathetic Alseans.

Ekatya took great comfort in watching her speak so freely at last. She wondered if perhaps this was what Lhyn had needed to finish her healing—access to the only people who could begin to understand what had happened. People who would not react with fear or judgment, but be excited at the potential, just as she was.

After several hours, Salomen proposed a light meal to absorb the spirits they had been drinking, Andira and Lhyn went to help, and Lanaril said that she would step outside for a moment if no one minded. Ekatya stood looking at the view of Pica Mahal, highlighted by the brilliance of Sonalia, then took a fortifying breath and walked onto the deck.

Lanaril was leaning on the railing, her forearms crossed as she stared out to sea. A soft, warm breeze ruffled her hair and stirred the leaves in the trees below them.

"Do you mind if I join you?" Ekatya asked.

"No, of course not."

They stood side by side in silence, watching the silver path that Sonalia was blazing atop the shifting waters.

"I've always loved that," Ekatya said. "Back on my home planet, we call them moon paths. You have to catch the moon at just the right time to see them. I hardly ever get the opportunity."

"Neither do I. And I have less excuse than you." Lanaril sniffed quietly and brushed a hand across one eye.

Ekatya looked over in alarm. Oh, stars, she was crying. Only a few tears, and obviously trying to hide it, but…by now she would have sensed her reaction and there was no turning back.

"Is there anything I can do to help?" she asked.

Lanaril made a soft sound of amusement, her gaze still on the moon path. "So very polite and diplomatic, as always. You are quite a study, Ekatya."

There was nothing she could say to that, so she remained silent. And though it wasn't intentional, her quiet presence seemed to be what Lanaril needed, for she began to speak.

"One of the great debates among templars—among all Alseans who believe, really—is why Fahla allows terrible things to happen to good people. I resolved that for myself a long time ago, because it never made sense to me that Fahla would be monitoring all of our individual lives. I cannot support the idea of our Goddess managing us down to the last soul. If she's powerful enough to do it, why would she? Surely she must be paying attention to the bigger issues instead, guiding us as a people, not as individuals. And I would rather believe that I have autonomy, that my decisions are my own and I'm not being nudged one way or another by a goddess who has already mapped out my fate."

She shifted, resting on one arm and facing Ekatya. "But I believe there are certain individuals she does monitor. Individuals who are important to the bigger issues. Andira is one. We needed her in order to survive the Voloth invasion, and we need her to see us through this difficult time as we learn to live in a universe that is no longer just ours. Her divine tyree bond with Salomen is no coincidence. It's what saved her during her challenge, what kept her on the State Chair when we need her so much. And I believe Fahla watches you and Lhyn as well."

Though startled, Ekatya said nothing. Lanaril had the look of one who was not done.

"She chose you, Ekatya. She brought you here to save us. And it was your passion and outside point of view that helped convince Andira to break Fahla's covenant. We needed you as much as we needed Andira—and we needed Lhyn to convince you to stay. It seems we also needed her to be our voice among your people."

She shook her head and turned back to the sea. "But if Fahla is watching Lhyn, how could this have happened? How could she allow such pain and terror to be visited upon such a peaceful, kind, loyal person? At first I thought perhaps Fahla's power doesn't extend past Alsea. Perhaps she cannot affect events in the Protectorate. But then I remembered that she brought you here from the Protectorate. And she gave you a bond, an Alsean bond, that saved Lhyn and pulled her out of that horrible place. So she *was* watching, and she did have the power to affect the outcome. Which puts me right back at the beginning of the question. How could she let Lhyn suffer like that?"

Wiping away another tear, she gave a shaky laugh. "So the Lead Templar of Blacksun is having a crisis of faith. And I have no idea why I'm telling you all of this."

Ekatya didn't either. She was the last person on Alsea equipped to handle this conversation. Instead, she focused on the one thing she was now certain of.

"You really care for her."

"Of course I do. She's my friend."

"She cares for you as well. Very much. She wants you to be our bond minister."

Lanaril straightened and faced her. "She told me earlier. I would be honored."

"The problem is…" Ekatya sighed. The words were not coming, so she tried a different tack. "I've spent too much time being suspicious of people who didn't deserve it. I wasted six months—I mean, a little over four of your moons—not trusting Ensign Bellows, and I regret that so much now. If I had known how soon I would lose him…" The breeze blew her hair across her face, and she idly pushed it behind her ear. "I just hate that I wasted so much time. And then I did the same thing with Dr. Wells. At least that one didn't take as long; we only wasted eighteen days. But it probably would have been much longer if she hadn't come to me with that bottle of iceflame. And now I'm doing it with you."

Lanaril's intake of breath was audible.

"Lhyn trusts you," Ekatya continued, watching her closely. "And I want to as well, because I know how much you mean to her. But I don't know how to do that when I can't forgive you."

Unlike Andira, Lanaril did not show her emotions in her eyes. "What have I done that requires your forgiveness?" she asked evenly.

"You agreed to empathically force her to leave me, to stay on Alsea. You would have betrayed that kind, loyal person you were just having a crisis of faith over. Yet you call her a friend and act like it was never an issue."

Lanaril took a step back, her whole body telegraphing shock, and Ekatya thought with some satisfaction that she wasn't entirely made of stone after all.

"You—how do you—oh, Fahla. Andira told you."

"Andira had the *integrity* to tell me immediately. I knew before the Battle of Alsea."

Lanaril stared, a symphony of emotions playing across her suddenly expressive face until she hid it in her hands.

"Great Goddess above," she murmured, her words slightly muffled. "Of all the—what a perfect lesson she is teaching tonight."

She lifted her head and walked to the door of the cabin. Sliding it open, she called, "Lhyn? Would you join us, please?"

Chills ran down Ekatya's arms, leaving bumps in their wake. "Don't you dare. Don't you *dare* do this to her; I swear I will—"

"What's going on?" Lhyn asked, stepping through the door. "Oh, wow. Look at the moon path. I didn't even notice that until now."

Ekatya glared daggers at Lanaril. If the woman had a speck of empathic ability, she was surely feeling the murderous thoughts.

Lanaril closed the door and said, "Ekatya knows."

"Knows what?" Lhyn was smiling as she looked between them, but when Lanaril tapped her own forehead with two fingers and then pointed them at Lhyn, the smile dropped. "No. No, what have you—Lanaril!"

Ekatya watched in confusion as Lhyn rounded furiously on her friend.

"You swore in the name of Fahla! Is this what your word is worth? How *could* you?"

"I didn't tell her! She's known since before the Battle of Alsea. And she knows whose strategy that was," Lanaril added meaningfully.

"She—what?" Lhyn swiveled toward Ekatya. "You knew all along? Everything?"

"Wait." Ekatya shook her head, trying to come to grips with a truth she could not believe. "Are we all talking about the same thing?"

Lhyn looked at Lanaril, who nodded.

Ekatya steadied herself against the railing. "How…?"

"I told her before you left Alsea." Lanaril had recovered her poise. "You expected me to ask forgiveness—I did. But I asked it of the one person who could give it."

Lhyn crossed the deck and took Ekatya's hand in hers. "You look like you just fell out of a shuttle. I'm a little shocked, too. I've been trying to protect you from this for two years."

"Why?" Ekatya managed. "Why did *I* need protecting?"

"Because Andira is so important to you. I thought it would destroy your friendship."

Ekatya laughed, because what else could she do? "Andira is the one who told me. When we had our challenge fight."

"You're kidding me." Lhyn's eyes brightened before her expression fell into a frown. "I don't understand, then. You were ready to kill her just because you *thought* she empathically forced me. Then you turned around and supported her in everything, so I knew you couldn't have found out the truth. But if you knew that was really the plan, and the only reason they didn't go through with it was because I decided to stay…how did you come out of that fight as friends?"

"Because—oh, Shippers, Lhyn, I can hardly explain it to myself. We talked about it, and then she Shared with me so I could feel your emotions, and after that I just…I didn't think I could judge her when she already felt so guilty. Especially when I had nearly done a terrible thing myself."

"But you judged me," Lanaril said.

Lhyn's head snapped around as if she had forgotten Lanaril was there. When she turned back, Ekatya cringed at the realization in her eyes. "Is that why you were so rude to her today? Right after she helped me with my panic attack? Ekatya—"

"I know." Ekatya held up her hands, trying to forestall the censure.

"You owe her an apology."

She knew that too, but it was the last thing she wanted to do right now.

"That's not necessary," Lanaril said. "She was protecting you. It's what a tyree does. I should have realized what that was about."

"No, you shouldn't." Ekatya could not bear compassion from this woman. "How were you supposed to know? Fucking Hades, I didn't even understand it myself. I knew it was hypocritical, holding you to a different standard, but I couldn't—" She released an inarticulate growl of frustration. "It just made me so angry that Andira has felt guilty about it all this time, and you…didn't."

"Oh, she did," Lhyn said.

"But it seems that I had an easier resolution, because I was able to go to Lhyn. If Andira was keeping this a secret with you, then…" Lanaril trailed off as Ekatya tipped her head back and groaned.

"I made her keep it a secret. I made it worse than it had to be. And Salomen knows now, and she thought I should tell you, but I made her promise, too."

Lhyn snorted. Then she bent over, holding her stomach, and laughed in a way Ekatya had not heard for months. "Oh, stars!" she gasped, and pointed at Ekatya. "Warship captain and diplomat." Pointing toward herself, she said, "Scientist trained to observe the smallest details." She turned to Lanaril. "Counselor and high empath. And Andira is a consummate politician and diplomat, and also a high empath. And somehow we *all* missed this. We spent two years killing ourselves keeping a secret that everyone already knew."

When she put it that way…

Ekatya began to laugh as well, and Lanaril soon joined in. When Andira and Salomen came out to see what the noise was about, Ekatya watched her friend undergo much the same reaction that she had, though she didn't seem to share the amusement.

While Andira was recovering, Salomen asked the impossible question.

"Yet you still feel safe here?"

Every bit of Ekatya's humor drained away as she waited.

"I do," Lhyn said. "I always have. And maybe I'm a grainbird, or a little insane, but I'd already made up my mind to die with all of you if it came to that. I never believed Ekatya would leave me here, but if she did, it seemed a just punishment for what I brought to Alsea."

"You were not responsible—"

"Andira, stop." Lhyn's voice was sharp. "Let's not discuss responsibility, all right? Or we'll be here all night comparing our mistakes and misdeeds. We all have things to feel guilty about." She gazed around the group. "When Lanaril asked my forgiveness, I thought, who can I ask forgiveness from? I brought an invasion on your heads. I would have done *anything* to save you from the Voloth. So finding out that you planned to force me to stay—it didn't really register as an event I needed to worry about. If I'm about to murder someone and they threaten me with a knife, am I supposed to feel aggrieved that they're defending themselves?"

Ekatya shook her head and smiled. Only Lhyn would come up with that.

"This is about something I wanted to do anyway. You didn't go through with it because you didn't have to. Even if you had, it would have been temporary. I've had more recent experience with someone trying to force me, and it was not temporary at all."

No one spoke. No one seemed able to look at her.

"I know what I'm talking about, because I asked Lanaril to empathically force me so I could see what that really meant."

"You *what?*" Ekatya almost shouted.

Lhyn shrugged. "I was curious."

Ekatya slapped a hand to her forehead. "I can't believe it. Wait, yes I can." She lifted her head, noting that Andira looked equally shocked. "What happened?"

"I forced her to stop asking questions and leave the temple," Lanaril said. "It was the most aberrant behavior I could think of that would still be harmless to her. Then I followed her out the door and reversed it."

"It was a remarkable sensation," Lhyn said. "You have no idea how much I itched to write about it, but that was one thing I never dared put into a file. What was so fascinating about it was that I really didn't want to ask any more questions. And when Lanaril reversed it, I couldn't imagine how I had ever thought that way. It was seamless, and there were zero lasting effects."

"That's not quite the same…" Andira began, only to be stopped by a look from Lhyn.

"Don't insult my intelligence. I know it would have been different. Probably by a few orders of magnitude, but it doesn't matter because *it didn't happen.* Can we all please just drop this? I'm the one it concerns, and the only reason I've given it any thought at all was because I worried about the two of you." She gestured between Andira and Ekatya. "But you're obviously fine, so let's just…be done with it. I want to be done. I'm not a shekking victim. Stop protecting me."

After a long moment of silence, Andira ventured, "That's a difficult order for two warriors who love you. One of whom is your tyree."

Lhyn's expression softened. "I accept that point. Let me rephrase: stop protecting me from this specific thing. There's so much else for us to think about! Like the reappearance of divine tyrees in Alseans—in mid empaths, no less—and the sudden appearance of a form of telepathy in at least two Gaians. And the fact that Ekatya crashing the *Caphenon* seems to have been the catalyst for all of it. Both of our cultures are changing, and we're right at the center of it." She pointed at the moon path dancing on the water. "We're standing here looking into our future, and we have no idea what it will be except that it won't be like the past. So let's stop looking back."

Salomen stepped up, pulled Lhyn in by her shoulders, and kissed her cheek. "Thank you. I didn't want to keep another secret." She turned toward the open door and asked, "Is anyone hungry? We have bread with grainstem powder, cheese, and sweetfruit. And a little bit of Jarnell's fruit drink."

Andira watched her go, then crossed over to Lhyn. "If you ever want a seat on the Council, tell me. I would take great joy in unleashing you on them." She kissed Lhyn's cheek as well, but did not let go of her shoulders as she spoke in a quieter tone. "I understand your need to move forward. And I will abide by it, but before we close this, please…let me apologize."

"You don't—"

"Please."

Lhyn closed her mouth and nodded.

After an awkward moment of hesitation, Andira stepped back and straightened. "That was the most difficult decision I have ever made. It was so unjust, sacrificing an innocent to save the rest. I know you don't see yourself as innocent," she added as Lhyn shook her head. "But I did. I still do. When you chose to stay, of your own accord, you—" She stopped, clenching her jaw.

"Andira," Lhyn said softly. She reached out and drew Andira's fisted hands forward, coaxing them open before holding them in her own.

"When you chose to stay," Andira tried again, her voice rasping, "you didn't just save yourself. You saved me, too."

Lhyn slowly pulled her closer.

"I'm sorry," Andira choked out as she gave in to the embrace.

"I know. I forgive you."

Andira closed her eyes and went very still.

"I'm sorry, too." Lhyn rubbed one hand up and down her back. "I guess I was trying to avoid this, because I didn't want you to feel this way, but I should have known better. And I should have spoken to you before we left Alsea, when Lanaril came to me. You've carried a burden you didn't need to. Will you forgive me for that?"

"Of course," Andira said instantly.

Lhyn smiled. "You say that like it's so easy."

"It is."

"Then believe me when I say it's exactly that easy to forgive you."

Ekatya watched them with an uncomfortably tight throat, thinking of all the times she had insisted on keeping this secret, so sure that she was right and never understanding the true cost. For two years she had tried to protect Lhyn, only to find that Lhyn had never needed it.

When did good intentions turn into arrogance?

"She spoke the truth," Lanaril murmured next to her. "She is not a victim."

Andira let go, turned without meeting anyone's eyes, and vanished into the cabin.

Lhyn stood looking after her for a moment, then gazed skyward and took a deep breath before facing Ekatya and Lanaril. "Are we done with this?"

Lanaril raised her hands. "I'm done."

"Ekatya?"

"More than done."

"Good. I'm ready for some of that bread. We need to find out how they keep it so fresh here; that's worth a treaty all by itself." Lhyn walked inside.

Ekatya rubbed the back of her neck, not quite able to look Lanaril in the eye.

"How is it that you warriors always seem to find bondmates who leave you with the same stupefied expression?"

She glanced up to find a knowing look trained on her. "Not all of us. Just the lucky ones."

"True words." Lanaril sobered. "Do I still need to ask your forgiveness?"

Ekatya shook her head. "Now I feel like an asshead."

"A what?"

Realizing that she had fallen into Common slang, she said, "A grainbird. Except stronger. Much stronger."

"Ah. A dokker's backside?"

"That'll do."

Lanaril smiled, the slow, serene smile that had so irritated Ekatya only yesterday. Now she found it oddly reassuring.

"You're not. You're just stupefied. I believe the cure for that is a late night snack with good friends…and family."

It was a graceful peace offer. As Ekatya led the way to the door, she said, "Do you think my crashing the *Caphenon* was the catalyst for all of these changes?"

"I think Fahla has her own plan. And whether you believe in her or not, you're a part of it."

That was exactly the kind of statement that made her uncomfortable around Lanaril. But then she entered the warmly lit, glassed-in room and saw Lhyn smiling at something Salomen was telling her. Andira stood behind them, filling two glasses with the fruit drink, and turned to hand one to Lhyn.

Andira and Lhyn were alive because of a bond she didn't understand. She owed her current happiness to that bond, and so did Salomen.

She remembered Dr. Wells saying *You're asking me to take a leap of faith*, and wondered if she was capable of making that same leap. Wells had done it in minutes. It wasn't just their bond that had saved Lhyn, it was also Dr. Wells and her willingness to set aside doubt and take a chance.

Lhyn was certain that a Shipper was actively involved with this planet. The existence of a powerful, pre-existing race was already accepted fact, so was it much of a leap to think that perhaps one of them really was here?

But accepting that also meant accepting the idea that this advanced alien might be responsible for her bond—and for what had happened to Lhyn.

Suddenly, she had much more sympathy for Lanaril and her crisis of faith.

Stopping her with a light touch on her arm, she said, "I'm not comfortable being a part of any plan that I didn't have a hand in creating. But I didn't have any control over our tyree bond, and I would never give that up now. So perhaps I can keep an open mind."

"Faith is not a blind belief," Lanaril said. "It's an open mind and a willingness to learn. I've learned a great deal tonight, and much of it about you. It seems you've learned quite a bit as well."

"Words for Fahla," Ekatya said with a small smile.

Lanaril looked startled, then broke into a brilliant answering grin. "We might make an Alsean out of you yet."

"I can think of worse things. Lanaril, I'm sorry about…" She gestured toward the deck. "I'll probably never understand your faith in Fahla, but I know something about questioning one's trust and ideals. I hope you find the answers you're looking for."

"Thank you. Of course, if I do, I'll just find new questions to ask."

"Lhyn can help you with that. She has a limitless supply."

"Now those *are* words for Fahla." Lanaril hesitated. "Lhyn was right. We need to look forward, not back. I would like to put our…misunderstanding behind us and not look back at it. Your future looks bright to me, and you have an extraordinary bondmate walking that path with you. I hope I can walk it as well, from time to time." She held up a hand.

Ekatya offered both of hers and enjoyed Lanaril's surprise. "Considering that I'm the one who owes you the apology, those were very kind words. Right now my path is leading me there." She pointed across the cabin to Lhyn. "But you're welcome to walk it with me."

They crossed the polished floor together, and Lhyn looked up with a smile that grew as she saw them side by side. Ekatya could almost hear her thinking, *Good. It's about time.*

Three days, she mused. They were three days into an eighteen-day bonding break and already some of her firmest beliefs had been turned inside out. What was it about Alsea? Every time she came here, it seemed that the person she had been before was not…enough, somehow. She was *more* here, as if the Alsean air unlocked parts of her that otherwise stayed closed and still.

Reaching Lhyn's side, she wrapped an arm around her waist, picked up a piece of grainstem-sweetened bread, and let the conversation flow over her while she thought about Lanaril's words.

She could not share Lanaril's or Andira's faith in Fahla. But she had faith in herself, and in the women in this cabin, and in Chief Kameha and Colonel Micah and Salomen's family downstairs. She had faith in Dr. Wells and Commander Lokomorra and the rest of her crew, somewhere overhead keeping guard on Alsea.

Perhaps the important thing about faith was not who it was for.

Perhaps the important thing was simply to have it.

GLOSSARY

UNITS OF TIME

piptick: one 100th of a tick (about half a second).

tick: about a minute (50 seconds).

tentick: ten ticks.

hantick: 10 tenticks, just shy of 1.5 hours (83.33 minutes). One Alsean day is 20 hanticks (27.7 hours) or 1.15 days.

moon: a basic unit of Alsean time, similar to our month but 36 days long. Each moon is divided into four parts called **ninedays**. One Alsean moon equals 41.55 stellar (Earth) days.

cycle: the length of time it takes the Alsean planet to revolve around their sun (13 moons or approximately 17 stellar months).

GENERAL TERMS

bondmate: a life partner.

dokker: a farm animal similar to a cow. Slow moving and rather stupid, but with a hell of a kick when it's angry or frightened.

dokshin: vulgar term for dokker feces.

Eusaltin: the smaller and nearer moon of Alsea.

evenmeal: dinner.

Fahla: the goddess of the Alseans, also called Mother.

front: a mental protection that prevents one's emotions from being sensed by another.

gender-locked: an Alsean who is unable to temporarily shift genders for the purposes of reproduction. Considered a grave handicap, denying the individual the full blessing of Fahla.

grainbird: a small black and red seed-eating bird common in agricultural fields. It is known for singing even at night, leading to an old perception of the birds as lacking in intelligence—hence "grainbird" is also a slang term for an idiot.

grainstem powder: powder derived from crushed stems of a particular grain, which yields a sweet taste. Commonly used in cooking; also used to sprinkle over fresh bread.

horten: an Alsean delicacy, often used in soup. It comes from a plant that, once harvested, stays fresh for a very short time and must be processed immediately. Due to that short window of time, fresh horten is very expensive and usually served only in the nicer restaurants.

joining: sexual relations. Joining is considered less significant than Sharing between lovers. The two acts can take place simultaneously, though this would only occur in a serious relationship.

length: a standard of distance equaling one thousand strides (about a kilometer).

midmeal: lunch.

molwine: the curved apex of the pelvic ridges on both male and female Alseans. A very sensitive sexual organ.

molwyn: Fahla's sacred tree. It has a black trunk and leaves with silver undersides. A molwyn grows at the center of every temple of decent size.

mornmeal: breakfast.

probe: to push beyond the front and read emotions that are not available for a surface skim. Probing without permission is a violation of Alsean law.

raiz: honorific for a producer.

Return: the passage after death, in which an Alsean returns to Fahla and embarks on the next plane of existence.

Rite of Ascension: the formal ceremony in which a child becomes a legal and social adult. The Rite takes place at twenty cycles, after which one's choice of caste cannot be changed.

shannel: a traditional hot drink, used for energy and freshening one's breath. Made from the dried leaves (and sometimes flowers) of the shannel plant.

skim: to sense any emotions that an Alsean is not specifically holding behind her or his front.

Sharing: the act of physically connecting the emotional centers between two or more Alseans, resulting in unshielded emotions that can be fully accessed by anyone in the Sharing link. It is most frequently done between lovers or bondmates but is also part of a bonding ceremony (in which all guests take part in a one-time Sharing with the two new bondmates). It can also be done between friends, family, or for medical purposes.

shek: vulgar slang for penetrative sex. Usually used as a profanity.

Sonalia: the larger and more distant moon of Alsea.

sonsales: one who is empathically blind.

tyrees: Alseans whose empathic centers share a rare compatibility, which has physiological consequences. Tyrees can sense each other's emotions at greater distances than normal, have difficulty being physically apart, and are ferociously protective of each other. Tyrees are always bonded, usually for life.

warmron: an embrace. Warmrons are shared only between lovers or between parents and children—and only until the child reaches the Rite of Ascension. A warmron is too close to a Sharing for it to be used at any other time.

winden: a large six-toed mammal, adapted to an alpine environment. It is wary, able to climb nearly sheer walls, and the fastest animal on Alsea. Winden travel in herds and are rarely seen.

wristcom: wrist-mounted communication device, often used in conjunction with an earcuff.

THE STORY DOESN'T HAVE TO END ON THE LAST PAGE

Take it with you—on a shirt, a phone case, a mug and so much more. Choose your caste, or give a caste gift to a friend. That way, Alsea will always be there.

HTTP://WWW.CAFEPRESS.COM/CHRONICLESOFALSEA

ABOUT FLETCHER DELANCEY

Fletcher DeLancey spent her early career as a science educator, which was the perfect combination of her two great loves: language and science. These days she combines them while writing science fiction.

She is an Oregon expatriate who left her beloved state when she met a Portuguese woman and had to choose between home and heart. She chose heart. Now she lives with her wife and son in the beautiful sunny Algarve, where she writes full-time, teaches Pilates, tries to learn the local birds and plants, and samples every regional Portuguese dish she can get her hands on. (There are many. It's going to take a while.)

She is best known for her geeky romance *Mac vs. PC* and her science fiction series, *Chronicles of Alsea*. Currently, she is working on the next books in the *Chronicles of Alsea* and as an editor for Ylva Publishing.

CONNECT WITH FLETCHER:
Website: www.chroniclesofalsea.com
Blog: www.chroniclesofalsea.com/blog/
Facebook: www.facebook.com/fletcher.delancey
Twitter: @alseaauthor
E-Mail: fletcher@mailhaven.com

OTHER BOOKS FROM YLVA PUBLISHING

www.ylva-publishing.com

THE CAPHENON

(Chronicles of Alsea – Book #1)

Fletcher DeLancey

ISBN: 978-3-95533-253-2
Length: 374 pages (165,000 words)

An emergency call to Lancer Andira Tal has shocking news: there is other intelligent life in the universe, and it's landing on the planet right now. The aliens sacrificed their ship to save Alsea—temporarily. Alsea is now a prize to be bought and sold in galactic politics. But Lancer Tal is not one to accept a fate imposed by aliens, and she'll do whatever it takes to save her world.

THE TEA MACHINE

(The Teatime Chronicles – Book #1)

Gill McKnight

ISBN: 978-3-95533-432-1
Length: 321 pages (97,000 words)

Spinster by choice, Millicent Aberly has managed to catapult herself from her lovely Victorian mews house into a strange future full of giant space squid, Roman empires, and a most annoying centurion to whom she owes her life. Decanus Sangfroid was just doing her job rescuing the weird little scientist chick from a squid attack. Now she finds herself in London, 1862, and it's not a good fit.

Catalyst
© 2016 by Fletcher DeLancey

ISBN: 978-3-95533-641-7

Also available as e-book.

Published by Ylva Publishing, legal entity of Ylva Verlag, e.Kfr.
Ylva Verlag, e.Kfr.
Owner: Astrid Ohletz
Am Kirschgarten 2
65830 Kriftel
Germany

www.ylva-publishing.com

First edition: 2016

No part of this book may be reproduced, scanned, or distributed in any printed or electronic form without permission. Please do not participate in or encourage piracy of copyrighted materials in violation of the author's rights. Thank you for respecting the hard work of this author.

This is a work of fiction. Names, characters, places, and incidents either are a product of the author's imagination or are used fictitiously, and any resemblance to locales, events, business establishments, or actual persons—living or dead—is entirely coincidental.

Credits
Edited by Sandra Gerth
Proofread by Cheri Fuller
Cover Design & Print Layout by Streetlight Graphics